The Cuddle Plan
Nathan Baylet

The Cuddle Plan

by Nathan Baylet

First edition : February 2026

Published in the United States by
Paper Beach Publishing, LLC, Portland, Oregon.

ISBN 978-1-959920-03-8 (paperback)
ISBN 978-1-959920-04-5 (ebook)

Editor : Erin Brown
Proofreading : Sara Fargo
Book cover design : MadliArt
Typesetting : Sabrina Milazzo
Map : Candace Rose Rardon

www.nathanbaylet.com

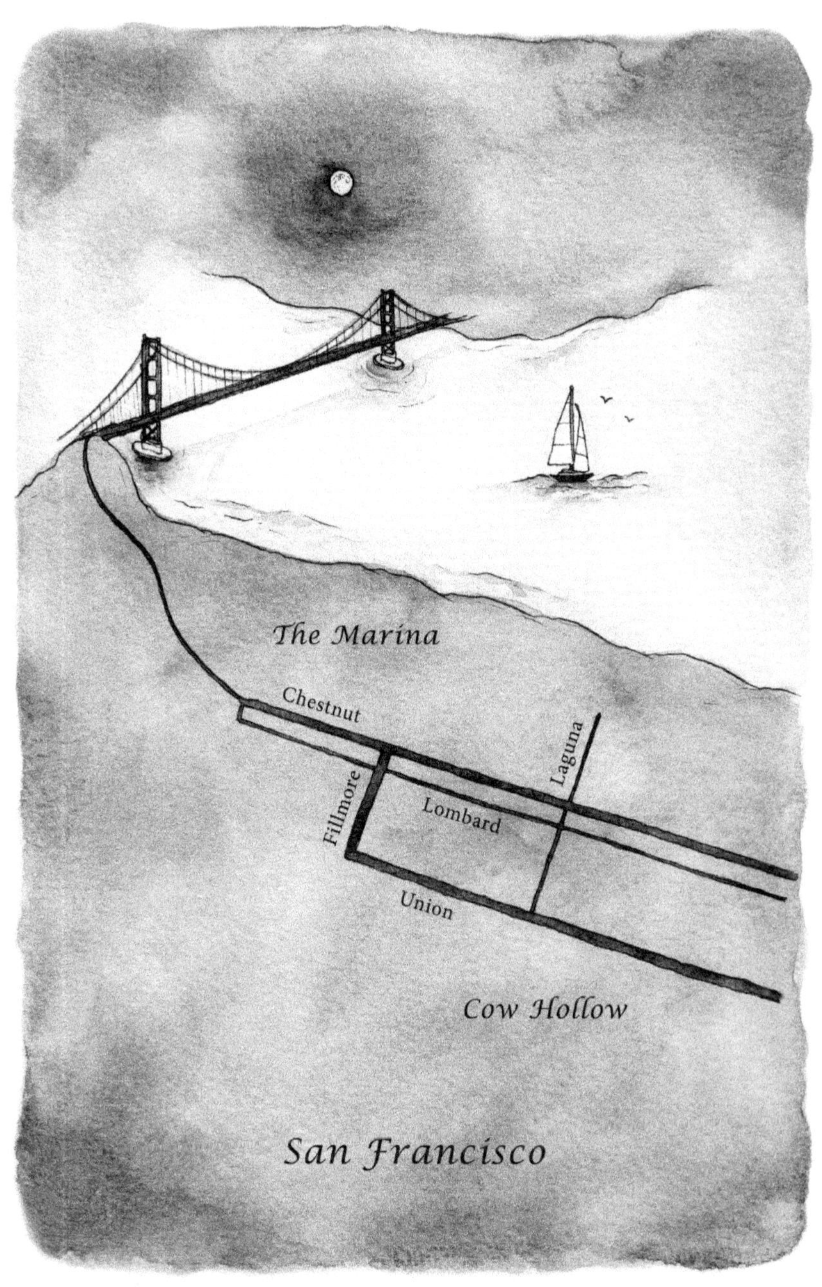

Map illustration by Candace Rose Rardon.

Author's Note

In December 2012 I had a thought, that amidst this ridiculously cold, endless, silent universe two people could find comfort by holding each other. I love that powerful image and I decided to write a rom-com story around it, and of course set it in my favorite place in the world: San Francisco. It took me 12½ years to finish *The Cuddle Plan*, but it's finally done and it's everything I hoped it would be. It is also the follow-up to my rom-com novel *Passion or Pancakes*. I thank my editor Erin Brown, proofreader Sara Fargo, and my family and friends and MadliArt and Sabrina Milazzo and Candace Rose Rardon for all their help and support on this adventure.

I hope this novel gives you laughs, feels, and a super fun reading experience. I hope you look forward to more novels in this Marina rom-com series, and I thank you very much for letting my writing into your life. I wish you wonderful things and lots of love. Cheers.

2014

summer

San Francisco

Prologue

May

Bren watched the balloon inflate, bigger and bigger and bigger. Then just before it couldn't pump up any more, she saw Nikki slip her silver balloon's hole from the nozzle, tie a perfect knot, and attach a lovely ribbon to it with firm gentleness, like a bizarre balloon-version of *Fifty Shades of Grey*. *Mmmmm.* Was balloon inflating really that sensual, or was she just super excited about tonight's fun with Greg?

"Someone's in love," Nikki teased as she floated the shiny balloon over to Bren's hand.

Bren smiled super big. "Very in love," she said.

"I'm jealous as hell," Nikki blurted, turning the heads of the older women in the party shop. "Lots of hotties here in the Marina. But hard to find a Mr. Right. What's your secret?"

Bren chuckled. "Total luck. I've also been looking for my Mr. Right in the Marina for years, and finally there he was in the mystery section of the bookstore. Mystery finally solved."

"I'm envious. But, I'm not a reader like you. I like guys who swim. Maybe I should hang out at the gym pool."

"Go for it. Who knows where you'll find love?" Bren encouraged, handing her cash. "Life is an adventure."

"Life's a monthly seesaw between passion and heartbreak around this party village," Nikki accurately summarized their bar-filled San Francisco neighborhood, handing the receipt and then grinning at the love-red "HAPPY BIRTHDAY" words on Bren's new helium friend. "Are you and Greg doing anything kinky with this balloon or is it just gonna watch?"

Bren blushed. "That *is* a secret."

Nikki grinned and rolled her eyes. "You're so Jane Austen-ish. What did you rename 'doggy-style?'"

Bren smiled and whispered. "Looking for earring."

Nikki laughed. "Well, have fun looking."

"Thank you. I hope you find your knight in shining Speedos."

Nikki chuckled. "Thanks."

Bren felt the older women's eyes staring at her, and felt their knowing of what wildness her balloon might witness tonight, as she grabbed its red ribbon, and zoomed out of the party shop and out into the freedom of the bright summer sunshine.

5:45pm. Right on schedule. She clacked her Prada pumps west, into the sun, up Chestnut Street's glittery sidewalk, her new silver balloon friend dancing in the crisp seaside air behind her. She reeled in the ribbon until Bren's balloon was near the V-shaped neckline of her breezy pink sundress, safely away from the pretty pruned leafy green trees she marched under, passing the big Baby Gap, the glass fronted Apple Store, and all the pretty restaurants, pretty people, then screeching her heels to a halt to ogle at all the pretty new books in the window of Books, Inc., so many wonderful, wonderful new books.

The new novels were beckoning their wild worlds to her in little rectangle shapes displayed like delicious cakes in a bakery's window, teasing her with new treats from Nora Roberts, Suzanna Young, Jenny Han, and a thrilling-looking one from Emma Pass. Her heart thumped and fingers tingled, aching to rush into the store and browse and touch and read and buy and rush home and lose herself in their new, fun adventures. But she didn't have time. *Wait, why?* Oh right, she remembered, tearing her eyes away, back into daylight, and resuming reality.

Darn. Now she was two minutes off schedule and so sweaty-palm excited from book browsing she felt even more eager to jump into Greg's arms.

She zoomed across Chestnut Street, between the crosswalk lines, past super-slow-walking people until there were none, walking north up Avila Street, leaving the busy part of the Marina and entering the lovely residential calmness with all the cute 1920s-style houses and occasional ornate four-story apartment buildings all painted pretty pink, white, tan, or sometimes light blue with the evening side-sun blasting them colorful or cooling with shade. She buzzed with excitement to give Greg the balloon, and the wrapped rare book she carried in her bag, and a fun night to remember. She was the only anxious element in this pleasant paradise as she marched towards the glistening blue bay and little sailboats way up ahead, with her workbag strap over her shoulder, balloon to her chest, and a thousand thoughts in her mind: books, work, friends, Greg, and also curiously wondering what the Golden Gate Bridge would be used for once everyone has flying cars, and of course thinking again about Kris's wedding. *Oh, right, the DJ.* She had to call Kris.

Four rings.

"I'm out of underwear!" Kris hollered over the phone.

"What?"

"I gotta meet Mark at Brixton in ten minutes and I have no clean underwear."

Bren rolled her eyes.

"It's National Star Wars Day," Kris cheered.

"Happy National Star Wars Day," Bren wished her.

"Thanks. Same to you. So after dinner me and Mark are gonna go to his apartment and dress up like rebels celebrating the death star blowing up while my stuffed Ewoks watch us get freaky."

Bren shook her head. "I don't wanna know the galactic details."

"But I'm out of undies," Kris panicked. "I'm a rebel without a thong."

"Don't go through my room trying to find mine."

"I stopped doing that years ago," Kris said. "You're a panty-hiding mastermind."

Bren grinned.

"Hey," Kris said. "That's a good thing about me moving out next month, you won't have to hide your undies from me anymore."

Bren laughed. "That's true." Then Bren's smile wilted. Not having to hide her undies was the only good thing about Kris moving out to live with Mark. Bren kept marching. Eight years as roommates over, the unimaginable end of a party-tastic era. Their apartment would be so quiet. Too quiet. Emotions swirled. She remembered C.S. Lewis writing about dreading an empty house, as she totally dreaded Kris and her empty apartment a month from now. Her shoes clacked forward on the hard wide sidewalk. She didn't have time for tears. She would stay positive, somehow see newness as opportunity, and "open every door . . . not knowing when the dawn will come" as Emily Dickenson wrote, or "just be happy; it's more fun" as her mom used to sing to her, usually when looking at a "past due" bill. Bren would be really happy if Greg maybe moved in with her after Kris left. She hoped Greg wouldn't mind the disco ball in the bathroom. Funny how life worked: when someone leaves there's room for someone new. *Hmmm.* That's a good saying, she thought; she should write that down.

"Underwear!" Kris exclaimed. "I need underwear!"

Bren snapped back to the productive present. "Use the emergency panty drawer."

"I used it last week."

"Use the 2nd emergency panty drawer."

"There's a 2nd emergency panty drawer?"

"I created it last month."

"You did?"

"Yes."

"Really?"

"Yes."

"Why didn't you tell me?"

"Because you would have used already."

"Where is it?"

"In the closet, in the cardboard shelves," Bren answered, "behind the vacuum cleaner."

"Why is it there?"

"Because you would never find it there."

"True."

"There's ten panties."

"You're a lifesaver!"

"And a panty provider."

"Yay!"

Bren took a breath. "I'm also the bearer of bad news."

"Un-yay."

Bren swung left and headed west on cute Capra Way. "Your DJ can't play your wedding reception."

"Why?"

"He got the part of a DJ in JJ Abrams' new movie shooting in June."

"TJ the DJ can't stay past May 'cause he playing a DJ for JJ in LA?"

"Yes."

"Damn."

"Don't worry," Bren said. "Anna will find a new DJ."

"Who's Anna?"

"Your wedding planner."

"Her name is Anna?"

"Yes."

"I thought it was Ann."

"It's Anna."

"I've been calling her Ann."

"I know," Bren said.

"Why didn't you tell me?"

"I did."

"You told me Ann."

"I told you Anna."

"Why is life so harrrrd?"

"It's gonna be fine," Bren comforted.

"Holly knows DJs."

"I'll talk to her."

"Call her now."

"I'm walking to Greg's."

"I don't wanna worry about this during dinner or Star Wars sexy time," Kris said. "The only thing I wanna be thinking about it is how hard Mark is x-wing-ing my exhaust port."

Bren cringed, grinned, and dialed. "I'll conference in Holly."

"I'll find panties."

Her balloon danced in the breeze and bopped Bren's chest as she swooshed right onto Scott Street and walked north again.

"Hello, Bren. How are you tonight?" Holly greeted.

"Good. Busy. Bonkers."

"Is Krista in a crisis?" Holly joked.

"Of course."

"I found the panties," Kris cheered.

"What?" Holly asked.

Bren grinned. "TJ the DJ is with JJ on the wedding day."

"Oh no," Holly said.

"Now we need a new DJ."

"I know just the girl," Holly said.

"I figured you would."

"She's spinning the music at my rooftop party in June. I'll ask her."

"Excellent."

"She's very good," Holly said. "She DJs swingers parties."

"Swing dancing?"

"No. Multiple couples swing parties. You know, parties for . . . sex," Holly whispered.

Bren grinned at Holly's cute discretion. "Swingers parties have DJs?"

"I guess so."

Bren chuckled. "Everyone's job is more exciting than mine."

"I'm an office person too," Holly said.

"Maybe we should quit our corporate jobs and become circus acrobats."

"Fun," Holly cheered. "We could hire Kris to be our physical trainer."

"Let's wait until after her wedding. She has a lot going on."

"I put on the green lace panties," Kris announced.

"Yes, she does have a lot going on," Holly agreed.

"These undies will go great with my forest rebel outfit."

"Kris," Bren said. "Holly may have a new DJ."

"Awesome."

"But I also have a new change to the wedding reception," Holly said.

"Un-awesome."

"What?"

"Calli is no longer bringing a plus-one."

"What happened?"

"She's bringing a plus-three."

"Three?"

"Not only is she dating Leon, she's now also dating Lindy."

"Calli's in a throuple?"

"She's in a quadrouple. She thinks she's also dating the ghost in my apartment."

"Oh lord," Bren smiled. "Well, the ghost doesn't need to sit at the reception. But I'll tell Anna we need another seat."

"Are you sure her name is Anna?" Kris said.

"Yes."

"Maybe don't bother with another seat," Holly said. "Calli is a flittery firefly. By the wedding day she will probably be single again."

"Or she might be in a quintouple," Bren joked. "Calli might break a world record for most dating partners at one time."

"Please don't tell her that. She might try to do it."

"These panties feel great," Kris announced.

"What?"

Bren's balloon bopped in the breeze as she veered west onto Beach Street, clacking towards the silhouette of the gloriously domed Palace of Fine Arts structure a few blocks in front of her and once again she felt so glad she worked her butt off through high school, college, a multitude of non-exciting jobs to be able to afford to live in this California paradise, so glad she found these friends, so glad she finally found the happy kind of love she had only read and reread about in books her whole life.

Holly softly cleared her throat. “I’m going on a date with Jacob tonight.”

“Good for you. Get back out there,” Bren said.

“That’s fuckin’ awesome,” Kris said.

Holly sighed. “But I have some bad news.”

“That’s un-fuckin’ awesome.”

“Calli lost another job.”

“What?”

“Seriously?” Bren said, adjusting her balloon that was blowing into her face. “Calli is getting ridiculous.” Bren tapped her phone, conferencing in Calli.

“Bless you with love. Calli speaking.”

“You lost your job?”

“Who is this?”

“Bren and Kris and Holly.”

“Breakfast bread and jelly?”

“Bren and Kris and Holly.”

“Oh hi. The drum circle is loud.”

“You’re at a – ? Nevermind.” Bren sighed. “How did you get fired from a hardware store?”

“A customer asked for caulk and there was a *big* misunderstanding.”

“Lordy.”

“But now I know about caulk.”

“Our girl is growing up,” Kris joked.

“Our girl is running out of places to work.” Holly sighed.

“This is your seventh firing,” Bren scolded.

"It's not my fault," Calli said. "It's the universe telling me I'm not supposed to work at those places. The planets want me to move on until I find the flower I'm supposed to be sitting on."

Bren rolled her eyes.

"We heard you're sitting on Leon *and* Lindy," Kris added.

Calli giggled. "And Maurice."

"Who is Maurice?"

"The ghost haunting Holly's bathroom. He's a sexy plumber from San Francisco's vintage past, and he vibrates the toilet sometimes when I'm on it."

"I told you," Holly said. "Those were earthquakes."

"Love-quakes."

Bren rolled her eyes again. "I can't listen to this nuttiness right now."

"Me neither," Kris said. "I gotta meet Mark."

"I need to meet Jacob," Holly said.

"I'm gonna meet Leon, Lindy, and Maurice," Calli said.

"I'm on my way to Greg's," Bren said, "and I think he's going to propose."

"Holy fuckadoodles."

"Oh my goodness."

"Propose what?"

"Marriage."

"That's wonderful."

"That's kick ass."

"You mean *propose* propose?"

"Yes," Bren cheered, as she passed Marilyn Monroe's old house.

"We could have a double wedding," Kris said. "I'll tell Ann."

"Anna."

"Right."

"How do you know Greg's going to propose?"

Bren felt butterflies flutter and her lips stretch up into a huge smile. "He's been reading romance books like crazy, he's been extra mooshy lately, he vacuumed, it's his birthday, and he wants me at his apartment at exactly 6:30pm, but I'm gonna be early and surprise him with – " Bren's feet screeched to a halt in his driveway, as her eyes saw Greg . . . in his doorway . . . kissing his ex-girlfriend.

Butterflies dropped.

Her smile fell.

"I . . . have to go," Bren said, clicking off her phone, her heart crashing to the ground, and feeling the ribbon slide through her limp fingers as her happy balloon flew away, up and up and up and . . .

Chapter 1

June 7 – Saturday

CLUNK! THUD, THUD, THUD!

Bren bolted up in bed!

Heart pounding!

Gasping for breath!

Darkness.

Thoughts racing.

Where am I?

Jane Austen poster. Shelves of books. Her bedroom.

My bedroom! Yes. I'm in my bedroom.

She clutched her covers.

Her thoughts were flinging!

She'd been dreaming, remembering Greg, *again*, remembering that day, that galactically heart-smashing, trust-crushing, nightmare-causing day.

Breathless!

Fighting for air!

Bren focused into logical-mode, whipping her eyes to her nightstand, grabbing her ready inhaler and sucking a hit!

She breathed . . . and breathed . . . and breathed . . . in bed . . . shaking.

Shaking so much that her inhaler in her hands was a *blur*.

This nightmare, every night since seeing Greg cheat, was again mucking up her sleep.

Mucking up *her*.

"Daaaamn," she groaned with a super big eye roll, as she sat up in bed.

It had been a month. Was the memory of Greg's cheating gonna keep hijacking her sleep *forever?* She sighed and tried to see the humor in this ridiculous reoccurring nightmare, again, remembering her mom's saying: "a smile kicks a bad day in the balls." But hard to find the funny after four flipping weeks of waking up devastated all over again. Her smile drooped, emotions welled, and still felt so damn duped by Greg.

But . . . sniff . . . pajama sleeve nose wipe . . . she fought her feelings, so much depending on her staying strong for just one more stressful week before Kris's wedding. She breathed and thought and fought to stay positive, listening to the happy birds chirping outside her apartment. She wondered if birds cheated. Were birds monogamous, or were the treetops below her window full of bird orgies and that's why they were all cheerily chirping?

She looked around at reality to have less weird thoughts, looked at her still ceiling fan as stagnant as her enthusiasm, at her special bookshelf of erotic poetry that used to be her favorite guilty pleasure, but now gave her as much joy as a vibrator with dead batteries. The morning sunlight trying to shine around her curtained window barely enlivened her shadowy shelves of happy-ending romance novels just beyond the end of her formerly romance-romping bed, shelves of total frickin' fiction her now-wise head reminded, as her now-broken heart grumbled and her now-numb sex gathered dust, swearing for the 34th morning in a row to never ever let herself be bamboozled by a book or boyfriend again.

"Ass penguins," her books said.

What?

Her books just talked?

Whooooa. Was getting no sleep making her delirious?

STOMP. STOMP. STOMP.

Now there was stomping.

No delusion.

Someone was out there. Beyond her books, beyond her room.

Bren scrambled to her knees, her heart pounding and fuzzy brain spinning its wheels trying to make sense of this. She went into logical-mode again. *Think. Is Madeline moving out? No, that was last week. Is Kris moving out? No, not until tomorrow. Is Barbara showing the upstairs apartment? No, not at 7am.*

"Oh goat balls."

She heard the voice again.

A *man's* voice.

A man's voice saying "Goat balls."

But no man and no goat balls should be in her stairway.

Was he a burglar?

Was he bad guy?

Was he Greg????

"Oh, screw *him!*" her brain announced like a blaring trumpet. This mystery guy was messing with the wrong sleep-deprived, not-gonna-put-up-with-any-more-crap woman.

All her faculties snapped to red alert as she flung her sheets and swung her feets wild into the air and onto her carpet and launched herself out of bed and into action!

She ooooh soooo regretted moving fast.

"Hello bachelorette party hangover," she said to her totally-throbbing head. Once again, paying the price for enjoying something fun. Adrenaline barreled her forward, wobbling and bumping around her bedroom in the dark to wrap her yellow fuzzy bathrobe around her sweat-wet pajamas. Just her luck to be woken up so early on a Saturday morning. She marched her bare feet from her soft carpet to the entry's chilly wood floor, out of the dark, snatched her pepper spray off her nightstand, unlocked her apartment door, yanked it wide open, and stomped onto the carpeted landing at the top of the stairs, ready to face this intruder!

Oh! Sunlight blasting below the long stairway was blinding

She squinted.

Through the building's open door down there, the summer rays were bouncing bright off the sidewalk and up into her blinking eyes. Her pupils fought to focus as she looked down the narrow stairway's twenty maroon carpeted steps. The light was so bright that Bren averted her eyes down to her feet, and saw Jane Austen on a stair.

Huh?

Pride and Prejudice was there on the stair by Bren's un-pedicured toes. And on another stair lay Verne, Plath, Tolkien, and Poe. Why were they there? She didn't know.

Bren's half-awake eyes traveled the trail of literature literally littering down her stairs, seeing books by all her favorite authors: Bronte and Alcott and Woolf and Shelley, all scattered around like a hurricane had blown through a library and then into her stairway. Or had Santa Claus generously come seven months early?

Intrigued, her eyes followed all the stunning classics down from Heller to Hardy to Agatha Christie, perusing the mystery until she finally saw a hand handling Dickens. There the plot thickened as she saw the silhouette of a guy kneeling in the building's open front door at the bottom of the stairs.

He didn't look like Greg.

This guy looked more beefcake.

Bren was startled to see a stranger in her familiar land. She didn't recognize him, and he was too young and toned to be Santa.

The blazing morning sunlight glowed gold around his masculine frame as her eyes tried to adjust to the brilliance below her. Her intruder was a muscled shape with his face in shadow, sporting short hair that the wild summer breeze teased while his strong arms reached and grabbed and tossed books into a box.

He filled up two cardboard boxes with book after book, until he got sidetracked with one and started to read it. The cover looked like *The Notebook*. If he was a burglar, then he was the worst one ever. Robbers don't usually break in to read a romance.

Maybe a book thief.

A mysterious hot guy reading a love story surrounded by golden sunlight. *Seriously?* This seemed like the kind of heart-flutteringly meet-cute start of some mushy-romance novel (ahem, she would know). But it was completely wasted on her now-wiser self, immune to such cheesy, romantic, erotic scenarios, no matter how . . . amazing . . . this guy . . . . looked.

Curious, confused, angry, vulnerable, and excited, she studied him, until her banging heart's yearning vaulted her voice out of her throat.

"*Who the heck are you?!*" Bren shouted down at him.

The stranger quickly looked up from one of Bren's favorite books.

She flipped a wall switch. The fluorescent light snapped on.

Illumination.

She saw his face. Handsome.

He saw hers too. He stared. He smiled.

Sparks.

Yep, he was holding Nicholas Sparks.

He stood up, tall, nodded like a gentleman, but also leaned to one side with an air of cockiness. His staring eyes never left her.

Her eyes adjusted to the light and his twenty-something face, Byronically handsome, as he stood among a mess of love-lit as if he had stepped right out of one the romance novels at his sneakered feet. *Good gravy.*

She had exposed him with the light, but unfortunately had exposed herself too. Now she felt vulnerable.

He politely raised his palm. "Hey," he happily called back up to her with a big smile, his deep friendly voice echoing warm up through the narrow passage and into her throbbing hungover head.

"Are you my new neighbor?" he said cheerfully.

What?

Neighbor? Oh . . . damn. Bren quickly spun around and saw the door to the upper apartment above hers was wide open, a foot away from her astonished face. She saw the long flight of carpeted stairs going up, up, up to the now vacant space since motherly Madeline moved out last week. The apartment door was open, and hot guy was moving in?

Oh no.

With only two apartments in the whole three-story building, Bren would now be living on the second floor above the Vento Cafe, and Mr. Hunky Book Man would be living in the top apartment above her? Above her *bedroom?!*

She had just woken up from a nightmare. Now she was in a real one! A good-looking guy was moving in. In the past this sexy Harlequin romance scenario would be a most welcome surprise. But now, gutted by Greg and grieving lost love, and lost trust, she felt absolutely noooo delight in welcoming her new handsome neighbor. Girl neighbors would be better, or some quiet old couple, not a hot guy who read books too. A man-temptation back to another heartbreak was whom she wanted out of her life not moving into it. She swung back around fast and stared panicked at the smiling male stranger.

"*You're* my new neighbor?" she threw down at him hot and hard.

"I sure am," he answered happily, starting to walk up the stairs toward her.

Yikes.

She tensed, her wide eyes watching him gently reaching down and nonchalantly picking up his litter of wondrous books as he slowly walked up, closing the space between his muscular body and her smaller, tightening one.

She clutched her pepper spray.

Step by casual step the sexy mystery man kept climbing up to her, closer and closer. His toned arm stretched down for *Bossypants*, showcasing his thick bicep while wearing a muscle-stretched t-shirt and blue jeans.

He got nearer.

She got nervous.

"Is your wife moving in with you?" she asked.

He chuckled. "Wife? I'm not married."

Damn.

Another book, another stair.

"Your girlfriend?"

"Nope. I don't have one of those either."

Damn damn.

"Your boyfriend?"

"Nope. I'm straight."

Another book, another stair.

Damn damn damn.

Another book, another stair.

"So. It's just *you*, moving in?"

"Yep."

Damn damn damn damn.

Another book, another stair.

Her heart thumped her chest.

Finally, he stopped only four unnerving stairs away; he stretched down and rescued up Jane Austen's masterpiece with a mighty, gentle hand and appropriately placed her on top of all his other authors as he looked up and gave Bren a smile.

She pointed pepper spray at him!

He looked surprised.

She was surprised too. She'd never seen her hand point a weapon at anyone before. This was *crazy!* She'd never felt this aggressive. Or this exhausted. Or this vulnerable.

"That's an inhaler," he said.

Bren looked at her air can pointing at him. "*Ooooh . . . crap.*"

His grin grew into a gorgeous smile, looking at her with his dazzling blue eyes . . . and his . . . his *everything* . . . There, on her stairs, was a man, a very fit and handsome man. His friendly face was strong and square, with fresh skin that couldn't have seen more than a quarter of a lifetime. He stood casually on her stairs, holding his books, looking up at her with his cool blues radiating calm intimacy and joy, like a happy dog messing with a porcupine.

She stuffed her inhaler back in her bathrobe pocket, folded her arms, and blocked his way. She was not about to give up the high ground.

"I guess we're not friends yet," he said humorously.

"I'm not convinced we're neighbors," she said serious. "Someone would have told me that you were moving in."

"Well, I just rented the place last night."

"Prove it."

"How?"

"Somehow."

"I can show you my rental agreement. It's upstairs."

"I can't let you upstairs."

"Why not?"

"Because I'm not sure you live here."

"I can prove I live here if you let me upstairs."

"I can't let you upstairs because I'm not sure you live here."

"I feel like we're caught in a loop here."

"A catch-22?" she quipped, eyeing his copy of Heller's *Catch-22*.

He glanced down at his stack and smiled. "I love this book," he said to her cheerily. "You ever read it?"

"Yes."

"Really? What's *your* favorite chapter?"

"The chapter where the guy in the stairway does not loudly wake-up the sleeping woman on a Saturday morning at *7am*."

A bell seemed to *ding* in his head. His eyes traveled around her messy bed-hair, bathrobe and probably dark circles under her eyes. He seemed to finally catch a clue. "Ah, damn. I woke you up didn't I? My bad. I'm sorry I woke you. You see, I tripped and my boxes and books went flyin' everywhere like a flock of birds. Pages like wings." He chuckled.

She didn't.

"I'm sorry I woke you, exceedingly sorry."

Exceedingly sorry, she thought, catching that he just quoted Darcy from *Pride and Prejudice*, chapter sixteen.

"But I have to move in this early 'cause the street festival is gonna be goin' on outside today and I needed to move in before the crowds flood the sidewalk."

Crowds? Oh, crud. Bren suddenly remembered. The annual summer festival on Union Street would be ruckussing below her bedroom for two full days. Six blocks of her cute quiet Union Street would now be a noisy crowded insanity of tents, grills, and 100,000 gabbing people. She then noticed the sound of clanging metal poles coming up from the open door below, hearing the tents being set up outside. Soon there would be a loud jazz band rockin' outside her window. So much for going back to sleep.

"I'm sorry I woke you up," he apologized again. "Hey. I'll tell you what. I'll make it up to you. I'll take you to breakfast."

"Breakfast?"

"Sure. I'd make you breakfast, but I'm a terrible cook. I see there's lots of great cafés on this street. I'll get you whatever you want, an omelet, pancakes."

"Pancakes?"

"I love pancakes."

She *tingled*. "I'm not going to breakfast with you. I don't even know you."

"I'm Trent."

"Trent?"

"Trent."

"Trent."

"And who are you?" he asked.

"I'm the woman you just woke up."

"How 'bout I buy you a beer at the festival?"

"No, I'm walking the festival with Kris."

"Oh. Is Chris your boyfriend?"

"No, I don't have a – . . . um . . . I mean. Kris is Krista, my roommate."

"Oh," he said.

She realized she'd slipped him way too much information. Damn his entrancing stack of hypnotic paperbacks.

He seemed to notice her constant ogles at his very impressive pack.

"You've, um, got a lot of books."

He grinned, proudly. "This is just the tip."

Intrigued. "Really?"

"Yeah."

"How big is your collection?"

He smiled, proudly. "Huge."

She swallowed. "Really?"

"Can I set these down?"

She found herself actually nodding, curious how he would treat his books. She watched him caringly glide down all those wonderful books that she knew, intimately, fifteen of her favorites, paper friends, like former lovers she had shared her heart with until they eventually came to an end. She watched Trent let his books go, gently setting them down from her stare to her stair. He eased them down with a pleasingly respectful grace, as if they were his friends too. Hmmm. Bren liked his respectful behavior and relaxed a little more.

He looked up at her. “Barbara.”

“My name's not Barbara.”

He chuckled. “Barbara, the real estate lady, she showed me the apartment last night.” He held up his key.

Crap, she thought. Barbara was the real estate lady. He was really moving in.

“The apartment is amazing. I signed the papers right there and then.”

She knew why. “The view?”

“Totally the view.”

“Better than the view from the Villa Diodati,” she said, testing his love of literature.

His blue eyes shined even brighter. “You know Villa Diodati?”

“Yes.”

“You've been there?”

“No.”

“Oh.”

“Have you?” Bren asked.

“Yeah.”

“You have?”

“Yeah,” he said.

She warmed. Her head tilted. Her heart pounded. “You've been to the Villa Diodati?”

"Totally," he said. "In Switzerland, where Byron and Mary Shelley had their ghost story contest. The contest that inspired her to write *Frankenstein*."

"I know where it is and what it is." Her heart really pounded. "You know it? You know about it? You've been there⁇"

"Yep."

"When?"

"Eight years ago."

"You . . . you . . . went there?" Her palms sweated. "What was it like?"

He smiled. "Rapturous."

She really warmed, super impressed. Too much *wow*. Her head was spinning. Her heart was pumping. Her body was becoming *un*-numb.

"What's your name?" he asked.

"Why the heck were you at the Villa Diodati?" she asked instead of answering.

"I took a trip through Europe in 2006, touring the homes of all my favorite writers: Verne, Byron, Dickens, Joyce, Austen."

She got hot. So hot. So damn *hot*.

He was suddenly more than a gorgeous book collector. He was . . . *gulp* . . . a book lover, like her.

"You know about Villa Diodati and Shelley? Awesome," he said. "Do you read the classics too?"

Did she read the classics? If he only knew. "I do."

"What think you of books?" he quoted *Pride and Prejudice*. "What's your favorite?"

She just stared at him, not giving up herself to this too-good-to-be-true troubadour.

"My favorite is still Jules Verne, *Journey to the Center of the Earth*," he said. "It's the one that got me into reading. Then Shelley. Then Austen."

"You got into Jane that fast?"

"I love her language: 'We will not quarrel for the greater blame annexed to that evening,'" he quoted *P and P* again. "What a great sentence of fun words."

"Like: 'Some people will believe nothing against the testimony of their own experience,'" she quoted *Journey to the Center of the Earth*, to impress him, and test him.

"You know Jules Verne?" he exclaimed, growing a great smile.

She grinned back. "I know Jane and Jules."

"*Jane and Jules* sounds like a fun romance book."

"I don't think they would have gotten along."

"Why not?"

"They had nothing in common."

"They both loved books." He grinned.

She smirked.

"They could have written a book together."

"*Journey to the Center of Pride and Prejudice*?" Bren suggested.

"Awesome."

"Elizabeth and Darcy could decode a poem that leads them into a volcano."

"Down into an enchanting world of adventure and witty banter."

"Risks of perils and prejudice."

“Desires and discovery.”

“And amidst all the wonders of chasms, crystals and creatures the most wondrous find found was romance.”

“So much so that the unusually aloof Darcy burst forth declarations of his affection for Elizabeth.”

“And overcoming her pride and misunderstandings, she equally disclosed her blooming desires.”

“They found the light of love in the depths of the dark.”

“And their descent into the earth became a metaphor for their descent into their relationship.”

“To the center of their hearts.”

“And finding love.”

“And dinosaurs.”

She laughed. “And a ballroom dance with dinosaurs.”

He laughed. “And when they emerged from the depths of their exploration they found themselves bonded to each other, and really needing a shower.”

“Entwined in a glorious happy union, they journey down a tunnel of love, a much funner hole then a volcano’s.”

“And they lived happily ever after.”

Bren’s smile dropped. He was making her feel that “happily ever after” was actually possible. Hope. Too much hope. Too soon. Too overwhelming! *Oh gosh.* What was she doing? Getting enraptured by another guy who could break her heart even more. She had to escape!

“I . . . I . . . I . . . need to sleep!”

Quickly Bren turned away from Trent's beautiful confused face, raced back into her apartment, and whammed her door shut!

Safe.

Not the most graceful exit, but really super necessary.

Out of their catch-22.

Bren was wide-awake now! Her heart banged like a bongo drum solo, adrenaline pumping, her left hand gripping her bathrobe, and reeling from the blood-boiling elation of their thrilling book-banter. Her whole body dripped with sweaty embarrassment, feeling hot like they'd been word-screwing! She'd been out of control. *Not good. Not good at all.* She felt frighteningly vulnerable. Euphoric feelings wildly overwhelmed her cold common sense.

"Nice meeting you," his jovial voice sounded through her thin wooden barricade, as she heard his big hands pick up his big stack and his big footsteps clomp up his stairs, into her life, and walk across her ceiling. Now *he* had the high ground.

Wow.

Her hot wet palm slowly slid wetness down her door. Breathing fast. Brain spinning, heart whamming, body tingling like a raw nerve in the wild, wild wind!

"*What the heck just happened?!*"

Chapter 2

Soooo, this was not the morning Bren had planned.

She washed her hair remembering Trent's smile. She shaved her legs remembering his eyes. She washed her hair remembering his arms and remembering that she already just washed her hair. *Gosh darn it.* She dried off remembering his chin, his chest, his cheerful charm invading her home, her heartache, and her whole new done-with-love thing. She wrapped her yellow towel around herself remembering how fun he made her think, how warm he made her feel, how wild he made her tingle. She brushed and brushed and brushed her teeth remembering their banter and bonding over books, oh books, all his beautiful books!

Spit, rinse, spit, toothbrush back in its holder where it belonged, back to normal, back to organized stability.

She stared at herself in the mirror, gripped the counter, and breeeeathed. *Dammit. Now? Really? Now?* A month after her heart had shattered and a week before Kris's wedding? Now is when Mr. Perfect-For-Her arrives in her life?

Debbie the Disco Ball shining star lights all around the bathroom did help keep her life a little bit lovely.

Feeling woken up in more ways than one, she opened her super organized and well-labeled drawer, brushed her hair and put on makeup while realizing this mix of elation and uh-oh is totally what Kris must have felt a year ago meeting Mark that magical night. The perfect guy at an imperfect time. Although, book-reading Greg had seemed pretty perfect too. But this meet-cute with Trent felt so much different: realer, easier, amazinger. Was amazinger a word? Such an instant and obvious connection. *The* connection. Romeo in real life. He was here. Now what? Date him? Deny him? Be denied by him? Do nothing? Let him date someone else? Lose him forever? Or date him and be cheated on and devastated all over again? She shoved her drawer shut.

Damn Greg . . . damn him . . . so much.

She saw Clark the Clock.

Ooooh life, you stinker. Timing, love, loss, temptation. Life was giving her the big dramas for some reason, when she really needed no drama, but she somehow had to handle it. She hoped her brain could muster up one heck of a plan. Everything was better with a plan.

She straightened tall, rolled her eyes, and marched out of the bathroom, into the earth-toned living room and achingly enjoyed all the colorful pillows and furniture being there for the last day ever, and half of the furniture all tagged with Kris's green Post-its – it looked like a leprechaun pooped around their place, this special place where Kris and her had laughed together at all the dumb TV shows, all their "what-silly-superpower-would-you-want?" cooking convos in their kitchen, all their getting ready to go out on Saturday night bantering under the spinning stars of their bathroom disco ball, and now all their roommate fun would end at noon tomorrow.

Life, you really big stinker.

Big exhale. Bren marched towards her front door where the wild verbal affair on the stairs had happened. *Yikes.* She turned away, right, into her bedroom.

She flipped her light switch on, breaking the dimness with her bright ceiling bulbs, enjoying blasting light on anything hidden. She disrobed and wished all her body's flaws in the mirror could be remedied as easily as making a bed. She covered her imperfect body with clothes. Then she made her bed, tucking her yellow bedspread tight, thinking of memories of her mom's sing-songy voice reminding her: "*When life is wind and rain and sleet, at least you know your bed is neat.*" Indeed, the sight of her smooth yellow bedspread soothed her, so did the sight of her alphabetically organized bookshelves, her clean silver desk, and her two nightstands on either side of her bed. Yet today it all felt like not enough. She toyed with the thought of rearranging things for the first time in eight years. With Kris leaving was it time for a radical change? Maybe redecorate with a Victorian theme, or spaceship neon lights, or paint the walls like a tropical island kinda like Holly had done to her living room. But after Kris leaves that tropical island imagery might make her feel marooned on an island, alone, like *Robinson Crusoe.* She wished smart people would invent screen walls that could project any environment she wanted: a forest, a beach, inside a castle, on the Moon. For fun she could project the inside of a grocery store on her wall, as if her bed was in a grocery aisle. She would probably wanna sleep in the potato chip aisle because if she woke up in the middle of the night the snacks would be right there. Fun thoughts.

Clomp, clomp, clomp.

Snapped out of the snack aisle and back into not-as-comforting reality, her new neighbor's creaking footsteps above her bedroom were un-soothing. Oh this was gonna drive her bonkers having him right up there all the time.

Clomp, clomp, clomp.

Wham!

Oh no, she thought, that *wham* sound wasn't above her, it was below, the downstairs door, and familiar footsteps bounding up the stairs. Kris's footsteps!

No, no, no.

Kris wasn't wasn't supposed to come home now.

Kris-the-matchmaker might run into Trent, talk to him, find out he loves books, then Kris would literally push him and Bren together to be in love; Kris might invite him to the fest with them, invite him to the wedding when Bren was soooo not ready for new love, thus shoving even more crazy into her already chaotic week. Work, the wedding, and this growing guilt of keeping her broken heart a secret from Kris felt like an over-stretched balloon, and blowing Trent into it might totally make it pop! Everything was becoming too much. *Daaaamn.*

What if she just unpinched this stupid big balloon and told Kris the truth, and let it fly wherever it flew? That glorious idea gave her so much relief as she exhaled out . . . then she inhaled logic back into herself. She couldn't, she reminded herself; she couldn't tell Kris about Greg's cheating until after the wedding. If she spilled all her heartbreak to Kris, if Kris found out that Greg cheated on her, Kris would sprint to Greg's apartment and kick-box the crap out of him, and he'd for sure press charges against her, and even if he didn't someone might see Kris's crap-kicking and call the cops. It would be Kris's third arrest for beating up jerk-guys. It'd be hard to have a wedding with the bride in jail. And Bren sure didn't want to yuck Kris's yum with her personal problems during Kris's fun wedding week. And she couldn't tell Holly or Calli or anyone because they might accidentally tell Kris. She felt alone. Bren *sighed* and gripped her sunny dress. Just a couple more weeks of keeping this balloon secret pinched tight, she told herself. After Kris's wedding, after Kris's honeymoon, then Bren could tie Kris to a chair and tell her the truth. Until then Bren had to keep faking a smile, and she had to keep Trent's existence a secret. Avoid anymore drama. Kris would move out tomorrow morning and never even know Trent moved in. Bren just had to keep them apart until noon tomorrow.

Lickity split, Bren swooshed open her curtains, letting the afternoon light brighten up her whole bedroom golden and turn her yellow sundress into a Bren-shaped sun. Time again to pretend for her friend that she was happy and not heartbroken, to be a good maid of honor, to be a good friend, and not make a mess of things.

Bren breeeeeeeeathed in and out, took another look at her calm-inspiring bed, and forced her frowning mouth up into a believable smile and . . .

Kris was still in the stairway?

Why?

Uh oh. Did Kris meet Trent?

Bren zoomed to the door and eavesdropped on a rattling sound, sneaking a peek through the peephole, then dropped her tense shoulders and rolled her eyes while seeing her roommate rummaging through her purse outside their unlocked door.

"Holy clit-lickers," Kris exclaimed. *Rummage, rummage, rummage.*

Oh, for crying out loud. Bren lit up a BIG smile for her bestie and flung open their door.

"Hi, Kris!"

"Heeeey," Kris sang out to her.

Whoa. Bren's jaw dropped when she saw Kris's neck.

"Wow," Kris cheered. "Yoooou look so fucking pretty."

Bren stared at Kris's neck.

"How are you, bunny?" Kris pulled her into a big squeezing hug.

"I'm great," Bren lied brightly, inhaling Kris's clashing mix of homemade green apple shampoo and magazine sample perfume while getting crushed. She hugged Kris back, while wondering what the heck had happened to her neck. Kris seemed extra mooshy today. Bren got released and watched Kris whoosh into their apartment.

"You're a fucking lifesaver," Kris said. "I'm so glad you're home. I was a second away from kicking in the door. Couldn't find my key. One of these days I'll clean out this jungle in my purse. Thank God *you're* holding onto the wedding rings, 'cause I'd sure lose 'em."

Bren stood open-mouthed.

"Happy National Play Outside Day," Kris wished her.

"Same to you. Let's go play outside."

"Totally. I just gotta do something first . . . but I can't remember what? What was I gonna do here?" While trying to remember, Kris flitted happily around their home. Her tall, athletic frame clacked over their hardwood floor to their round wood kitchen table in her stylish gorgeous green sundress which accentuated her lush, long hair as Kris tossed her Hermes purse onto a wooden chair while kicking off her Prada shoes willy-nilly over the floor, then turning back to Bren, *still* not explaining what the heck happened to her neck.

"Sweet fuck, you look great."

"Kris."

"Your face has an extra glow today."

"It does?"

"Yeah. And I see a sparkle in your eyes."

"I'll have to get that fixed."

"And that's such a cute dress. You look like a pretty little dandelion."

"Kris."

"I love it."

"Is it new?"

"You don't remember?"

"No."

"*You* bought me this dress?"

"I did?"

"Yes. For my birthday last year."

"Did I really?"

"Yes."

"Wow. I have good taste," Kris laughed.

"Cripes, Kris."

"What?"

"Don't you know?"

"Know what?"

"You've got a *hickey!*"

Kris's hand searched her neck. "Do I really?"

"Yes."

"Is it bad?"

"*Yes.*"

"Ooooooooh. So *that's* why people were pointing and laughing at me."

Bren broke out into real laughter at her friend's cartoonish revelation.

"And now *you're* laughing at me," Kris said, laughing too.

"I'm sorry." Bren smiled big for real.

Kris's bare feet vroooomed to their bathroom mirror, almost tripping over her shoes. Bren picked them up and placed them neatly on the labeled “Shoe Rug.” Bren’s heart broke a second time; how was she going to live without Kris’s comedy?

“Fuck my sweet cunt!” Kris shrieked with laughter at her reflection.

Bren chuckled into a smile as she hurried over to investigate today’s lunacy.

Kris stared open-jawed at her hickey. “It’s HUUUUGE!” Kris sang out.

“And red.”

“Like a rose.”

“Like a third areola.”

Kris laughed.

“Mark sure left his mark.”

“Beautifully.”

“Why did you let him do this to you?”

“Because it felt so fucking *gooood*.”

Why did *gooood* things always end up biting us, literately, Bren wondered? “He messed up your neck.”

“It’s just a hickey.”

“It’s a week before your wedding.”

“Oh it’ll be gone by then.”

“You hope.”

“Oh, whatever. Who cares?”

“Uuum. Your guests, your space-religious parents, and *you* when you look like a vampire victim in all your wedding photos.”

“I’m not worried, so you shouldn’t worry.”

“As maid of honor it’s my job to worry.”

"Bunny-Bren, I think part of you likes being maid of honor so you can worry for an actual reason."

"All my worries have reasons."

"Really? Not only are you having two paramedics at my wedding just in case someone has an allergic reaction to the reception dinner or falls off the roof, but you're also having guard-people stand around the wedding wearing baseball gloves to catch any fly balls that might get hit towards the ceremony?"

"You're having your wedding in a park with baseball fields; it makes total sense."

"You crack me up."

"You stress me."

"*You* stress you."

"For good reasons."

Kris cracked up again.

What was life gonna be like without Kris there to stress her out?

Clomp, clomp.

Uh oh. Speaking of stressing her. Bren wildly coughed to cover up Trent's clomping.

"Do you have a cold?"

"Um . . . *cough, cough* . . . asthma."

"Is it my perfume again? I used Kate Winslet's magazine sample scent today."

"I'm-I'm-I'm just so excited to walk the festival. Why are you here?" Bren calmly freaked out. "We were supposed to meet at the barbecue tent."

"Why did I come here?" Kris wondered aloud.

Bren secretly frantically fidgeted her fingers waiting for her friend to organize her thoughts.

Kris looked around, and around, then down. "*Oh yeah*, I decided to wear my sandals today instead," Kris finally epiphanied.

"Well, let's grab your shoes, wrap a scarf around your neck and go," Bren said while hooking her arm around Kris and playfully pulling her dawdling friend across their apartment to quickly find her darn sandals.

"What's the rush?"

"Um, it's 2:30," Bren reasoned. "We told Holly we'd arrive at 4:30. That means we only have two hours to walk the festival before we need to be at her party."

Kris bounced to a halt. "Fuck sake, bunny. Chill out. For once in your life be late to something. It'll be good for ya."

"I don't wanna be late. I'm really excited to go to Holly's party," Bren said sorta truthfully.

"You are?"

"And I want a bunch of pre-party just-you-and-me-time to celebrate our last full day as roomies," Bren said truthfully.

"Ooooooooh," Kris cooed sweetly, getting mushy. "It's our last day."

Oh dear. No time for tears.

Kris went in for another big hug.

Rock music.

Kris stopped.

They both looked up.

The Rolling Stones rocked their ceiling.

So, this was gonna need some explaining.

"Is someone upstairs?" Kris asked.

Hot embarrassment flushed Bren's cheeks.

Think. Think. Think. "Oh . . . um . . . " Bren stammered, her brain whirring. "That's um, Marvin. He's um . . . repairing the . . . thing."

"Marvin likes classical music. Why's he rockin' the Stones?"

Bren shrugged. "Uh, maybe he's . . . on crack."

"You can't do crack at seventy."

"And you can't find your sandals if you don't look for them." Bren ever-so-kindly yet quickly rotated her side-tracked friend. "Hurry so we can go."

Kris sniffed back feelings.

Bren flipped on Kris's bedroom light.

Oh . . . cripes. Kris would never find sandals in this massive mess.

The light let Bren see everything all right, everything all over the place. The dreaded land of clutter. Dirty clothes covered a smothered carpeted floor as Bren beheld a bedazzling junkyard of strewn skirts, shirts, shoes and skis. Underwear everywhere. Everything anywhere. Purses and pillows. Boots and bags. Trophies and towels. Mementos and mags. All exploded around like a kaleidoscope of holy geez.

"I've got hickies in *ooootber* places too," Kris giggled naughtily.

Bren smirked. "Ooookay. I don't need to see those."

"Sweetie, I have to tell you all about the incredibly romantic night Mark gave me after the bachelorette party yesterday," Kris said with glee. "And this romantic morning."

Bren polite-smiled. Her hardly healed heart couldn't take many more of Kris's successful-love stories.

"After the bachelorette party, I went to Mark's and found him sweetly waiting for me in his bed, wearing *only* a hat," Kris told merrily.

Bren missed the old days when their in-depth discussions about politics, business, and who might get kicked off *The Bachelor* next could pass the Bechdel test instead of convos about "Mark, love, Mark, wedding, Mark is gonna wax his balls for their honeymoon."

"Mark romanced me *soooo* fucking good last night," Kris jubilated, while Bren listened. "He had mint-scented candles and Elle Fitzgerald singing and a 'Happy Bachelorette' party hat was over his big beautiful cock."

Good gravy. What a visual she now had to carry around, happy that her bestie had found happiness, but having to hear about the splendor of Kris's romance after hers imploded was a silent torment. Though Trent's clomping was not a *silent* torment. And Kris finding *both* sandals in this bedroom mess would a take zillion years. They didn't have that kind of time.

Bren remembered Hippocrates: "Desperate times call for desperate measures." "Kris, you're never gonna find them. So . . . I'll loan you my Dolce&Gabbana sandals."

Kris looked up, eyes wide. "Seriously?"

Sigh. "Yes."

Kris smiled ear to ear.

"It's a special day. So."

"You're so fucking awesome."

Bren rushed to her closet and procured her $400 sandals that would probably get tragically lost amid Kris's bedroom junkyard, and a pretty silk scarf to pretty Kris's mangled neck. She returned to see Kris grabbing mini-booze bottles from their kitchen cupboards. Bren brought Kris the sandals. But Kris baulked at the scarf.

"I'm not hiding my hickey."

"Whatta you mean?"

"I want people to see it."

This did not compute. "Why?"

"To show it off."

"Show off that your fiancé is a werewolf?"

"Show that Mark loves me."

"Show that he mauled you."

"It's Facebook on my neck, displaying my relationship status."

"Your status is chew toy."

"My status is *loved*. And it'll keep guys from hitting on me."

"I think your soccer ball-sized diamond ring does that trick."

"But this is better. It isn't store-bought affection, it's real, ravenous affection."

Oh cripes. This was classic love-loony Kris. More sensibility than sense.

"Friend intervention," Bren declared.

Kris rolled her eyes. "Listening."

"I'm thinking people at the party will take pictures, post them online, and you'll go viral as the "hickey woman." The world will laugh at you, your clients will drop you, your easily triggered temper will flare, you'll yell for everyone to go F-themselves and the entire planet will explode in a cataclysmic apocalypse."

Kris smirked. "I'm thinking you're overthinking."

"I'm thinking you're *under*-thinking. This cynical world will totally twist your sweet love mark into a scarlet A."

"You gotta stop being so scared about what other people think."

"But what people think matters."

"What I think matters." Kris pointed at her big red hickey with a great big smile. "And I think *this* is love!"

"What?"

"My hickey is love."

"That's love?"

"Yeah. *This* is love. I'm proud of my hickey!" Kris announced jubilantly. "You're always yacking to me about stories and symbolism. Well this is a symbol, a symbol of Mark's love for me. Mark's mark of love. This is me and Mark's red fern that grew between us."

"That's not what the red fern meant."

"Whatever. This symbolizes that I found the love of my life and I'm happy and passionate and proud of my love, so proud that I'm letting my neck go full frontal to the whole world and I don't care what anyone thinks. I love my scarlet H!"

Bren burst out laughing.

Kris did too.

They looked at each other.

"Oh I'm gonna miss our daily bullshit," Kris said.

Bren nodded, silently thinking: *Then don't move out.*

Then Kris's smile thinned. "Friend confession," Kris said sheepishly.

Bren tilted her head. "Listening."

"I've been worrying too."

Uh oh. Now Bren worried about what Kris might be worried about. *Moving out? The wedding? Getting married? The odds against sixty-plus years of fidelity?*

"I'm worried about *you*."

Bren's eyebrows shot up. "*Me?*"

"Here. Alone. After I move."

Bren worried that Kris worrying would accidentally unleash all the emotions she was trying to hide. "I don't want you worrying. Not this happy pre-wedding week."

Kris's eyes got misty.

Oh dear, no emotions, not now.

"I feel so guilty." Sniff. "I'm ditching you."

Uh oh.

Sniffle. Nose wipe.

Footsteps continuing around their ceiling.

No time for this. Bren tried to hurry Kris along by taking the mini-vodkas and tequilas from Kris's hands and packing them in her purse.

"I worry – ."

"No need to worry. I'll be fine," Bren assured her. "Everything's fine. Let's go."

Kris stood still. "But I worry that when you're not at work, you'll just stay at home all the time, laying on your bed, listening to romantic movie soundtracks, and reading. I won't be here to boot your ass out the door. You won't go out and meet new guys and find the kind of amazing love I found."

Getting uncomfortable, Bren struggled to keep a good-humored smile pasted on her face.

Kris stayed still. "A month ago everything was fucking perfect. I was so happy you and Greg were working out so well. I figured he'd move in with you when I moved out so you wouldn't be here by yourself. But, then you dumped him because he decided he never wants to have kids."

Thank goodness Kris was still believing that lie, Bren thought. "Sometimes things don't work out," Bren said half-truthfully.

"But now you'll be here all alone and you'll never go out."

"I'll go out."

"Sitting in the cafe downstairs and reading is not going out."

"Technically it is."

Kris smirked, but then busted into ugly-face tears.

Oooh shoot, Bren thought as she fought back her own tears and hugged her big hearted bestie, a little cringed that her neck was next to that icky hickey. "Don't cry. California is in a drought. We have to conserve water," Bren joked.

Kris chuckled through sobs. "I'm gonna come back and kick your ass if you don't date."

Bren rubbed her back, and sighed. "I promise to sleep around."

"Good."

"I'll catch all kinds of chlamydia just for you."

"You better."

"I will." Bren felt Kris's tears drip down her back and into her dress. At least she hoped it was tears.

"Go crazy. Have fun. So you can find love too."

Kris's thinking was as messed up as her bedroom. Love was mangling Kris's mind. Bren fretted, now knowing a romance could just end instantly, now knowing the danger of letting your heart go all in and believing everything will be glorious forever, now knowing the pain when that belief in love is shattered. Suddenly Bren felt a hot whoosh of fear and guilt. Was this all *her* fault? For years Bren had filled her friend's ears with lovely lofty tales of all the romances she had read, to inspire them both to keep trying to find better guys, find the perfect guys. But now, after Greg, all that perfect love stuff in books seemed pretty much a bunch of flooplezoople, and Kris was thinking she had found Mr. Perfect, and was gonna marry him, and now wanted to wear his suck-mark in public. *Damn.* Had she duped Kris like Greg had duped her? Bren felt like Dr. Frankenstein. She had created a monster, a duped love-crazy monster on the loose and out of control!

They pulled out of their hug and Bren looked at her roomie's mascara smudged face. "Don't worry about me," she said, to ease Kris's stress. "I'll be fine here by myself."

The music upstairs stopped.

THU-THUMP, THU-THUMP, THU-THUMP, TH-THUMP . . .

Trent's footsteps thumped down from his upstairs apartment, and on the other side of her wall, Trent's embarrassingly squawky singing voice tried to swoon like Jagger as Bren heard him close his apartment door.

"W*oooooooo yeeah*," he sang as he bounded down the stairway and out the building.

WTF confusion raised Kris's eyebrows. "That doesn't sound like 70-year old Marvin."

Daaaamn. Bren looked at Kris like a deer in the headlights. Then . . . "Oh, yeaaaaah," Bren pretended to just casually remember off the top of her head. "We have a new neighbor."

Chapter 3

Sunshine, music, festival tents, and people-packed Union Street were a welcome relief from everything. Slow walking through the most fun day of the year in her favorite neighborhood with her bestie was better than a brand new book, or at least equal. Finally something she had planned to do today was working out wonderfully. Well, almost.

Instead of two roomies roaming the fest while reminiscing about their fun eight years together or debating what bubblegum flavor each day of the week would be, Kris kept asking about their new neighbor: "How'd you meet him?" "Do you like him?" What's he do?" Wanna have a double-wedding?"

Cripes.

Bren clicked the cap off a little gin and splashed it in her lemonade, as Kris kept asking. Bren kept sipping, walking three crowded shoulder-bumping blocks between the outdoor runway fashion show to the corner by the ice cream tent, Bren was starting to feel a nice relaxing buzzzz. It didn't take much gin to make her grin, more of a thinker than a drinker. She hoped this bit of booze might ease her stress today and get her mind off how madcap this overloaded week was going to be with work, the wedding, pretending to not be heart-wrecked, and having to live with – *oh crap* – Trent!

She actually squeaked out loud when she saw him standing across the street by the falafel vendor. She quickly dropped down behind the crowd, probably looking like a wacko. *Cripes.* In a throng of thousands, what were the odds she would see him? Kris was busy deciding between Chocolate Chip Mint or Rocky Road. She should steer Kris away quick, so Kris wouldn't try to matchmake Trent and her together.

But . . . Bren kinda liked what she saw.

Curious, she slowly poked her head up to sneak a peek at him. *Woooow.* He looked even more gorgeous in the sunlight. Handsome face, muscled arms, and sexy clothes. Yes, it was definitely Trent.

Her eyes savored the sight.

He stood tall and tan in the bright summer sunlight, his bulbous triceps kinda shiny as he drank a swallow from of his plastic cup like a hunk in a soda commercial. He looked like he could be in a soda commercial; he had changed out of his t-shirt and jeans and into some way better clothes. Her eyes read what they said: that he had style. His sky blue t-shirt fit perfectly over his brawny covered muscles and accentuated the showing ones. Not many guys could pull off multi-pocket tan cargo shorts, but they hung smart on his epic physique with ties below his knees, showcasing his toned calves, ready for adventure; *mmmm*, what would a jungle journey with him be like? The ready red long-sleeve shirt tied around his waist showed he was a smart

San Franciscan, knowing the temp would drop as soon as the ocean swallowed the sun. His brown man-sandals weren't silly flip-flops; they were those solid hiking sandals, like Achilles might wear when heroically sword battling. *Cripes.* Well-read, well-mannered, and also well-dressed . . . well, keeping her life uncomplicated right now just got even harder. His hair looked a lighter brown than in her stairway and she watched the breeze playfully toss his tips, and also play with her heart. So different to see him outside in the wild, primal. She breathed a big breath. Clearly she hadn't dreamt him; he was in real life, other people were seeing him too, like the three pretty twenty-something women talking to him.

Record *screeeeeeeeeech!*

Who?

Her eyes zoomed in on the enraptured faces of three laughing hair-flipping flirties googly-eyeing at his every word, as his exuberant hands helped animate some exciting-looking story he was telling them with bewitching hubris. His giggling audience smiled ear-to-ear watching The Trent Show. Was he discussing Bryon with them too? These girls seemed into Bieber, not Byron.

She was surprised to see him fitting in so well so fast, and with some of the neighborhood's prettiest pretties. They were hypnotized by his charm, the same charm she had accidently swooned to that morning in the stairway. Bren suddenly felt less special.

Sigh. *Darn it.* Just another player, she sadly thought, actually feeling her heart sink into her stomach, while her brain relished having a definite reason to reject him. But she couldn't turn away. Curiosity kept her eyes glued to his glitter of girls now snapping selfies with him.

Selfies? Why?

Lots of sunlight shining on this happening, yet still a mystery.

"*Who's that?*" Kris asked.

Bren startled and dropped her drink!

Kris laughed loud and apologized.

Bren stammered as she wiggled the wet from her toes.

"Do you know him?"

"Uuuum . . . " Really not wanting to lie.

"Wait," Kris said, grabbing Bren's arm. "He looks like the guy you described. Is *that* our new neighbor?"

Bren stiffened and didn't answer, but her blushing face must have said "*Yep, that's totally the hunk that hot-book-talked my vag back to life*" as Kris's mouth dropped open and her eyes sparkled!

"He's fucking cuuuute!" Kris overreacted. "You didn't tell me he was so fucking cute!"

Bren thought silently: *No, of course I didn't, because I knew you would make a HUGE deal out it.* "He's all right," Bren shrugged, wiping her palms on her dress.

"Those girls sure think he's more than all right," Kris observed.

They certainly did.

"What's his name again?"

"Trent."

"TREEEEEEEENT!" Kris shouted over the loud crowd and music.

Ooooooooh damn.

Her bestie's embarrassing barbaric yawp sounded past fifty head turns and verbally flicked Trent's ear. His head curiously bobbed up and around, looking a like a hound dog hearing his name called to dinner. He looked baffled until he saw Kris WAVING her arms like a lunatic!

Oh cripes.

He squinted, looking confused until *ding*; his eyes saw Bren and his mouth grew a smile.

Shoot. She should have worn sunglasses; but she had wanted to see everything clearly. *Gosh darn it.* Once again she had tried to see truth in the light but she exposed herself too.

Kris WAVED him over!

"What are you doing? Don't call him over here."

"Why not? I wanna meet him."

"He's not worth meeting."

"He sure as hell is. This guy's gonna be living alone with you in the building after I leave. I need to make sure he's not a psycho serial killer."

Bren wanted to say: *Then maybe you shouldn't move out and leave me alone with him.*" Instead she watched Trent politely wave goodbye to his hottie fan club, and walk away from them and towards Kris and her.

The Trentettes looked completely puzzled until their eyes locked onto Bren's face and scowled at her, and she scowled at Trouble with a capital T wading through the festival crowd to her, closer and closer. *Cripes.* Her separate worlds were about to crash together. Tragical!

Her heart banged another bongo solo. Her inhaler lay ready in her purse if she needed a hit of air.

Kris kept watching him.

Bren b-b-breathed nervous.

Trent walked up to them.

The front of his t-shirt read: *Stranger in a Strange Land.*

Exhale. What a cheeseball, she thought, a really gorgeous cheeseball.

"Heeeey," he said warmly to Bren.

She politely flashed a grin, with limited air to speak, while eye-touring his tan, toned bod, from his sandals to his smile.

"Good to see you again," he said smilingly as he glanced at her hand, seeming glad she didn't have her inhaler pointed at him this time.

"Uh huh," she murmured unencouragingly.

"You look very nice," he complimented.

She flashed a polite grin again, feeling Kris's eyes hot on her too. San Francisco's summer day was 68-degrees, but felt a sweltering 168 in this pressure cooker situation.

"Did you get some sleep after we talked?" Trent asked.

Bren secretly scoffed. How could she possibly sleep after their passionate stairway encounter? She had to take a cold shower.

"Noooo. I, uh, I was up, so . . . " Bren said, trying to not let Kris know that she had any sleep difficulties.

"I still feel bad about waking you," he said, then turned his attention to Kris's beaming face. "I woke her up this morning with my loud movin' in. I'm a dunce."

"I'm a Kris."

"Hi Kris." Trent's eyes popped bigger. "Oh. She mentioned you. You're her roommate, yeah?"

"Yeah. And you're Trent, our new neighbor."

"I am."

"Where are you from?"

"Oh. I was living over in Haight/Ashbury," he answered.

Kris's eyes wandered aaaaaaaall over Trent's gorgeousness too, not subtly, while Trent wide-eyed Kris's huge relationship status on her neck. Kris ogled him like if she wasn't engaged she might jump Trent herself. But she shot an excited look to Bren like "*you tooooooootally need to hook-up with this guy and tell me all about it!*"

Bren's polite grimace tried to chill out Kris's matchmaking before Kris –

"So, do you have a prison record?"

– made a scene.

Trent smiled. "Nope. No prison record."

"Are you respectful to women?"

He smiled more. "I am."

"And will you treat my bestie with total respect after I move out or will I have to *rrrrrrrip* off your lovely balls and toss 'em in the bay?" she said as sweet peach pie.

He looked shocked, then chuckled, then caught a clue that Kris wasn't kidding. "Kris, me and my balls will be on our best behavior," he assured her for the sake of his sack.

"Woooonderful," Kris elated.

Kris was once again one of Bren's heroes, and one of her worries.

Trent smiled at Kris's pleasant protectiveness. If he only knew the clobbering Bren's karate green-belt, kickboxing instructor, fierce physical trainer roommate gave to the boyfriend Bren dated before Greg for secretly sexting a coworker Trent might bolt back to the Haight like a bullet.

"You're moving out?" he asked, instead of bolting.

"You didn't tell him I'm moving out?"

"We didn't get to that," Bren said.

"I'm moving in with my fiancé."

"Oh. You're getting married? Congrats."

"You didn't tell him I was getting married?"

"We didn't get to that," Bren said.

"Bren's my maid of honor."

"Oh, your name's Bren?"

Kris's mouth fell open. "You didn't even tell him your name?"

Bren blushed. "We didn't get to that."

"What the hell did you two talk about?"

"Books," Trent blurted happily.

Bren winced.

Kris froze. "You like *books?!*" Kris flipped out with glee!

Dang him. Bren gritted behind her grin.

"I *love* books," he said, making things worse. "I even started a book club in the Haight," he said, making things more worse.

"A bookclub? Holy shit."

Uh oh.

Just as Bren feared, Kris immediately zinged into matchmaker mode.

"Oooooooh, that's amazing. Bren loves books too."

"I could tell."

Bren blushed so hot she felt like Joan of Arc getting cooked.

"So, you *both* like books," Kris exclaimed cheery. "Well, that sure is lucky. Isn't it, Bren?"

Bren struggled up a smile.

"It's an awesome coincidence," Trent said.

"It is. You two could talk about books all the time."

"We could," Trent happily agreed.

"You could even talk about books today. Couldn't he Bren?"

Oh, cripes, no.

"Or are you hanging out with your girlfriends over there?" Kris asked.

"Girlfriends? Oh," he laughed. "No. I just met 'em and we got to talking. I'm just wandering around checking out the festival on my own."

"All alone?" Kris said, half sympathy, half excited.

Oh super cripes.

"Our friend Holly is having a party. We're on our way there."

"Oh yeah?"

Bren cringed.

"You wanna go with us?"

Bren blushed even hotter.

"I'd love to," he said happily.

Bren sweated.

Kris turned to Bren. So did Trent.

Bren totally fake-smiled.

Kris winked playfully to Bren as if she had just done her the greatest favor ever.

Damn. Not today. Not this week. Maybe not this life.

"Follow me," Kris said merrily and led the way.

Trent flashed Bren a happy grin and followed.

Bren saw the back of Trent's shirt. It read: "*The Other Side of Paradise.*"

She shook her head. *Total cheeseball.*

A gorgeous, tempting, heartbreaker cheeseball.

This was such a mistake.

Union Street, usually quiet and charmingly laidback the way a Colbie Caillat song feels, had ka-boomed into a carnival of *woo hoo!* Bands and BBQ and crowds of zillions swarming either side of the big white tents stretching six city blocks like a white spine down the center of Union Street's back. Moving like molasses past one vertebrate tent to the next Bren, normally would be enjoying the chaos of fun, jazz, smoked chicken, weirdo art, laughter, and squeezing past endless chatty partiers. But emotion-stirring Trent was hijacking her last roommate day with Kris.

Instead, she was nervous and confused and eavesdropping hard on Kris quizzing Trent relentlessly to find out how fitting he was or wasn't for her friend. Bren listened and learned stuff she probably should have interrogated out of him in her stairway. Kris uncovered that he was twenty-nine from Boulder, Colorado, dropped out of college, wandered Europe, moved to Seattle, then to SF's Haight, that his mom is an astronomy professor and his younger sister is a trying to be an actress in L.A., and that he got all his muscles without a trainer, using free-weights and watching YouTube instructional videos.

Bren's bombarded brain processed so much info so fast, like reading Spark Notes instead of a slow novel.

And the more he talked and made Kris laugh the more comfortable Kris seemed to be with him, comfortable enough to happily share the stories of fun times her and Bren had spent at each restaurant, bar, shop they passed by: the dog-stole-Bren's-phone incident, the night they played panty Frisbee in a bar, the night drunk-Bren fan-fawned a stranger she thought was Katy Perry, and, of course, the classic beauty salon fart.

Uuuugh. Bren blushed every time Trent looked back at her with a "you seriously did that?" smirk. Bren knew that Kris wasn't intentionally trying to embarrass her; that their memorable memories were some of Kris's favorite times and she boasted them proudly. But it was a bummer that every mentioned memory that ended with Kris and her drunk-shouldering each other to late night pancake restaurants and back to their home for more laughs, reminded Bren that their roommate nights were about to end, forever.

Everything is changing.

Though, when they veered right and turned the corner, Fillmore Street was once again the same annual neighborhood-wide frat party gone supernova!

It was a PAAAAAAAAARRRRRRRTTTTYYYYY!!!!!!!!

Trent's jaw dropped seeing Fillmore Street freakin' with the wide sidewalks packed with party people spilling out of every bar and restaurant they passed.

"Abandon sobriety, all ye who enter here," Bren thought as they proceeded into the even stranger land.

They walked through the gauntlet of debauchery, squeezing through the billowing crowds spilling out of every pub, club, eatery and lounge. A thousand-plus revelers gabbed, schmoozed, drank, smoked, yelled, danced and sometimes drunkenly fell over on the sidewalks. Traffic-jammed cars honked their horns, buildings vibrated with boomin' DJ beats, and, this festival day, everyone was having the time of their lives!

There seemed to be a party in every house on the side streets too, and each bar's bangin' drumbeats tried to be louder than the other bar across the street. Beer and booze flowed into patron's glasses from never-ending waterfalls, and gobs of pretty pretty people waited outside every drinking venue just to get in.

Swarms of not-so-sober, horny, happy revelers clustered inside and in front of each carousing watering hole. Ginormous security guard bouncers in black suits and earpieces looking like secret service agents stood in front of each bar door, checking IDs and keeping out the uncool. The slice-serving pizza places had lines oodling out the door. And every so often some inebriated loudmouth would yell a sustaining howl and everyone would join-in with follow-up long-sustained *whoooooooos* until the entire neighborhood came alive as a great roaring party monster!

Bren and Kris instinctively "*whoooooed*" along with everyone else from conditioned tradition.

Trent seemed awed at it all. "Now *this* is a party," he said.

"You like?" Kris asked.

"Oh yeah. I love a good party."

"Well this party happens every June."

"Excellent," he said, sounding impressed and surprised. "I thought things would be calmer in a more affluent neighborhood. I had no idea it got so Gatsby in the Marina."

Bren and Kris smirked at each other.

"This isn't the Marina," Bren schooled him. "This is still Cow Hollow."

He looked bewildered. "What's a Cow Hollow?"

"It's where you live."

"I do?"

"You do."

"I thought I moved to the Marina."

"The Marina is further down here. You moved to Cow Hollow."

"I mooooved to Cow Hollow?"

Bren rolled her eyes. "You should put *that* saying on a t-shirt."

He smiled. "My mom sends me these shirts."

"Oh. That's sweet," Bren said, legit heart-squeezed and now finding the cheesiness of his t-shirts endearing. "What do you send your mom?"

"Pictures of me wearing the shirts."

Bren smirked.

"Why do they call it Cow Hollow?" he asked.

"There used to be cows here."

"Did the party people scare 'em off?"

"Yeah. When they tipped them over."

Trent laughed.

Bren realized that they were passing the bar where Kris and Mark first met and easy-bantered a year ago, like Bren and Trent had easy-bantered in the stairway that morning, just as magical, just as soulmatey? *Wow, life, you crafty romantic.* Bren felt tingly one-with-the-universe, then back down to Earth as she spied a guy peeing on a side street winking at her, then she almost tripped over a girl holding her drunk friend's hair while she hurled on the sidewalk. Bren felt glad to have outgrown sidewalk hurling.

A macho dude demonstrated his muscley buffness to all the ladies by doing pull-ups on a tree branch, until it snapped and Bren stepped over his dumb drunkenness. Then she passed a girl using pantyhose to pull her wobbly intoxicated BFF behind her like a water-skier up to the next party. Bren wasn't sure if it was her heart getting continually pummeled by love or soon turning twenty-nine, but all this fun just wasn't as *FUN* as it once was, especially with the stress of now having Trent with them.

Bren envied the seagulls gliding above them, gliding so free and easy without worry, unafraid of falling, trusting the wind, trusting that their wings wouldn't fail or that their boyfriend wouldn't cheat on them, break their heart, and send them plummeting down. Or did seagulls, like morning birds, have tree orgies too?

"Aaaaaaaawe my God!" girls exclaimed.

Ugh. The giddy shrieks of drunk girls was also losing its cuteness, especially from the giddy shrieking drunk girls clacking through the crowd towards Trent.

Huh?

More girls were flocking to Trent? Bren had never seen a guy with such pull.

"Excuse meeee," a hottie in apricot sailor shorts giggled up to him. "Are you that guy from the magazine?"

Bren and Kris both did a *whuuuuh?*

Magazine?

"*Hemp Times* magazine?" he joked with smiley smoothness.

"Nooooo," she sang back playfully.

"*Playgirl*?"

"Nooooo," her and her tipsy friend sang back like a drunken glee club.

"Perhaps *SF Knower*?"

"Yeeeeeeees!" the cuties freaked, totally losing their minds and stinging Bren's ears. Pink shorts-girl palmed his bare muscled arm. "You *are* the guy who wrote that *book*."

SCREEEEEEEEEEECH!

WHAT?!

Bren's head popped off and spun around a couple of times.

He wrote a BOOK????

"About the party house, and the girl."

What party house? What girl?

"Yep. That's me," he smiled shyly, but seeming to relish the attention.

"I loved your book so much!" the girl cheered, fawning all over him, just like the three giddy girls on Union Street had done.

Ooooh, Bren realized. So *this* was why girls kept swooning for him?

She and Kris shared a look of shock.

Then Bren watched Trent sheepishly look up at Bren, clearly embarrassed that she was witnessing all this flirty fuss the girls were giving him as they snap-snap-snapped selfies with his blushing face.

"Thank you," pink shorts celebrated with a bounce, almost knocking over her friend. "I'm gonna tape this selfie next to your picture on my fridge."

"Well, I'd rather be on your fridge than your dartboard."

His flirty fans laughed waaaay more than he deserved.

Bren's mouth fell open. *Women were taping his picture to their refrigerators?*

Trent-the-secret-famous-author thanked them for their kind words and politely excused himself.

His new girly friends waved bye bye and screeched "*Oh my God!*" giddily as he turned back to Bren and Kris as if nothing bizarre had happened.

Uuuuuuum, something bizarre *HAD* happened, Bren thought, standing stunned, now knowing that he had more interest in books than just reading them.

Bren circled around him, putting her body between him and the hotties and putting the bright interrogation-light sun directly on him, now seeing him way more clearly.

"*You're an author?*" she cross-examined him.

"Yeah," he admitted bashfully.

"What did you write?"

"A novel."

"What novel?"

"It's called *Helluva Party.*"

Bren's brain-circuits sputtered and sparked. She knew this title. She'd heard people say it. She remembered seeing the hardback in the bookstore window a few weeks ago, just before Greg bummed her so bad that she couldn't even look at a book, and now the gorgeous goofy-shirt author was living in her building, re-exciting her love of books and making her *feel* things?!

Well . . . this was a helluva shock.

Kris's giddy smile looked even more convinced that Trent was perfect for her single friend as they all got walking again. They passed by the four rockin' bars of the Bermuda Triangle while Bren immediately whipped out her phone and Googled his book title.

Ding. There it was.

Helluva Party by Trent Baxter, and there was his picture.

O . . . M . . . G.

Surviving the Inferno of drunkards, the adventurers departed Cow Hollow. They pressed forth and finally crossed o'er the great six-lane chasm of Lombard Street, the cleavage between the two bountiful trendy neighborhoods of fun, and miraculously stepped into the epically cooler Purgatorio land of milk and honey, beauty and money . . . *the Marina.*

They had crossed over into new territory in more ways than one.

Reaching the other side, Bren followed behind Kris and Trent, reading and researching. She saw the rave reviews for his successful novel. She saw it on *The New York Times* Best Seller list. She found an article on the bidding war for his debut novel and the $1.4 million deal. *Cripes*. Enough to afford the rent of the apartment above her.

"*You're famous!*" Bren exclaimed.

Kris took a look at Bren's phone.

"*You're famous!*" Kris exclaimed.

"I guess," he shrugged.

"How come you didn't tell us that?"

"People get weird when they find out."

Yes, they get bouncy and giggly, Bren's thoughts agreed. But she got peeved. He'd been hiding info from her. That's a HUGE deal, and a deal breaker. *Darn it.* Gorgeous, funny, fun Trent had done the one thing she just couldn't tolerate anymore: keeping secrets. He could have told her he was an author in the stairway or when Kris mentioned the girls on Union Street. Heck, he might still be keeping this secret from her if he hadn't gotten *caught* by those Fillmore girls. She was really hoping this good-looking good-booking guy was better than sneaky-Greg. But, alas, he might not be.

Exhaaaaaaaale.

She was peeved . . . but intrigued. She stared at the back of Trent's light-brown head. What other wild secrets was he hiding in there?

She tap-tap-tapped her phone finding out everything he hadn't told her. She found his Twitter page (122,447 followers), she found his Wikipedia page (age twenty-nine, from Boulder, Colorado), and found the interview he just did for *SF Knower* (June issue, "Hottest 30 Under 30", with a wowwingly, jaw-droppingly handsome full-page picture of him). So *that's* how all these women knew what he looked like. She scrolled through Google Images of him at parties, at the beach, at the park, with friends, and with women. *Hmmm.*

Especially one really beautiful woman.

She felt Kris's hands steer her away from crashing into sidewalk newspaper dispensers while she multitasked walking and Googling, then steer her left and around the corner onto trendy Chestnut Street and through a thick loud crowd with a thick cloud of cologne, perfume, alcohol, hairspray, and cocoa butter sunscreen.

Bren knew what was around her: a mega-monstrous swarm of the most stunningly beautiful-looking people in the city, as if someone pulled the fire alarm at a Paris fashion show and every gorgeous celebrity and supermodel was now standing out on the sidewalk, gabbing and flipping their fake-blond hair at the annual look-at-me gathering in the playground of the young, rich, and sexy who lived well, super-shopped, serial-dated, and partied trendy-bar hard in SF's loveliest chicest yuppitopian fairytale land that Bren still had to pinch herself to believe existed outside a *Sex and the City* episode.

Always an amazing sight for Bren to see. But today the interview Trent did for *SF Knower* was farrrrrrr more amazing to ogle and boggle her brain with by reading all the fascinating new things about Trent. Yep, he did drop out of college to wander Europe visiting the homes of famous authors, she read, then he went back to Colorado, then visited homes of American authors, then worked as a waiter in Seattle for two years, then moved to SF for two more years, got his writing in various magazines, then published his first novel just a couple months ago. And, *oh no*, his dad died when he was twelve. And, *oh geez*, his middle name was Copernicus?

"Bren," Copernicus's voice called to her.

She looked up to find his blue eyes in front of her as they walked.

"Are you all right back there?"

"Yes. I'm coming," she breathed out, her legs wobbling, then seeing all the beautiful, beautiful women all around them, but seeing his sparkling eyes and smile checking on her, instead, not them, . . . her.

Well, that's interesting.

She stuffed her phone back in her purse realizing that she was about to learn more about Trent by watching him right there in person.

Kris's hands playfully steered Bren like one of those Segway-things through all the glamorous carousing crowd-traffic blocking their yellow brick road while she glued her eyes to Trent's head as it gawked all around at the beautiful people and multitude of classy high-end stores and restaurants, bars and salons, manicured green trees, and cool posers.

"How would he handle all this temptation?" Bren wondered with mega-curiously. Did he have wandering eyes like Greg? She watched Trent intently. He looked but didn't leer or linger. But his man instincts did have him occasionally gandering all the smooth, exposed skin and beautiful faces of the women he passed by. He was a single man in possession of a good fortune, fame, a manly frame, and a kickass apartment, and he was probably in want of a girlfriend. But would he still look if he had a girlfriend? That was the *real* question.

The too-beautiful-for-words women certainly noticed him, turning from their boyfriends and tipping down their Ray-Bans at Trent spy-style. He smiled politely at them, but kept on walking.

Well, that's really interesting.

It felt like they would *never* get through this crowd of flirty fashionistas. All these Helens of Troy taking Trent's attention bubbled up Bren's nagging doubts about her too-common-to-be-cool looks, once again feeling like she didn't quite pass the hot-or-not test enough to live in this glitzy fairytale land. But with every PR stop Trent made she caught him glancing back at her, and blushing, confusing her head, th-thumping her heart, and rousing her primals as her lungs filled with more Chanel than oxygen.

Inching passed the glassy Apple Store, classy Marina Theater, the sassy high-end venues, and through the hullabaloo of hunks and hotties toward Holly's, they finally broke free and stepped off the curb at the street corner.

Air.

Yay!

Bren breeeeeeeeathed in.

Aaaaaaaawe.

Better.

They had survived.

"We're here!" Kris cheered, and pointed.

She watched Trent look up and behold what "here" meant.

"Wow!" he said.

Across the street, at the corner of Chestnut and Pierce, was an enchanting three-story building. Atop a high fashion dress boutique was a sapphire blue apartment building with cream wood shutters and dancing white curtains waving in the breeze, looking like a rectangle ocean with white waves foaming around the pretty windows. It seemed like a fairytale princess might live inside, or Smurfs.

But, the blue cute cottage looked like it had gotten invaded by a wild horde of rowdy revelers. The rooftop was lousy with tons of chatty people, drinking and laughing. From across the street Bren could hear and see the whole top apartment buzzing like a beehive with a hundred gabbing voices and pounding pop music. An attractive crowd spilled out of the street-level doorway, plastic cups in hand, another gauntlet of good-lookings awaited Bren's bravery, and thirst for more easing-alcohol.

Trent stood smiling ear-to-ear, like he'd found party Shangri-La.

And Bren had found that he was a rich writer, who liked to smile at her.

This day is just getting weirder and weirder, Bren thought, as they crossed the street. The big bouncer security dude Holly had rented at her apartment building's entrance gave a smiling nod to Kris and her and got the okay from Kris to let their new friend Trent in too as the three parched travelers entered the doorway and ascended up through the stairway of drunkards, unknowing what wackiness would happen next!

Chapter 4

Trent's butt was beautiful, hypnotic, and at eye-level.

Bren watched his perfect, taut cheeks take turns rising and falling, rising and falling under his tan cargo shorts like fluctuating pistons of a man-motor moving him up the stairs with her stares following behind his behind with his black Ralph Lauren undies peek-a-booing over the top of his trousers, classy clothes even underneath. *Hmm.* So far the things Trent meant to hide from her were good things.

She also wondered how good his peach within reach would feel in her palm. It had been a month since enjoying such pleasures. She felt conflicted. Feelings vs. fears. She thought Greg killed her lusts completely. Butt Trent was resurrecting them.

Step. Step. Step.

Boom. Boom. Boom.

Drum and bass got louder.

Feelings got wilder.

And they all hiked higher up Holly's tight stairway that was crowded with party people spilling down the familiar blue carpeted stairs. Fun stickers of colorful little fish decorated the sea-blue walls. It was like walking under the ocean. As they ventured up the stairway, entering this enchanting world, Bren remembered the fun mashup story Trent and her thought up of Jane Austen and Jules Verne, now they were kinda living it.

Coincidentally, Trent turned back to her and said: "Hey, Bren, this is like *Journey to the Center of Pride and Partyland*, going up stairs instead of down a volcano, huh?"

Wow. He and she were thinking the same thing?

Tingles.

She smiled at him.

He chuckled.

She tried to think smart as he tickled her heart.

Thinking.

Feeling.

Lusting.

Louder.

Higher.

Following his beautiful bottom up up up into *WOOO-OOOOOW!*

Paradiso!

Holly's cute-elegant top-floor living room was now a sonic zoo! The whole sunlit place was packed solid with partiers. Bren, Kris, and Trent had reached the heart of the Marina, and it was thumpin'. Bren watched Trent gawk around with wide-eyed wonder at the jubilatious scene. It was a helluva party!

Bright afternoon sunlight poured through the six-foot wide north window illuminating the talking, laughing, drinking and dancing mayhem with all the side windows open and the thin white curtains waving to Katy Perry's "California Gurls." Behind the DJ and the inflatable fake palm trees, and behind all of the Marina's prettiest pretty people Bren could still see the beautiful lifelike mural that Holly had commissioned an artist to paint all over her four living room walls.

Bren marveled once again at the soothing 360-degree painted panorama of Baker Beach with sand and trees on the east wall, coastline and houses to the south, the whole west wall with a horizon of blue ocean and sky, and the north wall painted with the Marin hills and the red Golden Gate Bridge. Gorgeous. It was always a lovely day at the beach at Holly's, and Holly was certainly going with this *spring break on the beach* theme by having the DJ dressed up as a lifeguard and the sexy drink servers dressed down in bulging Speedo briefs and buxom one-piece swimsuits as Bren ducked as a beach ball soared past her head.

She noticed Holly's comfy aqua-colored couch, matching chairs and coffee tables pushed against the painted ocean by the west wall to make room for the dance floor circus. The crystal chandelier still hung from the semi-high ceiling, but today it sported a variety of colorful hanging bras, and a chuckling couple were noticing the barely noticeable naked sunbathers painted on the east beach wall.

A large security dude guarded Holly's big beautiful fish tank. No one was gonna swallow her fish this year as the orange goldfish and some colorful exotics nervously swam around in their vibrating blue ocean-in-a-box, wondering *what the heck was going on.*

It was another Holly summer party, that's what.

Half the Marina was in Holly's apartment, humid with hot bodies. Even with all the windows open, all the hot bods pushed the heat up to mouth-parching levels, encouraging drinking, which encouraged dancing, and encouraged drunk horny guys to ogle Bren and Kris.

Bren totally did *not* want to get hit on today and her dry mouth longed for another drink. But between her and the liquor-filled kitchen was an impeding throng of dancing, drinking people. It would be slow going. They might make it to the kitchen by Christmas.

Trent looked right at home in partyland, nodding and smiling.

Slightly liquored, Bren's fake smile for Kris was getting a little easier to do. But she still wasn't in much of a party mood. Very confused, a little boozed, and full of questions, she would much rather interrogate Trent some more than pretend to be cheery for the next seven hours. But she would be upbeat for Kris, and hoped nothing else crazy would happen today.

Suddenly a loud shriek came singing towards them, and an *SUPER EXCITED* cute redhead bounded from the crowd and crushed into Bren's arms!

"Ooof."

"You're heeeeeeeere!" Red sang out, squeezing her friend tight.

Bren had to brace herself from falling over as Holly's tipsy pixie roommate slammed happily into her. "Hey Calli," Bren greeted back, chuckling for real.

Calli zinged out of their hug and zanged in and out of Kris's arms too. "Whoooo! You're here! Now it's a party!" Calli's twenty-three year oldness laughed and bounced around like a pogo stick in her adorable pink crop top and red skater skirt.

"You both look so cuuuute," Calli raved.

"Thanks," they both said.

"Your skirt is adorable," Kris complimented.

"Your skirt is on backwards," Bren noticed.

Calli blushed as red as her hair. "Oh my God you guys. You'll never believe the crazy week I just had."

"Yes we will," Bren joked dryly.

"I got a new job."

"Oh awesome."

"But I got fired."

"Oh un-awesome."

"I worked at a record store."

"Where?" Kris joked. "The 1970s?"

"Nope. This year," Calli said. "It was the perfect job for me, as a music lover, working in a record store. I was hired as a put-the-records-on-the-shelves person. But I told the manager that I could probably get the store more noticed if I stood by the street with the records taped all over me, take pictures of me, and put them on interweb. And he thought that was a great idea. So I took records out of their sleeves, and I taped records all over myself and stood by the street while the stock boy took pictures of me."

"Oh lordy."

"Did it work?"

"I caused a traffic jam."

"I bet."

"They should make a breakfast toast topping called Traffic Jam. You'd eat it in your car on the way to work," Calli said, sidetracked. "I have so many ideas."

"Why'd you get fired?"

"The manager was really happy with me. We got lots of new customers, lots of likes online, and people even sent me pictures giving me thumbs up, I think they were thumbs. But I got fired 'cause at lunch I sat down & my butt record cracked. I guess it was a really rare record called "Signed By John Lennon," but I didn't know John Lennon did an album called 'Signed.'" Usually breaking a record is a good thing, unless you work at a record store. I wonder if I could break the record for breaking the most records, but that would be a waste of records, I like records. Do you know what band's record I put over my hoo-ha? Bush. Which is ironic 'cause –"

"Got it," Bren said. "Wait. Where did you learn the word ironic?"

"From Alanis Morissette."

"And you used it correctly."

"Yay! That was my goal this week. Every week I've been trying to learn new big words and use them in sentences. Last week I learned to masticate."

"Oh my."

"I masticate three times a day."

"Um."

"And when I masticate I – *OH MY GOOOOOOOOD!!!!*

Calli stared at Trent, screaming!

People turned, Bren and Kris backed away, wondering "what the heck?"

Calli stood aghast, her eyes and mouth flopped open like she'd seen a ten-eyed space alien. But she was just seeing two-eyed Trent. She did a huge inhale and out of her mouth came "*YOOOOOOOOU!!!!*"

Trent looked back at her bizarre reaction, seeming as totally bewildered as Holly's fish.

Calli lit on fire with giddiness!

Bren shared a "Huh?" look with Kris.

"Do you know each other?" Bren asked to Calli about Trent.

"Nope," Trent answered.

Then Calli started laughing loud, no one getting the joke. "No way!" she exclaimed, waving her hands around. "Is it really *you?* Seriously?"

Trent smiled politely, still not understanding.

"Wait a minute," Calli gasped, her eyes ping-ponging between Bren and Kris's curious faces. "Did you all come here *together*?"

"Yeah," Bren said.

Now Calli looked super duper confused.

"*HOW?!*" Calli exclaimed. "*How* do know him?"

Bren looked to Kris. Who would answer? Kris seemed content to just enjoy watching Calli's entertaining conniption fit.

"Calli," Bren said. "This is Trent."

"I totally know who this is. How do you know him?" she asked wildly.

Oh cripes. Was Calli a Trent groupie too? *Oh no.* Not one of her friends. That was too close to home. Bren hesitated to explain, but all eyes were on her. "Trent moved into Madeline's apartment."

Calli didn't move or breathe. "Um. Did you just say . . . " She broke from her stillness and zipped zipped zipped around, danced with a random couple, then came scampering back. "Did you just say" big breath "that he *lives* with you?!"

"Above us."

"*Above* you? Are you kidding me? *Trent Baxter lives above you?!*"

Trent's face blushed even more with embarrassment. This seemed like much more of a reaction than he was used to.

Calli nervously stretched out her hands toward Trent.

"Um. Can I . . . can I just . . . welcome you, with a hug . . . oh my . . . " Calli said, moving in gently with open arms.

"Uh . . . sure. I guess," Trent obliged her, after she had already made a home against his blue t-shirt.

Calli starstruckingly hugged Trent the way Bren would love to hug Shakespeare, but with less leg wrapping around his. She nestled against him. And siiiiiiighed, staying next to his chest, as if she was taking a nap on it, like a koala bear to his muscle-pecked tree, then she opened her eyes and grinned big at Bren.

"Thank yoooou," Calli breathed out to her.

Whoa. What was happening here?

Trent wasn't a gift she brought to the party like a bottle of wine. But Calli sure was drinking him in. Bren kinda, sorta politely grinned back, not particularly liking Calli touching Trent. This day was getting even weirder.

"Did you read his book or something?" Kris asked.

"Ooooh yes," Calli cooed.

Calli read his book? Trent's novel was an odd genre for her. Calli only read erotic-romance, celeb mags, and pregnancy tests.

"You liked his book *that* much?"

"His book," Calli looked up at him, "and his looks."

Trent wide-eyed glanced over at Bren, like, "Help?"

"Ooookay, Calli." Bren gently took ahold of Calli's shoulders and had to slowly detaaaach Calli politely away from Trent like Velcro.

Calli sighed, then fanned herself fast with her hand. "Oh my gosh. Wow. *Trent Baxter*. Here. This is crazy!"

"*You're* crazy," Bren thought.

"Why is this so crazy?" Trent asked Calli.

Calli gasped at the sound of his deep, manly voice speaking directly to *her*.

Geez. She was acting like a dizzy boy band fan.

"I just finished reading your book last night. And . . . and . . . and . . . " Calli couldn't get her words out. She could only latch her hands onto Trent's arms excitedly and pull him into the party.

"Come on," Calli said to him feverishly. "I'll show you!"

Trent looked back at Bren with a "your friend is *nutty*" expression.

Yes. For sure. But never *this* nutty.

Bren watched Calli steal Trent away from her. What the heck? She watched him and his beautiful butt get pulled into the dancing crowd, with *Calli*.

Then he was gone.

Whoa.

Bren felt a strange emotion stir in her chest, like loss.

Kris laughingly smiled and started to tug Bren to follow.

But Bren said she had to pee. She needed a moment to think, then watched Kris curiously follow Calli and Trent eastward towards the kitchen, into the sea of dancing bodies.

Bren stood alone, surrounded by happy party people, feeling loss . . . and relief. Maybe this was for the best. Maybe Calli just saved her by taking temptation away, taking away his book-talking and writer-ness and his beautiful tempting butt so Bren's unclouded brain could think clear again and make smart decisions, not desirous ones. She exhaled a huge gust of *wheeeew*, and felt a little more in control. Yes, she thought. Calli just unwittingly saved her heart from again getting broke and her soul getting crushed. So. This was good. This was good. Yes . . . good. Her head was clearer.

Though, gone less than a minute, her other parts kinda missed him.

A lot.

But this was for the best.

She couldn't handle anymore crazy in her life right now.

"*Bren*," a male voice said behind her.

Her blood chilled cold. *Uh oh.* She knew that voice. That sweet, familiar, horrible voice. She hadn't heard it in weeks, and she would be awesome never hearing it again. Fear. Sweat. Now she really did have to pee. Her healing heart pounded like a war drum as she stiffly turned around in slow motion and saw *him*, the source of her secret heartbreak.

Greg.

She gasped. He was out of her nightmares and back in her life. Uninvited. His presence tightened her with panic! "W-w-what are you doing here," she stuttered out, barely able to breathe.

"*I still love you*," his beer breath said.

ZAP!

Right to her core.

Oooooooh no, she thought.

Three weeks of healing suddenly wasted as all the pain he caused her whooshed back in a *flash!* All those emotions swirled alive again, thanks to her distant ex, back from the past, to re-upset her, looking like he used to but less so, handsome, but heartbroken. His shirt was dressy. His words were pretty, but they couldn't cover up the unforgettable kissing-his-ex she had witnessed. The relationship they had was dead, but like a zombie ex he didn't seem to understand that. He clearly didn't understand that he had killed her ability to trust again. And she didn't understand how much upsetness she had been burying until now.

"You don't understand *love*," Bren finally released to him after a month of mulling.

Her words made him wince. "I understand love more than you think."

Bren fumed. If he did then he wouldn't have cheated. "I don't wanna hear this."

"You need to hear it."

The heck she did. Bren quickly looked around and luckily didn't see her friends, just happy people dancing around her screwed up situation. She stayed calm. Trying to not make a scene her friends would hear about. She had to defuse this delicately.

"You need to leave," she said calm, but coarse.

"We need to talk."

"No."

"Yes."

"No." She backed away.

He stepped closer.

Suddenly Trent's back was in front of her.

And Trent's front was in Greg's face.

Holy crap!

"She said '*No*,'" Trent told her ex.

Bren quickly looked around to see if her friends were there too, but it was just him who had come back.

Greg startled and stepped back, looking surprised and befuddled, totally caught off guard. "Who the hell are you?" he barked back.

"I'm the guy who's gonna show you the floor if you don't leave her alone," Trent said very calm, but very strong.

Whoa.

Greg cocked his head. "Oh, is that right?"

Trent stood still and calm. "Yeah, that's right."

Greg pushed up his sleeves in pre-fight fashion.

Trent clenched his fists.

Cripes! Her past and her present stared each other down hard, about to mess up her future, neither one backing off, the tension skyrocketing into the INSANE-OSPHERE! She didn't want a *Bridget Jones Diary* boy-brawl breaking out over her at Holly's peppy party on Kris's and her lovely last day together. This was worst-case scenario. Her worlds were *colliding!*

Bren quickly slid her body between her two testosteroning buffoons.

"Stop this stupidness," she ordered.

"Bren," Greg snarled. "You know this guy?"

"Yes."

Greg looked stunned. "Is he your new boyfriend?"

Her *what?* She just stayed silent.

Greg's face seemed to assume that Trent was her new love. His body wobbled backwards. His eyes darted between Bren and Trent and Bren and Trent, then he stared at the floor, then at the door, then he slowly wobbled towards the exit, then stumbled through it, and out.

Gone.

But not gone. Greg's awful ghost still lingered with her. Adrenaline tasted hot and bitter in her mouth. Shaking. Nerves tight. Needing air!

She fumbled out her inhaler and inhaaaaaaaaled.

And breathed.

And calmed.

And saw Trent seeing her use her shaking inhaler with his sympathetic eyes.

"Well, *he's* not very nice," Trent attempted humor.

Damn. Trent's concerned blue eyes had seen her secret, her emotions, and her damaged soul. She felt naked to him. And not in a good way.

Mayday.

She had to fix this.

But . . . she couldn't make him unread this. And, actually, it felt kinda good to have someone know her life was in trouble. She just hadn't planned it to be troublesome Trent. And it had to stay *only* Trent. "Please don't tell anyone about this," she asked of him, between breaths.

He tilted his head and looked at her with curiosity. "All right," he said casually, and easily, like he hadn't considered telling anyone. His cool eyes were on her, while she tried to be cool.

She wiped her slightly moist eyes. She let him see. Something about his protective presence felt comforting, and it helped her decide to stay at the party when she really wanted to run back home to a blanket, pizza rolls, and distracting YouTube videos of *American Idol.* Actually *The Amazing Race* was better, or *Survivor. Geez.* Maybe she didn't need to watch TV because her own life could be a reality show. Maybe it was. Maybe there was a secret writer's room where they said "Let's make *The Bren Show* more exciting by having her bestie get engaged, her boyfriend cheat, then she has to keep his cheating a secret so her engaged over-reacting bestie doesn't clobber her now ex-boyfriend and go to jail before her wedding, then let's have Mr. Tempting Awesome Author Guy move in above her to confuse her life even more, and her ex show up on her and her bestie's special last day as roommates and almost ruin it by audaciously declaring he still loves her, and then have Mr. Cheater and Mr. Author almost brawl in public for her and really cause a scene!" Now *that's* a great reality show. Bren eye-rollingly looked around her for hidden TV cameras. But her only audience was Trent, looking at her, nicely.

Exhaaaale.

It was good he now knew some of her secrets, and was there to give some comfort.

Then she worried that Calli might come looking for him and see her upset. "Where's Kris and Calli?"

"The kitchen."

She exhaled again. "Why'd you come back?"

"I had to pee."

Bren definitely needed to now.

"Then I saw you looking in need of rescuing."

She blushed and straightened up. "Well, that was nice. But not necessary. I don't need a rescuer."

He looked at her with a smile. "What do you need?"

She exhaled a huge exhale. "I need to go back in time and not date Greg. Do you have a time machine?"

"Nope. But I've got cool dance moves to get your mind off of things." He then began goofy-dancing, popping and locking, roboting, and hand movements of putting imaginary food in a microwave and pushing its buttons that actually worked as a bizarre dance move.

She felt her mouth curl up.

He smiled, a gorgeous kind smile.

Oh my. She quickly ducked her smile into the crowd. *Too many feelings!*

Chapter 5

Bren refixed her makeup in Holly's bathroom, trying to make her reflection look less frazzled.

Cripes, life, what are you doing to me today, she thought. Why don't you just have alien dinosaurs invade the world with laser blasters today too. I'm just kidding, she clarified to life, who knows, you might actually do that. I don't trust you either.

Now she was really on the look out for chaotic surprises.

Greg was gone. But his "*I still love you*" flew around in her head like a spastic bird trapped in a house. Was there a mind-window she could open to let the bird fly out? *Damn him*, for ambushing her at her friends' party, and for wearing his Polo cologne that soared her mind back in time to all their romantic snuggles, and reminding her how much she really had loved him. Luckily his bad behavior today helped that love fade away some more. And her feelings for Trent fade up.

Trent literally eclipsed Greg when he stepped between them.

Big exhale.

Love-drama was cute in high school, but not at twenty-eight.

Staring at Holly's blue hand soap shaped like fish. Where did Holly get fish soap? Was there also horse soap? Bird soap? Parakeet soap would be fun.

Partiers knocked on the door.

Sigh.

Visine to clear her red eyes.

Happy smile on.

She snuck out of the bathroom, hoping for no more surprises, and squeezed through the crowd to Holly's kitchen. Kris camped by the kitchen table, getting her heart and body squeezed by Mark-the-nice-vampire as he stood behind Kris looking handsome-as-a-movie star with his thick arms wrapped around her, his manly jaw gentle to her head, and – OMG – a huge hickey on *his* neck!

Kris had marked Mark, suck-tastically, branded him so big every party girl in the place could see he was totally taken. *Wow.* She hadn't even considered that Kris had ravaged him too. More than an extra areola, his gigantic symbol of love looked like a blazing asteroid klunked into his neck. *Well done, Kris.*

They looked like total dorks with his-and-hers-hickeys. But Kris and Mark didn't seem to care. Bren envied their carefreeness, so in love, so happy. The image Kris described of the baseball cap over Mark's penis bubbled up in Bren's mind while seeing Mark in real life. *Lordy.*

"Bunny!" Kris's voice sang out to her over the loud thumping beats while stretching her hands out for Bren to come over to her.

Bren weaved through the kitchen crowd to the canoodling couple.

"– smooth for our wedding night."

"But the last time I trimmed I got a ingrown hair bump on my balls," Mark said.

Bren smirked, Kris and Mark's conversations ranging from politics to ball-itics. From their convo Kris clearly was still debating the question: to vjazzle or not vjazzle, for their wedding night.

Kris's eyes flew wide and hugged Bren with her fiancé still attached to her, yanking Bren into a three-way embrace with Mark's massive hickey an inch away from Bren's face.

"Hey, Bren," Mark's too close face greeted her as Kris squeeeezed her so tight she almost needed another inhaler hit.

"Hey, Mark," Bren greeted, and wiggled out of their one-person-too-many cuddle.

Kris tipsily and smilingly still swayed in her soulmate's hug as Mark smiled big down at Kris in his big arms, providing a home her, a perfect-seeming home, a really great loving home.

This is what real happiness looked like, Bren thought, admiring their magic. This is what a perfect couple was: two marathon-running, baseball-loving, camping enthusiasts who also counterparted each other, with Kris's wild and Mark's calm, his idealism and her street-smarts, two soulmates whose kink was *Star Wars* role-playing on the other side of Bren and Kris's too-thin apartment wall, and who a year after meeting were even more hands-all-over-each-other with *LOVE!*

Forever?

Bren looked away and wondered how many fish soaps could fill Holly's kitchen, and wondered where Calli had taken Trent. "Where's Calli and . . . "

Kris suddenly laughed, kissed Mark like a rom-com finale smooch, then twirled away and grabbed Bren's hand. "Come with me. You gotta see this."

Bren got tugged through Holly's stunning state-of-the-art kitchen, seeing Holly's ocean theme continue with a kitchen under the sea. Bren once again marveled at the shiny blue cupboards, blue drawers, blue sink, even blue stools at the blue counter. The floor tiles looked like sparkly ocean-bottom white sand, with cute starfish and colorful corals painted in places to look like the bottom of a tropical sea. Up the walls deep royal blue faded into much lighter shades until Bren's neck craned back to see the bottom of a sailboat painted on the light blue ceiling, putting her underwater.

Appropriate imagery, Bren thought, she certainly felt in over her head lately. Though the colorful fish painted all over the walls did happy her up a little; that's probably why Holly had them painted there. It was always hard to stay sad in Holly's adorable fantasy-ocean. Maybe if she just hung out in there all day she would feel better.

She and Kris followed the fish and reached a gaggle of girls staring at Holly's fridge.

"Move aside, girls. We need to peek at this too."

"Wait your turn," a tipsy-girl said, waving her cocktail at Kris.

Uh oh, Bren thought.

Kris's hot-eyes gave the girl a glare.

The girl's eyes popped and she quickly stepped aside, as if realizing she was dealing with *the* Kris, the Marina girl you totally don't mess with.

Kris cooled and smiled. "Thanks."

Yep, Bren thought, seeing that primal turbulent temper swirling in Kris's eyes. Good thing Kris didn't witness the Greg drama a moment ago or she might have shoved the Golden Gate Bridge up Greg's tookus, and then get arrested again right before her wedding. Yeah, staying silent about everything was the best plan.

Kris's hands parted the party pretties bod's like human curtains and there was Holly's sea-blue refrigerator completely covered with pictures of friends and friends and – OMG – *Trent.*

Bren's mouth dropped open at yet another wild surprise.

There among Holly's vertical scrapbook was Trent's face, his very handsome face, on a full page from that magazine, taped up for everyone's viewing pleasure, and Bren's shock.

"Seriously?" Bren gaped at the mag picture of Trent looking super sexy in a t-shirt. Did he wear anything other than t-shirts?

"Why is he on Holly's fridge?"

"Calli taped his picture up there," Kris said. "Yesterday."

Bren double-taked. "*Yesterday?*"

"Yesterday."

Bren was way confused. "She knew he was coming?"

"No," Kris corrected her. "Calli saw his picture in the magazine just yesterday. She thought he was 'the hottest man-sandwich' she'd ever 'peeped' and put his picture up on the fridge so she could moon over him while she eats breakfast. She didn't know he was coming here. That's why she freaked out. She thinks this is divine providence."

Oh, geez. "Calli knows that phrase?"

"She really does now." Kris's hands turned Bren's shoulders and eyes around to see Calli's hands all over Trent shoulders and arms.

Oh lordy sakes.

Bren's eyes gawked at Calli's hands hanging onto Trent's arm and looked for his reaction. He just stood there, beside Calli, letting her possess his arm, while his hands stayed parked in his back pockets, not looking at Calli, but instead speaking with the hotties gathered around him taking more giggly selfies with the gorgeous author. All of them clearly wanted to leave the party early with him for a much more private party. But Calli, his most adoring new fan, was hugging him like a human fence so no other hottie could have him.

Bren wasn't sure she liked this sight of Calli with Trent, and she wasn't sure she liked the idea of Calli sitting at the kitchen table every morning and masticating to Trent's picture.

"If you want Trent, you're gonna have to pry Calli's fingernails out of his muscle arms," Kris advised her like Gandolf.

Bren tensed tight. "I don't want Trent."

Kris super duper eye-rolled at her like "Ooooh puh-leeeeeeeese".

Bren felt herself blush hot. "I don't want him."

Kris tossed her hands in the air. "Well, you *should* want him. It's so fucking obvy that you two have a vibe, and you both like books, and you're perfect for each other."

Calli stealing Trent.

Kris match-making Trent.

Bren uncertain about Trent.

Greg, the wedding, and Bren still peeved that flying cars still hadn't been invented yet.

It was all too much!

Being under the sea was no longer soothing.

She needed air.

Bren wiped her sweaty forehead. "I'm gonna find Holly."

Kris's face lit up. "We'll all go with you," Kris cheered as she grabbed Mark's hand. "Calli. We're all going upstairs to see Holly. *Bring Trent.*"

Oh geez. The madness was escalating.

Bright side: there was an open bar on the roof.

Dark side: too many footsteps were clomping up behind her.

Up, up, up the stairs they all went.

Bren's wandering mind wondered where Calli's hands were as she listened to her over-the-top giggles at Trent's joke that mirrors were invented because people got tired of falling in lakes.

BLAM!

Sunlight blasted Bren's eyes as she reached the roof, gold and great, promising hope, or causing blindness, as she stumbled out into the glare hoping not to crash into anything. Suddenly life was spacious, the temperature was cooler, noise was mellower, stress was lighter, and the air was cleaner. Though, if the breeze were any fresher she'd have to slap its face as it fiddled with her dress and tickled her skin.

Deep breaths also brought whiffs of pricey perfumes and colognes. Her ears filled with chill-out techno beats from the purple-haired DJ girl spinning records and blowing bubbles over the cheery chatter, as Bren's sun-adjusting eyes slowly made shapes into a whole village of party people mingling over every elegant inch of Holly's gorgeously decorated rooftop.

Her eyes beheld a razzamatazz of colors, shirts, dresses, hair, and skin, like a big square lake of happy humans, standing and talking and laughing under a glorious blue sky as if Holly had put in an order for the great weather weeks ago. Colorful balloons bopped in the breeze and helpfully flagged the railings where the party ended and gravity began. The sharp edges also sported umbrellas over tables and benches letting sitters socialize without getting sunburnt. The sweet smell of roasting coconut sunscreen breezed off the mostly unshaded partiers. Though the overcooked could always swim through the swarm to the shaded benches and big umbrella-canopied bar that was pourin' for all the smiling girls and peacocking guys. And everyone was awesomely awesome in so cooool sunglasses.

Strangers, friends, acquaintances, local celebs, top business people, city hall elites, models and sports heroes filled Holly's roof, rubbing all their shoulders so friskily there should be fire extinguishers. Calli pointed out all the famous people to Trent. He gaped when he saw two big name baseball players. Kris proudly mentioned that Mark lawyers for them. And Bren – *yikes* – saw her dating history in the flesh: some of her former dates, hookups and ex-boyfriends sprinkled through the crowd like croutons in a social salad. The Marina was like a chic small town.

She just couldn't escape her past today. *Attack of the Exes!*

There was Leo-the-liar, Brian-the-lazy, Hunter-the-hung-but-rude-to-the-waitress, Don-never-read-a-book, Chaz-only-talks-about-himself, Harry-howls-when-he-comes, and Katy-she-kissed-just-to-try-it. And these were just the exes who hadn't moved away to other cities. They were all giving love another try, and so were the hotties they were hitting on or holding hands with.

And now, Bren stood apart from all the shenanigans, like Nick in *Gatsby*, just watching, the shine and fun of dating now dulled, staring out at the Marina's tipsy tippy-top hot spot, the peak of SF's dating pool that she had worked so hard for years to climb up and play in and find her "Prince Charming," and now this glittery crowd just seemed so different to her.

All the wine glasses looked half-empty, not half-full. All this *wow* now seemed like theatre: pretty clothes, disguising make-up and polite smiles covering up doubts and insecurities and lies and fears and loneliness and heartbreaks and deal-breakers, deceiving aftershaves and fragrances, hyperbolized boastings and pleasantries, performances of characters presenting their seemingly-perfect-selves, their party-selves, their best-selves, the *sexy*-on-the-surface selves she used to fall in love with and then see the guy's real deal-breaking self weeks or months later.

Pretending led to heartbreak.

Now, like Hamlet or Holden she craved honesty.

Then she looked down at her pretty yellow dress that was disguising *her* inner sadness for her friend, and rolled her eyes at herself for being no better.

But, wanting better.

And wanting to find Holly, to maybe pull aside and confide some of this secret stressing stuff.

Bren eagerly grabbed Kris's hand and pulled her, with Kris's pulling Mark's hand around the railing's edge, staying out of the perilous ex-infested party waters, chin down but eyes all around trying to not be noticed while playing *Where's Holly?* as she scanned the crowd. Not easy since humble-Holly did her best to not be noticed, at her own party, being ghosty like Gatsby.

Weaving and squeezing though this masquerade, Bren finally found her Holly grail, cloaked behind guests, behind a palmy plant, under an umbrella, under big Gucci sunglasses and a stunning cobalt blue chiffon dress with a plunging neckline and sapphire high-heeled sandals, looking like an exquisite mermaid.

"Permission to come aboard, captain," Bren ahoyed.

Holly's head swung up, mouth popped open, and her enviable thin body leapt to her feet and into Bren's arms. "You're heeeeere!" Holly's blue dress hugged Bren's yellow so tight they almost made green. *Mmmmm.* Lovely perfume, lovely embrace, lovely Holly. "I'm so happy now," she cooed as she de-squeezed then squeezed Kris too. "Look at you two beautiful ladies."

Bren and Kris and Calli greeted Holly, the fourth corner of their friend-squad.

Then Holly hugged Mark. "So good to see you too."

He hugged back. "Excellent party, Holly. You outdid yourself again."

She blushed. "You think it's all right?"

"Are you kidding?" Kris raved. "It's great."

"Really? Are you sure?" Holly irrationally worried as always.

"Beautiful," Bren said.

"I just don't know," Holly doubted. "The caterers brought the wrong wine and there's only four servers and half the balloons flew away and two guys were juggling the cupcakes like in that party book."

"This is the guy that wrote that party book," Calli cheered, pointing at Trent.

"What?" Holly stopped and stared at Trent with "who the are you?" on her face, as her Gucci sunglasses perused this hottie party-crasher.

"Do you recognize him?" Calli's perky voice popped up as she pushed Trent toward Holly, his face blushing, his mouth awkwardly smiling, clearly trying to be a good sport.

Hol slid off her eyewear like a movie starlet, stared through the bright summer light and studied Calli's new man-candy, then suddenly lit up her "oh my gosh" face. "Oh my gosh!" Holly exclaimed with amazement. She looked proud at Calli. "Is this really *him*?"

Calli jumped up and down with delight. "It *is!*"

Holly looked shocked, and relieved that he wasn't a party-crasher but rather a party-enhancer, she instantly welcomed him with a big sweet smile and a pleasant handshake. "Did you send him an invite?"

"No," Calli squeaked. "Kris and Bren and Cupid brought him to me."

"What?"

Calli jabbered the whole story of why Trent was there.

Holly smiled as her eyes focused on Calli's hands clutching Trent's arm.

Bren sensed Holly's motherly protection over Calli kicking in, super-studying Trent.

"Sorry my writing caused the cupcakes juggling. But I'm secretly hoping its popularity grows into an Olympic sport."

Holly snort-laughed, spilling her chardonnay.

Wow. He got Holly to snort. He really was a wooer with his words, Bren noticed. She wondered how many other women he had wooed, on a rooftop, or in a stairway.

Now thrilled that this witty magazine celeb had come to her party, Holly's hand on his shoulder gave Trent her blessing to be there.

And to be with Calli?

Oh wow. This Trent-and-Calli-together thing was actually happening, as Bren watched Calli whisk Trent away from her again to impress him with sports heroes and cool peeps while steering him away from the pretty models and parade him around the party with her arm securely around his, as if he was her new boyfriend.

Mixed feelings: relief, envy, and wondering how many cupcakes someone could juggle. She hung out with Holly, talking and smiling, her eyes darting stealthily back to Trent every ten heartbeats to watch where Calli's hands were, watch where his hands were and how much coquetting he let Calli get away with. She watched Trent never stop smiling while talking with total strangers and quickly getting them smiling and laughing too. What a schmoozer. Total people-person. Clearly in his element. Friendly seemed to be his default position. Calli hung on his arm the whole time.

Bren watched . . . and felt . . . and thought . . . and concluded that it was good that Calli had Trent. Now he wasn't a temptation. Bren could relax and feel relieved of pressure and focus on work and the wedding and rediscover the joys of boyfriendless solo-fun with some of the sex toys their former neighbor Madeline invented. This totally simplified things. Yes. Calli and Trent being together was for the best. Absolutely.

Although she might have to hear Trent and Calli humping above her bedroom. *Yikes.*

Stress.

More drama.

She looked to Holly to maybe slip a little and confide some her stress to, but Holly was surrounded by guests and playing hostess, and Kris was busy upright-snuggling her cupcakes pressed to Mark so mooshily that Kris and Mark might screw right there on the roof in front of everyone.

Alone in this party, in this world.

Calli might be saving her by taking Trent. But that didn't mean it didn't hurt a little.

Bren saw Trent glance back to her.

Sigh. How many more hours of watching Calli with Trent before she could go home and not sleep? Too many.

"I haven't met *yoooou* yet," a cool guy in cool shades hit on her.

"You have met me," Bren said, recognizing brags-about-his-biceps-Brad. "We dated for a week three years ago."

"Oh yaaaay." Clearly not remembering her name. "You wanna date again?"

Not in the mood to be wooed, she polite smiled and zipped away.

Criminy. She couldn't be alone without getting hit on, she couldn't hang with Kris hanging with Mark, she couldn't talk to Holly, and she couldn't watch Calli taking Trent.

So.

She saw the sun heading west down towards the Marin hills, trying to exit this zany day; she totally understood that feeling and headed west too.

She kept her head down and squeezed through the horde of hopping partiers and found a vacant space of prime party real estate in the northwest corner of the roof, hidden behind a plant/tree thing, where the fresh ocean wind breezed her first before it got polluted by perfumes.

Pure air . . . truth, at last.

She breathed . . . and breathed . . .

The warm sun and the cool wind competed on her skin, all soothing stuff she hoped would un-stress her. She gripped the wooden railing, breathing easier, but feeling like life was not on her side lately, and not understanding why it wasn't.

Finally alone.

Hopefully her life-is-weird reality show was on a commercial break.

She stared out to the yellow western sky. She watched the dying sun slowly fall. She felt like a part of her was dying too, the part of her that had hope for everything to be like a rom-com novel's happy ending. She gripped the wood railing tighter. She tried to calm all her ricocheting thoughts, watching the Golden Gate Bridge become a silhouette as the warm sun started to light it from behind. And beyond the bridge lay the distant shadowed Marin hills. They looked like a far away magic land, and sort of like silhouetted mashed potatoes, mashed potatoes with no loud people, no problems, just fluffy easiness. Silent nothingness-nature always used to bore the heck out of her growing up on the muddy tree farm, she thought. But for the first time, the chaos of the city life made the quiet land out there seem like an exotically nice relief. Maybe after this week of wedding insanity she might actually visit outside the city.

Gentle breezes brushed her hair and she imagined it was a loving hand. It was nice, but it wasn't enough to calm her actual stress. She needed something more. Something as comforting as mashed potatoes.

"Brenda," a voice said.

She startled and spun around.

Trent.

He was alone.

Oh my.

"Bren is short for Brenda, yeah?"

She fumbly gathered her wits. "Yes. Bren. Is."

He grinned, handsomely, then casually sauntered to the railing beside her and looked out west. The blazing sun lit up Trent's gorgeous face glorious gold, reminding Bren of Bella in *Twilight* seeing sunlight glitter up Edward's sparkly diamond-like skin, making him look magical, and dangerously sexy. Suddenly Kris's surrender to a vampire's hot, wet suck seemed sorta fun. He looked out at the beautiful view. Maybe he saw silhouetted food too. But then he chose to look at her instead. "What does Brenda mean?"

She grinned. "The name Brenda means sword."

His grin grew into a smile. "So you're a warrior."

She smirked. "A survivor."

He nodded.

"And I'm also the inventor of the word flooplezoople. I'm hoping it catches on."

He smiled.

The yellow sun spotlighted his handsomeness, and his aloneness.

Hmmm. "Why aren't you with Calli?"

"I told her I needed to talk to you."

"You did? You do?" she said surprised, curious, liking his directness.

"Yeah."

"Talk to me about what?"

"I wanted to see if you were all right."

"Oh. Oh no, did you tell her about Greg?"

"Nope. Just that I had to talk with you."

Bren breathed.

"Oh good."

"How are you doing?"

"I'm . . . all right."

"Yeah?"

"Yes."

"After your ex left, you looked a little shaken."

More mixed feelings: trauma & butterflies. "Shaken, but not stirred."

He chuckled. "Good."

"So . . . you can go back to Calli." She watched for his reaction.

He grinned and shook his head. "Calli's very sweet, but she wants me to be in a five-person relationship that includes a ghost."

"Sure."

"She's planning our quin-ouple Halloween costume."

"Sure."

"As a hand."

Bren grinned. "She gets excited."

"About what?"

"Everything."

He smirked. Then took a breath. "What gets *you* excited?"

She shot him a look. Was he hitting on her? But a realness in his eyes made his question more like a curiosity than a flirt. She gripped the railing. Walk away? She stayed. Also curious. "I think you know what gets me excited."

He smiled. "The same thing that gets me excited."

Then . . . he didn't flirt. He just looked back at the breathtaking view of wispy fog flowing in over the distant hills, like the wanderer guy in that Caspar David Friedrich painting.

Interesting.

She looked at the view too.

Sharing it.

Silently.

Really silently.

Was he thinking about all the secrets he now knew about her? Her lust for books, her drama with Greg, her name meaning sword, or about his own life. Or was he also thinking that cloud above the ocean looked like two birds humping.

"Not too many Brenda's in books," he said.

Oh. "Sir Walter Scott," she helped him.

His eyebrows raised.

"There's a Brenda in Scott's *The Pirate,*" she answered.

"Oh."

"Yes. But she was captured by a pirate." Bren looked him. "I don't capture easily."

Trent grinned again.

She didn't.

"Do you like Sir Walter Scott?" he asked.

She smirked. "I like his most famous quote. From *Marmion,*" she quizzed him.

"Oh, what a tangled web we weave when first we practice to deceive," Trent quoted, then grinned again.

Impressed, Bren looked at him, telepathically telling him that she didn't like weavers of webs.

But he just looked confused.

"*You deceived me.*"

"I did?"

"You didn't tell me you were an author," she released. "I thought you were just a reader, but you're also a writer. A bestselling writer. A bestselling writer with selfie-craving fans decorating their fridges with your face."

"Only temporarily deceiving you."

"Oh. You're all right with deceiving me?"

"Temporarily."

"Why?"

"We were having so much fun talking about books, as equal readers. If I had told you I was a writer it would have changed the air. And it was fun talking to a woman who didn't know who I was."

Hmmm. He had fun talking to her?

"I didn't tell you 'cause I didn't wanna ruin our fun."

"But now our fun is ruined because you didn't tell me your full truth. You deceived me."

"Is that what that Greg guy did?"

"*What?*"

"Did he deceive you?"

"That's not your . . . that's none of your . . . that's . . . yes."

They shared the view again.

Silently.

"Then I won't ever deceive you again."

She scoffed. "You're gonna be completely honest from now on?"

"Yeah."

Doubting. "You won't withhold information?"

"Nope."

Curious. "You'll tell me *everything*?"

"Sure."

Serious. "How can I believe you?"

"I guess you'll just have to trust me."

Bren broke into laughter, then chuckles, then smiles, then studying him.

He just stood, his cool eyes looking at her, grinning. "You know what Hemingway said?"

"I like to write short sentences."

"Besides that."

"I hope my fourth marriage works out."

"Besides that."

"I like this bar's urinal so much I think I'll take it home and turn it into a fountain."

"I visited Hemingway's home and totally saw it," he said.

"Cool."

"Hemingway also said: 'The best way to know if you can trust someone is to trust 'em.'"

She rolled her eyes at him, and looked away, with *really* mixed feelings, and saw Calli standing in the crowd, staring at them, with her arms folded. *Oh dear.* Bren knew Calli's kryptonite; as long as her and Trent were near the edge of the building's three-story drop, near un-swayable gravity, Calli's terrible fear of heights wouldn't let her come anywhere near them. *Really really* mixed feelings: should she scoot Trent back to Calli or keep exploring this wild feeling of chemistry with Trent just when it was getting interesting?

A couple got up from a shaded cushioned bench under a big umbrella and Bren watched Trent race over and plant his butt on it before anyone else could.

"Wow, you're fast," she said.

He smiled. "Trent means swift."

She smirked. "Really?"

"Yeah."

She sorta believed him.

His open hand invited her to take the seat, right beside him.

She hesitated.

Calli still stared at them.

Bren gave her frowning friend the international index finger sign for "just one more minute." All Bren had to do was get Trent to deceive her with something different than the truths she'd researched about him, withhold info from her, or admit some furry costume fetish deal breaker, and she could toss him back to Calli and be free of his temptation back to feelings, trust, and heartbreak.

That shouldn't take long.

She sat down on the cushioned bench under the shading umbrella with him and got right to work, reading his gorgeous face as she quizzed him.

His past, his present, his future plans.

His family, his friends, his favorite bands.

His dating, his jobs, his fears and regrets.

His audition for *The Bachelorette*?

He went to the tomato fight festival in Spain.

He lost his virginity at Red Rocks at an Ani Difranco concert.

He dropped out of college and toured Europe.

He worked as a human statue for tourist tips.

His dad had been a geologist.

His mom taught astrophysics in Colorado.

His mom remarried.

His mom's hobby is making art out of colorful paperclips.

Trent moved to San Francisco because it seemed romantic.

He waitered.

He believes celebrating New Month's Eve should be a thing.

He dated a girl named Julia.

She left him for her old boyfriend.

He was heartbroken.

He wrote a book.

He got published and famous.

He book toured.

He thinks going to Mars is just an expensive camping trip.

And . . . he cheated. Only one time. In high school. He kissed another girl and got caught.

His sister, mom, and grandma gave him *hell*.

He felt terrible.

He vowed to never cheat again.

Skeptical, but intrigued, she . . . . stayed, and kept quizzing him.

And listened.

And added.

And shared.

And compared, his life with hers.

Her growing up in a small town.

Her having to be organized because her mom was so disorganized.

Her reading every night and morning.

Scholarships, college, her jogs at dawn.

Her blowjob brag with the work speakerphone accidentally on.

WOMP!

A throw pillow landed between them on the bench.

Night was all around them.

What?

They'd been talking for hours??

"Hey, you party poopers," Kris's voice hollered over to them. "Come join us."

Chapter 6

Flung out of their fun verbal trance, Bren and Trent were reborn into a Narnia of nighttime splendor. Bren blinked and remembered that there was a world outside their exciting conversation, but now it was a world of darkness and beautiful lighting. Holly's roof had transformed from bright and crowded to cute twinkly lights, and everyone gone, except Bren's friends.

Oh geez. She felt shocked and embarrassed that she hadn't even noticed that it was now night. *Damn.* She had lost control again with him, even *without* talking about books.

"Come join us, you two!" she heard Kris holler happily from the other side of the roof.

But she wanted to keep talking and laughing with Trent.

She was feeling so much freer and lighter; she hadn't felt this upbeat in a month. *Hmmm.* Maybe bringing Trent to the party wasn't so awful. He gave good conversation, maybe *too* good, she thought as she noticed that she was wearing the button-up shirt he had tied around his waist earlier. *Oh that's right.* He gave it to her to keep her goose bumping bare arms warm. She felt it with her fingers.

She felt calm and happy in this still point of the swirling world.

He looked even handsomer in this new nighttime lighting. The angelic white glow from the paper lanterns lit him up like an eye-candy Romeo, a lethal combination of funny, looks, and a brain that knew books, an amazing guy, at the worst possible time.

He grinned nicely at her. His grin this time had a knowingness, an intimacy. She felt closer to him, warm in the chilly air. Her bench-mate stood up, smiled, and offered her his big, beautiful hand.

Whoa.

Trouble.

Back to reality.

She stood up, handed back his shirt, and walked without him.

Breathing big, she bolted away from his blue bedroom eyes that stayed hovering in her mind as she wisely walked away from the dangerous pull of his magic, though the romantic lighting all around her sure wasn't helping her run away from romantic feelings.

Holly's roof was like a land of sparkling beauty. Around her was the magic of the city at night. San Francisco was now a glittering citadel. Thousands of little lit windows surrounding them shined like bright stars on Earth. The Marina streets three-stories below were a colorful neon carnival, all the two-story buildings and houses around them sprawled with little lights out to the golden domed Palace of Fine Arts, and way beyond it glowed the warm-red Golden Gate Bridge, and here at the neighborhood's heart, beat the drum & bass thumps of Holly's sparkly private after-party.

She walked under shiny little colored bulbs on ropes strung over her head lighting up Holly's rooftop with the illusion of a fairytale paradise. Green plants in fancy clay boxes decorating the scene, each getting their own spotlight, the railings were wrapped with luminous icicle light strings, and blue strip lighting around the edges of the whole roof defined the space as a plateau of fantasy.

The purple-haired DJ girl was now spilling her smooth lounge beats into the chilling air to an almost vacant rooftop while blowing bubbles. Bren read her watch, 10:22pm. *Geez.* Her and Trent had been talking for almost four hours, but it seemed like just a blink.

She heard the casual steps of Trent's sandals following behind her.

Bren saw all her friends seated in a campfire-like circle around a rectangle orange light illuminated coffee table in comfy patio chairs with colorful pillows. Translucent cube drink-tables beside each chair glowed blue, like blueberry lanterns with orange candles dancing atop their shiny glass-like surfaces, like little fires in the ocean. Holly had outdone herself again.

And next to the group, a chic little blue neon-lit bar had been created at the northeast corner, above Chestnut Street, and a lovely lady bartender in a sparkly silver dress served up cocktails, wine, and beers. She smilingly welcomed Bren and Trent over with an inviting wave. They walked towards the light and laughter and stood by everyone all relaxing under the stars for late-night drinks and looking like an elegant council of friendship seated in a circle atop the sparkly city in Holly's fancy furniture, lit with cool colored lighting, wearing spendy long-sleeve shirts, some under blue blankets and sipping wine and whisky, and deeply immersed in intellectual conversation.

Calli: So I peed in your umbrella stand.

Holly: *What??*

Maybe not so intellectual.

Holly: That was my *grandmother's.*

Calli: You two were hogging the bathroom in the shower, what was I suppose to do?

Holly: Go down to the coffee house.

Calli: Oh yeah, I could have done that.

Holly: Uuuugh. Sometimes with you.

Calli: I'm the best roommate ever and you love me, 'cause I'm loveable. Don't you think so Trent?

Bren quickly looked for Trent's response.

Trent smiled politely.

Trent: You're awesome, Calli.

Calli smiled up at him.

Bren: Sorry we talked so long.

Kris smiled.

Kris: You sure did.

Calli frowned.

Calli: You sure did.

Uh oh, Bren thought, Calli sounded upset with her.

Hot Bartender: What can I shake-up for you two?

Hmmm. The sexy way she said "you two" and the two-seater cushioned couch clearly left vacant for B and T to sit together made

Bren worry. She hoped her friends didn't get the wrong idea and think that they were a couple. She took a step away from Trent.

Bren: Oh, nothing for me.

Bren breathed in chilly ocean air deeply to keep her tired wits about her.

Calli: Trent, get a drink and come sit by me.

Calli's hand patted the side of the couch by her.

Hmmm, Bren thought.

Bren: I need to use the bathroom.

Holly: Hurry back up. We wanna spend more time with you.

Bren hurried and hurried back but when she returned Trent was sitting on the cozy couch and Calli had moved the drink table cube away and was squeezed as close to his left side as she could be from her chair.

Hmmm. This after party might be a little re-stressing.

Bren: Maybe I *will* have a Lemon Drop.

Holly's bartender friend gave her a "coming right up" *wink*.

Oddly, everyone looked *totally* engrossed in Trent's storytelling.

Trent: Villa Diodati is a beautiful villa by a lake, rented in Switzerland one summer by Byron and his guests Polidori, Mary Shelley, and Percy Shelley, and they all hung out with him there and thought up ghost stories, and the weather really influenced the stories. It was dark and stormy and cold. Cold because of the volcano that blew up a year before in 1815 screwing up the world's climate for a while. One thing can totally affect other things. It's like we're just trees swaying in the world's wind, 'cause the subject and style of a writer's story is so swayed by the conditions of the time. In fact, the first twenty years of the 1800's were the coldest of the Little Ice Age and that cold affected the writings then. That's why you have snowy Christmases in Dickens, and the icy river in Virginia Woolf's *Orlando*, and the arctic ice in Mary Shelley's *Frankenstein*.

How did they get Trent talking about Villa Diodati, Bren wondered.

Bren: How come all of you never look this interested when *I* ramble about literary stuff?

Kris: I'm always interested sometimes.

Calli: 'Cause Trent's dreamy.

Trent blushed.

Holly: Bren, sit and join us.

Trent smiled at Bren and motioned his open palm toward her side of the cushioned couch beside his right.

Bren sat on the couch next to Trent, beside Kris's chair, beside him once again, but now with lots of eyes on them. Probably best to not show that she kinda liked him and encourage them to match-make.

He smiled at Bren, as if glad that she was back.

She politely half-grinned, trying to keep her jets cooled because Trent looked damn handsome in the cool-blue and fire-orange lights. He did look dreamy.

Calli: So you're saying because there was a volcano thing, now tricker treaters dress up like Frankenstein?

Trent: That's a fun way to look at it.

Calli: Thanks. I like seeing things funly.

Bren: You know, that volcano thing also killed Jane Austin.

Trent's attention turned back to Bren.

Trent: How? Jane died of an unknown illness.

Bren: I think Jane's illness was worsened by the cold weather.

Trent: Interesting connection.

Bren: If Mt. Tambora hadn't erupted and messed up the weather that worsened Jane's condition then she might have been able to gift us with another great romance novel.

Trent: Or may have found romance herself.

Ooooh yes, Bren thought. That would have been wonderful. Jane missed out on that in her final years. Bren nodded.

Jane: Wow, listen to Bren and Trent book banter. When are you two getting married?

Bren tensed.

Calli leaned closer to Trent.

Chet: Oh no, now there's *two* people in our group talking about books. I need another cocktail.

Bartender beauty winked at Chet as she brought Bren a Lemon Drop.

Bren: Thank you so much.

Bren immediately drank.

Trent raised his beer bottle toward her. She politely nodded and took a sip of the sweetness while eyeing him. He smiled warmly. She smiled back cooly.

Calli: Trent. You need to meet everyone.

Bren stared at Calli's palm on his shoulder. Her feelings flowed. So did the booze through her bod. She straightened up.

Almost twelve hours left until Kris would leave their apartment forever; that's what she should be focusing on, she schooled herself. This was her and Kris's last night as roomies. Bren chose to enjoy their last hours as much as she could, instead of caring what Calli and Trent did . . . sorta.

Calli: Trent, you've met Holly and Kris and Mark. And this is Holly's ex-boyfriend Chet. And our friends Jane and Sara, and Andy.

Calli pointed around their al-girl-quin roundtable that tonight included their guys and . . . Calli completely skipped over Bren.

Was Calli that pissed at her for hanging out with Trent?

Calli: Chet is into computers now.

Chet: Tech marketing.

Calli: And he's one of Mark's groomsmen. Me and Holly and Jane and Sara are bridesmaids. Jane and Sara moved from here up to Oregon last year. Jane does cupcakes.

Jane: I have a cupcake shop.

Calli: And Sara does yogurt.

Sara: I teach yoga.

Calli: And Andy is Mark's old college roommate. He's in Hollywood doing CSI for movies.

Andy: CGI. Special effects.

Calli: Andy is also the wedding's officer.

Andy: Officiator.

Trent: Cool. Very nice to meet you all.

Kris: Where's Ash and Darce?

Holly: Ashley's photographing a wedding in San Diego, and Darcy and Mitch are vacationing in Europe.

Holly turned to Trent.

Holly: Ashley and Darcy are our downstairs neighbors. They're so sweet. Ashley is an amazing photographer. She's photographing Kris and Mark's wedding.

Trent: Cool.

Calli: Trent's a brilliant writer.

Chet: What brilliant thing did you write?

Trent: I –

Calli: He wrote a funny love-novel about people having house parties in the Haight.

Chet: Is there any sex in it?

Trent: Well –

Calli: OMG, the sex in it is *so hot!*

Kris: I would read that.

Holly: What kind of parties?

Trent: There's –

Calli: Crazy parties! Cosplay and fistfights and zebras.

Holly: Oh my.

Jane: Oh my God. *You're* the author of the book with the cupcake juggling? You're the reason my cupcakes got juggled?

Chet: That sounds fun.

Trent: I am. Sorry about that.

Jane: That's a bizarre coincidence that you're here.

Calli: It's an awesome coincidence.

Trent: It's a good sign I hope. I think coincidences let us know that we're on the right path in life, and to keep going in that direction. I think I'm supposed to be here and now with all of you nice people, eating your cupcakes and drinking your beer.

Trent chuckled.

Others did too.

Bren secretly rolled her eyes at his theory.

Trent: I really liked *your* party, Holly. You put on a really awesome shindig.

Holly put a legit-hand to her heart.

Holly: Thank you soooo much. That really means a lot to me.

Kris: Cheers to Holly for rockin' another rager!

Everyone agreed and lifted their glasses and bottles to her.

Calli: Hells yeah!

Bren: It was great Holly.

Mark: Top notch.

Jane: So glad we flew down a week early for it.

Sara: Totally.

Holly: Thanks for bringing the cupcakes.

Kris: You outdid yourself this year.

Andy: Amazing party.

Chet: And I didn't moon anyone today.

Kris: The night isn't over.

Holly: Do you really think people had a good time?

Kris: Are you kidding? Of course they did.

Holly: Was it better than my party last year?

Doreen: Yeah. It was great.

Calli: It was a 'Helluva Party' wasn't it, Trent?

Trent grinned.

Bren rolled her eyes.

Holly: I ran out of finger food too soon, and . . .

Kris: No one even noticed. Don't do your insecurity stuff tonight or I'll flick my drink at you. Deal with the fact that your party was a *hit*.

Holly: Uuuuugh. That just means my next party has to be even better.

Trent: I understand that.

Bren's eyes went to Trent.

Kris: Another great Saturday night!

Jane: And next Saturday night you two will be married.

Kris: Holy shit. *That's true.*

Mark: *Yeah we will.*

Bren felt the booze kicking in.

Bren: Actually, "Saturday night" makes no sense. It's no longer day at night. Logically, we should call it Saturnight.

Sara: And next Saturnight you'll be married.

Kris: Trent, Bren likes to rename things.

Holly: She calls grocery shopping "grocery hunting."

Mark: She calls drinking a soda slowly a "slowda."

Kris: My favorite are her sex position renames. Doggy is looking-for-earring. Missionary is heart-to-heart. Cowgirl is bumpy road.

Chet: Bumpy road?

Kris: Bouncing up and down like a truck on a bumpy road.

Chet: Is there a reverse bumpy road?

Kris: Yeah.

Calli: Why is it called looking-for-earring?

Kris: 'Cause that's the position you get in to look for it.

Calli: I shine a flashlight in the dark to look for mine.

Chet: Flashlight in the dark sounds like a sex position.

Kris: Bren saw me looking for mine one day. So, I have a sex positioned named after me.

Mark: I'm a lucky man.

Andy: But looking-for-earring only describes the position of one person. Doggy-style describes the position of two people.

Jane: Both people could be looking for the earring. One is crouching. One is kneeling.

Kris: You could cover more ground that way.

Jane: Exacly.

Sara: I might be dropping my earrings more often.

Jane: I might be wearing my strap-on more often.

Chet: There it is.

Andy: That's what she said.

Laughter.

Jane: Did I just say that in public?

Jane put down her drink.

Sara: What's scissoring?

Bren grinned.

Bren: Boomerang bumping.

Laughter.

Trent grinned.

Bren sank in her seat.

Calli held onto Trent's arm.

Bren silently named that position clutching-Copernicus.

Sara: Will you rename all the yoga positions for my classes?

Bren: I will put that on my to do list.

Kris: Fucking-A, Bren. I'm gonna miss your wacky thoughts every day. You have to promise to text me daily all the nutty thoughts you have.

Feelings swirled, but Bren kept smiling for the bride and groom.

Mark: We'll have to remember all those positions for our honeymoon.

Kris: For sure.

Jane: Where's your honeymoon?

Kris: Saturnight we're at a resort up in Napa, and then all week we'll be rockin' a tent in the woods.

Mark: Yeah we will.

Kris: This week I'm gonna vajazzle for my honeymoon.

Chuckles.

Mark blushed.

Bren: Mark, you get to live with Kris's un-censoring-ness for the rest of your life. Are you up for that?

Mark: I love Kris's boldness. It's one of my favorite things about her.

Kris kissed him!

Bren smiled.

Mark: Trent, you trekked all over Europe?

Trent: Yeah, it was fun.

Mark: It sounds great. Kris and I thought about Europe for our honeymoon, but we were more excited about hiking and camping through Sequoia National Forest.

Calli: I bet I'd love it too. I'm becoming worldly. Holly's been teaching me French, I can count to ten. On, doo, twat, cat, sank, seas, wheat, queef.

Bren: Um . . .

Mark: How long were you there?

Trent: Almost a year. Just traveling around. Touring the homes of my favorite authors.

Kris: Oh, I bet Bren would love to do that.

Bren sipped more of her drink.

Mark: You like baseball?

Trent: Denver fan.

Mark: You're from Denver?

Trent: Boulder.

Mark: San Francisco plays Denver on our wedding day.

Trent: I won't root out loud for my team that day.

Mark: Thanks. Did you know that in Boulder it's illegal to make a monkey smoke a cigarette?

Trent: I didn't know that.

Mark: It's true.

Trent: Well, shoot. I'll have to call my mom and tell her to stop giving menthols to her monkey.

Mark: That'd be wise.

Trent: And how is it that you're familiar with the primate prohibitions of Boulder?

Mark: I'm a lawyer. I find strange laws to be a fun conversation starter.

Trent: Well, nicely done, counselor.

Mark: Thank you.

Chet: Trent, did you come across any vjazzles in Europe?

Trent just grinned.

Trent: I don't kiss and tell.

Bren liked his answer.

Calli: Trent, tell me more about Lord Brian's vanilla.

Trent: No, no. I've talked enough. I wanna know about your wedding. The theme is baseball?

Kris sat up and smiled.

Kris: The whole wedding party will dress up in baseball uniforms.

Mark: Andy will dress as an umpire and marry us.

Kris: All the guests sit on comfy chairs in the infield.

Mark: And everyone gets a baseball signed by the bride and groom.

Trent: Sounds like a homerun.

Group *grooooan.*

Trent: My attempt at humor.

Mark: We've been hearing baseball-wedding puns for six months.

Kris: For example, out of left field Mark proposed on Christmas.

Mark: Best Christmas ever.

Kris: Also, Mark rounds my bases and I give him a double-header.

More *grooooans.*

Trent grinned.

Holly: They've heard it all.

Bren: And done it all.

Trent: You two must really love baseball.

They nodded and smiled.

Holly: And each other.

They really nodded and really smiled.

Bren hoped they would smile together forever as she drank her drink.

Kris pointed east, up the street.

Kris: Our wedding is gonna be on that baseball field in the park a few blocks from here.

Trent: Wow, you're getting married on a baseball field?

Kris: That's where Kris and I fell in love.

Mark: Above the park.

Kris: On a rooftop.

Mark: Actually I fell in love with you in the bar before we got to the building

Kris: Actually I fell in love with you in the bar before that bar.

Mark: Actually I did too.

Kris: Yep.

Mark: It was an amazing night.

Kris: A fucking amazing night.

Mark: That too.

Kris giggled.

They canoodled.

Trent: That's awesome.

Bren remembered that amazing night. There was magic in the air. Then she remembered her amazing conversation with Trent in the stairway that morning, and on the bench that afternoon, and wondered and worried they might have more amazing conversations.

Jane: That was the night Sara and I met you all.

Sara: And the night we first karaoked.

Kris: And that was the night of the big super moon.

Calli: And the night we mooned the super moon.

Chet: I've seen all of your asses. Except Trent and Andy's.

Andy: You saw my ass when we streaked through the park last night at Mark's bachelor party.

Chet: Oh that's right. Nice ass.

Andy: Thanks.

Kris: You streaked?

Mark: They streaked. I kept walking home.

Kris: Then you streaked in our bedroom.

Mark: I did more than streak.

Kris: Yeah you did.

They cadoodled, again.

Bren drank.

Calli: Trent you should show us your ass!

Jane: Is that our group's initiation ritual?

Trent grinned.

Bren blushed.

Holly: Um. Speaking of the Moon, when did people go to the Moon?

Kris: Nice segue, Hol.

Chet: Holly and me went to the Moon and back a few times.

Holly blushed.

Holly: Not since we broke up last year.

Chet: Good times.

Holly: Yes.

Chet: We broke up at Christmas time, and Kris and Mark got engaged on Christmas. Man, Christmas can make or break a relationship. And birthdays.

Bren drank.

Bren: We went to the Moon in 1969.

Calli: You know if you turn 69 upside down it's still 69?

Chet: I'll have to try that.

Kris: Why don't we ever go back to the moon? It's like right there.

Andy: The moon is so retro. Mars is the new moon.

Trent: Oh my gosh. There's a great new book you all need to read, about a guy marooned on Mars.

Bren: *The Martian.*

Trent: Yeah. It's a really fun read.

Sara: I'll wait for the movie.

Bren: It's really techy. They'll never make it a movie.

Andy: If they do I'd love to work on it.

Sara: I wanna go to Mars.

Jane: We have dogs now. Our neighbor's not gonna look after our dogs for a year-long Mars trip.

Sara: We'll bring the dogs.

Jane: Do they make space helmets for dogs?

Andy: Do you realize in our lifetimes, we'll see people land on Mars? That blows my mind. It's gonna be epic.

Sara: Isn't it like a year-long trip to Mars? What will the astronauts do for sex?

Chet: Sex robots?

Sara: Would *you* have sex with a robot?

Chet: Well, I've always been on top of technology.

Bren wondered if robots were the answer for people wanting to cheat.

Holly: Would anyone else like a blanket? Even with the heat lamps it's getting chilly.

Kris: Yeah, toss us a blanket too. I wanna cuddle with my fiancé and get my oxytocin flowing.

Chet: Your *what?*

Bren watched Mark smile as he draped the blanket around them and put his oxy-fixing arm warmly around Kris. She happily leaned her head against his, and sighed calmly. Kris instantly looked peaceful.

Kris: Oxytocin is the chemical in your brain that counters the production of cortisol, which is adrenaline. It reduces stress and calms you into a relaxed state of mind that induces sleep.

Bren sipped her drink, listening super closely.

Andy: Pot used to be my oxy-fix.

Kris: Hugs are better.

Calli: The ancient Egyptians made drawings when they smoked pot. That's why they're called high-roglyphics.

Trent laughed.

Bren: She's not joking.

Trent: Oh.

Holly: We'll have to talk about that, Cal.

Kris: Oxytocin's called the "love hormone."

Trent: Wow. Why's that?

Kris hugged Mark. He kissed her cheek.

Kris: 'Cause it makes you feel really close to someone. Like when you share an experience together, you snuggle or hold hands, watch romantic movies, sing or dance together, go on a roller coaster together, or even just talk with someone, you bond. You calm down. You feel close.

Mark: And puts her right to sleep.

Bren listened. She thought. She looked at Trent.

Kris: The week before our wedding, my stress level is gonna be off the charts. I'm gonna need a million oxy-hugs this week, baby.

Mark: I'm happy to hug you, baby.

Kris: I know, love-pumpkin.

Mark oxy-hugged Kris tight. People aaaawed.

Chet: I'm thinkin' *I* need a hug.

Sara: So do I.

Jane hugged Sara.

Jane: Kris, take it from a former bride. Don't stress about your mom or work or your wedding this week. Let your planner and your bridesmaids handle everything, and just have fun. This is *your* week.

Kris: Fuck yeah. Aliens could take over the world on our wedding day and I'll be like "whatever" 'cause all I care about is marrying this fucking amazing man.

Mark kissed her.

Bren watched them.

Sara: Kris, is your zany family coming to the wedding?

Kris: Ooooh yes. And I'm hoping they don't pray to planet Zoopa-Loopa to bless our marriage. We don't need a UFO showing up at our wedding.

Bren: And there's no room for aliens at the reception tables.

Calli: I think aliens at a wedding would be fun.

Holly: They would upstage the bride and groom.

Bren: You think aliens could upstage loud-Kris drinking, dancing, and hollering on the happiest day of her life?

Kris: Yeah. No alien's upstaging me on our wedding.

Laughter.

Bren: Mark, Kris's family is gonna be your family. Can you handle that?

Mark smiled.

Mark: I'm looking forward to it. Kris keeps making my life more fun.

Bren smiled.

Jane wiped her skirt.

Jane: Oh my God. I've still got sprinkles on me. This is the thing about running a cupcake business, sprinkles; they get everywhere. They get on the floor, my desk, my car. I even find sprinkles in my underwear. I don't know how they get there.

Sara: Lucky me.

Jane grinned.

Sara: We miss being down here with all of you.

Andy: Where'd you and Jane move to?

Sara: Oregon. Just outside of Portland.

Jane: Near Boring, where Bren grew up.

Trent turned to Bren.

Trent: You grew up in a town called Boring?

Bren sighed and nodded.

Jane: Near a Bigfoot museum.

Sara: It's fun museum.

Jane: Her mom's real estate boyfriend helped us find our house.

Bren: Now she is dating a tango teacher, if you wanna learn to tango.

Sara: I kinda do.

Kris: I still can't believe you two moved away from San Francisco.

Jane: It was time.

Kris: But this is where the fun is.

Jane: That's why we love visiting. But now we've got a backyard, and cars, and trees, and waterfalls.

Sara: There's lots of hiking. You and Mark would love it.

Kris: We love the outdoors, as long as we can drive back to San Francisco.

Andy: It rains a lot in Oregon.

Jane: It does.

Calli: Too bad it doesn't rain cupcake sprinkles.

Sara: That would be more fun.

Calli: Although the sewers might get clogged.

Holly laughed.

Holly: You know, sometimes I think you're a genius.

Calli: I do too!

Laughter.

Sara: I miss us all gabbing. I miss our monthly girl slumber parties in Holly's living room.

Jane: Oh my gosh, yeah.

Kris: Oh yeah.

Bren: Yes.

Calli: Totally.

Holly: I'm so glad you enjoyed them.

Jane: They were epic.

Kris: Sleeping bags in the living room.

Bren: Holly would have so much food and party favors.

Sara: Holly used to sing for us.

Kris: Holly stopped singing.

Sara: Why?

Holly blushed.

Holly: I didn't stop. I just sing for myself.

Kris: You reverted. 'Cause some comments called you "show off." Fuck those fuckers.

Holly: Anyway. I miss our slumber parties too. Remember telling ghost stories?

Sara: Calli couldn't sleep all night.

Calli: Neither could Bren.

Bren: Yeah, I probably couldn't have handled Shelley and Byron's nightly ghost story contests.

Kris: Or campfire ghost stories when you went camping with me and Mark.

Calli: Do ghosts sit around campfires telling stories about humans?

Chuckles.

Mark: It didn't help when Bren's ex-boyfriend kept trying to scare us afterwards.

Kris: Yeah. Actually Greg was kind of a dick. I'm actually glad you dumped him.

Kris smiled at Trent.

Bren tensed again, and drank again, and saw Calli's hand on Trent's arm again, and drank again.

Kris: Then I found out the mailman wasn't just happy to see me, he really did have a banana in his pocket.

Laughter.

Kris: I always thought he had the hots for me. Holy dick swings. I don't know what's true anymore.

Bren: *Right?* It's like you can't trust anything anymore. Who knows what or who is true? I mean, cereal boxes are only half full of cereal. The Sahara looks like a desert, but every 20,000 years it turns and will lush tropical jungle because the Earth wobbles. There's fish fossils on top of Mount Everest. Dorothy wore silver slippers in the book. Beautiful San Francisco is built on a shaky fault line. How are we supposed to live happy when we're full of fear and worry that everything we believe is solid might actually be a lie? Advertising, internet, relationships –

Bren froze! *OMG.* She almost said marriage in her list of things she didn't think were solid. She almost told her bestie bride-to-be that love and marriage and faithfulness might be a lie. And she realized the other reason she stopped talking was because she was out of breath. And feeling dizzy. And panicked.

Kris: Use your inhaler, sweetie.

Kris dug into her purse and pulled out an emergency inhaler she always kept with her and thrust it out for Bren.

Bless Kris, Bren thought, her heart beating wild. She grabbed the inhaler and sucked I needed hit! She felt the magic open her airways, her lungs devour air, her heart calming, her body shaking, and Kris's kind hand rubbing her left shoulder, inducing comforting oxytocin. *Ooooh wow.* She sweated hot with worry. She'd lost control. She's caused a scene. She'd said dangerous things, almost secret-spilling things. Did she throw a curve ball and mess up their wedding?? Trent's words haunted her: "One thing can affect other things." She had to fix everything fast. She gripped her inhaler, straightened tall, and smiled to everyone.

She felt a little embarrassed about Trent seeing her inhaler needs.

Bren: But.

She breathed big, in and out.

Bren: My point is . . . that . . . in this life of illusions, the one thing that *is* rock solid is the love that Kris and Mark have for each other.

She grabbed her Lemon Drop and raised it high in the air.

Bren: To Kris and Mark, our beacon of solid truth.

Cheers!

Everyone toasted.

Happiness, laughter, and talking again.

Wow, Bren thought, they bought it. She exhaled, still shaking, and Kris smiling, but then looking worried for her.

Kris: Bren, are you all right?

Bren worried again. Did Kris suspect she was secretly distraught? She looked at Kris, then at Trent, and at Calli still clutching Trent's arm.

Trent's eyes saw hers.

He seemed to sense her need. Suddenly he stood up. Calli's grip fell away. He faced Bren, unbuttoned his shorts, and mooned his bare ass at her friends.

OMG!

Cheers!

Bent over, he gave Bren a big smile while giving his butt to their group.

A modern Lancelot rescuing her in a modern way.

Bless him.

He then pulled up his shorts, rebuttoned, and faced his audience.

Chet: He's one of us now!

Kris: You're officially part of our group.

Trent smiled. Mark shook his hand. Everyone applauded.

Whew.

Her weird knight diverted attention away from her.

She breathed easier, then worried that she actually believed the rant she gave about this untrustworthy world, then wondered what Trent's bare butt that everyone got to see except her looked like.

Chapter 7

Criminy sakes. What just happened? She almost upset the bride and groom, and inspired Trent to pull down his pants? The insanity just kept coming.

Bren wearily worried while descending Holly's rooftop stairs like too-high-flying Icarus now tragically faaaalling, a still-tipsy Icarus, totally tired and gripping the railing, leaning, and clacking down the stairs, feeling like a limp noddle in a sundress.

"Bren, you look exhausted," Kris's voice behind her pointed out.

Oh, if Kris only knew.

"You wanna sleep on my couch tonight?" Holly's voice offered kindly.

Oh heck no, Bren thought, quickly straightening tall to project the perception of perkiness so she could leave and at last get back to her bed, bury herself under her covers and hide her embarrassment from everyone and never come out again. "Oh, thank you, but I can make it home."

Holly's kitchen looked incredibly clean and, *wow*, so did her living room. All the furniture was back in place, including the infamous umbrella stand. Holly's whole apartment looked like there had never been a raucous domestic dance club at all. Her cleanup crew had de-partied the place so spotless that forensics wouldn't find a drop of beer anywhere. And Holly's fish glided much calmer; they never seemed tired; Bren was so envious.

Bren bid the tireless tropical beauties goodnight, then turned and bid the same to her friends. Bren hugged Holly while Calli hugged Trent, and kept hugging him.

"Hey, Bren," Kris's voice took over the room. "I had one margarita too many and I'm gonna enjoy a nice vomit."

Mark gently rubbed her shoulder.

"But you should go ahead home without me."

"What? No. I'll – I'll wait."

"Trent, will you walk Bren home?" Kris asked him.

Whoa, Bren thought, what was happening here?

Calli's face had the same bewildered expression.

"Sure," Trent accepted.

Bren and Calli both looked at Trent, and then at Kris's smile.

"Bren, you look so tired. Go home with Trent," Kris matchmakingly insisted.

Bren looked at Kris with scrunched eyebrows. Was Kris actually sending her home with a new neighbor they both hardly knew?

Calli looked at Bren with scrunched eyebrows. Was Kris actually sending Bren home with a guy Calli liked?

Kris looked at both of them and smiled.

This was such a mess. Bren felt confused and torn and guilty for liking Trent. Now worried that she was about to cause a major rift between her and her sweet friend Calli, a rift a week before the wedding.

Kris hugged Bren and whispered gently in her ear. "Last year you brought Mark to me. You changed my life and I owe you. I'm matchmaking you with Trent. It's so obvy he's your soulmate. If I'm wrong and he's a dirt bag I'll kick the shit out of him. But I have a good feeling. I'll explain it to Calli. She'll be fine and in love with three new people by next week. I love you. Go."

Bren stood silent with soooo many emotions.

Bren and Kris shared a loving look between them, beyond words, but full of friendship.

Wow.

Kris waved at Bren and Trent.

Bren hesitantly waved at Kris and everyone.

So did Trent.

Everyone waved back.

Calli folded her arms.

And Kris looked at Trent and put her two fingers together like scissors.

Trent gave her a knowing nod, him and his balls clearly catching her protective warning.

The air was chilly even with Trent's warming red shirt back around her shoulders as she clacked homeward through the neon night. 54-degrees her shaky phone read and her cold calves felt. Up ahead party people were chillin' in the sidewalks of Chestnut Street, lots of them, still, at 1:22am.

Ugh, she thought, so not wanting to squeeze through more crowds of beautiful drunk people while she looked like crap and felt tipsy and tired, and saw all the man-hunting Marina hotties (looking even more beautiful at night with the pretty lights and pretty skin-showing clothes) that would ogle Trent and stop him for selfies and delay her getting home.

Screw that, she decided and headed north up empty Pierce Street instead, with confused Trent following her brisk wobbly pace. *Cripes.* She had been awake for like almost twenty hours. Trent's gentle hands sometimes had to guide her shoulders as she veered and he steered her straight and kindly kept her from marching out into Lombard Street's *zipping* cars.

What a crazy day. So glad to be going home. Though not so glad another night of Greg-nightmares awaited her. Her lead-heavy eyelids kept closing, then popping open, then closing then popping. Trent's continual yapping about how fun the party was helped keep her awake.

Green light.

He helped her south across Lombard's six lanes of bright headlights, crossing the wide threshold back into Cow Hollow, then turning left onto the sidewalk and having him follow her east past IHOP, and past the motel where she cried herself to sleep after catching Greg cheating, not going home to avoid Kris finding out. Bad memories flashed back, but she kept focusing on going home, Trent's pleasantly yapping voice sorta distracting her sad thoughts back to her favorite subject.

"Favorite book cover?" he asked her.

Her sluggish brain thumbed through memories. "*The Mists of Avalon*."

"Oh cool. I love that book. I like the cover of Bayard's *Lucky Strikes*. Cool artwork. What's your favorite new book?"

"I haven't read a new book in a month," she answered bluntly.

"A *month?* That's a dry spell"

Could he tell she was a little sad, she wondered? Or was he trying to help her stay awake? Or was he just talking to talk?

They crossed Steiner and passed Mel's restaurant, a place with much happier memories of pancakes and laughter, then passed the crowd outside the Hi-Fi Lounge, then they turned right and walked south up Fillmore Street, not sure more book talk would be smart to do with him, but it was helping keep her awake.

"Favorite opening line?" he continued, keeping her brain working.

"Anything but *A Tale of Two Cities*," she answered.

Trent gasped at her literary blasphemy. "'It was the best of times, it was the worst of times.' That's like the best opening line ever."

"Ugh. Worst opening line ever. You don't start a novel with the word '*it*.'"

"You don't like '*it*?'"

"'*It*'s vague."

"'*It*'s a summation."

"'*It*'s a snoozer."

"What's a better word than '*it*?'"

"Blaaaaaaaaaah . . . "

Bren puked all over a sidewalk tree.

People gasped and scattered from the splatter. Ick hurled out of her bowed over body as she felt Trent quickly gather up her hair and hold it away from her messy face. *Damn.* Maybe she hadn't outgrown public puking. All her booze and BBQ now fertilized the leafy maple. Trent's big hand consoled her shoulder as he stood between her and her unwanted "ewwww"ing audience. He sheltered her from them as she performed her one-woman vomit show at Fillmore and Lombarf. Now she felt *really* embarrassed.

Fortunately some people were nice and asked Bren if she was all right.

She nodded, though inside she felt *mortified.*

"Ugly alcohol can't live inside so sweet a person," Trent told them.

Oh, that was a nice thing to say, she thought as a wave of feelings tingled and calmed her a little. A good line too. He *was* a writer.

She saw the sexy night-out pants and puke-avoiding high heels of two girls now next to her and felt more caring hands touch and rub her back so kindly. All their soothing hands on her felt like love. She . . . she felt loved. *Ooooh no.* Emotions were coming out too.

Oooooooooh. She didn't realize how much she needed to feel loved, after Greg made her feel so *un*loved. It felt so good to feel loved and get a bunch of awfulness out of her. She wished she could have gotten such support from her friends, but she couldn't tell them, not now, so love from total strangers was the next best thing. She wished she could wretch all her heartache and bad memories out of her too. Muscles clenched. Mouth bent. Tears gushed.

"Oh, Bren," Trent breathed out.

Loving hands slid over her more, as she grooooaned a deep hurt out loud, in front of strangers. She felt so stupid and out of control, and that puddle of yuck below started to steam.

Ugh.

She stood up, dizzy and drained.

Trent handed her a cloth handkerchief.

She stared at it, *stunned* that he had one, then stared at him as she wildly wiped her mouth.

"Wow, a hanky," one of the beautiful girls totally complimented him. "You're a real gentleman."

"Yeeeeah," her giddy friend agreed.

Bren silently agreed too. Then thanked the two girls for their niceness, trying to not gleek ick on their cute sundresses.

"Oh, you're welcome, sweetie. I hope you feel better."

"Thank you."

"Heeeey," one of the girls exclaimed. "Are you the guy taped on my refrigerator?"

Ooooh, geez. Not now, Bren rolled her eyes. "Get me home," she nasty breathed to him.

He nodded to at her. "Thanks for your help ladies," he said politely to them. Then he wrapped his big arm around Bren and got her the heck out of there.

Cool rushing air dried her eyes and cheeks as she let her so-tired self lean against her muscled helper. She grimaced hard. She hated feeling weak. She hated needing help.

But his strong body braced her nicely and let her relax a little as they walk-walk-walked up busy Fillmore Street, past the beautiful bar where Bren had match-made Kris and Mark last year. Now here she was, match-made with this emotion-mixing, helpful guy as he guided her weary, shaking body walk through the chilly seaside air, with her stomach churning and her ears listening and liking his funny rambling about how the dude who invented roller skates probably thought that no one would ever want to walk in shoes again and probably didn't live in hilly San Francisco, and kindly asking her goofy questions about her favorite-tasting toothpaste, & if she wondered if the Golden Gate Bridge finds cars to be ticklish, clearly trying to get her smiling again and keep her awake as they trekked left at the crosswalk, veering onto barhopping Union Street. Trent's sandals kept a steady but considerate pace with her flats, their four feet finding a cooperating rhythm, an instinctive togetherness she hadn't intended. They warbled east as a four-footed creature.

They passed by all the white festival tents now in night, now closed and waiting for tomorrow's next crowd. He helped her past even more loud carousers outside the packed laughing bars. Bren couldn't relate to everyone else's jovial mood. She still felt isolated from the whole happy world, now more than ever. She sniffled and shivered against his warm body, under his strong arm as they hurried home, glad that she wasn't alone.

His presence with her by Holly's roof railing was pleasant. Leaning against him was even more pleasant, and protecting. She named this position: leaning-on-Copernicus. His tall body was really sturdy like a Parthenon pillar, and calming, and *wow*, her hand could feel his pillar's concrete-hard core muscles hiding under his flimsy t-shirt, and she could smell his no-cologne masculine Trent scent, and all things about him seemed good.

His kind continuous talking to her was good too, trying to pump up her dreary mood. His jokes were dumb, but his friendly voice was comforting, and so soothing she felt . . . sleepy.

Eyes closing.

Stress drifting.

His voice calming.

His body supporting.

Air flowing.

She felt like . . . she . . . was . . . flying . . .

"We're here."

Eyes opened. Head flung up. "What?"

"We're here, Bren."

Whoa. She whoozied awake. *Wow.* She had actually drifted off against him. *Oh, whoa.* That was unexpected.

His left arm held her while his right hand pulled out keys and unlocked and opened their front door. Up up up their stairs they went, up the unforgettable stairs where they met. That felt like so long ago, when he was a stranger, when she never would have predicted she would be back here with him again feeling so relaxed with him that she could nod off while walking.

She almost did again . . . but blinked herself awake at the top of their stairs, and she quickly found her jangly keys in her very organized purse. But her keys' woozy aim was off.

She tried to stick it in.

She tried to stick it in.

Trent helped her stick it in.

Oooh, his guiding hand felt so good.

Turn.

A lovely *click.*

She swung her door open, stumbled inside, and flipped on her bright lights.

She beelined to her bathroom and shut the door.

Peed. Washed her hands and face. Brushed her teeth.

She texted Kris: "Home safe."

Kris texted back: "glad u r. have good nite :) me still drunnk"

Odd way to end their last night together as roomies: apart.

Who was this messy-haired, weary-faced woman looking back at her in their mirror? She attempted to brush the mess on her head presentably straight, but, *screw it,* she just didn't want to stand up anymore.

Brush went back into its labeled place. Light off. Opened door.

Trent was sitting at her round kitchen table, smirking at her wild hair. Her apartment door still wide open.

Hmmm. She felt both cared for and weirded out to have him inside her place. This morning she hid from him behind that door. Now he was on the other side of it, with her, alone. Super weird day.

Trent's eyes looked past her and upwards as he chuckled. "Why do you have a disco ball on your bathroom ceiling?"

Bren smiled. "That's Debbie the Disco Ball. She keeps things fun. You haven't lived until you've showered among spinning stars. There's a seat belt on the toilet to avoid falling off if the stars make the toilet-user dizzy"

He laughed. "You're an ever-unfolding mystery."

"So are you, refrigerator author."

He smiled, then stood up, like a Jane Austen-ish gentleman, like when she first saw him stand for her in that golden light at the bottom of the stairs. But now they were standing on the same level.

She stood and he stood. Looking at each other.

"How you feeling?" he asked her with his low, caring voice, staying standing by her table.

Not a simple answer. She felt a jungle of feelings more messier than Kris's bedroom while looking at him.

His muscled arms were muscley. His t-shirt stretched tight over his chest and hung loose over his flat stomach. But his flatness didn't fool her; her hand had ventured like Columbus and discovered no flatness; she had found abs. She definitely remembered feeling abs. Like cute square cobblestones that her fingers could almost hook onto like a climbing wall. She wondered what his climbing wall looked like. Then she realized *why* he was just in a t-shirt. "I'm still wearing your shirt," she blurted out.

"No worries. I'll get it from you later."

"After I clean it?"

"I can clean it. It's all right."

"I should clean it. I got yuck on it."

"Whatever you'd like."

Odd pause.

Looking at each other.

Silence.

Despite her blocking his way on the stairs, this writer, this wordsmith, had so "awe shucks ma'am" easy-goingly talked his into the building, into her circle of friends, into her psyche, and now into her apartment. Now, what would he try to sweet-talk his way into next?

"Have a good night, Bren," he tossed out casually, turned, and walked out while closing her door.

Really?

"Wait!" Bren called out, unintensionally.

Her door opened and Trent's curious face came back. "S'up?"

She stood surprised at her call to him, and surprised that he wasn't gonna try to make a move on her. He didn't even seem interested in messing with her vulnerableness. Interesting. Relieving. Calming. Perplexing. And she felt a slight whoosh of happiness to see him again.

His presence stayed standing there, in the room with her, as she realized that when he was in her apartment there was one emotion she did not feel: lonely.

"Um . . . Oh. Where's my purse?"

"You're wearing it."

She looked down and saw it hanging around her. "Oh. Good. Thank you."

"You're welcome."

"All right."

"All right. Goodnight." He was closing her door again. It almost shut.

"Wait."

Her door opened, again. Trent's handsome face came back. Another *whoosh* of comfort that he was back.

"Hi."

"Hi."

"S'up?"

Her hands hugged her bathroom doorframe, almost needing to so she wouldn't topple over. She felt safe that he was fifteen feet away. " . . . Um . . . I . . . can you . . . water?"

"Water?"

"A bottle of water. Bring it to me?"

"Oh. Sure."

"In the refrigerator."

He opened the fridge and she saw him see the left side labeled "K" and the right labeled "B." He snatched a bottle from the B-side and walked it to her. He had a good, confident, yet casual walk as he walked that beautiful body back to her.

"Must be strange to *not* see your face on a refrigerator."

He smirked. "It's nicely un-embarrassing."

"Oh please," she doubted him. "You love it and you know it."

He rested the chilly water bottle into her open hands. "I don't know what to think."

Her weaker-than-she-thought fingers futzed with the cap while he watched.

"Need help?"

"I can do this."

"I'm rooting for you."

"Thanks."

Finally she snapped the cap with a *click. Mmm.* She loved a good click.

"Well done."

"Your support was crucial."

"Happy to help."

She drank the soooo good cold clean replenishing water. And breathed.

"Good?" he asked.

"I'm good." *Hiccup. Eww.* Vomit and toothpaste taste.

"Okay," he said nicely. "You all right to walk?"

"Of course I'm all right to walk."

"All right."

"All right."

"Goodnight, Bren."

She watched him good-walk that beautiful body away from her, watching his strong strides, his thick hair, his broad shoulders, his beautiful taut butt again under his tan cargo shorts. *Ooooh*, that butt. It got further and further away. Then it disappeared behind her closing door along with the rest of him.

"Copernicus!" she teasingly shouted out, much more urgently than intended.

Her door opened, *again.* Trent's handsome and laughing face came back.

Another wonderful *whoosh* of comfort.

"S'uuuup?" he chuckled, leaning against her front door doorframe with her leaning against her bathroom doorframe, looking at each other across the apartment, laughing at each other.

Logic and feelings found unexpected words. "I'm *not* all right to walk."

He nodded, like he had figured that out many minutes before she did.

"And this bottle is freezing my hand."

He walked back to her, still looking good, and grinning. He relieved her freezing hand of the bottle.

She warmed her hand on her Trent-shirt-covered tummy. Then slowly wiped her palm down her body to her dress-covered thigh while she looked at those two blue pools of his, wondering what thoughts were swimming behind them, then remembered that he promised to tell her everything, honestly. "What are you thinking?"

He grinned. "That you need sleep more than anyone I've ever seen."

She grinned. "You have no idea."

He held out his hand.

And . . . this time . . . cautiously . . . surprisingly . . . she decided to take it.

She slid her sandals across her wood floor, her balance supported by his hand, probably looking like a wobbly drunken dance couple, across her apartment, and helped her slothy wobbles towards her dark bedroom.

"Why in the heck did they name you Copernicus?"

"Because Copernicus proposed a one-sun solar system, I'm the 'son' around which their 'heliocentric lives joyously revolved around.'"

She laughed. "For real?"

"Yep."

"Woooow."

"My mom's endearingly wacky. And an astronomer."

"Oh, right."

"But she also loves *Back to the Future*, so she might have named me after Doc Brown's dog."

"I thought Doc's dog was Einstein."

"His dog in the '80's is Einstein. His dog in the '50's is Copernicus."

"You're named after a dog? Like Indiana Jones?"

"We're talking about movies now?"

Tired sigh. "I'm off track."

"Let's get you back on track." He got Bren to her bedside.

This was so pulse-poundingly odd. This morning Trent was on the other side of her wall, now he was on the inside of her walls, inside her bedroom, in the anything-can-happen dark, with her.

Confused between tension and comfort she slowly untangled off her purse and dropped it on her nightstand, fumbled out of Trent's button-up shirt and hung it on her chair, then fumbled out of her shoes. Bare feet on soft cool carpet. Then, so flipping happy to be home, she finally let go, and fffffffflopped onto her soft cushy mattress that caught her fall like a big loving hand. Bren's wacky mom was right, her neatly made bed felt soooo good when everything else in life was a mess. Her bedspread was cool on her cheek and palms and feet. She presssssssssed them into her mattress and moved herself around until her whole so-thankfulto-be-laying-in-bed body was fully on her glorious cloud. She lay spawled out on her stomach, looking right, and gazing up at him.

Trent stood near with his hands in his back pockets.

Her heavy eyelids fell closed.

"You're about to fall asleep, so I'll leave you to it," his voice gently said. She heard the thick, empty hum of silence and his sandals clomp her hardwood floor outside her room, then heard his voice casually say "sweet dreams."

DREAMS!

She popped awake. Wide awake. Fear surged through her like an electric current, the fear that kept her awake every night, fear of the returning Greg-nightmare.

"Wait!"

His head slowly peeked around her doorframe, yawning.

"You know, Bren, at some point *I* have to sleep."

"Not yet, " she panted. "Um . . . um . . . " She soooo needed him to stay, and keep keeping Greg away, like at the party. Maybe if Trent could scare Greg away in real life he could scare him away in her dreams too. That sorta made sense. Sure. Total sense. Now, she needed to find a reason to make Trent stay.

His silhouette leaned in her doorway like a sexy cowboy on a pulp romance paperback cover. Once again he looked like a literary romance hero come to life. Actually, he *was* a literary hero, she remembered. He was writer.

Ding!

"You need to tell me a bedtime story."

His head tilted like she was nuts. "Really?"

"I have trouble sleeping," she admitted. *Whoa.* It felt so great for her to finally say that out loud to someone, like setting down a big stack of heavy books. "I need noise," she explained. "To distract my thoughts. TV or a singer or something softly."

"You want me to sing?"

"Not if it's like your singing voice I heard as you went down the stairs today."

"Oh," he chuckled. "I like that you're blunt with me. No fluff. Lately I get a lot of nice compliments. It's relaxing to hear the truth."

"The truth is that I need a happy story. And you're a storyteller. It's my bedtime. So, I need you to tell me a bedtime story."

His head then tilted more, probably still thinking she was nuts.

She still lay on her stomach, mentally patting herself on her back for coming up with such a brilliant excuse to have him stay with her a little longer. It was perfect. She had a writer at her disposal. She might as well put him to good use, and she got to enjoy his company some more, and find out more about him.

"I don't know if I can just make up a story."

"Why not?"

"Well, for one thing, I've been up since dawn and I'm about to nosedive onto your floor."

Bren hadn't considered that he was tired too. But she really needed him to not leave, knowing Greg would re-haunt her dreams again if he left. Her heart was thumping, practically punching a hole in her bedspread, while her weary, fuzzy brain pushed its gears to clunk up a plan.

"Well . . . " she said.

She thought how resting against him vertically while walking relaxed her to sleep.

" . . . then . . . "

She thought being horizontal with him might really help her fall asleep.

" . . . um . . . "

She thought about Kris's oxytocin-cuddle tip.

" . . . I . . . "

She thought about him scaring away Greg, while she was awake.

" . . . have . . . "

She thought about him saying: "I guess you'll just have to trust me."

" . . . an . . . "

She thought of a crazy plan that totally made logical sense.

" . . . idea . . . "

A few minutes later, Bren's tired head rested comfortably on her pillow in the darkness. Her body lay on her left side, warm under a blanket, and Trent's fully-clothed front cuddled protectively against her fully-clothed back.

Ooooh, this feels soooo good. His oxytocin-hug was more soothing than any sweet cocktail, and less sickening. The really nice feeling of this new man's body behind her was unnerving at first, then kinda nice, and then soooo wonderfully relaxing. So surprisingly, something about his friendly presence made her feel relaxed more than nervous, feel so comforted, and a little guilty about laying with the guy Calli liked; she hoped Kris would fix that situation as her softening body softened next to his.

Trent's spooning support was exactly what she hadn't known she needed but now that she knew she totally needed it she snuggly cozied her back against his hard chest and her backside against his –

"Once upon a time," his deep calm voice whispered friendly behind her ear. "Um . . . there was a really, lovely, um, park, and in the park was a, uh, a lake, and in the lake lived, um . . . a duck."

She listened to his effort, wondering where this story was gonna go. It sounded like he didn't know either.

"Yeah, a duck, and it swam and stuff, in the lake, with its duck friends, and their lives as ducks was awesome, swimming, and sometimes flying, and getting fed bread."

She smirked. His story was simple, it's delivery cute, and oddly calming.

"And the ducks got fed bread by a nice lady named . . . uh . . . Mrs. Whistle, wood, Mrs. Whistlewood, and every day she would go to the park and had fun feeding the ducks, after work, at the lava lamp factory."

Bren tilted her head. What the heck kind of story was this? He was supposed to be a brilliant author and he was stammering about ducks and lava lamps? Silly, but oddly calming, and intriguing, as she wondered what bizarre stuff would he ramble out next?

"Then one day Mrs. Whistlewood was shopping at the store and saw some really boring shower curtains, and she thought that shower curtains could be way more exciting then they are. And so she decided to invent new shower curtains. She invented shower curtains with fun pictures on them, like a pretty forest, or a rock concert, or in a library, and you could have fun pretending to shower in a library. Although if you sing in the shower the librarian and might tell you to 'shhhh.'"

She chuckled out loud. His story was so ridiculous, and so what she needed, and she was so curious to hear where the heck this acclaimed author took her imagination next.

"And Mrs. Whistlewood invented other shower curtains with fun pictures on them that could make you feel like you were a participant in fun environments while showering, like a dog show, or in a grocery store, or at a poker table in a Las Vegas casino, and she put her fun shower curtains on the market. But unfortunately no one bought them, and she said 'Oh dang.' But then one day she met a wizard whose robe was stuck in an ATM machine, and she helped him get his robe unstuck. And to thank her, the wizard turned her clever shower curtains into Magic shower curtains, so not only could people shower in front of fun pictures, but they could literally walk through the shower curtain into the picture and gamble at the casino poker table, and attend the dog show, and then people started buying Mrs. Whistlewood's shower curtains, and they became very popular. And, oh, she made enough money to build a mansion that had a lake in the backyard where lots of ducks came and she could feed them bread all the time, and, yeah, a happy ending."

Bren lay there wondering *what the heck?*

She lay with her heavy eyes closed, smiling into her pillow at his silly story. What the flip was happening here? Women were throwing themselves at him in the streets over *this* ridiculousness? That morning he was quoting Jane Austen, now he was blathering the a tale of a duck-feeding shower curtain entrepreneur? She wondered if the moral of his story was that you should follow your passion, and even if it looks like you fail, you might find a wizard that helps you the rest of the way. That seemed way too deep of a lesson to be yielded from such a ridiculous story. She wondered if he was the wizard in her story, to help her the rest of the way to some happy ending. But that also seemed way too ridiculous.

Whatever the story's takeaway was supposed to be, at least he was with her, distracting her thoughts. She chuckled at his funny absurdity. Then eventually she became less interested in the details of his bizarrely cheesy story and just enjoyed the comfort of his soothing voice, and enjoyed the gentle tickles of his whispers on the back of her neck as he continued rambling about Mrs. Whistlewood and the wizard falling in love and learning to surf together, becoming more and more comfortable with him as his silly story unfolded on and on . . . and on . . . and laying with him was even better than when she rested against him as they walked home together, because now she didn't have to walk and be upright and awake and stuff. This was exactly what she wanted, this not-being-aloneness.

Take *this* you taunting nightmare, she secretly thought, fighting Greg's ghost with this new guy's presence, and with a smile as she melted like cheese into her pillow, melted under Trent's protection, under his muscly arm wrapped caringly around her, fully relaxing in the shielding glory of his rock solid body behind her, his heart beating gently upon her back, and his wonderful thought-distracting words filling her head . . . and kindly keeping her company . . . and relaxing her body . . . and helping her feel a serene peace she hadn't felt in . . . ever . . . with oxytocin goodness flowing through her . . . her thoughts fading, broken heart beating, and her body releasing . . . as she felt herself drifting . . . and drifting . . . and drifting . . . wondering if this wonderful feeling could last forever . . .

Chapter 8 – day

Sunday

Stomp. Stomp. Rattle. Stomp. Stomp. Stomp. Rattle. Rattle. Rattle.

"Ooof!" *CRASH!*

Bren bolted up in bed!

What the heck?

Sitting up.

Bewildered.

Breathing fast.

Darkness.

Looking around. *Where am I?*

Jane Austen poster. Silver desk. Yellow bookshelves.

My bedroom . . . right. I'm in my bedroom.

It's fine. What day?

She grabbed her phone. Sunday. Relief. *Good.*

10:04am.

Really?

A whole eight hours of sleep. Wow. That never happens.

Ooooh. Baaaad hangover. That does sometimes happen.

Her head ached. Alcohol had seemed like such a brilliant idea last night, but it had turned against her, like good things can do. Bren eased back down onto her mattress, her head sank into her soft cotton marshmallow for comfort. She exhaled, getting her bearings, her bare feet discovering a warm blanket was over her, feeling hungry, thirsty, her body still tired, but *woooow*, one thing about her felt good; she felt shockingly well rested.

A full night's sleep!

It was a miracle!

She hadn't slept so long in so long, and so delightfully.

But how?

She sat up!

Trent.

She had slept with Trent.

Or Trent had slept with her.

Either way.

They had slept together!

Damn.

Bren frantically slipped her hands under her covers and touched her body all over to see if she was wearing clothes. She was. Her palms slid fast over her sundress. Her underwear was on. Her shoes were off. She felt normal and good.

Her brain-wheels squeaked past her headache, recalling: after-party, vomiting, walking, feeling needy, then . . . *asking him into her bed.*

Oh geez!

She sat frozen in a state of uh oh. She had totally broken her promise to herself to stay away from guys for a recuperating long while. A long while had turned out to be only a month. Too soon. Not healed. Not hardened. Not headstrong. Not un-hurtable. But also not having had a nightmare last night.

Another frickin' miracle.

Trent in her bed and no nightmare. Coincidence?

CLANG!

Bren whipped her head left to her closed door.

There was a noise.

Clink, clank, clang.

For real. She hadn't dreamt it. A noise was there.

Outside her bedroom.

Bren threw off her blanket and swung her bare feet to her floor. She raced out of bed and threw open her door.

"Aaah!" she gasped, looking down.

Trent was kneeling at her feet.

He looked up at her, on bended knee, with jeans and t-shirt and muscled arms, and smiled sweetly, with something shiny in his fingers. Her heart flew into her throat. Oh my gosh. she thought. Was he *proposing?*

She rubbed her waking eyes.

"Good morning," he greeted her cheerily, booming her throbbing head. Then his hands went down to pick up a mess of clinking shiny silverware scattered all over the wood floor and softly clanging them into a cardboard box.

Ooooooooh. Bren sighed out loud with realization and much relief. She relaxed against her doorframe. Trent had a fork, not a ring. *Wheeeew.* "So that's what that feels like," she thought, her heart thumping fast and hard and trying to calm so she could face the super weirdness now between her and her no-sex one-night stand man . . . down there . . . looking handsome . . . as handsome as the first time she saw him below her, yesterday morning, looking like a romance novel stud come to life. Except *this* morning she knew the feel of this stud's gorgeous tan muscled arms around her: strong and protective, caring and comforting, warm and wonderful. *Uh oh.* Now she was feeling connected with him, knowing him more intimately. She broke a sweat. *Danger.* Feelings and desires mucking up clear thinking and –

What the fork? Why was there silverware?

"Hey! You're up," Kris called out, carrying a box out of her bedroom. "Sorry," Kris said. "I didn't mean to drop the silverware. Thanks for picking that all up, Trent. You're handy to have around. I bet Bren agrees." Kris winked at her.

What? Oh no. Bren suddenly remembered. Kris was moving out today!

Their time was up.

Her roommate and best friend was leaving her.

Right now!

"Oh, Kris. Oh my gosh. You're moving. Oh shoot. I'm so sorry. I overslept. And I forgot about your moving today."

Kris laughed. "*You're* disorganized? Well that's a first."

Yes. It was.

Kris laughed, as she crossed to Bren, stepping over her silverware and Trent's fingers. "We decided to let you keep sleeping.

Except I tripped over my shoes and dropped the box. I finally appreciate you keeping shoes safely in the labeled shoe area, ironically at the end of me living here."

"OMG!" Bren exclaimed.

She looked around in dismay at their now way-empty apartment. Sophie the Sofa was gone, so was Clark the Clock, Tess the TV, all of Kris's patio plants had vanished, along with dozens of pictures and decorations now off their walls and stuffed in boxes that Mark was carrying out . . . forever!

"Oh gosh," Bren gaped in astonishment, as her heart sunk to her gut.

"I *know*," Kris exclaimed in agreement. "It looks different."

It looked *wrong*, Bren secretly shrieked.

Her shriek must have shown on her face because Kris gave her a look of empathy. "You'll fix it up. You finally get to put your chair by the window."

But Bren didn't care about her chair; she cared that her best friend in the world was really leaving her. Bren again losing someone she loved. Her chest crushed with sadness. This was gonna be harder on her heart than she thought. She breathed in deep and totally tried to not cry so Kris wouldn't feel bad about leaving her.

Trent rattled at her feet.

Kris went and stuffed her clothes in big garbage bags.

And Mark walked in and picked up more boxes and bags.

They were all like busy bees buzzing Kris out of her life, and all of them audaciously smiling because now Kris got to live with Mark and Mark got to live with Kris and Trent seemed to be happily helping.

Whoa. Now it would be just her and him in their building. Maybe he liked that. Maybe he liked last night. Maybe he thought last night would happen again.

Uh oh.

Now Bren *really* wanted Kris to stay, not leave her all alone with this gorgeous temptation. Bren wanted to shout "Kris, don't go!" But too-helpful Trent and Mark were smilingly picking up her boxes and carrying them out their door and down the stairs and joking together about strange laws and baseball like man-besties.

This was all too nuts. She had to get away for a second and get a grip.

"I'll go put on some sweats and help," Bren said, turning away.

She felt the bottom of her dress yanked back like a horse's tail, then felt Kris's superhuman strength spin her around and lock onto her shoulders.

"*You two slept together!*" Kris whisper-yelled, super excited.

Oh cripes.

Kris's eyes were as big as her smile. "Tell me *ev-er-y-thing.* Quick, before Trent and Mark come back."

Good gravy. "We *didn't* have sex," Bren insisted. "I just let him hold me."

Kris smiled even bigger.

Did Kris not believe her? "I was drunk and vomiting and he just stayed with me, in case I needed help."

Kris smiled even bigger bigger.

"*We didn't have sex,*" Bren affirmed.

"I know," Kris laughed.

"You know?"

"Your door was open when Mark and I came home and we saw you two spooning and sleeping with Trent's arm adorably around you while you were clutching it like a Teddy bear and he was cute-snoring."

"He was?"

"And you had this hilarious smile smeared across your face."

"I did?" *Oh dear.*

"And I'm *soooo* happy for you," Kris squealed.

"What?" Bren worried.

"Bunny. This is such a fucking relief. Now I don't feel so guilty for leaving you all alone. You've got *Trent!*"

She had Trent? No. Kris was mistaken. She didn't have Trent. Trent wasn't with her. She wasn't with Trent. They weren't *Trenda.* This was just a dumb drunken error in judgement, a slip, a snafu, a gaffe, a blunder, a really enjoyable and practical nightmare-preventing spooning.

"I'm not going to do anything with Trent again. Calli likes him. I'm not gonna mess up my freindship with her."

"Calli's over Trent," Kris said.

"What?"

"After you left last night I talked to Calli. I explained how you and Trent have a thing."

"There's not a thing."

"There's totally a thing."

"There's a slight thing."

"Calli was grumpy, but she understood, and now she's fine with it."

"Really?"

"I talked to Holly this morning. Calli met a hot guy playing soccer in the park this morning and now they're dating. She might be dating the soccer ball too."

"Really?"

"Yep. It's all good. So go bang Trent."

"I'm not banging him."

"You should bang him. He's totally bangable."

Bren started to protest more . . . but Kris seemed so happy and guilt-free thinking that Trent was there to fill the void she was leaving her BFF and wouldn't let her be lonely. *Ooooh cripes.* Pretending she would hookup with Trent would help Kris feel less bad about leaving her, and since keeping Kris happy this wedding-week was Bren's maid of honor duty, well, *sigh*, what the heck, Bren thought? What was one more little lie if it made her friend happy this pre-wedding week?

Bren smiled and let Kris believe whatever. After all, she did promise Kris that she would sleep around.

Trent came back in.

Kris smiled at Trent.

Trent smiled at Kris.

They both smiled at Bren.

Wait. Did Trent also think she and him were now together?

Madness!

Up and down the twenty maroon stairs Bren walked out Kris's bags of clothes and clothes and more clothes and also teetered the tightrope between pretending to like Trent for Kris's benefit but not so much that Trent thought she liked him. *Ugh, exhausting.* She also hovered between being super sad and incredibly awake.

Her full-night's sleep had zinged her almost back to her old energized self. Even with a throbbing hangover she hadn't felt this energetic in the morning in a month. Trent had actually been helpful, but she didn't dare tell him; he might think she wanted another sleepover.

Mark and Trent led the way, pulling the last cart-full of bulging boxes and bags down the less-festival-peopled-today sidewalk, laughing loud and brotherly bonding while Bren and her friend were so sadly about to part. Opposites were everywhere: the happy sun and Bren's wounded heart, the merry festival and Bren's hung-over head. Life was ridiculous and so was Kris for picking the worst two days to move on Union Street, during the fest when the street was totally blocked off and the moving truck had to be double-parked two blocks away. Sometimes Bren felt like the only smarty in life's crazy party.

A mishmash of boxes, bags, and furniture with green leprechaun poop Post-its cluttered the moving truck's gullet as Mark did his best to arrange the last of Kris's bulging bags in an organized system then he noisily rolled down the back door and locked it.

Normally Bren liked the sound of clicks, but she hated this one. The lock's little *click* was a huge crack in Bren's already broken heart. So was Kris handing Bren her apartment key.

Oh no.

This was it.

Goodbye.

Bren so tried not to cry, but Kris's hug was so tight it squeezed Bren's sadness to the surface, more easily than she expected. Tears falling, feeling fragile, seeing Trent see her vulnerable. *Ugh.* She totally blamed him for these tears. For three weeks Bren had been getting so good at not showing her sadness to Kris, then he crashed in and frenzied up her feelings. Troublemaker.

She also eye-rollingly blamed Mark for this sad moment. He was taking Kris away. *He* was the culprit of this friend-theft. Her loss was his gain. And she blamed her silly past-self for matching Kris and Mark together resulting in Kris moving out to be with Mark. No good deed goes unpunished. She gripped Kris's back, so hoping this move out wasn't all for not, hoping Mark and his soon-to-be-waxed balls really appreciated who they had and could love only Kris tender and true, for a lifetime. A whole faithful lifetime!

She didn't know what the heck to say at this sentimental turning point. Now, there they were, at the big climactic end, tearfully closing the book on their amazing roommate-ness, swirling with woe and nostalgia, living this monumental moment into her memory. Always priding herself on her planning, she didn't plan this moment of saying goodbye. It was too sad to plan.

"I can't believe you're moving out on National Best Friends Day," Bren said, her emotions whirling.

"I know that's so iconic."

"Ironic."

"That too," Kris said with watering eyes. "We'll still see each other all the time," Kris's half-sorrowed half-excited voice reassured her through tears. "But you won't be alone. Now you've got Trent!"

Oh cripes, Bren thought.

"Oh," Kris said. "Your spendy sandals I borrowed yesterday are in one of my trashbags. I'll find 'em . . . both of 'em . . . hopefully."

Bren just smiled and nodded, quite unsurprised, and finding that classic-Kris statement a fitting punctuation on their *Odd Couple* time together. Then she watched her messy, mind-challenging, heart-squeezing, soulmate friend that she shared every fun-fighting-farcical-fantastic-friendship-filled day with for the past eight years now share a sweet tearful look with her, and then wildly wave goodbye, jump in a truck with a neck-mauler, and drive off into the west.

Just nine blocks.

But it felt like nine light years.

Bren stood alone, watching the moving truck get smaller and smaller.

Kris was gone. Their roommating now just a memory. Their glorious time together just –

Trent yaaaaaaaawned beside her.

Bren slowly turned and scowled at him for messing up her meaningful moment.

"Sorry," he said, then flung his arms open to her for a consoling hug.

Oh, the heck with this, she thought and walked away.

She could drop the act now of pretending they were a couple, not wanting to encourage him. She wanted to get a zillion miles away from him and the super dumb mistake of intimacy she made last night, declaring her life now a Trent-free zone. He had served his purpose and now she needed to be alone.

But up the sidewalk incline back to Union Street his pesky footsteps followed and his motor-mouth motored, asking her how she was and if there was anything he could do to cheer her up. Yeah, she thought, move out. That would cheerily uncomplicate things.

She turned right at the corner and marched up Union Street, the sun and wind drying her tears, but not her sadness. Into the building, up the stairs, into the apartment.

"I'll leave my door open for you, if you wanna hang out," Trent said. "Come up anytim –"

WHAM!

Door shut.

Silence.

Exhaaaaaaaale.

No more Trent. Good.

No more Kris. Bad.

Silence.

Emptiness.

Talk about a bleak house.

Bren lonely-moped around Kris's finally clean but empty bedroom, actually missing Kris's mess, though Kris's sweet magazine sample perfume still floated in the air. Bren's chest whooshed with emotion seeing that Kris had left Debbie the Disco Ball in the bathroom, so symbolizing their amazing memories, still sparkling. And that was all that was left of her former roommate, just air and a sacred disco ball in her too silent, too empty apartment. *Her* apartment. Super weird. It really was *her* apartment now, hers alone. All alone.

Clomp, clomp.

Except for her new neighbor's bothersome footsteps above her. Life must love messing with her. She had lost her BF then her BFF, and now left alone with tormenting Trent she was just effed.

Then she noticed something on her kitchen table. Did Kris forget something? No, she soon realized. Kris didn't leave something behind. Trent did.

His novel.

* * * *

She did anything but read it.

Showered the feeling of Trent off her.

(Even though it felt wonderful.)

Washed any scent of Trent out of her bedding.

(Even though it smelled sexy.)

Made her messy bed neat.

(Making her life organized again.)

Cleaned her whole apartment.

(Playing Taylor Swift over his footsteps above her.)

Worked on her laptop at the Starbucks.

(Missing his calming voice near her ear.)

Brought back groceries.

(Feeling lonely that he wasn't with her.)

Made dinner

(Alone without Kris.)

Watched TV

(Alone without Kris, without Greg, without anyone)

She ignored Trent's book.

She ignored Trent's book.

She ignored Trent's book.

She ignored Trent's book.

She wondered what in the world he could have written that would exhilarate the hearts and parts of all those women so much that they fell over each other fawning him.

What?

What?

What?

Dammit!

She raced from her couch to her table.

This was not her taking his bait, she convinced herself.

This was not a read for fun.

This was the *Art of War*, the gaining of insight of her enemy to gain advantage, she justified.

She studied his book's dustcover, his funny cover of two hipster lovers googly-eyeing each other, surrounded by a raucous mishmash of bonging, dancing, orgy-ing, singing, beer-chugging, brawling, cosplaying, cupcake-juggling party people!

But she had been fooled by handsome covers before.

Like Nancy Drew cracking open a mystery she flung open the hardback cover, and saw his inscription to her.

Hey Bren,
I wanted to give my book to you as a thank you for making my first day in a new neighborhood a friendly and happy one. Also, from one booklover to another, I tender to you a less silly tale than last night's attempt at a bedtime story, my bungling effort to enter the aristocracy of great literature. My ego awaits to hear your astoundingly impressive book-smart critique. I hope you enjoy reading my novel, or it can help balance a wobbly chair.

Sincerely, Copernicus
415-555-0122

Hmmm.

His message was sweet, playful, and just for *her*. She guessed that none of his fans had an inscription like this, with his middle name, or his phone number. Special, personal, intimate.

She flipped a crisp page and saw the title page, promising a *Helluva Party* in a funny font.

Curious to see if he would keep his promise to give her a helluva party, she flipped another page, and saw the acknowledgments to his mom, dad, sis, and Julia.

Hmmmm.

Curious why he dedicated this story to his ex, she peeled back another page.

Chapter 1.

She read the first line.

Gasp!

Damn.

It didn't suck.

It hooked her.

She reread his jaw-dropping first line:

Geeeeeeeeeez, heartbreak sucks donkey balls.

Whoa.

It grabbed her funny bone, and her heart.

She totally related to this.

She didn't expect that.

Her eyes eagerly followed his funny first-person-written protagonist guy from a Midwest college heartbreak to a spontaneous trip to San Francisco, and into the entertaining lives of Trent's deep, wacky and touching characters.

His plot structure wasn't totally solid; the action forward was certainly secondary to his humorously insightful commentary. He tended to meander and stream-of-consciousness a bit too much, but the enjoyably lush way he described people and places and heart-thumping exchanges was delicious, lusciously detailed, enticingly sensual, easily involving and . . . surprisingly *arousing.*

She met rascally roommates, and bed-breaking lovers
A stuffed toy zebra, a treasure discovered
They were dancing on rooftops and streaking through clubs
Debating Descartes and falling in love

She lived parties and passions and clumsy romances
With spirited people who took kooky chances
She laughed at their hijinx, swooned with their words
She felt all their yearnings as if they were hers

Swept up in their world so fun and intense
Of wittiness, mayhem, sex and suspense
A guy and a girl, and a love so zany
So erotic, so funny, so wonderfully crazy

Page flipping, eyes zipping, ever-gasping and giggling
Her happy heart pounding, her tingling toes wiggling
Yes, crying at heartbreaks and laughing at wisecracks
As Trent's wild tale crescendoed to climax

She cheered for the fate of her new written friends
And hoping so hard they find love in the end
Her muscles all tensing, her mind so delighting
Feeling excitement shoot through her like lightning

The big party, the fight, the chase in the rain
She ached with their pain, their dilemma insane!
Love had to find triumph, just HAD to, but *how?!*
"Oh yes, Trent, oh please, don't let me down now!"

Oooooooooh YEEEEEEEEEEEEEEEEEEEEEEES!!!!
He did not disappoint.
She gaped and gushed over the last page of his story
As it finished in heart-thrilling, skin-quivering glory!
Ooooooooooooh wow!
This was a grrrrrrrreat boooooooook!!!!

Sh-sh-she . . . laid . . . sweating . . . and . . . sh-sh-shaking . . . on her bed that she had shared with him . . . now in more ways than one.

Mind-screwed to satisfaction, she let Trent's girthy hardback sssslip out of her wet, weak, trembling hand and tumble to her floor. *Kuh-lunk.* If Bren smoked she certainly would've celebrated the afterglow of her book-gasm with a soothing cigarette. But all she had was air and a needed inhaler hit. Breathing and reeling from reading Trent's mighty magnum opus that Calli and all his giddy fan-girls had fingered before her, now Bren finally knew what all the hoopla was about.

This golden-penned troubadour was the dumb-joking goof who lived above her? Who book-bantered with her? *Who slept with her last night?!*

O. . . M . . . G.

* * * *

Bren couldn't sleep.

At all.

Dark room. Eyes open. Suffering readers remorse.

She had done the deed. Read.

Now wildly awake.

For hours.

Brain buzzing. Heart thumping. Body still tingling.

She felt impregnated with his words.

His powerful pen had put 'em in her. She could feel his potent prose swimming deep inside her, all through her, now a part of her, his characters, his story, his style and his book's *wow* was as *wow* as her and Trent's hot book talk on their stairs. Now she knew his soul-shaking affect on her in their stairway yesterday wasn't a fluke. Now she knew he was a legit literary master who enraptured her with one of the most stirring love stories she'd ever let in. Now she knew whom she was dealing with. Now she knew how much danger she was in, in danger of being enraptured outside of his book, in danger of falling for him, falling all the way down down down this wonderful real-life Trent-rabbit-hole that could lead her to an even worse heart smashing.

She gripped her sheets, trying not to fall further.

She felt changed.

Dangerously changed.

She wished she could UN-read him, forget him, and just go the heck to sleep. She didn't need the distraction of these zinging flinging thoughts and sexciting feelings this week. But her now messed up mind kept mulling his story's protagonist and his quest to be a good man, how respectful he was with women, how faithful, and how *passionate*. Was Trent like this too she wondered and wondered and wondered? And if he was . . . *wow!*

His realistic happy ending love story had reignited her hope for real life love having a happy ending, and if Trent was as ideal as his protagonist then . . . *gulp* . . . there might be hope in real life after all. This revelation kept her awake. Should she avoid Trent, or (at great risk to her heart) explore him?

Did he want to explore her too?

What to do?

She lay confused, in her bed, on her back, reeling, staring past her bedroom's open doorway at the little nightlight on out there in her kitchen, and looked at the almost darkness in her bedroom, up at the horizontal line where her wall met her ceiling, remembering looking at the wall/ceiling line in her childhood bedroom, pretending it was the line the between the lips of a mouth of a big friendly wall/ceiling being who would talk and sing and say happy things and advice that comforted her after a confusing day.

But now at age twenty-eight it just looked like a line, a silent line, in a silent apartment, so silent without Kris clanging in their kitchen before bed. *Sigh.* Bren was on her own.

Alone.

Creak.

Well, not totally alone.

She heard his footsteps in his apartment above her.

She heard him be above her and not be in her bed like last night, not holding her, not comforting her, not talking her to sleep, a deep wondrous sleep.

Instead she lay unproductively awake.

He was doing it again. Nothing. Annoying nothing. Like his novel on her table, just existing, he was up there just existing, near her, his simple presence getting her all worked up. Brilliant because he could claim he wasn't doing anything. But he was *soooo* doing something. His presence up there and not down here was *affecting* her. She wondered if he knew it. Did he know what his novel would do to her? Is that why he left it for her? To get her all worked up? Was he a total manipulator? *Breath.* Or was he just a nice neighbor who wanted to share his writing with her?

Either way, he was totally trouble.

And he was absent from her bed.

She missed his arm around her, holding her, comforting her, protecting her. She missed his body behind her, supporting her, relaxing her, letting her know that she wasn't alone. She missed his soothing voice by her ear, telling her a mood-lightening silly story, distracting her flying, flinging, zinging, over-thinking thoughts, whispering her to sleep. She grew anxious as she lay dying to feel him again.

But, alas, he was not there. This amazing man was upstairs.

Creak.

She tried counting sheep. Then counted Trents. Then counted the *creaks* his feet made over her head, over her bed, over her lonely body. Hearing his creaky footsteps instead of a bedtime story; not nearly as good. Her ears ached for the soft whisper of another funny, lulling story, especially now that she knew what stories he could do. And all that do-ableness was above her, just one story away.

Creak.

Ugh. His tell-tale-creaks were driving her mad.

Damn. Her brain wouldn't shut off.

She struggled to sleep.

She needed to sleep.

As good as last night's sleep.

She had to bring her A-game for her 8am Monday meeting.

She *had* to sleep.

Creak.

She put a pillow behind her and pretended that Trent's body was with her.

She pulled her covers around her tight, imagining him holding her.

She tried to remember the warmth of his chest on her back.

She pretended that his strong arm was around her again, cuddling, and protecting.

Creak.

She couldn't smell his manly Trent-scent in her pillow anymore.

She regretted washing and changing her sheets.

Creak.

She remembered the delightful tickle of his breath on the back of her neck.

She remembered the soothing sound of his whispering.

Creak.

She missed his voice, his feel, his caring, his Trentastic-ness.

Creak.

She remembered what would happen if she fell asleep without him.

The nightmare would come!

Now she could logically justify!

Creak.

She flung off her covers and stormed out of bed!

She could bear sleeplessness no longer.

And there was only one crazy solution to this problem.

She turned her lamp on and gentle music off.

Marched out of her bedroom.

Click click click went her locks.

Swooooosh went her door.

Knock knock knock went her knuckles on his doorframe.

NEED had broken past her rules and was now runnin' the show.

Hot with adrenaline, exhilarated, terrified, determined. The nightmare didn't come last night. Both at Holly's party, and in bed with her, Trent had chased Greg away. *Gosh darn it,* Trent was her solution, but also her risk. This was so messed up. She needed her nemesis.

She stared at his open door, breathing shallow, her heart rat-a-tatting, totally knowing this was an absolutely absurd crazy wacky wild exciting wrong dumb foolish desperate dangerous deed she was about to do. But also a very logical solution, she hoped: she needed Trent so she could sleep.

His door was open, open for her, just like he promised it would be.

Impressed.

She heard his big footsteps womping down his stairs.

She saw his legs . . . his body . . . his face.

Beautiful.

Her body heated.

Her heart bammed her chest.

Her brain tried to overrule.

She thought of Faust's dangerous deal.

Stay strong, she told herself.

STAY STRONG!

He stopped.

He stood.

He smiled.

Ooooh my, she thought.

There he was, the author of her angst, the biggest threat to her heart, with pizza slice in hand and tomato sauce on his cheek, and handsome as heck even with smeared food on his face. He assumed a pleasing shape in a white t-shirt, gray sweat pants, and bare feet. His t-shirt said: *Not dumb. Just missing some pages.* Bren rolled her eyes. How could such a talented wordsmith be such a goof? He looked different to her now that she knew how hot he could write and excite. He seemed even more alluring, almost glowing. She was in the presence of an excellent author.

He burped into his fist. "Sorry," he said.

Okay. Now he had a little less mystique.

He looked surprised to see her, then pleased, then concerned. "You all right, Bren?"

She didn't answer.

"Is everything cool?"

Tired, nervous, and desperate, she stared back at him in her yellow jammies, bare feet, frazzled hair, and hands on her hips. She didn't answer. She just stared, teetering on whether to Trent or not to Trent.

He tilted his head at her. "What's up?"

I am, she thought to herself.

And took the risk!

She reached towards his heart and grabbed his shirt. She gave him a look of "you know what I need" as she pulled him to her, without a word, though his curious eyes seemed not entirely sure *what* she needed.

She backed away, pulling him down from his tower, onto their stairway landing, through her doorway, and into her apartment. He seemed surprised and thrilled, as he totally let her take him back into her private world once again. He uncaringly left his door wide open, but she closed hers and locked it.

Now he was inside.

Chapter 8 – night

Sunnight

This was happening.

Wow.

Electric!

Still gripping his front, she silently pulled her solution-to-sleeplessness very willingly back into her bedroom.

He was now *more* inside.

She looked at him. He looked at her. Together again, in her bedroom. This was nutty, but necessary. So. Straight to business. She gently grabbed his pizza slice and tossed it into her trashcan, gave him a tissue to wipe his gorgeous face and a Wintergreen Lifesaver to suck. He sucked. The only thing about him that sucked, she hoped. She watched him suck.

Stare.

Suck.

Stare.

Suck.

Stare.

Suck. Silly grin. *Crunch.*

Geez. This goof was her bedmate? He wasn't taking this serious enough. She stepped forward, close to his beautiful body, focused, fought her *excitement*, and looked right into his eyes.

He crunch-crunch-crunched.

She tried not to laugh. "I can't fall asleep. But I need to sleep. And your cuddling helped me sleep. So I need you to stay the night and cuddle me so I can sleep," Bren explained.

He grinned. "Okay."

"We are just sleeping together, *literally*," she instructed.

He swallowed his Lifesaver.

"No sleep. Just sex," she Freudian slipped. "*Damn.* I meant . . . no sex . . . just *sleep*." So much for being cool. "Got it?"

He smiled, happily, as he looked into her eyes and nodded. "I totally understand," he said to her with cool fresh breath. His friendly smile seemed to understand.

She felt more relaxed now, as she stared into his sweet baby blues, like staring into a delightful summer sky, staring into forever.

Forever stared back at her, kindly.

She nodded and released him.

Oddly, she felt incredibly comfortable with him.

He definitely seemed comfortable as he happily plopped onto her bed like it was a bouncy castle and merrily crawled under her covers. "Aaaaaaaawe," he exhaled, spreading out over her plush mattress in hedonistic bliss. This favor to sleep with her was clearly no hardship for him. It was super strange to see him making himself at home in her bed, her private place, this semi-stranger. Then he rolled onto his side, his hand propping up his head, and smiling up at her, looking pin-up sexy in sweatpants and ready to assume the position.

Now he was *really* inside.

She watched him grandly open up the covers for her like a blooming rose, or a venus flytrap, inviting her to lie down with his sexyness for the night.

Oooooooooh myyyyyyy.

This crazy decision would either be the solution to her slumber troubles, or just *trouble.* She took a nervous, excited deep breath . . . and slipped into bed with her amazing neighbor again, and clicked off her lamp.

Darkness.

Together again.

In bed.

Laying beside each other on their backs.

Their breathing filling the silence. Feeling the realness of having him there, and the oddness, enjoyably odd, but odd. She breathed in and out. Just two neighbors hangin' out in her bed, no big deal, she told herself, her heart th-thwapping her chest. Why did this bedshare feel awkward compared to last night?

Oh right, she realized, tonight she was sober, and also now very aware that beside her was an author whose words had wowed her to the Moon. She felt her whole body blush. Oh, if he only knew what his book made her do, on this bed, and now he was in this bed with her, this gorgeous prodigy of prose, about to wrap his wow-body around her and whisper more words, words just for her, from his magical mind, through his perfect lips, into her ear, into *her.*

She felt even more *electric.*

Too *electric?*

Maybe this was a dumb idea.

She thought she should cancel and panicked and prepared to kick him out, not caring what he would think about that. This was *way* too intense!

"I was at the Haight Street festival today with my old roommate Derek," Trent's interrupting voice tossed out casually. "A guitarist on stage sneezed, and he strummed the guitar as he sneezed. It was the coolest sneeze I've ever seen. A rock 'n' roll sneeze."

Bren smirked.

"Then Derek and I debated what part of a sneeze we enjoyed the most."

"What?"

"Well, there's pre-sneeze, sneeze, and after-sneeze. Derek likes after-sneeze. But I like pre-sneeze the most. The suspenseful build up. You know? What part of the sneeze-trilogy do you enjoy the most?"

Bren chuckled as she rolled her eyes. "I've never thought about it."

He chuckled. "It's fun to think about."

She smiled, feeling more relaxed with him now, and rolled to her left side, giving him her vulnerable back. Just when she thought he was anxiety-causing he said silly stuff like that.

She inhaled deep and heaved out a whole bunch of worry. He was Trent. She wasn't quite sure what that meant, but somehow he again relaxed her fears of him. Enough to let him stay, and she re-committed to her crazy plan.

She faced her open doorway to her dimly lit kitchen. Heart pounding, she waited. She had never been so aware of nothing against her back. There was nothing. . . nothing . . . nothing . . . and then *oooooooooooh*, there he was. Warm, wonderful, manly, muscled, living and fresh-breath-breathing Trent fitted his perfect body to hers like a delightful human blanket.

His arm around her, his body behind her.

Oooooooh yesssssss. She relaxed. This was soooooooo what she needed: Trent.

He was with her, in her bed, for real. Five minutes ago he was above her, now he was beside her. Out of her head and into her bed. A day ago she would have never predicted *this*. Truly, her life had become so crazy lately that it was impossible to plan ahead. Who knew what would happen tomorrow? Soon she would know, but first she had to sleep, and his amazing-feeling physique was preparing to help her do just that as she felt Trent's warm body settle in with hers under her cool covers, their bodies once again clicking together into a perfect fit, their four legs slowly finding agreement and his wide chest gently pressing to her pajama-ed braless back. Ooooh, this was *wild*.

So was the sizeable *hello* his brontasuarus impressed upon her butt cheek. Last night's jeans kept it vague, but tonight's thin sweatpants let it feel much more THERE! Untalked about, this dino in her bed, this Trent-osaurus, stirred up thoughts of her abstinence, excitement, worries, all messed together like a twisted pretzel, confusing her, unnerving her –

"I wish I could detach it like old people do with dentures at night," he said.

She broke into a smirk, then a smile at the bizarre visual of Trent unclicking his dino from him and putting it in a plastic penis-sized case. She untensed a little more; he could probably feel her relaxing even more. *Wow.* Could he read her mind or feel her tense muscles?

"Still want me to stay?" his whisper asked her right ear.

She inhaled, liking that he asked, liking him being there, and exhaled "stay."

She felt his body relax, all but one undetachable part of him. "Cool," he said, sounding casually happy with her answer.

His humor had given her some comfort, and, for more comfort, and inspired by Kris's fondness for naming things, she decided to label Trent's dino with a name . . . something to calm her nerves . . . something pleasant . . . she thought of Trent pleasantly handing her his hanky last night . . . Hank. Yes, she thought, Hank. A comforting name for his unnerving penis. A fitting name, sturdy yet friendly. A friendly name that might ease her anxieties of it. She pictured his Hank smiling bestride her buttock like a happy cat to a warm leg.

The image relaxed her a little more. She let Trent stay wrapped around her as they lay on their left sides. She let herself be calmed by him, protected, eased, and sleepy. She breathed, grinned, and listened.

"Once upon a time . . . " his deep velvet voice whispered.

She smiled with glee. Oh gosh, she thought, what amazing story would this brilliant storyteller fill her with tonight?

" . . . there lived a . . . "

A lonely princess?

" . . . a . . . "

A searching prince?

" . . . a guitar-playing kangaroo," he whispered.

Say what?

"No, not that," he revised. " . . . a robot afraid of pogosticks . . . no, not that . . . um . . . a clock and a sock that go for a walk . . . no . . . an astronaut's toothbrush . . . no . . . oh . . . a cowboy alien from Planet Western," he finally settled on, and settled more into their snuggle as he distracted her thoughts and drifted her mind away once again on whispers into another ridiculous fantasyland.

Not what she expected, but trying to trust his writer skills as his tongue tripped and tumbled out an odd story for her on the fly. She listened. He rambled, slowly and gently distracting her thoughts away from his big hard Hank by making up a bizarre bedtime story about a cowboy space alien who visits planet Earth and invents floating houses, so every day people enjoyably wake up in a new location, although that did make the drive to work a different distance each day, but an issue easily solved with audio portholes that play a fun sound effect when you step through them, most enjoyably if the sound is *bloooop.*

And she liked the feel of his gentle cool breaths on her hair and neck giving her a tingly lovely shiver, liked his silly story, liked inhaling Trent's pleasant scent, liked his sheltering embrace, liked his protective body behind her. He had her back, and she slowly relaxed, while clutching his forearm like a Teddy bear in the dark; Bren remembered Holly's roof and standing atop the dangerous heights, but as long as she could grip the railing she felt okay. She felt okay with the dark while gripping Trent's sturdy arm, while letting go of everything else, more and more, worrying less and less, listening and listening to tales of floating houses, slowly floating . . . into . . . his . . . care . . .

Chapter 9 – day

Monday

buzz . . . buzZ . . . bUZZ . . . BUZZ . . .

Bren's eyes flew open. Red neon 5:00am.

Familiar alarm.

Foreign arm!

A *man's!*

What the heck?

Startled!

Confused!

Sigh . . . relief once she remembered whose big tree limb was lounging over her. She reached over and bopped the top of her clock.

Buzz killed.

Silence, except for Trent's light snoring behind her. *Yawn.* Crisp morning air rebooting her brain. Eyes blinking to pre-sunrise dimness.

She relaxed back down to her pillow.

Under her warm comfy covers, under this weird and wonderful arm, this muscled affection, this promise of protection, she lay calm but perplexed under this new guy's flesh of security, amazed that it was there, glad it was there, but still weirded out that it was there, a caring arm, caring for her as a friend, as more than a friend, as her own personal cuddler?

Her eyes studied the beautiful, emotion-triggering manliness blanketing her: the t-shirted shoulder, the sexy thick bicep, the bulging round tricep, the tan forearm of this man she hardly knew wrapped around her, thinking about how wild this was, to wake in the nook of her new novelist neighbor, a semi-stranger, and feel his bulging GOOD MORNING Hank still guarding her rear, like a patrolman keeping one eye open.

She thought about her crazy choice to invite him back in bed with her. Had she done a dumb thing? Was she encouraging him? Was she compromising herself? She thought and thought.

And the more she thought the more she realized how awake she was. *Wow.* She was really awake. Vibrantly awake. More awake than yesterday. More awake than in weeks. She had always been a morning person, but this amazingly felt like her awakest morning ever!

Excellent. This was great. Her cuddle plan with Trent had worked. The guy who had woken her with bumbling book and fork crashes was now helping her wake wonderfully with a heavenly hug after a gloriously deep full night's sleep *with no nightmares.* Yes. Teddy-bear-Trent was now less of a woe and more of a *wow.* He had become super useful. For the second time in weeks she felt AWAKE!

Her work clothes waited anxiously on her big chair. Her open bedroom door beckoned her to begin a brand new day. She felt unexpectedly hopeful. And everything in her fresh, rejuvenated, energized soul said: "GO!"

She so went! Flinging his big branch back to him and springing out of bed. He was no longer necessary. She was free and eager and flew around her apartment like a canary free from a cage. She had so much pep that she passed right by her work clothes and instead yanked out her sportswear for an early morning jog that she hadn't been awake enough to do in forever.

This was so exciting. She felt recharged, revved and ready to start her day! All she needed now was to get Mr. Open-Mouth-Messy-Hair out of her bed.

"Trent."

"Hmm?"

"*Trent!*"

" . . . soup or salad?" he murmured.

"Wake up."

"Mmmm. Would you like a baked potato with that?"

"No. I'd like you out of my bed."

"Oh," he said, finally waking and realizing and standing up.

She helped him scoot a little faster by pulling his arms and pushing his back until his perfect butt was out of her apartment. She saw bewildered Trent groggily turn back to say: "Have a good – "

WHAM!

Door shut. Ready for action!

* * * *

It was such a GOOD a day! Bren got soooo much stuff done!

She jogged, ate, showered, dressed, caught the bus, grabbed a coffee, got to work, and got to WORK!

She made revisions, fast decisions, managed with precision. She was functioning efficiently like her old machine self again. Her meetings were constructive, her workday productive, and her verve was so impressive that she got two conventions organized ahead of schedule.

She got so much done she even had extra time to text with Kris that it would be fun if a city had a lava lamp as tall as a building, and they wished each other happy National Strawberry-Rhubarb Day.

Everyone was wowwed at how alive and surprisingly effective Bren was at her job. They hadn't seen her so *take-charge* in weeks. Neither had her boss, Pam, who at the end of Bren's speedy ten-hour day deigned to her a rare approving smile.

"YES!"

All because of a full night's sleep!

* * * *

Bren's knuckles knocked on the frame of Trent's open door once more, he clomped down his stairs with burger in hand and ketchup on chin. Bren shoved five packs of pajamas at him.

"My bed, in one hour."

Trent stood stunned. Then a goofy grin inflated his face.

"No sex. Just *sleep*," she made it super clear.

His gorgeous eyes smiled into hers.

8:59pm.

Knock, knock.

Bren pulled tight the drawstrings on her yellow flannel pajamas, took a big breath, and opened her door.

Oh . . . *wow.*

She had spent the last vexing hour pacing and debating whether she really should or shouldn't sleep with her neighbor *again.* This whole plan was wacky. But finally her logic had justified the wacky. Trent = sleep. Yes. This was a very logical decision. But as soon as she opened her door, logic flew out the frickin' window.

He . . . was . . . *HOT.*

New and improved hot Trent stood before her, handsome as heck, bordering on gorgeous, in his sexy new blue cotton jammies. Her nightly knight had arrived, in *style.*

Her unblinking eyes toured all over his royal blue magnificence from his big bare feet, up his pajama pants, lingering too long on his Hank, shook her eyes loose, then slid up to his wide pajama-ed chest, his manly neck, his stunning face, and beautiful crystal blue eyes looking at her happily. *Oh, damn.* He looked good. She had never seen him dressed so nice. He looked . . . dashing.

She had gotten comfortable with goofy Trent.

But she wasn't prepared for *dashing* Trent.

Oh, cripes.

She felt her mouth hanging open.

He grinned.

She quickly locked her lips closed while she remembered how to, um, say words and stuff. She tried to calm her br-br-br-breathing, her th-th-th-thumping heartbeat and her warrrrming body. She could see that he saw that she saw that he saw her blushing face. *Oh geez.* She couldn't even think straight. And obviously he could tell. This was so embarrassing.

He then began stylishly striking funny men's pajama-model poses: the hand-in-pocket, the fists-on-waist-Superman, The Thinker, and the *did-I-button-my-fly?*

She laughed at his foolery.

Then he struck a sexy, silly bedroom-eyed hunk pose. "*Roooom service*," he joked.

Ooooh, criminy. This was the goof she was stressing over? He was such a buffoon, the most flickin' frackin' gorgeous buffoon she'd ever seen, and he was *her* buffoon, for the night, if she wanted him to be, and she nervously, fearfully, skeptically, longingly and . . . ahem . . . very logically wanted him to be. She suddenly remembered why she liked hanging out with him, why she felt so comfortable with him: he was Trent.

She relaxed a bit, breathed, and smirked. "My goodness, who is this stylish man at my door?" she found herself playing.

He opened his arms with ridiculous presentational grandeur. "I'm your cuddler," he announced proudly, then chuckled, clearly feeling the absurdity of their arrangement too.

Bren chuckled. "My *cuddler*? Is that what you are?"

"According to my sister."

"What?"

"That's what she's calling you and me: cuddlers."

"You told your sister about us?"

"Sure," he said.

"Why?"

"I tell her everything."

Oh, geez.

"My sis says you sound awesome," he continued. "She says if you're ever in L.A. and need to cuddle that she'd like Donna Karen silk nighties."

Oh. Bren chuckled. *Wait. What?* Bren's brain whirred and wondered. "Um. Does your sister think we're weird?"

Trent grinned. "She called us 'sweet.'"

Bren's eyebrows raised. *Sweet?* Their arrangement was supposed to be productive, not sweet. Wait. Did Trent think they were sweet?

"Do you still want me?"

"*Want* you?" Bren shuddered.

"To come in," he said.

"Oh," she said, relaxing, sort of. "Right. Um . . . "

He waited.

She looked at this sweet-looking, totally tempting man.

He still waited.

She realized the carnal risk of *HOT* Trent in her bed, enthralling her body to want to do more than cuddle, and confuse her life even more.

He still waited.

But, she reminded herself: Trent = sleep. And she could resist temptation. She took a big breath. Then smartly, or super foolishly, stepped aside to let this dangerous dashing Darcy into her evening, into her apartment, and soon into her bed. But, that was *all* she would let him into she reminded her warm-blooded body.

Smilingly, he entered.

Chapter 9 – night

MONNIGHT

His presence changed everything.

His body passed by hers.

Mmmm. She breathed in his clean, showered scent.

His pajama-ed back looked as fine as his front.

She sensibly looked away, but festered with feelings.

He was inside.

She shut her door. She locked it. She had committed.

She heard his naked feet behind her casually stepping, then stop, while her heart kept thumping. He was in her home once more. She slowly turned around, and found her gentleman cuddler looking even hotter in the light. Tanner, taller, manlier.

Oh, criminy.

She stood statue-still, trying to not let her mouth flop open again, straightening tall and stiff, trying to keep her excited body in a business-like demeanor, not encouraging any air of sweetness, even though he looked damn sweet. She had guessed his pajama size correctly, at her own peril; she should have gotten him a size too big so he looked goofy instead of gorgeous. His pjs had no crease lines; did he wash and dry them? Nice, and courteous.

"I'm glad your previous Trent-experiences were so positive that you want more," he joked.

She smirked. "Getting a good night's sleep was a positive experience," she said, keeping things unromantic.

He grinned. He was standing in his place once again beside her wooden kitchen table, as if she had properly trained him to do so. *Hmmm.*

She saw him look down at her table and see his novel not there. Then his excited eyes flicked back up to her, as if he sensed it had been *experienced*. He gave her a cocky smirk. "Read any good books lately?"

Hot flash *whoooooshed* through Bren's body! She clenched everything tight to stay poker-faced while her tingly being recalled all the giddy guilty pleasures his novel had thrilled through her. And now the thriller writer was back with her for a personal appearance, staring sexy at her, and waiting for an oral book review. Stay cool, her brain said.

"I haven't had time to read it," she sidestepped.

His lips fell and eyebrows flew. "Oh . . . " he breathed out, sounding surprised. "I'm hoping to hear your opinion."

"You are?"

"Yeah."

"Why is that?"

"I think you're the one reader in the world who'll tell me the real truth."

She looked at him.

He looked at her.

"I've been busy," she sidestepped again. "Work. The wedding."

"And cooking," he added while sniffing her apartment's air.

"Yes."

"Halibut?"

"Wahoo."

"Gazoontite."

"It's not a sneeze, it's a fish."

"A gourmet fish."

"Oh, you know it?"

"I know its spendy."

"It's Monday," Bren said. "After a long crazy Monday I reward myself with a gourmet-ish meal. It makes starting a work week more delightful."

"Was your dinner delightful?"

"It was."

"So delightful that you went '*wahoo*?'"

She smirked. "Not *that* delightful."

"Well, can I help make your Monday more delightful?"

She steeled herself. "How so?" she asked, wondering if she might need to kick him out. Then she watched her handsome guest wink and not walk into her bedroom, but instead walk into her kitchen and over to her messy cookware. "Can I help clean up?" he offered.

Really, she thought? He impressed her again. Though the thought of his hands touching her dishes and stuff seemed wildly intimate. "Oh, you don't need to clean my mess."

"I don't mind," he shrugged, his big palm hovering under her panhandle, looking eager for a green light.

She took a breath, and found herself saying "all right." Then she watched him smile and begin working his magic. *Hmmm.* A guy who liked to clean? He got points. She reminded him of California's current water restrictions and to use her faucet sparingly while she watched him scrub, rinse, and dry, and wondered why? Was he hoping she would reward him with *wahoo*?

"Why *are* you washing my dishes?"

"You were nice and bought me pajamas. Which I will repay you for."

Hmmm. "Nope. They're on me."

"Actually they're on me. But you shouldn't have to pay for 'em."

"We're even. Five nights. Five pajamas. That's our deal."

"That's our deal?"

"Yes."

"Oooh," he reacted with a grin. "So we're cuddling for five nights?"

Bren felt a little forward. "Just so I can get sleep this crazy wedding-week. Would five-nights be all right with you?"

He smiled at her, ear to ear, and nodded.

Hmmm. She felt both glad and nervous.

He did her dishes, well. "I'm surprised you invited me back," he said.

"Why?"

"You threw me out of here so fast this morning, I thought I snored too loud or something and upset you."

"I just needed to start my day."

"And how was your day?"

"Very productive. Thanks to a good night's sleep. Hence your invitation to return."

"Glad I could help."

"I am too."

"So," he said, getting her plate wet and soapy, "why can't you sleep?"

Crud. She figured he would ask eventually. "Um. Stress."

"Got a lot going on, huh?"

If he only knew. "Everything happening all at once."

He nodded. "When sorrows come, they come not single spies – "

"But in battalions," she finished his *Hamlet* quote.

He looked impressed at her, as he scrubbed her soapy dish in a circular motion.

Yes, everything sure was battalioning into her life recently. Including the handsome battalioner who wet her plate, dried it good as new and put it on her shelf labeled "plates," then turned to her, smiling proud-ish of his good deed and hopeful-ish as he gazed into her eyes.

"How else can I make your Monday night delightful?"

Gulp.

Her romance book filled databanks thought of lots and lots of delightful ideas.

Butterflies fluttered her tummy as her cheeks burned warm.

Now she felt *wahoo.*

And hypnotized by his beautiful eyes.

Sharing a stare, her hand pawed-pawed-pawed for the light switch.

Click.

Darkness broke her Trent-trance.

Whew.

"Bedtime," she announced loudly, as she skeedaddled her heated body the heck away from her dashing helpful guest and beelined to her bedroom, her brain warning not to let him give her *too* delightful an evening.

Behind her his following feet patted as her heartbeats banged, *really* stirring up her butterflies. Her whole insides became a fluttering frenzy knowing that she was about to be in bed with his phanominal-feeling body again, and his sexy lulling voice. She exhaled, while making her room totally un-encouraging by clicking on her bright ceiling light, her desk lamp, and her tall standing lamp, plus the elegant, yellow shaded lamps on both sides of her bed. All that blasting light everywhere made super sure that there was not a shadow of romantic mood, and no misunderstandings.

She stood with her bed between her and him as she watched her fun/intimidating guest stroll into her clinic-ish atmosphere like a cocky suspect into a bright interrogation room. She wished she could shine her lights on all the hidden parts of him she couldn't see.

His feet stopped center-room. He was *really* inside now, like a Trojan horse that could unleash a battalion of sorrows or a friend who could end her current ones; her brain still didn't know which he was, but her heart and other parts didn't care, they just liked having him there.

She watched his curious eyes tour all around her room. She watched him take her private life into his brain like an art lover absorbing a Monet, with a slight smile. She saw him see her cheery yellow bed spread, her silver desk and Herman Miller chair, her posters of authors, her Howie Day concert flyer and ticket, her pretties of perfectly arranged fabric flowers and literary figurines, all her To Do Lists taped to her walls, and her three big, yellow, seven-shelved bookcases.

He smiled giddily. "Wow. I didn't see all these Bren-isms the other dark nights I was in here," he said. "This room is very *you*."

"What does *that* mean?"

"You and your room are charming, sassy, and . . . complex."

"Complex?"

"You got all these cute decorations going on everywhere, and then there's this metal desk. Like a military tank in a flower shop."

"It's a workstation. It's not supposed to be cute."

His eyebrows raised. "That statement says so much about you."

"It does?"

"It's kind of like you got a duality, between your profession and your pleasures."

"Cripes. I let B.F. Skinner in my bedroom."

"Nah. Skinner rejected freewill. I prefer Maslow."

"I prefer you cuddle me, not analyze me."

"Sorry," he said. "I'm totally happy to just with cuddle you."

"I bet you are."

He grinned.

She smirked, kinda feeling conflicted between her defenses and desirers as she walked around his stillness, to finish checking her *Nightly To Do List* taped up on her wall and did the next thing it reminded her to; she plugged her cell phone into the charger.

"What are those?" he asked.

She hesitated, but was curious if he would respect her paper helpers or mock them. "Those are my to do lists."

"All those?"

"Yes."

"You just keep getting more interesting."

She smiled.

"Can I look at 'em?"

She really hesitated, interested in his reaction. "All right." She felt her breathing thin seeing him wander over and curiously take her private lists into his eyes, into his mind, and judge them.

"You got a lot of to do lists."

"I've got a lot to do."

"Looks like it. Out the Door List, Workout List, Yearly, Monthly, Weekly, Morning, and Nightly To Do List. Wow." He smiled. "Yep, you're interesting."

"In a good way?"

"Totally good."

She smiled.

"Could you memorize your lists instead?"

"I don't trust myself to remember."

He chuckled. "You wrote 'rename yoga positions for Sara.' That just happened yesterday. You're very organized."

"I try to be."

His smile seemed impressed with her.

She secretly smiled, feeling thrilled that someone appreciated her organized-ness.

He read her Nightly To Do List. "Did you brush your teeth?" he asked.

"Yes," she said, rolling her eyes and playing along.

"Did you text your mom goodnight?"

"Yes."

"Did you lay out all your clothes for tomorrow?"

She grimaced. "Are you making fun of my lists? My friends do that plenty."

"I'm not making fun of you. I like your lists. I think they're cool."

She perked up. *Hmmm.* He got more points.

"Kris says my all lists around the apartment are like living with a senile 90 year old."

He chuckled. "Well, we all have our quirks."

She pounced on that. "What are *your* quirks?"

He grinned. "*Not* having lists."

"But they're helpful."

"They seem awesomely helpful I'm totally inspired." He looked back at her list. "Set clock alarm."

Bren walked to her clock and set it.

"Teamwork," he said, kinda making himself part of her life.

Hmmm. Not totally keen on being a team, but she tried it, putting her guest to good use. "Next?"

He grinningly took a look. "Lint roller."

Bren snatched up her roller and crossed to tomorrow's laid out work outfit hanging on her sliding closet door hook and proceeded to de-lint while she ogled him ogling her bedroom some more, thumbs hanging on his pj pockets and his eyes looking all around at her private world. His wandering eyes saw everything, and not glancingly. Slowly. Smilingly.

She wiped her fingertips' perspiration on her pajamas, both nervous and thrilled to have her hot neighbor standing among her lights, among her life, open, exposed, almost more intimate than holding her body. He could see all her stuff, symbols of herself, all her inside desires all over the outside: the furniture she chose, the knickknacks she loved, the pictures that empowered her.

"De-linting done," she said. "What's next on my list?"

He grinned. "Tell Trent about pictures over bed," he pretended to read.

Her mouth came open to breathe. She tried to stay cool and cocked her head. "I don't think it says that."

"I'd like it to."

"Really?"

"If you don't mind."

She paused, not sure if she minded.

His beautiful eyes had found her visual, long-term to-do list: five framed portraits hanging inspiringly on the wall above her bed. *Darn.* Once again, shining all her lights on him also meant shining lights on herself and her private life too. She hesitated, unsure of revealing too much of herself, but revealing herself to him felt *fun*, like walking naked in the warm sun. Butterflies fluttering, she let her life show a little more skin.

"You traveled to the homes of your heroes," she told him.

"Yeah."

"I hung up my heroes in my home."

"Oh," he reacted. "Well, that's less expensive."

She grinned.

"So these women are your heroes?"

"Role models."

"Really?"

"Yes," she admitted, studying his reaction.

"Cool," he said, as he studied the five-framed portraits, seeming genuinely interested, once again respecting and not mocking her stuff. He looked at Bren. She felt him study her. "Why these women?" he pried more, with a tilt of his head. "Do they have something in common?"

Wow. Bren grinned wider, but tried to hide it. No one had ever asked about their commonality. And he was the only person who truly seemed interested in her private display. Her heart beat faster and she found herself excited to explain to a true inquirer their commonality. "June 18th."

He grinned at her grin. "What's up with June 18th?"

"It's my birthday."

"Your birthday's June 18th?"

"Yes."

"That's next week."

"Yes."

"Do you celebrate just your birthday or do you celebrate your birthday-week?"

"Just my birthday. I can't imagine celebrating for a whole week."

"It's a great excuse to do at least one fun thing a day all week long."

"I don't know. That might be fun-overload."

"You might enjoy some fun overload."

Mmmm. She imagined enjoying all kinds of fun overload with him. "Wouldn't a birthday-week be called a birthweek?"

He grinned. "I like the way you think."

"Thanks."

"So you're a Gemini."

Bren rolled her eyes. "Really? You're into star signs?"

"Sure, mostly to see people roll their eyes when I talk about star signs."

She smirked.

"Of course you would be a Gemini. Intelligent, always on the go, can't settle down unless it's with a soulmate."

She tilted her head. "You believe in soulmates?"

He smiled at her. "Absolutely."

Electricity. She stared back at him.

He smiled even bigger, then turned back to her pictures.

She wiped her fingers on her pajamas again.

"All these women were born on June 18th?"

"No," Bren corrected him. Then inhaled, super excited that someone was actually interested. "On June 18, 1429: Joan of Arc defeated the English army at the Battle of Patay; on June 18, 1872: Susan B. Anthony attempted to vote in a presidential election and was fined $100; on June 18, 1928: Amelia Earhart became the first woman to fly in an aircraft across the Atlantic Ocean; and on June 18, 1983: Sally Ride became the first American woman in space."

Trent looked impressed. "Wow. They all did that on June 18th?"

"Yes."

Trent looked at the portrait of Mary Shelley in the center of the other women. "And what did Mary do on June 18th?"

Bren paused. "She thought up *Frankenstein*."

His eyes swung back to Bren. *That's* the night she thought it up? I thought Mary Shelley thought up Frankenstein on June 16th."

"Well, no one knows the exact date. Some say June 16th. Some say June 22nd. I like to think it was June 18th when she thought up Franky, after a nightmare." Bren realized another thing her and Mary had in common: nightmares. Bren wished that something great would have come from *her* nightmare, to justify having it. Something good from bad, like spring from winter. Though because of her nightmare she needed Trent. He was something good from bad, she hoped. Maybe? This was all just so –

"Wild," he said.

"What's wild?"

"You and all these famous women, and June 18th."

"Oh, yes."

He looked at her with a grin. "Cool coincidence."

Bren rolled her eyes at his illogical belief that coincidences tell you that you're on the correct path in life. She ran her hand through her hair.

His big hands hung from his pj pockets, almost framing his Hank. "So why are they your role models?"

Bren winced that he couldn't figure out *that* commonality. "They're all great. They're all great achieving women who said: "Screw you. I'm not gonna just be a common woman with common thoughts. I'm gonna think bolder and do something great. And they did."

"And they did it on your birthday."

"Yes."

"Hmm. That's a lot to live up to."

A new light popped on in her mind. She took a deep breath. "Yes. It is."

He still stood respectful by her sacred pictures. "Have you accomplished your greatness yet?"

She scrunched her lips. "Not yet."

"So what great thing are you gonna do?" Trent asked her with a smile.

Bren sighed. "I don't know." She played with the lint roller in her hands. She used to know. She used to have her whole life planned out, until a month ago, be an accomplished CEO, happy wife, awesome mom, and an inspiration to others. Maybe some girl would hang Bren's framed picture on her wall one day. But now, everything in life seemed so unreliable, her future so uncertain.

"I bet you will do something great," he said.

She looked up. "You do, huh?"

"Definitely," his voice's confidence comforted her. "You seem so driven. So organized."

"I am," she said proudly. "The first rule of success is organization."

"Although *I'm* not organized and I'm having some success."

"You had to be somewhat organized to write your book."

"Actually no," he said, he said, chuckling up toward her ceiling, then looked back at her. "The whole story for my book just fell out of me. I was sitting alone at a bar one night, months after breaking up with Julia, but still heartbroken."

Bren's ears perked up.

"I was just feeling the bar's vibe, just being there, and suddenly, out of nowhere, *blam*, I got this idea for a story. I didn't finish my beer; I just raced home and started writing. It was this crazy stream of consciousness thing. I couldn't stop writing. It was such an organic process. It was like an artistic orgasm."

Bren's eyes perked up.

"I just knew what the story should be and how it should start and journey and end, and I finished the whole story in a month. I rewrote it over the next few weeks, my editor helped consolidate it all, and ta-da, I had a novel."

Bren looked back down, shaking her head with disgruntled envy. Lucky bird, she thought. She had worked so long and hard for her successes and Trent just fell ass-backward into his: his long relationship with Julia, his successful novel. "So great things just *happen* to you?"

"Sometimes," he said. "Lots of nothing. Then *ta-da*, something magical happens fast and spontaneous."

She remembered how magically spontaneous he *blammmed* into her life. A rare unpredictable fluke. "Well, I don't wait around trusting life to *ta-da* me. I make my own *ta-das*," she said firmly, as she efficiently put her lint roller back in its labeled place in her drawer. "What's next?" she asked him.

He looked at her list. "Read."

Warmth whooshed through her, remembering his book. Then she stood up straight. "Um, no reading tonight."

"Don't not-read just 'cause I'm here."

She fizzed between excitement and sense. "I – I don't feel like reading tonight."

"All right."

Total lie. She totally *wanted* to read. *Wow.* She never thought she would feel the urge to read again, but what Greg ruined Trent resurrected, the pleasure of reading. But no flipping way should she read in front of Trent; she might feel too much pleasure, in bed, with him and get really *excited.* And *excitment* before cuddling would not be smart, because bed was like books, between the covers soooo much fun could happen, and all she needed to happen was sleep.

He smiled at her. "Can I look at your books?"

RECORD NEEDLE SCREEEECH!

Ooooh cripes. More excitement and nervousness. More reasons to go right to sleep. If she was smart she would say "no" and have them go to bed right now.

Although . . . she was curious to see *how* he would look at her books. His looking might tell her a lot about him. Like stories, behavior = character.

She hesitated.

He waited.

She found logic in letting him look at her books, and nervously and curiously nodded "All right. Go ahead."

He smiled giddily. If he were a puppy his tail would be wagging wild.

With bated breath she watched her new favorite author turn his gorgeous eyes to face her private litany of literature. Then she beheld the stunning sight: *Trent looking at her books.*

Time stopped.

Woooow. Seeing this handsome, delightful man, this brilliant author, her cuddler near her treasure of pleasures was the sexiest damn thing she'd ever seen! Her favorite guy with her favorite fun. His back and great backside faced her while he faced her three tall yellow bookcases on her east wall, looking over her collection, her private entertainments, her *indulgences.* He was looking at them! Her endorphins *rushed!*

She had figured her fellow booklover would gravitate to her books. She had planned some extra time for him to browse. But she sure hadn't planned on feeling so aroused.

She by the head of her bed, him at the foot. Both of them motionless. Both of them looking. Both of them rapt in awe.

And silence.

Wild silence.

Reverently silent, like they were in a church of books, a church of pleasure.

Their wild, reverent silence grew as big as her bedroom, as her torrent of tumbling thoughts totally filled the space.

Did her collection impress himm?

Should she care?

How many of her books had he read also?

What was he thinking?

She soooo wanted to know!

So, slowly she softly strode back across her room and pretended to tend to some papers on her desk. There she could spy a side view of him. She could see his wandering eyes and where they wandered, seeing how long they stayed before they strayed, and their reaction to what they were seeing.

His reaction was a look of focused fascination at all her fascinating titles in her genre-labeled shelves, each shelf packed with a long skyline of vertical wonders, perfectly alphabetized by author and title. Her arousing browsing guest could easily find any tome in her home as his eyes roamed all around, browsing and browsing, un-swiftly lingering, interestedly, really looking at her books, more than anyone ever had looked at her books.

Wow.

He was staring and caring, as if he understood how important and personal her paper friends were to her. These were the books she had chosen. These juicy, ripe fruits picked from the bookstore shelves were her nourishment. These word resorts were where she languished in language, floated through another's mind, got rejuvenated with fresh ideas, and improved herself. These paper parties were where she met fascinating new characters to detest or emulate, and define herself. These literary twilight zones were the fantasy worlds she escaped into, time-traveled, and explored, and the thrilling stories that she played in with her fun imaginary friends. These mental battlegrounds were where she vicariously confronted life's calamities, learned secrets, lived out brave adventures, and vanquished angers against insurmountable odds. These emotional rollercoasters were where she felt mystery and wonder, fear and romance, madness and revelation, fury and epiphany, and hate, love, desire, passion and debauchery, scandal, indulgence and rapturous sex! These books were her delights, her loves, her inspirations and excitements. These re-read, bent, torn, dog-eared, bookmarked, underlined, sweat-stained, memorized magic pages were where she *L I V E D!*

In her socially acceptable, restricted career world she was appropriately presentable. But inside a book she could live a wild, heroic, tragic, lustful, or pristinely perfect life. These were her fantasies.

And Trent was seeing her *books!*

Like having his eyes see her naked body; this felt *that* intimate. And no one, no man, had ever looked at her body of books with such gazing and smiling appreciation of what she had.

Exhilarating!

This time she wasn't reading about an adventure, she was *living* one right then, in real life, with the man who allured and thrilled her.

He said nothing. He just explored, perhaps unaware of the powerful effect his looking was having on her. *Electric silence!* Nothing felt more important than this wild moment. With his hands in his back pj pockets, on his perfect buns, his eyes drifted and his lips grinned at her sci-fi section, at *Hitchhiker's* and *Dune*, smiling at her whole shelf of Louis L'amour westerns, and chuckling at her two shelves of vintage pulp paperbacks: *Marijuana Girl*, *Lust in the Big City Jungles*, and her fave: *Those Sexy Saucer People*.

He beamed at her bios, her cookbooks, her classics. He smiled at her dramas and self-help and graphics. Hung out with her histories and sleuthed through her mysteries and her palms were so soaked as he perused her poetries. The pleasure on his face had her tingling so tingly. Him thrilled with her thrillers thrilled her so thrillingly. Up in her business, into her fantasies, going down on her erotic anthologies. Gripping her pajama fabric in fists, she hadn't planned on feeling such bliss. Loins shaking wild, heart rat-a-tat-tat, mind realizing – OMG – what he was really smiling at:

Her.

He was seeing *her*.

Who she was by what she chose.

Books = character.

Oh wow. He was seeing what all her likes, loves, and lusts had in common: her soul.

Ooooooooh my, she thought.

He was reading *her*.

Getting to know *her*.

She felt so vulnerable. *Cripes*. This was getting crazy. *She* was the one who was supposed to be in charge with all the power right now. Her nervousness grew.

His smile grew too. Smiling at *her*. Appreciating *her*. Seeming to like the soul he was seeing, liking as he kept looking, as if looking for something specific, as he stopped still in front of all her romance, perusing her through her Alcotts, Atwoods and Austens, and smiled at his novel now in her B's section.

Oh geez. Is that what he was searching for? His book among her likes and loves?

But her knight continued his quest, his eyes roaming through her romance, down, down down. He knelt. He paused. He smiled. He looked up at her, with a big, big smile like Tom Sawyer finding the hidden treasure in the cave.

Heat *whooshed* like a wave!

He'd found her fave!

Her blood got hot!

Her blushing cheeks totally telling his smirk that he had found it.

He had totally Sherlocked her!

Damn. He was good.

His eyes asked her for permission to handle her holy book.

She . . . nodded, giving him another green light.

He nodded back her.

Now she felt *really* vulnerable, and *soooo* embarrassed.

He hadn't been looking at the spines of her books for titles, but looking for her most dog-eared, bookmarked, spine-cracked, well-worn guilty pleasure, and found it within minutes. Trent really was swift.

But was he respectful?

How would he handle her favoritest favorite? If he didn't treat her book with respect she would kick him out, swiftly! But so far he had treated her body with respect, and she hoped that's how he would be with her books, as she inhaled the electric air. Her wide eyes followed his big hand as it slowly reached for her precious. Her body blazed! Her new hot neighbor was reaching for the story of two San Francisco neighbors, who screw. Wow. This was not the simple evening she had planned.

The air was on fire as his hand reached closer and closer and then – *OH*, she gasped! He touched it! He was touching it! *Oooooooo* – his pointing appendage was touching her *Wallbanger*!

She clutched her pjs tighter as his fingers gripped her very banged up *'banger*, and gently and ever so tenderly slid it out of its slot.

Soooo damn hot to see her new favorite author touching her favorite book!

Wow!

Bren watched Alice Clayton's funny heart-throbber happily surrender itself into his strong but gentle grip. He lifted her book away with his care. She watched his hands treat her book gently, respectfully supporting her pink paperback spine. Then he carefully turned her flat onto his four fingers to admire her front, holding her firm as her pages arched limp around his tips like a ball-gowned beauty dipped back by a strong tuxedoed dancer, trusting him to not drop her.

Bren was trusting Trent.

Her book lay helpless in his hands as he gazed down upon her alluring cover of a woman's legs wrapped around a suited man. Trent's grin at Bren's actual favoritest book cover seemed to sense the promise of delights that awaited him inside.

But, he looked over at Bren, as if asking for permission to proceed.

With a st-st-stuttery inhale . . . she totally nodded.

His smirk and eyes went back to her book. Her book's thin cardboard cover easily fell open to his seductive gentleness. His sturdy left hand kindly held her rectangle body safe as his right thumb caressingly slid over her fast flipping pages; her pages seemed to love the wild ride, almost sighing with pleasure as they flew. This clearly wasn't the first book his thumb had caressed.

She couldn't tear her eyes away from watching him work his magic. Bren loved the way he handled her: kindly, supportively, and his eyes explored her as slow and thoroughly as they had with Bren's library, pausing on pages with folded corners and blue ink underlines. Bren knew by the dog-ear where he was in the story; she knew what he was seeing, and he was finding out that she didn't just dog-ear the sex, she had flagged all the other stuff that fed her desires for story, suspense, relationship, playfulness, and of course steamy hot romance. He was learning so much about her, skimming her, reading her, learning her, as he fingered her fave lovingly, seeing her underlined passages and bookmarked pages, finding out what parts Bren liked the most. *Ooooh.* He was learning what she liked. He was learning *her*, intimately. *Wow.* She watched. Both troubled and turned on.

She thought about stopping him. But . . . but . . . she didn't. Her nervousness was devoured by how damn erotic this felt. He looked at what she adored. He smiled. He seemed to *like* it too.

Okay. *This* was the sexiest damn thing she'd ever seen.

He was giving her book the same gentleness he gave to her in bed. *Ooooh.* Bren soooo looked forward to feeling his gentleness with her again. But his eyes kept looking at her book as his hands slowly spread her pages w i d e open. *Like legs. Like sex. Like Greg had done with his ex before kissing her outside on that devastating day! Whoa. Bren no longer liked Trent with her book. Bren PTSD-ed! Now wildly jealous!*

"Library is closed!" Bren blurted out.

Trent looked up at her, seeing her flustered, and he quickly closed the book on this madness.

But she still felt mad and sad and excited and conflicted. She turned away. She breathed.

Silence.

Weird silence.

She heard Trent gently return her favorite book back to her slot. Bren slowly, slowly calmed. *Geez.* Greg's betrayal still haunted her, *big time*. Not just in dreams, but with a new man. She totally got triggered seeing Trent just look at a book. *Damn Greg.* Her love life had become a dangerous mess. She had to be more careful. She couldn't let Trent get her all fluttered and vulnerable. She had to keep control. She chided herself for letting things progress way too far too fast. She throttled back, and . . . breathed some more.

His silence let her, for almost a minute. Then his calm, concerned voice gently brought her back from the brink. "What's next on your to-do list?"

Yes, she thought. Her list, her reliable rock, and a way out of this intensity. She rushed to her lists like a girl on fire needs a lake and slid her sweat-wet finger down all her smearing to-do's and saw her last to-do of her day.

Gulp.

She turned her flushed-feeling face back around to this new, stirring man in her life, and in her private bedroom, as he stood with empty hands and his eyes on *her*, and only *her*.

"Bed," she said.

Bren clicked off her lights.

One by one.

Until only one of her bedside lamps remained lit.

Shadows shooed him and her closer in the limited light.

He stood on his side of her bed and she on hers.

His handsome face softly aglow. His bedroom eyes sparking at her.

Just him and her and a little bit of luminance.

Ooookay, she breathed. Now it was romantic.

Her emotioned bubbling. Her heart p-p-pounding. Her thoughts flinging all around. All stirred up before bed. Not smart.

She would so need to calm down.

He stood waiting, looking angelic, an angel come to help her sleep.

Right, good luck falling asleep easily tonight, she thought.

Slipping out of her fuzzy slippers, her bare feet now as naked as his on her cushy carpet, his eyes dancing with hers, she calmed with a big inhale of courage. Beginning her last to-do of her night, leaning forward her fumbling fingers found her soft bedspread and peeled it open. He did the same with his side, opening up this cover together, then both of them slipping inside her cool crisp sheets to create a living story with their warm bodies.

Legs accidentally touching. Gasping. Tingling. Breathing. Readjusting. Two busy bedmates finding their place in each designated space. She sat upright, then lowered her back onto her mattress, her head smushed upon her pillow, she pulled up her wonderful covers, then rested her hands on her stomach, and exhaled, then stillness.

Her guest not so still. Flat but fidgeting, kinda wriggling around.

"What *are* you doing?"

"I'm not used to pajamas. Usually I sleep naked."

Hot flash!

Cold logic.

"Well you're not sleeping naked tonight," her voice accidentally squeaked with excitement.

He chuckled. "That's cool."

She tried to be cool too, now reminded that his bare body was just a few thin pajama layers away. She needed to quickly change the subject from nakedness to . . . anything else. "Do you like my bed?"

"Oh my God, I love your bed," he said, as he settled in. "By far the most luxurious bed I've ever had the pleasure to sleep in."

How many beds had he slept in? With how many women? How much pleasure? "I'm glad you like it."

"What kind is it?"

"It's a Worthington fourteen-inch innerspring-dream quilted mattress," she rattled off. "Gel memory foam layer, with a Gideon box spring of multiple-motion individually wrapped coils for a sensuously luxurious slumber."

"You describe things very thoroughly," he complimented.

"I try."

"*Aaaaaaaawe*," he sighed out with pleasure as he finally stilled his body down into her bed's softness. "It feels like I'm nestled in warm butterscotch pudding."

"You describe things like a writer," she teased.

"I try," he joked back, exhaling blissfully and nestling himself into her "pudding," on their backs, his pajama-ed body beside hers, looking at her ceiling, then looking at each other for a nice stirring moment, as he began pillow talking.

"What books do you usually read before bed?"

Uh oh. He wanted to talk books, *in bed*. Bad idea. "I read something that makes me smile," she replied randomly and ridiculously. Then, before she could change the subject, she wondered what *he* read in bed, then pictured him in bed with a book, *naked!*

"Actually I thought you'd have more books," he mentioned. "If I pulled on one of your novels does your bookcase swing open to reveal a secret athenaeum of literary storage?"

She grinned. "No. But I can swing open my apartment door and walk a couple blocks to Green Street's cute little library."

"Oh, cool," he said happily. "There's one that close?"

"There is," she said more excited than she meant to. Excited that someone besides her really cared that there was a nearby library. Too excited. "I also read a lot of ebooks," she explained.

"I can see you as an ebook person. Always on the go. Endless titles at your fingertips. And it's very 'organized.'"

And no one can see that she was secretly reading erotica on the bus, she thought.

"But ebooks have no smell of ink and timber," he said.

"Maybe ebooks will come with smells one day."

"Oh, that'd be cool. And you could choose the smell of your ebook: floral, woodsy, or *moldy*."

"An ew-book," she quipped.

Trent laughed so silly that Bren laughed at his silly laugh. Endorphins flowed and filled her. She felt good. Too good.

"But no artificial smell could be as awesome as a real book," he continued. "I love slipping my nose between the pages of a good book and inhaling the year it was printed."

Mmmmmm. Bren felt tingly. "I understand that guilty pleasure."

"Really?"

"Yep. Bibliosmia," she said.

"Bib-what?"

"Bibliosmia is pleasure from smelling books."

"I didn't know it had a name." He chuckled. "So we're bibliosmia-ers."

"I think so."

"You should smell my first edition Austen," he invited. "She's a time machine back to 1813."

Ooooh. That sounded wonderful. She would love to smell his Austen. She could just imagine burying her nose deep between Jane's first edition pages and sniffing and time traveling into her actual world. Surge of excitement! *Whoa.* Feeling out of control. *Darn him.* Like his arousing writing, his words were once again making her *feel, in bed, with him beside her.*

She quickly sucked in a long breath trying to calm as much as she could with this exciting man just a lusting lunge away. She reminded herself of her own rule: no sex, just sleep. So, that was enough hot talk of page-sniffing. It was time for them to focus on bed not books. Her brain finally overpowered her desires and smartly switched topics. "Are you really all right sleeping with me all week?"

He playfully rolled to his side and faced her, his head on his pillow, giving her his bedroom eyes and his big grin.

Oh my, she thought, sexiest man alive laying next to her. Things getting even more exciting. Her heart did flips.

"I have happily penciled 'sleep with Bren' into my mental Nightly To Do List," he said to her playfully.

She grinned over at him. "Very good."

He nodded. "But can I add something to your Morning To Do List?"

She tilted her head, curious. "What?"

"I wanna add: Treat Trent nicer in the mornings."

Whoa. "Oh I *bet* you wanna add that."

"Not anything spicy," he explained. "I mean a tap on my shoulder, instead of shaking me awake and shoving me out your door."

"Oh." Relief. "Well. You weren't getting up and out fast enough."

"I'm not a morning person. It takes me a while to wake up."

"I thought you do things swiftly."

He looked at her. "In bed I take my time."

Oooooooooh my. How should she interpret *that*, she wondered? Her head filled with all kinds of wonderful ways he could take his time in bed. This cuddle plan was getting hard to stay just platonic.

Staring at his eyes looking at her so nicely intimate. A little silence. More nice than awkward. Enjoying him being there. Much more fun than being alone. Kinda super glad he moved in. She adjusted how her hair lay, and wondered, and got curious. "Um. So, I'm not interrupting you sleeping with your fans, naked?"

He laughed lightly. "No," he said shyly. "I don't sleep with fans."

Whoa. Bren wasn't expecting that. She turned toward his tempting body beside hers, still on her pillow, now facing his pleasant face, just inches away. Just her and him in the whole building, in the quiet city, in the sensuous night, in this romantic light. And all his flirty fans were without him, because he was here instead, in bed, with her. "You really don't sleep with your fans?"

"Nope," he said softly to her.

"None of them?"

He shook his head. "None of 'em," he said, his eyes never leaving hers.

Her heart thumped harder. Her brain got curiouser, finding his claim impossible to believe. "But they're all over you."

"Sometimes."

"You could be having sex with a fan right now instead of having no sex with me."

He smirked. "But they wouldn't have bought me fancy pajamas."

She smirked. "That you would never wear."

"Except with you."

She warmed and swallowed and realized he was only clothed because of her rules, and if she loosened her rules then he'd be naked. She warmed more. She blinked, and tried to stay sensible, and her sensible brain tried to shout above her thumping heart that there had to be more to his unexpected story. She needed to keep Nancy Drew-ing. "Why don't you sleep with your fans?"

His eyes fell away. Then returned to her with unusual shyness. "I'm hesitant to tell you."

Uh oh. "Why?"

"You'll think less of me."

Double uh oh.

He glanced beyond their feet, over at her tall bookcases, then back at her. "But I told you I wouldn't withhold info. So. I'll tell you."

Oh cripes. She worried.

He took a breath.

Bren held hers.

What horrible thing was he hiding? What deal breaker? What heartbreaker? What was so embarrassing that he didn't sleep with his fans?

"I feel like a fraud," he finally answered.

Bren's skin bristled. *Uh oh.* He was a fraud? Aaah, balls, she thought, feeling a deep sinking in her chest. He was doing so well: looking gorgeous, helping clean her dishes, liking her lists, liking her role models, appreciating her books, loving her bed, getting her as hot as the sun, and now he was about to mess all that up. *Darn it.* She knew he was too good to be true, a pretender, a liar, a fraud, and now he was admitting it, and, shoot, now she would have to kick him out of her bed and sleep alone. This sucked. Why was he a fraud? Did he lie? Did he steal? Did he cheat? Did he time travel and redirect history to not include unicorns? She tensed.

"I can't write," he confessed.

She paused . . . not expecting *that* . . . and waited for a much more mammoth shoe to *thud*. But no more thudded. She only heard their breathing. Feeling confused. She had read his writing; she knew he could totally write. Unless . . . she suddenly jabbed her elbow into her pillow and propped herself up, looking down on him.

"Did you not write your novel yourself?"

"What?"

"All those parties and the kiss in the rain. You didn't write all that?!"

"I thought you didn't read it."

"Of course I read it. You didn't write it?"

"Of course I wrote it. You read it?"

"You really wrote it?"

"I really wrote it. You really read it?"

"I read it."

"Did you like it?"

"How are you a fraud?" Bren insisted, ready to grab his pajamas and yank him back on track.

"I can't write my next novel."

"Your *next* novel?"

"Yeah."

"Why can't you write your next novel?"

"It's like Holly was saying about her party. It was a hit. Now she's got to top herself with her next one. I gotta top my novel with my next one. All my fans are expecting this amazing follow up, and . . . I can't write."

Oooooooooh. She suddenly realized. "Writer's block?"

"Yeah."

Was *that* all? She exhaled long and loud, both tremendously relieved and frustrated with her scatterbrained bedmate. She blinked her tired eyes and tried to organize this sloppy conversation into some sort of understandable order. "So, you feel like a fraud because you wrote a popular novel and now you can't follow it up because you've got writer's block?"

"Exactly," he said energetically. "And I've got all these cool characters and story ideas, but I can't bring 'em all to life as easily as I did before. I'm not feeling my magic. That's why I moved here, to shake my mind loose with a new environment. But I'm still writing nonsense. So, fans are complimenting me while I'm secretly failing, and the more they gush the more grandness I have to live up to, and I find that I can't live up to their compliments again, so I feel like a fraud, and my first draft is due in a month, and I can't deliver, and I'm gonna just be a one-hit-wonder, I'll be Howie Day of the literary world."

Oh for crying out loud, Bren thought, having enough of his helluva pity party. She leaned close to him and looked him right in the eyes. "First of all, Howie Day had more than one hit."

"He did?"

"To me every Howie Day song is a hit. And second, it's just writer's block. You'll get over it, and if you don't you'll be fine. You had a major success that most people don't. I read that you made a bank-load of money that you can invest wisely and live fine. So why is this such an embarrassing big deal?"

He lay silent, looking into her eyes with a realness she'd never seen him share with her before as he answered her softly. "I don't wanna let anyone down."

Wow.

That statement told her so much about him. And, *dammit,* he made her adore him even more. A guy who kept himself fit, offered to help clean, treated her books with respect, and also, didn't want to let anyone down. Well, he sure wasn't letting her down. He just kept being more perfect. Except right now he seemed more insecure than her, and that wasn't helpful tonight.

"Thank you for sharing your secret with me. I appreciate your trust, and I feel for your dilemma," she said.

His shoulders relaxed as he exhaled. "Thanks. It feels awesome to finally tell someone. It's nice to tell you. You're kind. It's been a bummer keeping that locked up all to myself."

She for sure understood that. She wished she could tell Kris and her friends her Greg-secrets right frickin' now and feel the super pleasant relief Trent was feeling. But, she couldn't think about that right now or she would never get to sleep. She refocused. "So," she said, focusing her eyes to his. "It's bed-o'clock and I have to be up in eight hours, and I need to sleep. So, I must ask you to not think about your troubles tonight, and instead be my weapon against awakeness. Right now I need confident-Trent, jovial-Trent, storyteller-Trent, to cuddle and comfort me. I need you to earn your pajamas. We gotta stick to the cuddle plan," she said with a grin.

His reaction was instant.

Like a snap she saw his attitude change. His soft lips grinned, his eyes brightened, and his whole being manned the heck up. He propped himself up with his elbow, rising to her level and facing her, eye to eye. "I won't let you down," he calmly vowed to her.

Wow. His words to her *zapped* right to her soul. It's what she wanted most of all: to not be let down. He seemed to mean it, and got her feelings fluttering again. Confident Trent was back, and that he had quickly shazamed from Clark Kent into Superman just for her was really hot. His blue jammies just needed a red cape. And now . . . staring into his eyes, his lips close enough for her to feel his minty breaths on hers she once again, slowly, smartly turned away from Trentacious temptation and laid back down looking up at him laying up there beside her, his blue eyes watching over her, the line between his lips smiling down upon her, making her feel looked after and cared for and not alone in this big quiet building, in this big messy world, in this big empty universe, seeing his kind eyes give her hope, then seeing his eyes flick to her lamp, ready for confident, funny SuperTrent to save her again, letting his blue pajama arm reach over her, give her one last look and smile and click off her last little light.

Darkness.

Focusing hard on sticking to her rules too, she rolled to her left side once again, and felt Trent's body cuddle behind her, comfort her, dutifully wrap around her like she was a hotdog and he was her bun, a bun with an instant big beautiful boner.

Oooooooh. So pleasant to have him blanketing her again. So close, physically, and now so much closer personally too, letting him know her room and her life, learning his respectfulness and his embarrassing secrets. The invisible wall between their souls was thinning. He was knowing her more; she was knowing him more, and she was liking him more, loving the way he didn't make fun of her lists, or her pictures, or *Wallbanger*, and instead seeming to appreciate all of her quirks. This guy was getting lots of points for his good behavior, and for his handling of *her* as he cuddled her close, holding her as gently as he had held her favorite book.

Soon his perfect presence helped her feel as relaxed as she was the night before. Her body weakened under his soothing, familiar touch. She slowly breathed out tension and accepted his gloriously useful companionship once more.

"Once upon a time," he whispered near her ear, beginning a new bedtime story. "Um . . . a wacky scientist built a magic

TV . . . no, a flying scooter . . . um, no, he built a morphing machine." His words goosebumped the back of her neck. She breathed calmly. She focused on the comforting sound of Trent's voice, her soul held onto his friendly low tone; its hopeful confidence chased all her other thoughts away, like light scoots away shadows. Sadness was no match for Trent's silly bright story. Writer's block, huh? No wonder his bedtime stories were so much less brilliant than his novel. She listened to him try and tell a story with a lot of ums; it sounded like he needed the practice.

Mmmm. she smirked happily. His silly bedtime stories had become the best part of her whole day. She loved listening to his fantastical mind whip up wonderfully silly stuff out of thin air. She lay there listening to him making up some bizarre random-plotted tale about the scientist's morphing machine falling out of the back of his truck, rolling down a hill and through a restaurant, toy shop, and music store, picking up a hamburger, a skateboard, and an electric guitar along the way and morphing them all into an electric hamburger-board.

It was actually good that his bedtime stories weren't good so they wouldn't keep her super interested and awake. Silly and tedious was great. Ridiculous, meandering, and distracting was soothing. His effort to think up a story for her was valiant. His struggling to come up with a good bedtime story just for her, so he wouldn't let her down, was very sweet.

"And then the electric hamburger-board signed a record deal and went on tour," Trent whispered to her. His heart seemed in it, and that's what made it wonderful. He was giving her a delightful evening.

Her thoughts fizzed like a settling soda, busy, less busy, less less busy, until calm, and quiet. His voice distracted. His body comforted. His Hank guarded. She relaxed, more, and more, and more.

She listened to him with eyes closed, as her breathing slowly calmed. She felt herself nodding off, and falling into nothing. The nothingness was unnerving. She felt her fingers searching for something. Her fingers found Trent's thick, solid forearm wonderfully wrapped around her waist; she clutched onto it for safety. It wasn't going anywhere; she had it; she felt more secure, secure enough . . . to let herself . . . fall asleep.

Tonight she didn't take a favorite book to bed, instead she took a new favorite writer, a new favorite neighbor, a new favorite friend, a friend who helped her feel happy that she had let him back into her apartment, back into her bed as his silly yarn helped her yawn, and relax, as she listened to his funny story, and listened, and listened, and listened, and fell asleep smiling . . .

Chapter 9 ¾

TUESMORNING-ISH

Bren woke in the night, slowly, warm and smiling. She lifted her lids a little and saw darkness. But she felt no fear, no loneliness. She had a warm body to hold onto. His.

Oh.

She realized that she had turned around in her sleep. She was facing him. Both their heads on her pillow. Her irises adjusting, she could dimly see his closed eyes as he slept, felt his mint breaths on her mouth, his arm around her, her arm around him, their lips oh so close.

Wonderful.

Her unconscious seemed to have a whole other agenda going on. It had rolled her around to him. It wanted her to hold him, not just be held. It wanted her to face him, front to front, heart to heart, junk to junk, like lovers lay.

This should have been too intimate for her, she thought. But somehow, it wasn't. She felt peace in this position. Safe, fun, and, for the first time, silence was relaxing. Maybe nighttime wasn't real life. Maybe it was a magical time when everything was all right. At least that's how it felt while they embraced. Bed was like a bubble. Nothing bad could get in. Not with him, her helper, her solace in the dark, her nighttime friend, and cuddler.

She wondered if her friend knew that they were facing each other. It would be best if he didn't know. She watched his closed eyes and motionless mouth. She felt his chest expand and deflate steadily against her. She listened to him softly breathing. She really liked holding him. She almost loved it. She secretly held him a little tighter.

He farted.

Her eyes popped open. Her lips pursed tight, trying not to laugh. *Oh geez.* She felt her face getting chipmunk cheeks. Her stomach muscles quivered. She slowly, slowly calmed, feeling delighted. She relaxed her wind inducing hold on him.

He just kept breathing and sleeping, completely unaware. Classic.

It was just a little toot, but it was enough to make him human and less of a potentially heartbreaking monster. It made him less threatening, even endearing.

Trent, she thought, you gorgeous loon.

She liked him even more now. She liked having him down from his tower over her and *with* her in her bed. She kept him close, out of any other woman's arms, parked in her bed while she figured things out, while she figured *him* out, and while sorting her mess of emotions about him, including a new deeper joy than she'd ever known.

She enjoyed their wonderful embrace just a little longer, until she felt sleepy again. Then, not wanting him to wake and find her being too intimate, she slowly detached her arm from him and rolled over to her left side again, re-pressing her back to his chest, her hiney to his Hank, and resuming their sporking. She gently draped his big arm around her body, to protect her from bad dreams. She felt safe. She felt relaxed. She exhaled. Then her hand lovingly held onto his thick wrist like a strong rope, as she lowered herself back down into the depths of sleep, smiling . . .

Chapter 10 – day

TUESDAY

buzz . . . buzZ . . . bUZZ . . . BUZZ . . .

Bren stopped her clock with a click, not a bop.

Feeling powerful to cease an annoyance with just a touch. Wonderful feeling to wake up embraced by Trent's big arm around her once again. His warm body behind her. His face nestled in her hair. His light breaths pleasing her neck. His Hank guarding her butt cheek. Under the toasty warm covers. Inhaling chilly air.

5:00am.

Bren clutched her covers to fling them off.

Although . . . she wouldn't mind just one more toasty minute.

The warmth felt nicer than the chilly air. Really nice. Nice enough to maybe appreciate this rare joy. She pulled her blankets around her tight, burrowed her head into her super soft pillow, snuggled her back to his solid front, melting against warrrrrrrrm wonderfulness, and softly groaning with pleasure. She liked them fitting together, so fittingly, feeling so right and relaxed and rested again. Another full-nights sleep, and no nightmare.

She smiled. Their odd plan was actually working out, brilliantly. She began thinking that she was really onto something with this. Why weren't other people just cuddling with their friends and neighbors? If you can set rules then it's a win-win for both cuddlers. No problem. She lay there feeling brilliant and awake.

5:01am.

Sigh. She needed to get up.

Although . . . she wouldn't mind just one more lovely minute.

One more therapeutic minute, languishing in luxury. This felt so healthy. So enjoyable. And justifiable. Starting her morning pleasantly was a good thing. Setting a happy tone for her day. *Yes.* This was good, and smart, and *so* delightful. And after enduring a month of miserable mornings, this was *so* earned.

She had missed these kinds of cuddly mornings. She missed feeling this happy. And her body missed what a morning cuddle usually progressed into. And in all the warmth she felt an even warmer urge. A wanting urge.

5:02am.

Sigh. She really needed to get up.

Although . . . she wouldn't mind just one more sensual minute.

One more glorious minute of feeling the sexiest guy she'd ever slept with sleep with her just a little longer. Feel the comfort of his companionship. And this feeling was really good, enjoyable, fun. And safe? *Yes.* This felt safe. They had rules. She and he would not get amorous.

5:03am

Sigh. She *really* needed to get up.

Although . . . they could get amorous, for just a recreational minute, maybe just a few minutes.

And what would be the harm? Really, she truly wondered, what would be the harm? She'd gotten physical with other guys just for fun and no commitments and no repercussions. She and Trent could do just a little more than cuddle and be fine. It would almost be silly not to. Getting physical might make her feel even better. Awaker. Energizeder.

She felt Hank's big readiness against her, just inches from where he could be if she let him. She *imagined*. She imagined helping herself to some morning-Trent. She imagined kissing and touching and groaning and grinding. She felt her blood grow warmer, her breathing shorten. She could do that. She could let that happen, so easily. Hank was clearly up for it. All she would have to do is roll over and initiate. *Oh*. She felt a *zing!* Her heart thumped faster. They could do it. *Oh, wow.* They could. They could amend their plan a little bit. For fun. He was right there. In her bed. Ready. Just pull down their pajamas and they could be doing it. Right now. She breathed thinner. Her eyes darted around. She slightly pushed her butt against him, just a bit, against his hard Hank.

Oooooooh, he felt goooooooood.

This . . . could . . . happen.

Right now.

Sex.

Morning sex.

Wonderful sex!

Greg and his ex had wonderful sex.

Flashback!

Greg's smile with his ex, after having sex.

That smile and kiss she saw.

That horrible moment.

That horrible pain.

That pain still hurt.

That pain still lived in her.

So much.

Killing happiness.

Dammit!

Her thoughts were hijacked.

Like ice water cracking through her hot veins, Greg's indulgence rushed back to her, Hank-blocking her, ruining the joy of sex. Muscles tightened. Heart froze. Anger and sadness returned. She breathed harder. Felt her forehead sweating. *Criminy.* She had almost succumbed to temptation. And isn't that what Greg did? Didn't he think: "Oh, a little sex wouldn't be harmful." Selfish jerk. She wanted to be better than that, better than Greg, better than urges. Desire was such a deceptive lure into trouble. She had a good thing going with Trent. She didn't want any trouble. She wanted to stay uncompromised and in control. But her relationship with Trent was different than Greg's cheating on their relationship. But both relationships had rules, and rule-breaking desires, and everything seemed confusing, like why aren't upside down words considered a language?

5:04am

Uuuugh. Now she *really*, *really* needed to get up!

"*Mmmmmmmm,*" Trent lightly moaned into her hair, into her thoughts, into her emotions. His presence re-comforted her . . . re-calmed her . . . and re-confused her. Still weirded out that he was with her. But so glad he was, distracting her Greg-thoughts, mostly. With Trent there she didn't have to suffer alone. She had someone to hold her, and comfort her, and talk with, and keep her from slipping down into despair so deep she might not care if her work clothes had lint on them. And right now she needed him, her new friend, her new friend who she didn't pull and push out of her apartment again this morning, but instead nicerly tap-tapped his blue polyester bicep hanging over her.

His embrace gently squeezed her closer.

Mmmmmmm. So caring.

Ooooh. He made her want to stay.

But, now she *really*, *really*, *really*, needed to get up. And get him up too.

She asked into the air, "Are you awake?"

No answer.

Then Trent's forearm slowly slid off her and out of sight. His arm's ghost still warmed her waist. Why did his arm leave her, she worried? Then, relieved, she felt the tickle of his finger on her pajama-covered braless back, softly tracing letters:

Y . . . E . . . S.

Her lips stretched into a smile. His answer was cute. His touch was soft, and so welcome. Tingly shivers through her body and goose bumps on her arms. Such a sweet and amusing way to wake up. Much nicer than yesterday morning.

"Excuse me," she said. "But, did you just give me the finger?"

She heard Trent chuckle his silly chuckle behind her. She smiled more and stretched her body awake, slowly, comfortably, rolling onto her chest, then turned her head on her pillow into a jungle of her hair.

His fingers gently brushed her morning mop from her eyes, his fingertips skimming her face. *Ooooh yessss.* Electric chills. Instant urge to grab him and kiss him! She clutched her sheets instead.

She saw him, her handsome cuddler. She was glad to see him, his familiar face so close to hers. His warm friendly eyes and smile greeted her. Clearly glad to see her too.

They shared the same pillow.

They looked in each other's eyes.

The moment was full of potential.

Then Trent's teeth *crunched* a Lifesaver.

Bren chuckled.

Crunch, crunch, crunch, crunch.

Swallow.

Inhale.

"Good morning," he whispered cool, minty breath upon her face.

She tingled again and re-warmed, then hid her non-minty breath. "Mormming," she misspoke, then cleared her throat. "Morning."

He grinned.

She grinned.

They stared some more.

Shared her pillow some more.

While he lightly caressed her back.

While she let him. Keeping things simple. Letting the moment be about her receiving his touch on her back, but not giving him her moans that would reveal how much she liked his splendorously soothing hand trilling sensations through her as he continued his caresses; his touches were new, and so nice.

His gentle touch spoke a language of kindness to her body, a kindness that seemed to flow from the depths of his soul to the tips of his very likable fingers. She longed to touch Trent too, but there was just no way that her prudent brain would let her hand do that. She abstained, and ached, trapped between dire yearning and agonizing restraint. *Oh.* She missed the blissful naiveté of not knowing how good he felt in bed. She wished she could give in to the wonderfulness he was giving her.

Was this the wonderfulness Trent used to give to his ex-girlfriend, she wondered?

His grin seemed pleasantly surprised that she wasn't tossing him out of her bed so aggressively again. Hank seemed pleased too as his hard plumpness rested on the side her thigh, like a third person nestled between them. But her sensible brain was also between them, not inviting Hank to do anything but exist, while other parts of her yearned for Hank to exist out of Trent's pajamas and inside hers and –

Oh, hey, whoa, she startled as Trent surprisingly peeled her covers off of her steaming body.

Cold air chilled her, she scrunched up closer to him. Why was he doing this?

"It's 5:20," he whispered.

Seriously, she thought?! Surprised at how fast time flew with him. Oooh you nice, nice man, her thoughts praised his sensiblenss, his kindness, his surprising restraint, while her heated parts frickin' hated him right now. He could've tried to have her right there, right then. But he didn't. He was gentlemanly releasing her.

Wow.

He just earned more points.

Reluctantly she rose up and slowly backed away from his so-hard-to-leave warmth and got herself standing in the chilly air, her eyes never leaving his. She stood and stretched and breathed and cooled, away from their hotbed of temptation, away from making a crazy mistake. She folded her arms and beheld the beautiful man she almost succumbed to, as he still lay in her bed, on his side, propping up his head and gazing up at her like a sexy pajama model; it was her new favorite pose of his: hunk in bed. He flexed his bicep, hamming it up. She smiled, liking him in her bed. But it was 5:21am, she needed to scoot him out of it.

Without Bren saying a word to him, Trent scooted himself, as if knowing the drill, casually sliding out of her bed and standing up. *Hmm.* She had trained him to be a gent. *Hmm.* Not *all* of him. His mighty erection tent-poled his pajamas like a jousting lance aiming right at her.

"It's not polite to point," she joked.

He laughed.

She looked at his cock-a-doodle-doo. She looked at her clock. So conflicted.

"Go save the world," he said, turning and then following his pointer towards her door.

"Go write your masterpiece," she said back.

He scoffed.

She stepped in front of him.

His eyes came back to her.

She thought for a moment. "When do you write?"

"Um. When I feel inspired."

"And when is that?"

"Um. Whenever."

She nodded. "That's what I thought." She raced to her desk and quickly scribbled on paper. Then handed him:

Trent's Daily To Do List

1) *Workout*
2) *Breakfast, shower, dress*
3) *Do something different for inspiration*
4) *Lunch*
5) *Text Bren if needed at* 415-555-0147
6) *3pm - 7pm write at Back Scratch Bar*
7) *Dinner, shower, pajamas*
8) *9pm bedtime with Bren*

He looked at her with a big smirk.

"I'm putting you on a schedule," she told him. "You're not a morning person, and you thought up your last novel in a bar. So try it again; write at Blue Light Bar in the afternoons. But don't get drunk." She instructed her favorite blocked-writer, then she pulled a book from her library and thumped it to his chest. "This is a great book on story structures. Put your story ideas into them and come up with plot ideas and outlines. First rule of success: organization."

He inhaled deeply, seeming slightly sentimental as his eyes sparkled. "You're helping me?" he asked.

"I want to read another great novel by Trent Baxter."

His smirk broke into a smile. "You thought it was *great?*"

She blushed. "And now I have great expectations. So, don't let me down."

His face transformed from appreciative to determined, determined to not let her down.

Good.

Now she was determined to get to work on time. She got him out of her apartment and said to his happy face, "Wear your cinnamon-colored pajamas tonight."

He smiled.

She smiled. And whammed her door shut.

* * * *

Work, work, work

And texting with Kris about how there should be a talk show with the host and guest each in bubble baths, and hearing that the wedding planner was doing a great job, that Calli was now dating a saxophone player, and Holly was complaining that the loud saxing and sexing is vexing, and Bren and Kris wished each other happy Ballpoint Pen Day.

Bren now felt so glad that Kris had hired a wedding planner. She could let Anna efficiently take care of all the wedding stuff while she could efficiently focus on work this week, and enjoyably focus on Trent.

Work, reports, managing, meetings.

Bren's mind kept drifting back to cuddling with Trent.

Each time interrupted by horrible Greg-memories.

Dammit.

Clients, emails, deadlines, calls.

She thought of Trent's pointer.

She thought of Greg's cheating weasel.

Dammit.

She texted with Kris.

Work, work, work, work.

Trent sent her a text: "Heading to Back Scratch Bar with fingers crossed. Thanks for your help."

Wonderful, she thought, so happy he was really following his to do list.

An organized man was so hot!

She warmed at the thought of him writing another amazing book for her to *experience*.

Bren texted back, not-flirty: "Excellent."

Work, work, work, work.

Trent was doing everything right.

Work, work, work.

Too right?

Work, work.

Too perfect?

Work.

No deal breakers?

She stared out her downtown window.

Her curiosity fling flanged.

She had to find out more about him, by getting closer with him.

Maybe take things to the next level.

* * * *

8:22pm

Knock, knock.

Bren stood before open Trent's door.

His door, just as he promised, was always open for her.

She heard his feet thumping.

She felt her heart pumping fast and happy and anxious to see her cuddler, her booklover, her new friend once again, to not spend the night alone, to hang and joke and talk.

She watched him walk down his stairs.

Wowza. He walked down wearing nothing but a towel. Jaw dropped. Knees buckled. Eyes liked. Red towel. Tan chest.

Muscles everywhere. And a gorgeous smile. He looked like paradise.

"Hey, Bren," his uplifting familiar voice said to her, happily surprised.

She was happily surprised t-t-t-too. His naked, muscled, chisled, wet, ab-tastic, peck-perfect, manly upper-half also said "Hey, Bren!"

Her gaping mouth grunted. "*Huhhh.*"

"You look really nice," he complimented her.

"Oh – thanks, uh, you look, um . . . fit."

"Thanks."

Really fit. A good fit. A really good fit. A really, really good –

"I thought you wanted me at nine," he said.

Bren wondered what kind of cheese would grate best on his cut abs.

"Bren."

Munster?

"Bren."

Mozzarella?

"Bren"

"What?"

"What's up?"

Her dopamine level was up. "Oh. Hiiii!" she sang, struggling to sound casual.

"Hello," he said, cheeriness and confusion in his sweet low voice.

"Yes – um – oh my gosh – did I, um, interrupt you?"

"I just took a shower."

"Shower . . . yes . . . good . . . to be clean . . . for *me?*"

"Yeah."

"Oh . . . well . . . um . . . "

She fixated on a little drip of water as it playfully dripped from his reckless hair and cutely splashed onto his thick shoulder, then watched naughty gravity slide that sexy droplet teasingly down his sun-kissed skin, over his hard muscled chest, off his perfect peck, down the rocky Alps of his abs, one defined rectangle at a time, drip past his naval, down his thought-provoking treasure trail, until it disappeared into the secret wonderland inside his lust-red towel. Her imagination slipped down there too. Then found waaaay too much down there to take right now. She quickly glanced back up at the slippery little stream the droplet left down his adonisly sculpted front.

Oooh, gosh. This was so unfair. He had such a perfect weapon against her will. Testing her, and getting harder to resist.

"Bren?"

She snapped back to reality. Eyes up. "Huh?"

"You were saying something."

"Was I?"

"Did you come here to cancel?"

"Oh *heck* no!" she blurted. *Whoops.* "I mean – " She struggled to get a flipping grip. "I just, um, uh, . . . I had an idea."

"Lay it on me," he said.

"*What?*"

"Your idea," he chuckled at her cheeks that felt as pink as her pajama bottoms and tank-top.

"Oh . . . " Fumbling, embarrassingly flustered. But she couldn't help it. His beautiful bare chest was beaming like the sun, and just as hot; it kept distracting her attention. She should have brought sunglasses. Huh, she thought, maybe that's why all the Marina people wear sunglasses, to dim the brightness of all the sexy people they see so they don't go crazy from arousal overload. Looking at super sexy Trent, she sure felt super aroused, and super nervous to be at his door again suggesting another crazy idea. "Uh," she said to him. "I thought, uh, just for variety, we would, um, sleep at *your* place, tonight."

His eyes lit up, lips smiled, and head slowly tilted in disbelief. He shifted his weight, causing his bulge to shift against his tight towel.

Golly damn. Eyes back up to his.

"You wanna sleep at my place?" he said with surprise.

"Would that all right?" Bren asked anxiously.

"Hell yeah," he said enthusiastically. "Bring your pink pajamas up here."

Relieved.

Then wowed as she watched him and his barely there towel turn around and walk upstairs, bedazzled at his beautiful naked muscled back, his toned calves, his well-sized feet, and his perfectly perfect alternating butt pistons steadily motoring his brilliant body up each stair, moving him further and further away from her, making her miss him the further away he went.

Whoa. Get a grip, she told herself.

She looked away to compose her ridiculousness. Difficult to do knowing that her naked feet were standing on the landing where Trent had first *thrilled* her to the Moon, and had been floating her hopes even higher each magical night since then, and now she was about to float up into his home advantage, so hoping this wasn't a stupid choice as her curiosity stepped her feet into the lion's den and shut his door.

Chapter 10 – night

TUESNIGHT

She was inside.

So excited, but keeping cool, as she casually walked her bare feet up his soft maroon carpeted stairs while wiping sweat from her damp forehead, climbing up his tower, entering his world, as she stepped up the eleven stairs that she knew well from visiting Madeline all the time, trying to not nervously trip as she turned left 180º on his landing, then stepped up nine more stairs, until she arrived into his large living room.

She gasped.

The big room was a wow of warm orange as the sunset blasted through his open west side windows, and so . . . empty. All of Madeline's many fine furnishings were gone, and so were all her framed pictures of her flashing her breasts in front of every major monument in the world, and Trent had zero furniture and zero topless pictures. Instead, his walls were as naked as his real life chest, just sherbet sunlight and a blonde hard wood floor filling the forty-foot long studio with the stylish maple-wood deck beyond the northern ceiling-to-floor windows and tall open glass door above all the flattop 1920s-style three-story apartment buildings outside, with the beautiful bay and hills glistening in the distance. Such a stunning view. Such a penthouse compared to her 2nd floor place. Such a talented, kind, sexy man with a whole top floor apartment needing to be filled from scratch, like a blank page ready for beautiful language. She saw a lot of potential.

"I love what you haven't done with the place," she joked. Her words bouncing all around his large vacancy.

"Thanks," his voice echoed back from his bedroom.

He was probably naked right now, her imagination ventured. She heard the snap of an underwear waistband flick skin and a rustling of pajamas being put on, getting ready for her, ready to sleep with her, ready for another night of fun, cuddly bodies touching, and silly soothing storytelling; in *his* bed.

Ooookay. She palmed her pajama sleeves to dry her hands. The evening breeze from the bay blowing through his open patio door and side windows and through his big room helped cool her as his rotating ceiling fan up high spread around the fresh fun scent of summer. The perfect scene for a romance novel. Paradise up high. Beautiful view, beautiful city, beautiful summer. She always loved watching the distant little sailboats out there on the blue bay from these windows.

Trent entered.

Beautiful man.

Gosh damn.

He stood before her staring eyes, looking even hotter than last night.

Her palms re-perspired, blood surged, and fingers urged to touch his silken physique. He had his cinnamon jammies on tonight, keeping his promise, and they were unexpectedly short-sleeved, wonderfully showcasing his mighty muscled arms, but hiding all the rest of his gorgeous man-sculpture that she now knew was under there. She wondered what color underwear.

"Welcome to my home." His warm hello clicked her eyes back to his, as the amber sunlight lit his face up like a beautiful bronzed Apollo.

"Hiiii," she breathed out with an unstoppable smile.

"You have good timing, coming up here tonight," he said enthusiastically.

"Why?"

"Because I bought a brand new bed today and had it delivered."

"You did?"

"Yep," he beamed. "I bought a bed just like yours."

"Seriously."

"Yep."

She didn't know what to think of that.

"You've changed me for the better," he told her, smiling.

"Really?"

"After sleeping on your amazing bed, I just can't ever go back to my crappy futon. So, thanks for broadening my horizons."

Wow. "Oh. Um. I'm glad."

He stepped a little closer. "And, honestly, on the off chance that we might sleep up here, I didn't wanna subject you to my futon."

Surprised. "You planned ahead?"

He smirked. "For once in my life."

She smirked back.

"Your to do list said for me to 'do something different,' so I did."

He did something for him and *her*.

Super impressed. "Well done."

"We can break it in together," he said.

Her eyebrows shot up.

"So to speak," he said with his big, silly grin.

She couldn't help but grin too. *Hmmm.* His joking with her was getting more flirty, as if testing her limits, fluttering her. It was getting easier to do. Their comfort zone with each other clearly widening. Too wide, she wondered?

"You're shivering," he noticed. "I'll close the windows."

Very gentlemanly. But restraining her desire was shivering her, not the cool air.

He passed by her, taking his grin and sexy pjs towards the north end of his big bachelor pad, breezing his wonderfully clean soapy Trent-scent to her as he walked by like human poetry towards his open patio door. She leaned in to sniff his air, secretly taking eau-de-Trent into her lungs like a new guilty pleasure, and held it in there dearly, letting his aroma perk up her spirit; *mmmm*, it smelled like bedtime. That'd be a fun name for a cologne, she thought.

She fell forward, *criminy*, almost tripping, but quickly faked like she was dancing or something. His focus was on his door, thank goodness. She straightened, and stood in the center of his orange, bright, big empty space, high above Cow Hollow, feeling like she was standing on top of the world, and in the center of his life.

He shut his tall glass patio door then smiled at her as he came near again, seeming totally happy to have her there in his private place, the only other thing in his empty space. And she felt happy to be and many other soaring emotions, as he pulled his glass side windows down closed, then looked at her.

"It's all right to look around. I don't have a red room or nothin'," he joked.

Tiiiingles. Well, good to know, she thought (though, um, not a total deal breaker if he did). Bren just grinned back at him, and casually (but eagerly) took the tour to see what he did have. Not much, she came to find as she snooped into his bedroom and clicked on his ceiling light.

Woooooooooooow.

Trent didn't have a red room. His was blue, soothing blue, sky blue bedroom walls with a cloud-white plush down comforter draped gloriously over a duplicate of her queen bed, arranged against the same west wall as hers, maybe so she would feel at home up here in his heavenly home; she instantly did. She imagined herself sleeping in that soft majestic cloud soon, with him, in his perfect bed, with his perfect bod. More *tingles.*

And, *oh goodness,* laying randomly in tons of boxes he had tons of books, lots and lots and lots of used paperback books.

Ooooooooooh. This *was* heaven, above her bedroom.

His HUGE collection of books was like the cave filled with heaps of shiny gold in *Treasure Island,* multitudes of paperback jewels just randomly hidden in boxes. These glorious gems should be displayed, and organized by genre, and in alphabetical order by author. Oh, she soooo wanted to put his books in alphabetical order!

And the smmmmell . . . *aaaaaaaawe* . . . was like a lovely old library.

Memories flashed back of having sex in her university library whenever she had a boyfriend. So much fun. She wondered if Trent ever bopped in bibliography. She wondered how she would manage to not bop Trent tonight while cuddling among this erotic musty smell.

Ooooh. She could stay up here forever and be happy.

Hmmm. Was that his intention?

His books' chaotic disorder totally made her want to sort, sort, sort! But sort into what? He had no shelves, just an old brown dresser with drawers and with the story structure book she had loaned him sitting on it, a closet half-full of casual clothes, a laptop, video game stuff, a TV, and very little else.

His bathroom was still moistly warm from him recently being nude. She liked his clean no-clutter countertop, and it was nice to see that he was a put-the-cap-back-on-the-toothpaste-tube guy. And the book beside his toilet was Andy Weir's "The Martian." *Oh geez.* He was a toilet-reader-guy?

His second bedroom had mats and barbells and a tall metal fitness gym-thing for pull-ups and whatnot (Fifty Shade-ish whatnot?). So minimalist. Just diet, jogging, and gravity sculpted his Michelangelo's David-esc physique? Impressive. His carved perfection definitely took dedication, evidence of commitment. He just kept being a guy she couldn't dismiss. Gorgeous, well read, funny, upbeat, kind, accomplished, amazing cuddler, and able to commit. Such a great, potentially more-than-seven-month guy.

Too good to be true?

She became Nancy Drew again.

She spun toward his kitchen, took a deep breath, and ventured further into this mystery, super curious, super hopeful, and kinda super horny.

Light acoustic guitar music played from speakers and her pitter-pattering bare feet echoed around his big sunset-lit studio as she followed the melody and his clinking dish sounds across his living room's shiny polished wood floor towards all the windows and the amazing view of the Marina rooftops and the bay. She walked to the marble countertop by his welcoming babe-magnet, bright, state-of-the-art modern kitchen. She found him illuminated angelically by modern hanging lighting, looking like a domestic dreamboat in his jammies.

"Hi," he said.

"Hello."

He washed his dishes.

She stood by his kitchen counter, watching him wash. She loved watching him wash. *Why was this erotic? Who knows? It just was.* "This apartment looks different than when Madeline lived here."

"Was Madeline your friend?"

"Yeah. Madeline was a hoot," she said, memories swirling in her mind, recalling Kris and her sitting over there on plush chairs and laughing and loving all of Madeline's crazy San Francisco stories of her cocktail waitress days, of her four wild marriages, and of her fortune-making turn as creator of fun sex toys. "Kris and I would hang out with Madeline up here all the time. We'd laugh so much. She's almost sixty and still dates like a horny twenty-year-old, well, she did; this year she married a doctor. Her life stories, oh my, gosh. She did everything, traveled the world, met everyone in the world, dated the whole world, invented . . . stuff." Bren smiled, then sighed. Maddy and Kris moved out, Greg gone, everything good ends, she thought. "And now this room is empty."

"Well," Trent's voice said.

Bren turned left to him, seeing possible new beginnings.

"I hope you're as happy up here with me."

She looked at handsome Trent and his silly smile. Time with Trent felt like a different kind of happy.

"Would you like something?" he offered. "Ice tea? Juice? Half a sandwich?"

"No thanks." *Hmmmm.* Now he was being a perfect host. She was continuing to run out of excuses to run away from him, and keep her life safe and simple. But undeterred, for the sake of her fragile heart, she absolutely kept looking for an excuse, his big silver refrigerator was bespeckled with pictures. She zipped over to his fridge and sleuthed every one of his pictures, and everyone in them. No pics of his ex Julia. *Good.* She recognized a few of the pictured people from all her internet searches on him: his mom piloting a small airplane, his beautiful sister on stage dressed as a singing flower, and lots and lots of his friends in SF and London and Madrid and all over, trying to see if his life that he told her about on Holly's rooftop matched the pictures of his past, and they did, and she saw his to do list that she gave him taped up on his fridge, and . . . OMG, his invitation to the wedding. "Oh my gosh. Kris sent you an invitation to their wedding?"

"Yeah," he said drying a dish. "That's nice of them."

"You're going to their wedding?"

"Sure."

"Oh."

"Ooooh," he said. "Do you not want me to go?"

"Um, I don't know."

"If you don't want me to go I won't go."

"I don't know if I want you to go."

"It sounds like you don't want me to go."

"Do you *wanna* go?"

"Sure. But not if you don't want me to go."

"Oh. I don't know."

"How about you think about if you want me to go, and then let me know, if you want me to go."

She exhaled. "I like that plan."

"Cool."

"Okay."

"I just need to finish these dishes and then we can cuddle."

Tingles.

She liked that plan too.

His mighty man-hands handled his plate.

She imagined his hands handling her with her looking for earring. *Super tingles.*

"Would you like to sit down?" he offered with his right, big, beautiful hand.

Her mind spun with a gust of thoughts: cuddles, being in his apartment, him maybe *coming to the wedding*, as her bare feet patted out from his kitchen tiles to his living room's hard wood floor, her pink pajama-ed seat took a seat on one of the cushioned wooden stools at his marble kitchen counter.

He looked at her.

She looked at him.

Oh goodness. This almost felt like a date, alone together but not in bed, a lovely, casual, yet nervous date. She grinned; she felt more comfortable with him in bed; *geez*, their relationship was so backwards, like organizing all her books in reverse alphabetical order. In bed she knew the plan, knew he would follow her rules. She knew exactly what was going to happen: nothing. Safe, uncomplicated, wonderful nothing. But out of bed she didn't know where the heck things would venture.

She listened to the serene guitar music playing through his iPod speakers. *Good taste.* Soft music, pretty lighting, evening. This *did* feel like a date.

She looked at the time on her phone. Twenty minutes until bedtime.

Tingles.

Gotta keep things formal and totally not date-like.

"So," she said, breaking the silence. "How was your day?"

"Awesome. How was yours?"

"Productive."

"Cool."

"Was yours more productive than usual?"

He smiled. "It really was."

"Oh good. Did you write?"

He smiled as he dried a bowl gently, firmly. "I stuck to the plan," he said, looking at her with such a super proud smile.

She couldn't help but smile back.

"At 2pm I went to Back Scratch Bar. I sat and thought, had a burger and beer, sat and thought some more. And also I decided to get a couch for that corner."

What? He didn't perfectly follow the plan. He only got half points. Bren rolled her eyes. "You were supposed to write."

He grinned. "Half of writing is staring at a wall, wondering what to write. I got a lot of wall wondering done."

"I thought you had ideas. You were supposed to use the book I loaned you to put your ideas into a story structure."

"I looked at my story ideas. They all suck. I gotta start fresh."

"Ah geez."

"But I was starting to feel a comfortable vibe there. Maybe inspiration will come."

Bren tossed her hands in the air and flopped them on his counter.

"What?"

"I got a hundred things done today and you stared at a wall and make a million dollars more than me?"

He smiled and dried. "That's what writing is like: hours of nothing, nothing, nothing, a slightly interesting idea, then more nothing. Hopefully that slighting interesting idea can expand into a whole novel.

Bren exhaled. "It's a process."

He nodded. "It's totally a process." He put his dry bowl in his cupboard. Then he looked at her.

She looked at him.

More soft music, more pretty lighting, more feeling like a date.

Yikes.

"So you're gonna get a couch?"

"Yeah. Totally. What else do you think I should get?"

Oh, she thought, interesting question, a fun question. She spun right on his stool, smiling, looking at his big empty living room, with lots of potential . . . *wow* . . . the potential to build a boyfriend from scratch, build the perfect boyfriend. *Oh my.*

She remembered Greg's pristine apartment, with such spendy, classy furniture that it felt like a museum where she dare not scratch his leather sectional, or clink dishes on his icy glass-top dining table, or make love too wild on his expensive bed. She thought it was love. And she thought Greg's fancy furniture was so impressive, evidence of maturity. But looks are deceiving, she remembered, still hurting, still healing, still wanting to toss Greg in a time machine and feed him to a T-Rex.

She looked left at Trent, her friendly-smiling, healing helper. His evidence of maturity was all the committed effort and time he spent on building his beautiful abs, his devotion to his to exploring what he loved, and delightfully what she loved too: books, his openness to reading a variety of genres, his dedication and passion to writing a spectacular novel, his humbleness at fame, his politeness to her and her friends, his joy of talking about his mom and sister, his interest in her answers rather than just talking about himself, his teammate ability to banter, his kind cuddles, his gentle touches, his respectfulness of her boundaries each night, his restraint, *oh*, his restraint was so *hot*, and his, just, his whole happy, easy-going, friendly, comfy vibe, as if he wasn't just a potential boyfriend, he was a real, honest, dependable friend, that she really wanted to *bang!* And love? Make actual, real, fairytale-come-true love? *Ooooh my.*

Looking at pajama-ed, to do list sorta-following, silly smiling Trent, she saw a solid foundation of maturity she could build on, build an actual wonderful relationship, build a fun life with. Maybe a blenda of Brenda and Trent into Trenda would be awesome-enda.

Whoa. Overthinking.

Don't get your hopes up in the air, Icarus, just to be burnt by the sun again.

Build step-by-fun-step.

She took a big breath of Trent-apartment-scented air while looking at her possible future and exhaled out: "Shelves."

"Shelves?" he said.

"You need shelves, for all your books. Get those literary treasures out of boxes and onto shelves."

"Wow. I've never had shelves, or room for shelves. Shelves would be fun."

Yes. "And carpet. But only in your bedroom. Keep the living room hardwood. Really soft comfy carpet you could lay on, um, you know, to read books on."

He grinned. "That sounds awesome. I always thought shelves were extroverted cupboards," he said.

"What?"

"Cupboards have a door; they keep their goodies private." He closed his cupboard door, giving his dried dished privacy. "But shelves have no door, very exhibitionist, they like people seeing their goodies."

Bren chuckled, then wondered. "Which are you? Do you like people seeing your goodies?"

He chuckled. "If it's allowed."

Oh my. She warmed, blushed, and totally changed the subject. "And, um, you need a proper writing desk, wood, with a comfy chair." *Ooooh, this was fun.* She jumped up and wandered his living room. "And you need a dining room table that is *not* glass, it's wood and solid and you could even sit on, if, you know, you wanted to."

He smiled, seeming to like this fun as much as she was. "And a telephone booth."

"What?"

"A telephone booth, from the 1940s."

"Why?"

"For fun."

She grinned.

"You know what I've always wanted?" he said. "First class airplane seats."

She chuckled. "What the heck?"

He zipped into his empty living room and pointed at places to put things. "The publishing company flew me first class and it was awesome. I totally want to watch TV in first class airplane seats."

She smiled as she pointed to places too. "Well, if you want fun, go even wilder and make this big room into a roller skating rink."

He laughed. "Oh yeah. I'm on board. And should I get a disco ball for my bathroom?"

She grinned. "Take it from someone with dizzy disco ball bathroom experience, go with Christmas lights instead."

He grinned. "Awesome advice. How about a pinball machine?"

She laughed. "How about ten pinball machines?"

He laughed. "And a mechanical bull."

"And a juke box."

"And a Ferris wheel."

"A rocket ship."

"And a slide," he said.

"A slide?"

"So I can slide down from my apartment right into your bedroom."

Whooooa. "Oh. You think you're gonna be down in my room enough to warrant a slide?"

"Maybe."

"Huh."

"You push a button that rings a bell up here, and I slide right down into your bed."

Bren chuckled, excitedly, cautiously. "You want to be that available for me?"

He paused, seeming to realize the super-availability he was implying, standing figuratively exposed in his wide-open room.

That's what happens when you don't think before you speak Mr. Does-Things-Swiftly, she thought. But glad his blabby mouth was giving her clues to his true thoughts, glad his thoughts were being like an exhibitionist shelf and not a closed cupboard. He looked caught and on the spot. A guilty grin decorated his face, then a playful grin. "How long do you want me to be available to you?" he casually tossed back to her.

She paused. Their deal was until the end of the week, she reminded herself, but grinned at his grin and zipped out of the spotlight by continuing their imaginary-decorating. "And you could have Holly's mural-painter paint a tropical beach on your walls."

"And install trapeze to swing from the ceiling."

"And fill the apartment with blowing bubbles."

"And I could fill the place waist-high with balloons."

Bren tensed.

"It might be fun to walk through balloons every day. Balloons bring happiness."

"Not too me," Bren said, her smile dropping.

"You don't like balloons?"

"I used to." She took a deep breath. "Sorry."

"What?"

"Um. I was taking a balloon to Greg when I caught him kissing Abby."

"Oh."

She fell silent remembering. "I was holding it and then it was gone. Like love."

Silence.

"Well that's no good," he blurted. "We gotta get you feeling good about balloons again."

She chuckled, scoffingly. "Good luck."

"I'll put that on my to do list."

She wandered his space as her mind floated through thoughts like a balloon through clouds, then looked him in the eyes. "Do you know the book *Sex at Dawn*?"

"I've heard of it," he said. "Is it part of a romance series: *Sex at Noon, Sex at Dinnertime, Sex at Super Bowl Halftime*?"

She rolled her eyes. Do you take anything seriously?

"I try not to."

"I'm . . . I'm just not sure . . . maybe humans aren't meant to be monogamous," she said, looking at the floor.

"Hmmm," he hmmm-ed, as he leaned his shoulder to his wall while looking at her. "So you think people want lots of balloons instead of just one balloon?"

"Hmmm," she hmmm-ed back, looking up at him. "Maybe."

He casually sauntered across his big empty apartment filled with only him and her, and stopped in front of her with a smile. "I'm a one-balloon guy."

Ooooh my. Her defenses deflated, and her heart inflated, full of hope and feelings for him, too many hopeful feelings, *too much*. She stepped away from their monogamous moment and rushed passed him to his glass door, opened it, and exited out to his big back patio for some much needed air!

Wow. It was twilight. The sun had gone down. Where'd the time go?

Outside, she grabbed his wood railing. She breathed in the evening air in the darkness. She fumed, feeling overwhelmed. She focused on the silhouette of a bird flying over the bay, on the other side of the lit up baseball field in the park where Kris and Mark would get married on Saturday, where Trent would be with her . . . maybe.

She looked left. The distant Marin hills were now dark round silhouettes and the distant Golden Gate Bridge was now lit up passionately red.

She wondered if this view really was better than the view from Byron's Villa Diodati.

She heard Trent's bare feet clomping onto his patio balcony behind her.

He slowly moseyed up beside her and rested is forearms on his railing also.

Silence.

Wild silence.

It felt like the two of them at Holly's railing all over again, this time at twinkly twilight, and with so much more intimacy between them now, and so much more intensity. She felt his eyes tickling her cheek as she stared forward watching the distant boat lights glide around way out there in the deep purple bay like passing dreams, was her dream love life out of reach? Or maybe he was right beside her. No fog. The view was so clear. She wished her future was too. Such mixed feelings, passion or safe aloneness. She stared out into the darkness, seeing lots and lots of little lights in that darkness. It wasn't completely dark. She breathed in lots of fresh cool ocean air, absorbed whatever help it could give her, and exhaled it out long and slow, until she felt ready for whatever wildness was next.

"I think I should also get one of those water dunk machines like they have at county fairs," he said. "So you can throw a ball at the bulls eye and dunk me in water when I say something stupid to you like I just did. What'da you think?"

She smirked. "You didn't say anything stupid. You just joke a lot."

"I wanna keep seeing you smile."

She smiled. "I appreciate that."

"I believe monogamy is totally possible. I see lots of people do it. I know I can do it."

Woooooooow.

Exactly what she wanted to hear.

Exactly what she needed to know.

Exactly what she longed to believe.

He smiled at her smile. "Do you have any more questions?" he asked.

She laughed, loud. "I have a million."

He smiled. "I'm an open shelf. Ask me anything."

She paused. "Really?"

He nodded.

She paused again. "How did your dad die?"

He looked down then up at her. "My dad died from getting hit by an ice cream truck,"

"Oh my gosh."

"Not a big one, one of those little cute ones that plays the music."

Bren tilted her head. "Are you joking?"

"No," he said. "For real. He was wearing music headphones. He didn't hear it coming. It whizzed by him, scared him, and triggered a heart attack."

Geez, Bren thought. "I'm so sorry to hear that."

"Thanks."

Bren thought of her not knowing Greg's cheating was coming and that shock to her heart, and how that now seemed a bit less dramatic, but she didn't dare tell Trent her comparison.

"So I don't like ice cream," he said.

Hmmm. "Calli's family is into ice cream. They have an ice cream store in Missouri. Things probably wouldn't work between you and her."

He grinned. "She's sweet, but I don't think that's the only reason she and me wouldn't work out."

Bren nodded.

"Is your family in ice cream?" he asked.

"No," she answered. "My dad's in a truck somewhere, and my mom is in and out of relationships."

"Awe," he said. "Any more questions?"

"Do you think ski lifts throughout the city would make it easier to get around?"

He laughed. "I think that awesome idea merits discussion."

She laughed too, then exhaled, and looked at him, her potential boyfriend. "Do you still love your ex-girlfriend?"

Silence.

He smirked.

Oh . . . damn.

Her heart dropped through his patio and onto hers.

Damn.

Damn.

Damn.

Tensing so tight she couldn't breathe.

She fumbled fast to her pajama pocket.

Yanked out her inhaler!

Her shaking hand dropped it!

Trent dived down and brought it back up to her!

She swiped it from him and shot a blast of survival into herself!

Trent's hands steadied her while the asthma medication worked its magic.

"It's all right," he said.

She was jealous of his ability to breathe and speak.

"It's all right," he kept saying softly, between her hyperventilating breaths.

Slowly her throat opened up enough to get air freely in and out.

Her lungs sure liked being able to breath.

Deeeep breaths.

Calming.

Realizing.

Leaving.

"Please stay."

"I have to go."

"Why?"

"Because."

"'Cause why?"

"Because you *smirked!*"

She rushed toward his back stairs.

"But you don't know *why* I smirked."

Her bare feet patted fast down his back patio's chilly wood steps. "*You still love Julia!*"

"No. I smirked 'cause I'm falling in love with *you!*"

FULL STOP!

She stood frozen at the bottom of his stairs, on her dark patio, shocked.

Those were the most amazing words to come out of him *ever!*

Staring away from him, she stared at her wooden deck, hearing his perfect words echo around in her head, her hand still clutching their stairway railing, barely hanging onto her relationship with him, feeling *elation*, and *fear*, and reeeeally needing some more info.

"I smirked 'cause you're so off-base," she heard him say, up there behind her. "I don't love Julia anymore. I'm falling in love with *you*."

Ooooh wow.

"I laughed because me still being in love with Julia is ridiculous. It's so ridiculous because when I met you on our front stairs my heart completely switched gears, from her to you. It was an amazing moment, so damn easy. Falling for you was just effortless, and instant, and . . . now we're on our back stairs. We've come along way, Bren. Let's see where this goes. Let's go to bed."

Bren started laughing. "How the heck can we just go to bed? We're talking about love. *Criminy.* Love? Already? After knowing each other only four days, and three nights, three amazing nights, and this head-spinning night? This is so intense."

"I agree."

"Ooooh, I wish Kris was here," she said out loud, looking around her patio with so many Kris memories of dating talks. "I need to stop time, and analyze the heck out of all this with Kris, figure it out, then un-stop time and do the right thing, organize this messy emotional storm."

"Kris isn't here," he said. "But I am."

She slowly turned around, put both hands on the railings, and looked up and saw Trent standing at the top of his stairs, lit by the warm golden light from his home, looking sincere, and beautiful, their roles reversed from when she first met him on their front stairs. They had totally come a long way.

She stayed still, standing, studying him, hearing him, wanting him, fearing him, and kinda falling in love with him too.

Her foot stepped up on a stair.

He looked happy about her step toward him.

She felt happy to step toward him too.

They had gotten close, so fast, so easily, so funly, so close that now it hurt *so much* to try to leave him. Their simple arrangement had become so complicated. She had told him 'no sex,' but she hadn't forbidden falling in love. Maybe she should have been more specific. So much for another quiet evening together.

After all this, how could they just go back to cuddling?

But . . . she began realizing what she didn't want to do. She *didn't* want to go back to her dark, empty, lonely apartment and sleep alone. Thus, she now wanted to risk heartbreak more than being alone, and she used the word "thus" in a thought. *Wow.* She thought. She'd crossed over into a whole new realm, as her foot floated up another stair.

His face lit up.

Her heart beat so hard that it pushed her forward, toward him, toward her now more-than-a-neighbor, more-than-a-friend, slowly, cautiously, back up the stairs. Her wide eyes watched his hopeful smile as she slowly walked up. Step by cautious step she kept climbing up to him, closer and closer, looking up at the top of these stairs, at her perfect-wording cuddler and potential new boyfriend that was looking at her with affection in his eyes, waiting for her, his face full of hope, in the glorious golden light, with her cracked heart longing for healing.

Night around them, air chilling her bare arms, longing for the warmth of his body and bed.

And longing for love.

He might really believe his feelings now, she thought. But, would his feelings for her last or be enough to not screw her over in the future. She was not an easily moveable feast, still unconvinced. Of course he said the perfect words, he was a writer, and his words were getting better. But his actions would speak louder than his words. Behavior = character.

"Are you and I okay?" he asked her.

She stared at his loving eyes. She stayed strong. She exhaled. "Let's sleep on it."

In his bed, that felt as wonderful as her bed, she nestled next to him, right on schedule, cuddling again, *way* better, much more intimately. This crazy night of confessions changed their connection, and their sleeping position, as she lay with him face to face this time, on their sides, sharing a pillow, no longer giving him her back, but still too cautious to give him her heart.

So much still uncertain with him, in this darkness, feeling her way around. Her fingers finding his shaven cheek, freshly shaven just for her. Her pajama-covered legs entwining with his, bare feet softly stroking his big clompers. Feeling his minty breath cool her warm cheeks. Feeling his hugging arm comfortingly supporting her back, his hand lovingly caressing her shoulder blades, his hard desire for her respectfully staying on her thigh, and his body parts all cooperating to calm her, successfully. She felt so uncommonly calm with him. Not because of a single caress or a hug, but of how all his equally-caring touches together added up to an un-hurrying, un-pressuring, caring man. A sweet man. A good man, who genuinely wanted to make her happy.

Even better than shining every light in her room on him, cuddling in the dark was revealing his true character. Like city lights dim the stars, only when the lights were off could she truly experience the truth of him, feel the truth in his touches, who he was. He was how he touched her, how he made her feel, and he made her feel really good, as good as that elusive fairytale prince she had always read about and longed for and maybe was finally with, in his brand new bed that felt as comfortable as her own. She wondered if Trent was her soulmate; she was feeling *that* comfortable with him, more and more each comfortable night.

Feeling truly cared for in this self-interested-filled world, in this unhelpfully silent universe. Feeling herself caring for him too. Feeling a united caring. Feeling strengthened by their unity. Feeling empowered as a team. A cuddling team. And this rare empowering, caring, cuddling teamwork feeling like . . . a weapon, a non-violent weapon against everything negative in life, a quiet fight! Fighting Greg's nightmares with another man's embrace, fighting loneliness with companionship, fighting life's indifference with luxurious feelings from someone who cares. Cuddling was a couple-sized SCREW YOU to everything that made her feel weak!

Like the perception of a charming Austen novel, their bond only *seemed* passive. For in the still center of all the mighty universe's vast, dark, silent, cold nothing, caring Trenda was a tiny, fiery, body-talking, warm *SOMETHING!* "Take *this* life!" she thought secretly to herself with a vengeful giddily smile, under his ceiling sprinkled with glow-in-the-dark star stickers . . . really hoping that what *felt* good and true *was* good and true.

This felt like love.

It did.

Happening so fast, but feeling so real.

Geez Louise. So much said tonight. Too much said. Too wild.

She looked into his beautiful eyes, now full of caring, and hopefully truth. She sighed. She had told him she didn't like to have anything wild right before bed, especially a declaration of *love*. How the heck was she supposed get to sleep tonight?

"Once upon a time," his caring voice whispered, his minty breath breezing her lips.

She instantly relaxed, Pavlovian-ishly.

"It was a beautiful day," his gentle voice continued, "sunny, warm, wonderful, some fluffy clouds floating through the wide lapis blue sky. It was a beautiful day to . . . fly . . . to . . . skydive," his creative mind decided. "Marcie, buckled on her parachute stuff and stood ready at the airplane's open oval door, enjoyed solidness beneath her feet, then relaxed as she released herself out the plane door and into the air, unafraid, and thrilled. She flipped around and faced the stretching green earth below her. She smiled, floating, flying. She was an angel."

Bren exhaled long and fully, listening to his silly skydiving story, trusting that he would give it a happy landing, so glad to think of something not about their confusing situation.

"The rushing air helped spread Marcie's smile even wider for her 400th jump as she did somersaults, twirls, and reveled in the euphoric freedom. As the closing distance from the ground turned fun into reality, she switched gears from play to smarts, and at the perfect time, she popped her parachute. It burst open, beautifully, powerfully, hoisting her upwards, then gently lowering her down, softly, gloriously . . . but a little off course."

Bren grinned, now even more interested.

"The field Marcie had aimed for was way over there. She was way over here, above a stadium, filled with people, and music, and she glided down closer, closer, closer, into the stadium, over the crowd, toward the stage, right into the rock band's drum set, with a comical cymbal crash."

Bren chuckled, then thought. "What if you reversed the POV?"

"What'da you mean?" he asked softly.

"You could tell the story from the band's point-of-view. Then her comical crash is a surprise. They're playing to the crowd, maybe singing about how love can just happen out of the blue, and then out of the blue a parachuting woman suddenly crashes their concert."

"Huh," he said. "That's really good."

"Thank you."

"So let's pretend I said that." He chuckled. "Now what?"

Ooo. Now she was a participant, not just a listener. *Interesting.* She wondered, and fantasized, and joined in. "Marcie fumbled through all the parachute's poofy fabric, and found her way out of . . . aloneness . . . and into the arms of the gorgeous lead singer."

"Oh my."

"Oh yes," Bren continued with a grin. "His big arm muscles gently helped her to her feet, helped her shed her tethers, and held her waist, sweetly. His caring eyes looked like a happy ending, and of her 400 jumps, this was definitely her favorite."

Trent smiled big, and rubbed her back, as if thrilled with her addition to tonight's bedtime story.

She smiled, thrilled that this wonderful author liked her part of the story, as they finished together.

"And the crowd cheered."

"And they kissed."

"And the band played."

"And Marcie and Brock sang."

"Brock?"

"Brock."

"And their voices blended beautifully," he said. "And they lived happily ever after."

"I hope so," she added.

"They totally did," he assured her.

Bren's fingers touched Trent's cheek, as she enjoyed his sexy dish-washing hand holding her waist sweetly, and his loving eyes looking at her, and enjoyed his belief in happy endings.

"And," Trent continued. "Marcie, Brock, and their band toured the world, sold millions of records, and made so much money that they built a spaceship that took them all around space on a galaxy-wide concert tour that united hundreds of alien worlds together in peace through the power of music, and love . . . and pepperoni pizza."

Bren laughed, and calmly shook her head at her silly bedmate, appreciating his jokes keeping things lighthearted.

He smiled and continued softly rubbing her back.

She closed her eyes, keeping his smile the last sight of her day, ending her Tuesnight with a positive vibe, as she let him care for her, in his loving arms, slowly relaxing into his care, forgetting her fling flanging thoughts about life, his ex, their wild words, worries, the wedding, his hard Hank on her front thigh, and all his boxes of unorganized books, as she listened to his even more confident storytelling whispers of another bedtime story of a time traveling robot, letting his words gently enter her and fill her with happiness as she fell asleep with him once again, feeling even more hopeful . . .

Chapter 11 – day

WEDNESDAY

. . . thump-thump . . . thump-thump . . . thump-thump . . .

darkness, soft pillow, warm solid body

. . . thump-thump . . . thump-thump . . . thump-thump . . .

Bren smiled.

Waking in the wonderful warmth of Trent's sheltering embrace, finding her chest on his mattress and her ear to his heart. His steady beats pleasantly eased her back into consciousness. His calm thump-thumps were far more friendly than her alarm clock's cruel buzz.

Blissfully beside him, she listened to the audiobook of his heart: word – space – word – space – word, a comforting story about consistency, never fearing that his next beat for her wouldn't come. She liked this bedtime story in his chest the best. She liked hearing him be reliable, and worthy of her heart too if his actions continued to be reliable, as reliable as the sun rising again outside and filling his living room over there with pink pre-dawn light.

Would his inspiring words of love that he proclaimed to her last night also continue into the day?

It sure felt like it as his spread hand gently caressed her tingling back.

He was awake, and rousing her too, most kindly.

Lovingly.

Stirringly.

She snuggled into their bond, enjoying this delightfulness, her cheek pressing his chest, her hand sliding over his flannel top, feeling the hard-as-rock wall under his cinnamon-colored fabric. Arms around bodies, hands sliding on backs, fingers feeling, legs entwining, cuddlers saying "good morning," silently, sweetly, physically, funly, in a language she couldn't learn from books, a language only learned in bed, with someone very special. Their cuddly conversation was delightful. His caressing palm said: "I sure like you a whole bunch." Her toying fingers said: "I like you too, but I'm cautious." His light squeezes said: "You're safe." Her relaxing but not kissing said: "I want to believe that." His hard Hank said: "I REALLY like you." Her indented tummy said: "Yeah, no kidding."

Snuggling, cuddling, then rolling to her side, pajamas to pajamas, her breasts to his chest. Her fingers found his fabric and latched on, hanging on him like a koala bear to a tree, gentle at first, then tighter and tighter.

Ooooh. It had been weeks since she enjoyed such pleasure with a man, and never with such an ideal man. She tried so hard not to think of her last man. She focused on *this* one, this amazing one gently massaging her back with his firm but gentle hand, exploring her back, learning it, finding her most pleasurable spots, his fabulous fingers finding her knots, and sweetly working them, circling them, lulling them tender, freeing her being into surrender.

She mooooooaned, feeling his hand slide to her side, and lightly grip. Sensing where this was going, she felt so comfortable with him now that she took things to an even higher level and rolled on top of him.

He on his back. Her front on his front.

Now she had the high ground.

But he had the upper hands, magic hands, massaging marvelously, making her mmmmmmmelt all over him like oozy Velveeta. Not the cheese she had imagined on him, but soooo good, loving garnishing his abs with her tummy, and her pelvis upon his – *woooow*, Hank was VERY there, like a fallen redwood under her, exciting her, and his man-hands spanning over her, spoiling her. *Ooooh, yes.* His Hank and his hands, her body pampered between two pleasures.

Such a wonderful way to wake her.

Such a wonderful waker.

Oooooooh, and such a masterful massager.

His tender touches were like words said softly, a lovely language. His touches said "I hope you like this."

Her moans replied "*I totally love this,*" as she lay splayed on top of him.

Whole handfuls of her wings getting *squeeeeeeeezed soooooooo goooooooood*.

She became putty as he sculpted, gripped and glided, rubbed and slipped and slided, remolding her tight mangled muscles into mushy mush with the most majestic massage she had ever marinated in.

Oooooooooh wooooooooow, he was gooood.

Liquifying her upper back, then loosening her lower. So needing his kneading. Her lat dorsi so agreeing. "Yeah. Just like that," her moaning said.

"I love pleasing you," his giving hands replied.

Oooooh. She loved being pleased, pleased so *goooooooood*, so good her moans grew to groans, slightly grinding down on Hank in this new hedonistic adventure, mooshing together.

Oooooooooh. Yes. Any more pleasure and he could just have her!

His radio clicked on, unfairly filling the air with one of her most favorite songs, Howie Day's "Collide." *Oh wow.* A perfect moment, getting totally seduced with so much heaven all at once: hands, Hank, and Howie's enchanting light guitar strums and wispy voice serenading her and Trent's most luscious cuddle ever as dawn was breaking, her whole pleasured body shaking, her head flopping down by his neck, spilling her hair down around him, emptying her lungs with moans into his ear, while gloriously breeeeathing in Trent's manly scent and the majestic scent of his zillion paperbacks, her now soft-as-paper back getting spoiled by his glorious grips as her fingers clawed his linen sheets into fists. Senses overwhelmed with wonderful!

Ooooh. She had no idea that his hands were *this* talented. *Daaaamn.* Here, she had been sleeping with him for four nights now and she could have been getting this luxurious back action the whole time??

Sublime.

Smiling wide and happy.

Cared for so divinely.

Limp limbs fallen.

Soul floating above him.

Pelvis pressing down on him.

Chin into his shoulder.

Mouth hanging open.

Heat and sweat under his covers.

Feeling so much more than cuddlers.

Almost, almost, almost like lovers.

"Don't stop," her pelvic pressing told his body, as his hands kneaded her perfectly to the easy breezy melody, persuasively, elatingly, erotically, oh so loving being his guest, getting lost in so much *yes* of flesh and sight and scent and sound, oh such sensory overload. Feeling his hands, smelling ink and soap, tasting earlobe, seeing hope, and hearing Howie so sweetly singing with their thumping hearts colliding, bare feet playing, mouths panting, her entranced and him enchanting, him pleasing and her so letting, so swooning and sweating, caressing and meshing, lightly grinding and pressing together in a slo-mo collision, soft rocking in rhythm to the music, in the magic of this marvelous marvelous marvelous morning.

Howie faded.

The radio DJ interrupted and promised another sunny day as she felt her masseuse's hands softly slide away and turn off his clock radio and felt his humid covers gently peeeeeeeeled off her once again.

She shivered.

Cold air chilling her damp skin.

No, no, no. She didn't wanna leave heaven.

Ever.

His clock read 5:04am.

Daaaaaaaamn.

Her head fell to his pillow, felt him gently roll her weak-as-a-noodle body off his and back down to earth upon his soft bed, felt his body roll away, felt his bed lightly shimmy, heard his bare feet pat over his hardwood floor around her and then stop beside her.

On her back, she slowly opened her eyes up and saw her tall smiling tease towering above her, extending to her his hand and his pajama poking Hank. Torn between which to take.

His smile could so tell she was torn.

Her limp hand lifted.

Her instincts *wanted.*

And . . . her hand passed up his poke and, *whew*, passed this test.

Slipping her sweaty palm into his big hand, feeling his strong but kind grip gently resurrect her from his bed like a droopy rag doll.

He wrapped his strong arm around her waist and helped her stand.

Standing so close to him, this seductive man, who seduced her to his hard limit, who loosened her limits, loosened her so much. He could have had her. They could have had sex at dawn!

But, once again, he surprisingly restrained himself. Respectfully.

Impressive.

Shocking.

Flabbergasting how much he could restrain himself.

She almost abandoned their rules. Wildly!

Blushing that she had kinda humped him. Although, it was hump day.

And a *new* day.

Morning light behind him filled his big living room with the promise of wonderfulness, his caring eyes promised all the happiness she had ever wanted.

Wow.

Brain boggling.

Heart throbbing.

Legs wobbling, having to hold onto his dresser.

He slowly backed away, grinning at her, as if proud of his work.

Dr. Franken-Trent was bringing back to life her once broken spirit and amazingly enlivened her into a stunned, standing, tingling, wobbly, willing, wet, reborn being who finally saw actual non-fiction hope in love, in him, who wanted to passionately leap into that hope with him . . . but who now had to go to work, ALL HEATED UP!

* * * *

Work was work.

She texted with Kris about how Kris and Mark were still trying different arrangements of their furniture in their living room, and bantered about how floating-furniture would be much easier to move around, and they wished each other happy National Corn on the Cob Day.

Back to work.

She clicked her pen.

She liked clicks.

She liked how her and Trent were clicking, really clicking.

She liked Trent.

She maybe even was starting to *love* Trent.

Wow.

She typed a report and thought of his hands.

She talked in a meeting and thought of his lips.

She finished a call and thought of his voice.

She saw a building and thought of his tall skyscraping HANK!

Flashbacks of Greg's penis cheating on her interrupted, but less than yesterday.

Her thoughts fought back to Trent.

She could do that easier now. Progress.

She felt proud, yet nervous, yet comforted.

She thought about their magical morning together.

And couldn't wait for a magical night!

* * * *

Bren faked ill and broke out early from work, eager to get back home! She just had to see her magic man again.

Taxi. Sidewalk. Stairs, on the phone with her four friends about pre-wedding stuff.

His door was open. Always open for her. She smiled.

She rang his doorbell and knocked and called up to him, but no answer. She glanced at her watch: 6:42pm. He was probably still at the bar, probably be back soon.

She waited inside her apartment, laying on her bed, wishing Trent was cuddling with her right then, continuing her 4-way phone convo with Kris, Holly, and Calli.

Holly: The wedding's baseball hats arrived.

Kris: Awesome.

Holly: But there's a slight issue.

Kris: Not awesome.

Holly: The pre-marriage hats do say: "Team Kris" for the bridal party and "Team Mark" for the groomsmen.

Kris: Cool.

Holly: But the hats for after you're married, that everyone then puts on are supposed to say: "Kris & Mark" in a heart.

Kris: Right.

Holly: They say: "Kras & Mirk."

Kris: Kras and Mirk?

Holly: Kras and Mirk.

Kris: Oh shit.

Calli: Is that an ai problem?

Holly: Anna's fixing it.

Bren: Does she need any help?

Holly: Nope. It's all under control.

Kris: Well, as long there's the only one wedding glitch, we're doing great.

Holly: Well, there's also a roof issue.

Bren: Roof issue?

Kris: Roof issue?

Calli: That sounds like a dog sneezing.

Holly: A seagull built a nest in the middle of the rooftop and a tenant in the apartment building has vowed to protect the nest instead of letting us move it for the wedding reception.

Kris: A seagull cock-blocked my reception?

Calli: Can we make it a wedding guest?

Holly: Anna's fixing it.

Kris: I think her name's Ann.

Bren: It's Anna.

Calli: I thought her name was Hanna.

Kris: Well, as long there's the only two wedding glitches, we're doing great.

Holly: There's one more issue.

Kris: Holy ball dangles.

Holly: Andy's wife just had their baby girl, so he flew back to Los Angeles.

Kris: Oh that's awesome.

Bren: That's wonderful.

Calli: Yay, I won the bet.

Kris: What'd they name her?

Holly: Candy.

Kris: Andy and Sandy named their baby Candy?

Calli: I think that's dandy.

Holly: But Andy's supposed to officiate the ceremony, and he might not make it back here by Saturday, so someone else might have to officiate.

Bren: Can we get the seagull to do it?

Kris: Holy dick swings.

Calli: I'll do it.

Kris: Well, you're a bridesmaid, sweetie.

Calli: I could do both. I'd officiate you soooo good.

Holly: Let's play it by ear.

Bren: It sounds like we're working without a net.

Calli: Who's Annette?

Holly: Um.

Bren: Hats, seagulls, and Candy.

Calli: Oh my.

Kris: That's three glitches. Not good for a baseball wedding.

Holly: Everything will get worked out.

Kris: Holy nipple slips. This is supposed to be my week of no-stress pre-wedding pampering, so I'm gonna leave it up to all of you to handle it, while I go have fun styling my pubes with my new vjazzle kit.

Bren: Ooookay then.

Calli: Happy pubing.

Kris: Bye.

Kris hung up.

Calli hung up.

Holly stayed on.

Bren: Should I be helping out with the wedding more?

Holly: Nope. Anna has it all covered.

Bren: Her name's really Anna, right?

Holly: Yes.

Bren: Oh good. Is Calli okay with Trent being with me?

Holly: Yeah. She's got a date tonight with a physician or magician or maybe both. I don't know anymore.

Bren: Good. I just wanna be sure about things.

Holly: How are things going with Trent?

Bren: Oh. Good.

Really good, she thought, really really good, possibly in *love!* Bren wondered if her and Trent were moving too fast. She stared up at her blank ceiling, feelings swirling. She wondered. Should she calm things down and sleep alone tonight? She stared at her ceiling/wall line. It didn't give an answer. She stared at her bookcases, remembering the last time she was looking at her bookcases alone in bed, when she first heard Trent enter –

Sqeeeeak.

She heard their building's front door squeak open on the other side of her books. Then heard Trent's footsteps clomp up their stairway. Her heart *thumped.*

His feet clomped, casually climbing and climbing up to their landing, returning to her. *Yay!* Bren stood up.

Bren: I hear Trent coming home.

Holly: I'll let you go. I've got a good feeling about you two.

Bren: Thanks.

Holly hung up.

Bren had a good feeling about them too. But she'd had good feelings before. She really, really wanted her good feelings for his amazing guy to be right. She just wished there was some way to be 100% sure about him.

DING DONG!

Doorbell rang. Not hers. *His.*

"Oh my God," his voice reverberated through their stairway.

Bren froze, curious.

Bzzzzzzzz.

She heard him buzzing their front door unlocked.

It *squeeeeaked* open again.

"*Julia?*" he said.

Bren's heart launched into her throat!

What?

JULIA WAS HERE??

What the flipping crap was happening?

Trent's ex was in their building! This was insane!

Bren scurried her socks quietly across her carpet then hardwood floor, and stood by her door, listening, worrying.

"What're you doing here?" she heard Trent exclaim down to his ex.

Bren was all ears for her answer.

"Hiiiiiii!" Julia's voice sang out loud and happy through their stairway. "I saw you walk out of the bar and I – "

"Followed me?" he said.

"I just wanted to say hi," she replied gleefully. "It's been so long."

"It has."

"I can't believe my bohemian boy is living in the chichi Marina."

"Actually, I learned that this isn't the Marina. It's Cow Hollow."

Bren smirked.

"Awe. Well. I saw your picture on the magazine cover. I'm very impressed, with your move here and, of course, your novel. I read it and *love* it and I'm so happy for you."

"Thanks. That's really nice of you."

"Um, do you think I could come up?" she asked.

Lightning bolts of worry fired through Bren.

Was this the end of their wonderful nights together and their possible future? Would he be a cheating heartbreaker like Greg? Was there no hope to ever find a faithful, monogamous guy and fairytale love????

"I'm sorry, Julia, no," he said. "I'm not gonna let you up."

Lightning bolts of hope zinged through her!

"I'm in love with someone else now," he said.

Bren's mouth popped open!

"And." Trent continued. "I totally don't mean to be rude, but if she sees you here it will really mess things up. So I have to say goodbye, and I wish you the very best."

Shock!

Bewilderment!

Lightning bolts of elation rocketed through Bren!

"Oh," Julia reacted. "I'm so sorry. I didn't mean to . . . well, I wish you the very best too. Great to see you."

"You too," he said.

Front door slowly shut.

Silence.

Trent exhaled.

Bren's heart whammed wild!

Trent's footsteps clomped up his stairs.

Criminy WOW!

Bren burst from her apartment, onto their landing, and stared up his stairs at beautiful, wonderful, trustworthy Trent!

He spun around.

His face looked totally surprised.

She threw her arms open for him!

His blushing face was filled with elation!

He raced down his stairs and threw his arms around her!

They embraced for an eternity!

A really awesome in eternity!

Ready to love again!

Amazing!

So this is where their first kiss would happen, she thought.

Her heart pounded a drum solo.

Her lips prepared.

She loosened to let him have her.

But instead he took her hand and smiled huge. "Come upstairs," he said gleefully, inviting her up, not Julia, inviting *her!* "I wanna show you something."

Chapter 11 – night

WEDNESNIGHT

Smiling big, Bren let his hand lead her up his stairs and through his sun-filled empty living room, wondering what he could possibly show her that would be as amazing as hearing him choose her over his ex?

"My bedroom," his voice said, leading her in, then extending his arm out, inviting her to go into his room.

Hmmm. Were they going to bed early, she wondered, as she clacked across his wood floor towards his sunlit bedroom, until her clacking suddenly stopped.

Something was odd.

She looked down and around and –

Her jaw dropped.

Eyes popped.

She smiled with delight.

An incredible sight.

Carpet!

Shelves full of books!

Organization!

Wow!

He clicked on his ceiling light, brightening the beautitude even more.

She stood flabbergasted and gaping at his brand new bedroom, re-feeling a flutter of *awe*. It was just so beautiful. Tall, tan wood shelves all the way up to his high ceiling and stretching the whole length of his long east wall to his blue-curtained window. Fifteen feet long, and eight shelves high, and every slot packed pleasingly with paperbacks. Books, books, BOOKS. *Organized* books. She exhaled with such pleasure at his new and improved bedroom. Neat and nice and no more books stuck randomly in boxes. Now gorgeousness!

Her shoes floated on a sky blue carpet from her tingling toes to all his horizons, and among all the majesty lay a puffy white made bed, like a fluffy cloud, ready for them to unmake and cuddle upon or maybe even *more*, all night in the sky.

This truly was heaven. Everything sorted and soothing and smelling of books.

Wow.

"I've been busy," his voice said deep and proud behind her.

"I see that," she cooed.

"I did this instead of get a slide to your bedroom."

She laughed.

"You can come up here anytime," he invited.

Oh. She totally wanted to.

"You like it?"

"Oh my gosh yes."

He chuckled.

"How did this happen?"

"I rented a truck," he told her soft and plain. "And I bought some wood."

"*You* built these shelves?"

"With my bare hands."

"Criminy. Are they gonna collapse?"

"No way," he assured her. "The internet taught me real good."

"Oh geez. *And* you wrote at the bar today?"

"I did."

"You built all this in one morning?"

"I work fast."

"Yes. Yes you're definitely swift. And you keep surprising me and – and now you can build things?"

"Well, I can't rebuild you a house like Noah built for Allie. But I can build you shelves."

Ooooh, wow. Such a perfect thing to say. Bren felt herself weaken. "You built your bookcases for *me?*"

Trent smiled so sweetly. "I want you to feel comfortable here, so you'll wanna come up all the time."

Oh, it *did* make her wanna come, up! ALL the time!

"And maybe, stay."

Ooooh, it *did* make her wanna stay.

Too much?

Too fast?

She stood, in heaven, wondering . . . and now worrying.

He looked at her, smiling.

She had wanted to kiss him soooo badly. But . . . she didn't.

He looked at her, worried. "What? Did I do bad?"

"No," she assured him. "You did good. Really good. Really, really good." She slowly sat down on his bed, beholding him, his organized books, and aaaall his perfectness, stunned.

Silence.

He sat down on his carpet, beside his glorious shelves, and looked up at her. "I hope you won't withhold info from me, and tell what you're thinking, and feeling."

She thought, smirked, and tried to find the right words. "The guys I've dated, if they seemed to good to be true, eventually they were. You . . . you seem really, really too good to be true."

He nodded and exhaled. "I overdid it, huh?"

She looked at him and his overwhelming shelves and started grinning.

He laughed. "Oh man, I did, didn't I? I went too far, too fast. I'm so sorry."

"It's not a sorry situation. It's just so perfect. I'm feeling a lot."

"I was so convinced I was doing the right thing," he explained. "I thought you of all people would truly enjoy a really pleasant reading room," he said.

She nodded. "Well, I am a book nerd."

"If you're a nerd, I'm a nerd," he said.

She smirked and almost rolled her eyes, then looked at this big beautiful place Trent had created for her, like Noah creating a beautiful room just to resurrect Allie's love of painting; Trent had created a room to resurrect her love of reading.

Ooooh wow. Emotions welled up.

"I'm sorry, Bren. I just wanna make you happy."

"You are. You make me so happy that I'm waiting for the other shoe to drop."

He took off both his shoes and tossed them aside with a thud, thud. "Both shoes have dropped."

She grinned.

He smiled at her grin. "Just so you know what I'm thinking," he said. "When you smile, it's the most beautiful thing I've ever seen. When you don't smile, I wanna give you a smile. It's that simple. Making you smile makes me happy. That's how it's always been in my relationships, and that's especially how it is now with you. And I'm not perfect. I mean, at some point I'm probably going to not be able to live up to your expectations and accidently disappoint you. But I promise you I don't have a hidden agenda, all my good words and actions are not masking some horrible side of me, and I'm never going to cheat on you, and I'm always going to tell you what's up. So, no disappointment is going to come from those things."

Wow. She exhaled long with relief and hope.

"So, if you let me, I would like to keep making you smile, because I really love your smile."

She looked at him with swirling feelings.

He nodded. "It's gonna take some time, huh?"

She sighed. "Are you in a hurry, swift-Trent?"

He smiled, and shook his head. "For you I've got all the time you need."

She smiled.

He smiled at her smile.

She paused and breathed deeply, regaining perspective over emotions. She almost let herself get swept up in elation. Thank goodness he overdid it, snapping her back to sensibleness. Smartly, she still needed to know more about him before she could let herself love again. She *had* to, because if a guy as great as Trent disappointed her that really would devastate her hope in love. So, she returned to proceeding with caution.

She looked at his beautiful new room. A bed in a library. *Dangerous.*

And thrilling.

She turned her smile back to him. "Can I look at *your* books?"

His face lit up. "I would love that."

Mmmmm. She would love that too. She smiled wide. But she tried to not let feelings excite her so much that she lost sensibleness as she left his delighted eyes and cautiously, heart-thumpingly explored his books, to snoop, and gain perspective.

She approached his towering, spanning cathedral of literature. Inhaling the light tease of his library's marvelously musty-sweet scent, as it lured her nose and eyes to look again at the wondrous sight of his thousands of now pleasingly organized paperbacks, all calling to her like Waterhouse's painting of the water nymphs seducing Hylas into the deep, to help her or to tempt her in deeper.

Ears hearing an imaginary choir of "aaaawes" as she beheld such glory.

Fifteen-foot-ish long, five feet tall sections, eight shelves each, sixty-ish books per packed shelf. Over two thousand paperback wonders in his wonderwall, all gloriously organized alphabetically by genre, author, and title *for her pleasure*.

And her eyes felt soooo pleasured as they funly flitted all over his massive body of works. He had everything. From Homer to Green, Kinsella to King to authors that even she'd never seen. But it wasn't just his awesome size that mattered; it was also his awesome choices. Her eyes danced a path from Atwood to Plath, from Plato to Sendak to Updike to Zusak, from Walker to Bettelheim to Le Guin to Jong; his library was soooo lustfully long.

Keeping cool, saying nothing, just exploring, wondering if her looking was having a powerful effect on him the way his Monday night book-looking did on her. She loved seeing what books he appreciated and enjoyed, what was most dear to him, with her hands hanging at her sides, sometimes touching her thighs, her head drifting, sometimes tilting, sometimes nodding, and her lips curling up. Grinning at his made-up genre of "books with castles:" *Castles in the Air*, *The Blue Castle*. Smiling at his whole shelf of Alexandre Dumas's heroic tales. And chuckling at his two shelves of cheesy choose your own adventure books: *The Cave of Time*, *The Third Planet of Altair*, and her new favorite title: *Your Very Own Robot Goes Cuckoo-Bananas.*

"If I pulled on one of your novels does your bookcase swing open to reveal a secret athenaeum of literary storage?" she witted back to him.

He grinned. "Nope. What you see is what there is."

Hmmm. She hoped that was true, as she perused his used and sometimes new books for clues as to who he was by what he read. And seeing how he presented his wares to her; seeing that he had lined the whole frame of his library with unlit strings of colorful icicle Christmas lights as she ogled all over, smiling as wide as his library.

This was soooo sexy.

She felt warm and tingly.

She saw his copy of *Wallbanger*, he had great taste. She saw his thick *Moby Dick*. Ooooooo, she saw his rare first edition of *Pride and Prejudice* up there. Oh, but she didn't dare touch it for fear of feeling too much, even though she so yearned to learn its vintage smell divine and be transported back to Austen's time, to see his signed copy of *Color of Magic*, and read all his rares and touch his fun graphics, to thumb through his thrillers and probe and inhale, to fondle his folios, feel books in braille, explore every inch of his erotica section, and then lose herself in his OVERSIZED collection.

What book was his favorite?

She stepped back and took it all in. She looked for wear and tear on spines. Her eyes skimmed the tops of his books for dog-eared pages, bookmarks. She used her powers of guessing. But it was still a grand mystery.

But, she thought, Trent did have a terrible poker face, and a giveaway grin. She would use it to discover him.

She looked left at him, at is face, his beautiful, and honest face, as she slowly walked left, then right, then middle, watching his reactions. She pointed up, down, and all around, watching his eyes sparkle, his mouth smile, and his legs shift his confessing hips. And his behavior led her down, down, down, as she lowered her knees and hands to his soft carpet. *Oooo.* It was wonderful, and so was how much he was grinning as her finger slid over his erotica section, sensing that she was getting close to the book his big hands handled most. Warmer and warmer. His stretching lips smiled. His quick inhale gave him away, as if her fingers tickled a sensitive spot; she knew she was HOT! He was blushing, sweating, and looking caught.

She smiled proudly as she pointed at: *Erotic Exotic Untamed Tales.*

Oooooooh my, she thought.

She floated her trembling hand through the air, toward the waiting tome, hearing Trent's deep breaths behind her body, knowing she was affecting him. She grinned, and gripped her fingers around the vertical plaything's smooth surface, and lightly pulled. It came with her willingly, back to her warm body. She turned it slightly and saw the very enticing cover of blurry bare bodies. An anthology of sexy tales all clustered together, an orgy of stories and poems for a booklover to enjoy. *Oh my.*

She ventured past the cover to discover its wonders. The table of contents listed many sexy tales. And there were so many dog-eared pages. But which tale was his fave? Her fingers thumbed through the pages, story after story after story, until Trent's face got super red.

JACKPOT!

She left his turned-on eyes and read the dog-eared, underlined poem. *Wow.* He liked erotic poetry too?! *Fantastic! Ooooh.* It was a really good spicy poem, about a woman undressing for her lover, sexily, working him into a frezy before she let him ravish her!

Soooo. *This* is what got Trent hot.

Hmmmm. Interesting, she thought, now seeing him totally turned-on from her seeing what turned him on.

She gently returned his fave back to it's proper slot, stood, and stared down at him.

He stared back up at her, smiling, his eyes electric.

Good.

She slowly stepped out her strappy shoes, pivoted as sultry as she could, walked her stocking-covered feet around his luxuriously soft carpet, loving the feeling, and loving the feeling of her handsome librarian's curious eyes hot on her as she turned off all his lights, and pulled closed his curtains until only the ricochet of sunlight bouncing off the walls lit his room a bit, with just enough light for him to watch her saunter over to his tan dresser like a flirt, open the drawers until she found his t-shirts. She fingered through them for a wonderful while, until she found one that said: feeling the Call of the Wild. *Excellent.* Then, feeling hot too, with her back to him, she took off her skirt, took off her tights, and took off her shirt. Her flesh felt the cool air, and the heat of his stare. She took off her bra and heard him gasp "*awe.*" She happily grinned, her bare back still to him. Such a *zing* to have her breasts out in his room, just her yellow panties on, was Hank flying up towards the Moon? Then she slipped on his t-shirt, covered her skin, and she slowly turned around, for their night to begin.

His mouth was wide open; his eyes flew all over her.

She stared at her heated man. "Time for bed."

He nodded, a lot.

This was fun.

She opened up his covers and slid inside his fluffy cloud.

He exhaled and grinned as he walked towards his dresser. "Are you teasing me, testing me, or torturing me?"

"Maybe all three," she flirted, getting comfy and grinning up at him. "Or maybe I just like making you smile too."

He laughed, and definitely smiled, as he pulled out tonight's pajamas, red, the color of his blushing face. Then he started to leave the room.

"Change in here," she said.

He turned around. "Really?"

"I did."

He smiled even bigger. "Yes, I remember. And I'll never forget."

She smiled.

He inhaled a big breath.

The room was *electric.*

He unbuckled his belt and slid off his jeans, revealing the most toned man-legs she'd ever seen. He looked right in her eyes as he slid off his socks, pulled off his shirt, his torso hard as a rock, and so was Hank, pointing at her again, this time through black boxer briefs, and then Trent slipped on his red jammies, and struck a hot pose that could be called: "who knows where this wild night goes."

She watched him pop a mint into his mouth, then open up his covers and slide in bed with her.

Together again.

In his dim room.

A little less clothes this time.

Closer this time.

Sexier this time.

Crunch, crunch, crunch, swallow.

Very sexy.

They lay on their sides, facing each other, staring at each other, *not* having sex.

Not celebrating their new closeness with wondrous kisses and bodies flailing.

Their bare toes touching, playing.

Her naked legs floating around his pj-covered pins.

And the heat between them was the hottest summer ever.

She wondered. Could Trent restrain himself? Could he take things slow?

Could he keep his promise of having all the time she needed?

She wondered more. Could *she* restrain herself and take things slow?

Could she *not* mount him like a motorbike and ride him into rapture?

Exhaaaaaaaale.

Maybe?

"Once upon a time," his minty breath interrupted her wondering, "in a hot, steamy jungle."

"Hot and steamy?"

"Soooo hot and steamy."

They both chuckled.

"In a super duper hot and steamy jungle, a butterfly named – "

"Beatrice," Bren added.

Trent grinned. "Beatrice the Butterfly was so hot and steamy in the jungle and she yearned to cool down."

"So she could sleep."

"Totally. So, flapping her beautiful blue and yellow wings, she flew out of the trees and over the awesome blue wispy ocean," Trent continued. "The winds off the water dried the sweat from her wings."

"Butterflies don't sweat."

"Beatrice was a very rare butterfly that sweated."

"Did Beatrice use deodorant?"

"Beatrice didn't need deodorant because her sweat smell was sweet and pretty."

"Well that's lucky."

"Indeed," Trent said. "Beatrice was a rare, sweet-smelling, sweating, beautiful butterfly that yearned to cool herself from the hot, steamy jungle, so she flew to the ocean and cooled down, and – "

"She had globophobia."

"What's that?"

"Fear of balloons."

Trent laughed. "Yes, of course she did. And a big birthday party for Tad the Tiger was happening later that day. She yearned to avoid all the balloons at the party, so instead she sent Tad a happy birthday text and she flew out to a cruise ship sailing on the ocean."

Bren gently played with his hair while they faced each other. "What if there's balloons on the cruise ship? Beatrice might freak out."

"Then we will have some drama."

"But a relaxing bedtime story needs to be drama-free."

"Then she will avoid rooms with balloons and her life will be drama-free."

"I hope so."

"We're in charge of the story, so we can decide to have her be all right."

"We can have her get over her fear of balloons, if that's possible," Bren said.

Trent smiled. "We can do anything."

Bren smiled, as she rubbed his back.

He rubbed hers too, his eyes sparkling at her. "So Beatrice flapped her wings to the cruise ship and hung out with the other happy passengers by the swimming pool," Trent said.

"And she watched shuffleboard."

"And she sipped on people's drinks."

"And she laid beside the cool pool in the delightful sun," Bren added.

"Then on the ship deck, buy a lounge chair, Beatrice saw lots of other butterflies having a party together and flew over to hang out with them. But they were all hanging out by a balloon."

"Oh no," she said.

"But it was all right because as she flew closer she realized that it wasn't a balloon, it was a bald man's head and he was wearing a shirt with butterflies on it."

"Wow, what a crazy plot twist."

"Right? And she saw that one of the butterflies was actually real. He had also flown to the bald dude's shirt thinking they were real butterflies," he said. "And Beatrice got over her fear of round shiny things in order to land on the bald dude's shirt and meet her new friend."

"Named Brock."

"Again, Brock?"

"I've always liked the name."

"Very well," he agreed, smiling. "Butterflies Beatrice and Brock met on a bald dude's butterfly shirt and fell in love."

"Yes," Bren agreed, her heart pounding. "Somehow, someway she got over her fear so she could love."

"An amazing love," he agreed with her, with his hand lovingly sliding over her hair. "And they lived happily ever after."

Bren hoped they did. "But Beatrice getting over her fear sounds so easy."

"Well, she may have flown around bald dude and Brock a few times before finally landing. But everything worked out in the end."

"You think?"

"Totally," he assured her.

Bren smiled wide, and breathed a big breath, feeling so much, as she squeezed him closer. "I like that story."

He also smiled wide. "I like it too."

She touched his cheek. "You do make me smile."

"I'm so glad," he said, looking thrilled.

They lay together, looking at each other.

"There should be a detective show called Bald Dude and Brock."

Trent chuckled. "What if Beatrice and Brock started a detective agency?"

"No, they start a bed and breakfast for other butterflies."

"But first," Trent said. "They discover time travel and make friends with dinosaurs."

"Oh lordy."

"Once upon a time," he began Wednesnight's second bedtime story, as she nestled her cheek to his chest, and closed her eyes, and listened, and cuddled. His gentle voice told a story about a dog that learned to play chess and toured the world and fell in love with a singing cat and they invented a new game called singing chess.

Bren smiled while listening and snuggling under his cool covers that quickly warmed from their heated bodies facing each other, caressing, enjoying story time with her favorite author, once again, so wonderfully filling her ears with his fun words, easing her busy thoughts away, so calmingly, as only Trent's caring voice and ridiculous stories could do. And slowly she began to like that his story was ridiculous and didn't have anything to do with anything, floating her off to a completely different place and time, a different life, sweetly.

She lay. She listened. She lulled.

His wonderfulness slowly eased her pounding pulse to a medium/delicate rhythm, laying with him in his dim, cozy room, under his ceiling decorated with stickered glow-in-the-dark stars, and smiling. With Trent she always fell asleep smiling, and now smelling the sensuous scent of paperbacks and fresh wood and new carpet.

She could sense Trent's desires for her. She felt his wanting hardness restrained on her thigh. She heard heat in his cool minty whispers, and she noticed Trent's bedtime stories, though still humorous, were a tad more charged with romance and yearning, and she could feel more comfortableness with her in his touch as he unhesitantly caressed his hand over her head and down her hair, so lovingly. They were both restraining themselves, so their growing love balloon didn't pop too soon, or something romantic like that.

Her ears focused on the soothing enjoyableness of his voice and his distracting silly story, as her hand felt the hypnotic steadiness of his heartbeats under his pajama-covered chest, thump-thump . . . thump-thump . . . thump-thump . . . relaxing . . . loving . . . trusting . . . as she slowly let go of this day . . . looking forward to another amazing day with him . . .

Chapter 12 – day

THURSDAY

blee-blee-dee-dee . . . blee-blee-dee-dee

warmth . . . pillow . . . dimness . . . Trent's clean scent . . .

blee-blee-dee-dee . . . *blee-blee-dee-dee* . . .

Trent's neck . . . jaw . . . cheek . . . ear . . .

blee-blee-dee-dee . . . *blee-blee-dee-dee* . . .

wall . . . nightstand . . . clock . . . 8:07 . . .

8:07?!

"OH CRAP!"

Bren flung off Trent's arm!

"What the heck?" Trent exclaimed.

She jumped to her feet! Tumbled to his carpet!

blee-blee-dee-dee

Adrenaline surging, mind fighting to focus and fix this screw up!

She realized the *blee*s was her phone.

Blee-blee . . . Blee –

"H-H-Hello," Bren answered frantically.

"*Bren?*" her boss's stern voice boomed.

Whoosh of fear.

Bren panicked and rushed to her feet.

"Where are you?"

"I'm – I'm not there."

"I know."

"I'm late."

"I know that too."

"I'm on my way."

"Are you all right?"

"Yes. I-I-I-I'm . . . "

"Bren. Why aren't you here?"

Palm to sweaty forehead. "I – oh, Pam. I overslept. The alarm didn't go off."

Trent looked around groggily, in confusion.

"I just woke up."

"*Are you kidding me?*" her boss's disappointment *stung.*

Bren felt the hot, gut-churning humiliation of not being organized that she hadn't felt in years. It felt so awful that she suddenly remembered why she had tried so hard every damn day to be super-organized and avoid this horrible feeling, and with one absentminded slip up she'd fallen back into this painful horror again. Today she wasn't perfect. *Dammit.*

"We need you in here. *Now,*" Pam's restrained anger pierced. "We need you here for *your* meeting."

"I know. I know. Oh my gosh. I'm so sorry. I can't believe this."

"I can't believe it either. You're late. Today. Of all days."

"I know. I know. I'm so sorry."

"I'm sorry," Trent offered.

"Vicki stepped up and is doing your presentation for you right now."

"Can I help you somehow?" Trent bothered.

"Vicki?!"

"Yes, Vicki."

"What can I do?" Trent pestered.

Voices in both ears. Madness!

"I'm guming. I mean – I'm going – I'm coming. I'll be there in twenty."

Bren turned off her phone.

She paused . . . *shaking* . . . "Damn!"

"I'm so sorry," Trent apologized. "I forgot to set my alarm. I'm so sorry I let you down."

Bren grabbed her bag and all her scattered, un-hung, foolishly-unorganized-in-the-heat-of-pleasure clothes and raced away from him. She had no more patience for sorrys. Greg was sorry, Trent was sorry, and now she was sorry she had let herself be messed up. Angry, guilty, scared, and frantic, she flew out of his apartment, fleeing the trap of fun she had foolishly let herself get un-perfected by!

* * * *

Work was not great.

But she did have a fun text with Kris about how personal robots might greet Santa for you in your home on Christmas Eve and give him cookies and milk directly with a smile and a chat instead of just leaving them out for him to find, and that this might inspire Santa to leave more presents for you, and they wished each other happy National Peanut Butter Cookie Day.

* * * *

Clouds gloomed over pretty Cow Hollow. Fog had slipped in like a meanie and took away the sun. Trent had slipped into her life and was taking away her control, her time, her thoughts, her feelings, her resolve, and now her reliable reputation at work. So much for him being perfect, his unorganizedness couldn't set an alarm clock.

She scolded herself too for letting herself get so caught up in all his wonderfulness that she also forgot to set his clock.

Angry-clacking up charming Union Street, passing all the happy people eating yummy salads that her empty stomach ached for. Cute dog she wanted almost tripping her. Slow stroller in front of her with an adorable baby she didn't have. Dropping her keys. Squeaky front door. Too-many stairs. Clomping up them. Darn gravity. Trent's tempting open door above her invited her. Her body wanted to go up and get embraced and held and healed and charmed back into his distracting paradise.

But no, her brain overruled.

She had to put her pleasure-providing but smarts-fuzzing Trent routine on pause. She had become a Trent-o-holic and she hoped in the next twelve steps she would find the strength to resist her want to walk up his stairs and let his intoxicating arms wrap around her, warm her, melt her, sooth her and –

Rolling Stones music rocked down through his open door. The upbeat song clashed with her messed up mood.

Wait, she thought. It was 5:49pm. He was supposed to be writing at the bar right now. What the heck?

She heard laughter. A *woman's* laughter.

Whooooa.

Bren absolutely walked up.

Hearing voices as she climbed.

The woman's voice called out: "Fuck *me!*"

World stopped!

Heart dropped!

That was the last thing she wanted to hear.

Terrible chill froze her blood and her feet.

No, no, no, she thought. Not again.

Was Julia with Trent?

Feeling like a total fool.

Feeling sick.

Stomach clenching. Face scrunching with pain.

Completely stunned.

Couldn't move. Couldn't breath. Couldn't believe this was happening. Why was life punishing her again and again and again?

Feeling like dying.

The woman giggled, mockingly.

Fury unfroze her feet! This wasn't a dream.

Terrified to see the truth, but she just HAD to!

Bolting up his stairs, into his living room!

Bren saw the woman . . . with Trent!

Her heart fell through the floor!

DAMMIT!

It wasn't Julia.

It was some other hot, skinny, long brown-haired woman.

This twenty-ish girl was real. This was actually happening!

The giggling hottie in cute pink shorts and a cream tunic top was cozily shoulder to shoulder with Trent on a new blue couch, as the little skank held up her phone and took a selfie of the two of them.

Bren stared daggers at them in total shock!

She saw Trent see her . . . and see her anger!

Her bag dropped.

His smile dropped.

Click.

The selfie caught his look of horror.

Her anger became *ANGER!*

He flew to his feet!

She clenched her fists.

He waved his palms!

She didn't wanna hear it. She wouldn't believe *anything* he said!

"*She's my sister!*" he yelled.

Whoa.

His words hit her momentum like a finger into a bubble, her *rage* wrapping around, around, around, until . . . POP! She got it.

Bren b-b-breathed – b-b-breathed – b-b-breathed –

Oh . . . his sister . . . she might believe *that.*

He ran over to his stereo and knocked the damn thing over with a *CRASH* as he scrambled to turn off the music!

Silence.

"*She's my sister!*" he howled again, totally frantic The look of panic on his face told her just how much he really, REALLY wanted her to NOT think the wrong thing!

"Fuck *me,*" the hottie exclaimed in response to all the commotion.

Ooooh. Now Bren understood that phrase's context.

Cripes.

Bren whipped out her inhaler and sucked in a deeeeeeeep organizing hit.

Boiling blood through cooling nerves. Lightheaded. Dizzy. Breeeeathing. Shoulders slowly deflating down. She swallowed. She focused. She gave the giggling girl a deep study, her face, her hair, her eyes. Her eyes looked like Trent's eyes. She glanced between Trent and the girl. She could see the similarities. Then, yes, relievingly yes, this girl *did* look like the picture on Trent's refrigerator of the girl on stage dressed as a singing flower and the actress pictures Bren had seen online when researching Trent.

Chill out, she told herself, her chest heaving, breath blowing. This . . . this might be true.

Trent came rushing over to Bren. "This is Lucy, my sister. Everything's cool. Please don't freak out, all right?"

Already freaked out, Bren looked at him. She looked at the hottie.

"Lucy, please tell her," Trent said.

Lucy just giggled at Trent's insanity, remaining completely calm. "Fucking-A, Trent," she mocked him. "Get a grip."

She sure spoke bluntly to him like a sister.

"*You're* Bren?" she squeaked in a pippy tone, as if Lucy had heard everything about her.

Bren both tensed and relaxed, still unsure. "Y-Y-Yes."

"You *aaaare* beautiful," Lucy sang out freely.

"Oh. Um. Thank you," Bren said back, not used to such a sweet compliment from a stranger. Bren's heartbeat and breathing were still spastic, but slowly calming as she wiped her sweat-drenched forehead and tried to regain composure.

"I can see why Trent's head over heels about you," Lucy said.

Bren was flattered, and confused. *Whoa.* What had Trent been saying about her? Clearly good things, because she watched Lucy spring her tan toned body away from Trent's couch and practically skip with joy over to her and smother her in a tight, warm, wonderful hug. A really crushing hug. Bren felt like *she* had a fan. *Oh, wow. This felt good. So good to be hugged. Ooooh.* It felt wonderful to be held this sweetly, especially after her incredibly awful day, Lucy's tight jovial embrace *squeeeeezed* out some of Bren's anger and *squeeeeezed* in a really nice feeling of friendship, and by the time Bren was released she felt so much more relaxed, like after one of Kris's hugs felt, and accepted that this actually was Trent's sister.

"Yowza. You look like you've had a shitty day," Lucy said bluntly.

Bren re-tensed a little, now self-conscious.

"*Luce*," Trent got after her. "Give her a break."

"I'm just sayin'. It seems like she's had a shitty day at work. Maybe she wants to sit down or a cold drink. You should be a nicer host."

"I'm a *great* host . . . except when I forget to set my alarm clock."

"What?" Lucy asked.

"Never mind." he said, looking ashamed.

Bren and Trent shared an uncomfortable knowing look.

"I'll get you a water bottle," Trent offered.

"No, I'm fine," Bren told him. "I'll let you and Lucy hang out."

"No," Lucy said. "I gotta leave now to meet my friends."

"Oh, you have friends in SF?"

"Yeah, I'm staying with some from friends in North Beach." Lucy said. "Don't worry I won't stay here and third-wheel your guys's cuddle thing."

Oh geez. Bren felt her face blush.

"Oh my God. This picture of us is F-ing hilarious," Lucy laughed, holding up the bizarre phone pic of Lucy smiling and O-faced Trent looking horrified.

Bren grinned, sorta seeing the humor in that insane moment.

"I'm totally sending this to mom."

"We should take a better picture for her."

"I'm sending *this* one."

"Will you explain to mom the story behind it?"

"Oh hell yeah," Lucy pipped. "Bren, can I send my mom a picture of you so she knows who Trent's been raving about?"

Bren swung big eyes and a smirk to him. "What have you been saying about me?"

He blushed pink. "Just, you know, that you're my neighbor, and you're really cool."

"And that he thinks you and him should have a book-themed wedding."

"*Luce.*"

OMG, what? Wow. He *does* move fast, she thought, super fast.

He blushed deep scarlet.

Lucy cackled jubilantly at his embarrassment.

Having a sibling looked like fun, but also troublesome to have someone tattling your secrets. *Good gravy.* Trent already talking about a wedding was way too wild. Gotta slow things waaaay down, she thought. Gotta change the subject, fast.

"So, Lucy – "

"Smile."

Click.

Lucy took her picture.

"You gotta smile."

"Luce. Don't bug her."

Bren stretched her lips up for a good first impression to Trent's mom.

Click.

"Oh that's a keeper."

Bren doubted it was a flattering keeper.

"All right. Enough pictures," Trent announced.

"So, Lucy. Trent said you're an actress," Bren asked.

"*Ex*-actress."

"Oh, cut it out," Trent scoffed, rolling his eyes. "You're not quitting."

"I'm quitting."

"You're quitting?"

"She's not quitting."

"I'm quitting."

"After every bad audition we have this conversation," Trent explained.

"Oh?"

"I mean it this time."

"You're totally talented," he encouraged. "Keep auditioning. Show 'em your soul."

"My soul wants out of Hollywood." Lucy insisted. "I'm done fooling myself. I'm no good at being characters," Lucy said. "I'm better at being me."

"You could just be yourself in a movie. Plenty of actors just play themselves," Trent encouraged.

"Trent. I can't act. I screw up every F-ing audition."

"You're not screwing up," her big brother comforted her with smiling positivity. I told you. You're knockin' on doors, and an awesome door is gonna open for you soon. You just gotta keep knockin'."

"My knuckles are tired."

"You gotta keep trying."

"I'm done arguing 'bout this."

"*Bren didn't quit,*" Trent announced.

Bren's eyes shot to him. *What? Huh?*

"Bren came from Boring, Oregon, on a mud farm."

"Um, we didn't grow mud."

"Life said 'stay in the mud, stay and be boring.' But Bren didn't wanna be boring. She wanted to be great. Like Amelia Earhart and Sally Field."

"Sally *Ride*."

"Her too," Trent hyped enthusiastically. Then he wowingly continued building Bren into some kind of Katniss for his sister to emulate, in a grandiose storyteller style. "So, with her soul aspiring for greatness, Bren didn't stay stuck in the mud, she set a target and boldly ventured her mind into a million books and learned and earned lots of scholarships and worked in stores and dedicatedly studied and pulled herself out, out, out of the muck and up into college and did awesome and valiantly graduated and then bravely began knocking on the cold steel doors of San Francisco's mighty, highly selective corporations to get her dream job. Knocking and knocking and knocking, relentlessly, determinedly, facing the bitter sting of rejection over and over, but *never* quitting, always courageously pursuing her dream."

Lucy looked at Bren with raised eyebrows.

Bren bashfully gave her a "he's embellishing a bit" smirk.

But Trent kept soapboxing, cranked to eleven. "And through denials and doubts and depressions Bren devotedly still persevered to manifest her dream into tangible reality, day after daunting day, until *finally*, just when all hope seemed lost, in one *magic* moment, a welcome door swung open for her. She landed a job as a conference manager organizer person at . . . a big office place."

"Corporation."

"Right. Which allowed her to showcase her talents and knowledge and zeal. Unstoppingly from assistant to, uh . . . more important assistant, to manager, to department manager with her own high-rise windowed office in San Francisco, an awesome apartment in Cow Hollow, awesome friends, and an awesome life. Her dream became real, because *she didn't quit.* And all her years of diligent striving through strife and never-giving-up-ness finally, gloriously, paid off!"

Trent stood before his one-person congregation with a smile as wide as his spread arms, bright eyes full of hope, and looking like a breathless Olympian after jumping out of a gold medal-worthy performance.

Lucy just looked at him, unmoved, as if she'd heard this kind of *Rocky Themed hyperbolized* speech from her wordy-as-heck author brother waaaay too many times.

Bren's cheeks blushed red realizing how emotional *she* had become from Trent actually sounding in awe of her rising up from the "mud" to a glass office, her reading, her striving, and all her accomplishments.

She felt really appreciated.

Respected.

Loved.

As if for the very first time by a guy, truly *loved.* Emotions swelled. Face tingled. Eyes watered. And though Lucy wasn't moved, *Bren was!*

Lucy's eyes stared at her weirdly.

So did Trent's.

Bren felt a cool tear sliding down her hot face. *Oh damn.* She smeared it off fast and sniffled.

Too late. Now *really* in the spotlight, Trent's arms came down and his eyes were now focused completely on *her*, as she watched him reach into his back pocket like he was gonna pull out a ring.

What?!

His hand returned . . . with a clean, folded handkerchief.

She exhaled with *relief* and smiled. Bless his hanky having.

He politely handed a hanky to her once again.

She wiped her tear as his feeling-inducing speech continued in a gentle, sweet voice. "And not only did Bren become a successful manager, she became an amazing person."

Oh my, she thought, her throat tightening.

Trent stepped closer to Bren with a grand smile, gazing lovingly at her, smiling at her, seeming impressed and calm and starstuck. "She's got a beautiful heart," he said with seemingly deep sincerity. "And she's kind, and quirky, and feisty, and smarter than me, and beautiful, and inspiring, and all around amazing, and now her life isn't boring at all," he complimented her. "And she makes me want to be my best self for her."

Bren trembled with feelings as more tears slipped out.

"And, she's got a foolish neighbor, me, who almost screwed up all her accomplishments by stupidly not setting my alarm clock last night. And I deeply loathe myself for that screw up, and I vow to be flawlessly organized for you from now on and never let you down again, and hope that you can forgive me, give me another chance, and still hang out with me, and talk and laugh and cuddle with me, 'cause you're the most awesome woman I've ever had the privilege of knowing . . . even though your twitching legs kick my shins as you fall asleep."

She chuckled.

He stood smiling at her with such hope in his glorious eyes.

She stood smiling through her tears. "Ooooooooh, darn you, you amazing man," she thought, feeling Trent and Lucy's eyes on her drenched, messy face. "Darn you and your vastly-improving, perfect words."

She could see him seeing her soul with so much love in his eyes. All her striving and not-giving-up-ness to find a great guy had finally paid off. Trent had opened his welcome door to her, and she had walked through and up and found what felt like . . . home.

Bren and Trent stared into each other's wet, sparkling eyes as sunlight brightened! The floor felt solid. Tears fell. Mouths breathed. Stars exploded! World turned again! Hearts pumped! AND HOPE FILLED THE AIR!

"Oooooookay. Looks like you two are gonna sex," Lucy blurted out. "I'm outta here."

Bren and Trent stayed staring and staring and –

Trent took out his wallet and pulled out a wad of cash. "Luce. Here. Take taxis, not the bus."

Bren stared trance-like at his motions and moving mouth, that mouth that said such incredibly wonderful things to her that she was still wiping tears.

"Oh, stop taking care of me."

"Never," the big brother told his little sis. "Don't do anything more than pot. And don't let Vickie's cynicism get in you and corrupt you. If she gets to be too much then come crash on my couch."

"Oh yeah, you and Bren would love *that.*"

"Oh," Bren said, breaking from her trance and wiping her burning eyes. "Lucy, stay on his couch." Sniff. "That's totally fine if you need to."

Lucy winked playfully at her with a "that's-nice-of-you-but-no-F-ing-way-I'm-gonna-stay-here-while-you-two-are-doin'-the-nasty" look.

Bren grinned.

"And don't let Leslie belittle your accomplishments just because she's insecure," Trent continued parenting his sister. "Remember, *you're* the one brave enough to climb the mountain while she's still lost in the woods."

"Ugh," Lucy snarked. "Enough with the hokey storybook imagery."

"Bren likes my story imagery."

"That's 'cause she's *in love with you,*" Lucy blurted. "Why else would she be so mad for catching you with a girl?"

Bren's shocked face stared at Trent's shocked face.

Totally uncomfortable silence.

"Ooookay. Now I'm *really* outta here." Lucy grabbed her suitcase and bounded down Trent's stairs and out of the building while Trent stared lovingly at Bren.

Chapter 12 – night

THURSNIGHT

"So . . . that happened." Trent's joke lightly echoed around his bare-walled living room full of sunlight, as he smiled at her.

Bren grinned.

Wild silence between them.

Her heart thumped so hard she wondered if he could hear it as she stared at him, now breathing both calmer and exciteder.

His beautiful eyes looked at her filled with believable love, and caring, and concern. But he had absolutely nothing to be concerned about.

She trusted him.

It was official. She now trusted him. Easily now. Completely now. No doubt, no fear, no worry. His behavior with her, with Julia, and with Lucy had convinced her. This cloud of misery she had been living under for a month was blown away. Now she saw clear blue skies as crystal blue as his eyes. She felt like she could move around freely with him, be happy with him, and she totally wanted to! She exhaaaaled any remaining doubt and reveled in this wonderful, wonderful relief and belief in Trent, and love. Yes, the fairytale love in books was actually possible in real life. Trent was proving it. And trust was possible too.

His sister's confirmation was the last safety check she needed before their airplane of love could fly. Probably the most ridiculous metaphor ever, but that's what it felt like. What a heck of a boarding procedure it had all been to finally get to this magical moment.

Instead of doing the normal dating thing, it was like they had super-dated, cuddling together for five nights in a row, without sex to mess with their minds or feelings, and bonded faster than any guy she had dated for a month. And those other guys weren't even close in amazingness compared to Trent, which intensified their magic even more!

So now, here they were, convinced, alone, and ready to fly.

She smiled at him, big.

His eyebrows raised, curious.

Her eyes smoldered at him as she stepped forward, towards her loving cuddler, and . . . breezed by him, clacking across his living room, and unbuttoning her shirt as she entered his golden sunlit bedroom. Her shoes silenced on his pretty blue carpet and she kicked them off, pulled off her shirt, unbuckled, unzipped, and slipped out of her skirt. She noticed there were now four alarm clocks on his nightstand. She smiled and shed her tights and bra, sensing that he saw, and wearing nothing but undies, ready for funsies, slipped into his bed.

She watched him walk his big smile into his bedroom too. He pulled closed his curtains and his book-scented room dimmed. He funny-danced around his bed, hurrying out of his shirt, and his shoes, socks, and jeans, posed in his undies like a flirt, then slipped into bed with her, their bare chests finally touching, wanting each other soooooooo muching!

Laying on their sides.

Under his covers, embracing.

Glorious heat.

Staring at each other.

Totally trusting.

Her hands clutched him in bliss.

She pulled herself close towards his smile.

Her thoughts spun.

Her feelings felt, deeply, wildly.

She felt new feelings, intense new feelings.

And stopped.

And felt.

And realized.

Uh oh.

Their love plane . . . had a new problem.

Now, with all of her doubts about trust accomplished, there was something on the runway, something unexpected; a hidden feeling underneath; now she felt something new: *anger.*

Not at sweet Trent, but at something else she wasn't sure of.

A new mystery.

Dammit.

She thought she had solved everything.

Her smile faded as she slowly slid away from his concerned face and heavy breathing.

Poor Trent. She was really putting him through the ringer.

But she didn't wanna hurt this wonderful, caring man with what she was now feeling. She didn't want to take out her anger on him. For some reason, this moment just didn't feel right to shed the rest of their clothes quite yet. She looked into his loving, honest eyes, and put her palm to his hard, amazing-tastic chest, over his heart, his th-thumping th-thumping heart, and smiled lovingly back at him, hopefully letting him know that she cared for him as much as he cared for her. "I'm so sorry," she exhaled. "I'm torturing you. I don't mean to torture you. I'm so sorry."

He immediately sat up and caressed her hair and arm. "There's nothing to be sorry about," he assured her. "If you're not ready then you're not ready. It's all right. It's too soon. It's all right."

She flopped onto her back and stared up at his ceiling, feeling frustration, love, guilt, horniness, and this unexpected *anger*, at Greg, at . . . something more. "I don't know what's going on with me. I don't know why I'm not ready."

"It's all right, Bren," he comforted. "You don't need to give me a reason. There's no pressure here. Sex doesn't need to be on our to do list today. I'm not going anywhere."

She believed him.

"What can I do to help?" he asked.

She exhaled out, so damn confused, not even knowing how to help herself. She stared up at the silent horizon line where his ceiling met his wall; no answers there. She was going to have to figure this new mess of feelings out on her own. She laid in his bed almost naked with him, so close to her life being awesome, if it wasn't for this new, stupid obstacle of anger, that she hand't expected and didn't understand.

So she thought about it.

For a while.

In silence.

He patiently, lovingly, amazingly caressed her hair, cuddled her side, turned on the pretty Christmas lights decorating his book shelves creating a comforting atmosphere, ordered dinner delivered, ate with her, laid with her, and was the most perfect guy in the world for her.

"I like your new blue couch."

"Thank you," he said, returning from putting their leftovers in his kitchen and got back into bed with her, wearing only his boxer briefs. "Sorry you had to see it under such awkward circumstances."

She nodded.

"Next I'll install the skating rink you suggested."

She chuckled. She took a breath, and tried to finally find words for what the heck she was feeling.

"When I saw you on your couch, with who I thought was another woman . . . I was so *angry.*"

"I'm sorry."

"You don't need to be sorry," she said. "You were just fine. But the anger." It was an anger undefined, an anger she didn't want to accidentally take out on wonderful Trent. She had to sort this all out, and feel ready for him, free of this fury before she could let their cuddles become kisses and looking for earring positions.

"It's like Verne's Journey to the Center of the Earth; I didn't realize there was this whole underworld in me, of hot molton anger about stuff. When I saw you with her it erupted out of me like Mt. Tambora. I don't wanna spew all my lava anger at you, so we need to go slow again. I hope you're all right with that."

"Of course I'm all right with that. You're the woman I wanna be with. We'll go at your pace. I don't want you to spew on me. Well, not with lava."

She smirked. *Zing of heat.* Best to cool down. "I'm sorry to talk about my ex-boyfriend in your bed."

"You can talk about whatever you want my bed," he said.

She smiled at him through her hurt. She wanted to kiss him so badly just for saying that. But not now, not like this. She touched his arm instead, and kept her hand on him, for support, as she continued figuring all this out.

"I'm really sorry," he said. "I didn't mean for Lucy to talk about love and weddings. I was just talking my thoughts with her. You excite me, and I'm totally going too fast for you."

Bren grinned. "Out of curiosity, what kind of wedding did you plan for us?"

He grinned, and blushed. "I was thinking a big library would be a cool place for us."

"Oh. A library wedding would be fun. I bet it would smell amazing."

"Totally. Right? Perfect for us smell-loving bibliosmias people."

She chuckled. "Maybe we could get a famous author to officiate."

"Oh yeah. Brilliant. And – " He laughed. "Your bridesmaids could dress up as Jane Austen characters and my groomsmen could dress up as Jules Verne characters."

She laughed. "Yes. I love it. Oh my gosh. The guests can dress up too, as literary characters."

"At the reception Juliet might sit next to Frodo."

"Scrooge might dance with Mary Poppins."

"Bridget Jones with Humpty Dumpty."

"What?" she said. "I think Bridget can do better."

"Robin Hood?"

"Zorro."

"Oh."

"I've always had a thing for Zorro," she admitted.

"Really? His mask? His sword? His mustache?"

"He's dashing."

Trent paused. "Am I dashing?"

Warm rush tingled through her, as she stared at his kind eyes, his kind, dashing eyes.

She smiled and nodded at him.

He smiled big.

He was Darcy, Zorro, and goofy Charlie Chaplin all at once. He was loving, but not pressuring. Smart, but not smug. Manly, but gentle. A good brother, a good son. He got along with her friends. A fantastic cuddler, massager, and he vowed to be a better alarm-setter. He was caring, fun, and incredibly F-ing hot. He was absolutely perfect for her. So what the heck was holding her back from ravaging him right now?!

"Once upon a time," he said.

She grinned. Of course, he'd know the perfect thing to say.

"In the year 4012, astronauts left Earth in a polka dot spaceship to travel to a planet called – "

"Awesomest," Bren said. "Planet Awesomest was the awesomest planet ever, and everything was awesome. Everything was beautiful, everyone was nice, and there were no problems whatsoever. No misunderstandings. No cheaters. No confusion; all questions were answered, and everyone was really good to each other and happy."

"That sounds nice."

"Totally."

"And there was free cheesecake," he added.

"The best cheesecake in the universe."

Trent continued their bedtime story. "The crew of the polka dot spaceship, some of them were human, and some of them were puppets," Trent said. "Long ago humans thought that machines and robots would be the next major inhabitant of Earth, but it turned out to be puppets. And for a thousand years humans and puppets had learned to get along with each other in peace. And now they were space traveling together to Planet Awesomest."

"But," Bren said, "during the trip the astronauts got into a farcical marshmallow fight, and one of the marshmallows floated into the electrical system and malfunctioned the space ship, diverting it off course, and the crew had to land on an unexpected planet for repairs, Planet – "

"Funny Sound," Trent added. "On Planet Funny Sound everything had a funny sound. And when their ship landed on the ground it sounded like *sploosh*. And when they walked around the planet their footsteps sounds like duck *quacks*."

Bren chuckled. "So the human and puppet crew *quacked* their way to the nearest Funny Sound City where car horns sounded like slide whistles and the people's language sounded like squeaky toy sounds. And the crew couldn't understand the squeaky toy people."

Trent chuckled. "Luckily, one of the puppets spoke squeaky toy and was able to translate that they're ship needed repairs."

"Unluckily, the puppet translated incorrectly and accidentally told the funny sound people that their genitals were ugly."

Trent laughed. "Luckily, the translator was able to realize the mistake and retranslate correctly and complement their genitals."

"Unluckily, the funny sound people didn't have the gear for the repairs they needed and the crew was stuck on Planet Funny Sound."

"Luckily, a funny sound spaceship was scheduled to go to Planet Awesomest and the crew could catch a ride there."

"Unluckily, it wasn't scheduled to leave for another 20 years, so the human and public crew had to steal the funny sound spaceship, and fly into the air with a tremendous deflating balloon fart sound."

Trent laughed. "Luckily, when they landed on Planet Awesomest with a *bloop* sound, they were able to reprogram the ship so it could fly back to Planet Funny Sound, and all was forgiven."

"No it wasn't," Bren challenged. "The funny sound people were pissed off and flew a squadron of their ships to Planet Awesomest to give the human/puppet crew a strong squeaking to."

"But because nothing bad ever happened on Planet Awesomest the funny sound people changed their minds when they got there and all was forgiven."

"No it wasn't."

"Yes it was."

"No it wasn't."

"It's Planet Awesomest. Nothing bad can happen there."

"Well . . . *dammit!*" Bren inhaaaaled deeply and vented out a huge exhale, but slightly smirked, realizing she was arguing ridiculousness. But she still felt uptight, and stared hard the ceiling/wall line in his bedroom.

"Bren," Trent said softly. "Is everything all right?"

She exhaled again. Feelings swirled. Answers seem nonexistent.

His hand gently caressed her back.

A really nice feeling. There was some awesomeness here on Earth. She began breathing normal again. She looked in his eyes, his eyes full of caring. She wished she had an answer for his question. "I don't know if everything's all right, or if I'll ever feel all right, because I'm not sure why I wanted the funny sound people to be angry."

Trent continued gently caressing nicely. "I don't know either," he said softly. "But maybe the free cheesecake made them happy again."

Bren grinned.

"I wish I could make you happy."

"You gave me cuddles, built bookshelves for me, bought a nice bed, and got me a nice chicken dinner tonight. You've made me pretty darn happy."

"It doesn't seem like enough."

She nodded. "I appreciate all you've done. There's nothing more you can do. I gotta figure stuff out myself. I just hope you won't get tired of waiting for me."

He hugged her into a delightful embrace.

She felted loved, and slowly, more relaxed.

"I'm here," he sweetly whispered.

She smiled, but silently worried: for how much longer?

"Once upon a time," he said.

She relaxed into their skin-to-skin cuddle, let him solo story-tell, and let her mind clear of everything fizzing around in there. She really needed to figure things out, but not right now. She needed to feel his arms around her, and his comforting voice lulling her, so she could fall asleep. Her eyes closed, listening to her loving neighbor's improved silly bedtime story skills.

Trent softly told her of the ancient continent of Buttocks, a round continent with a crease through its center, dividing the inhabitants into two separate tribes: the Booty-Shakers and the Tushy-Twerkers. And every June the two tribes would meet on either side of the big crease and throw Frisbees back-and-forth to each other. Until one day, someone started building a bridge on one cheek of the continent, and so the other tribe decided to starting build a bridge on their cheek too, and eventually the two building projects met and formed a bridge over the great crease, and now the two tribes could travel back and forth and share each other's cheeky civilizations, and they could all dance together, shaking and twerking. And then the inhabitants of continent Buttocks invented their own Olympic games that they called the Olymp-ocks.

Bren grinned. Wow, he was really going for it tonight, trying to get her smile. Bless him and his bizarre sense of humor, exactly what she needed to help her calm . . . and stay positive . . . and slowly fall asleep . . .

Chapter 13 – day

FRIDAY

Trent lightly snored. Cars softly passed. Birds blithely chirpped, enjoying their bird-orgy.

On her back, Bren blinked her eyes open to see pink dawn light-painting his living room, and four alarm clocks on his nightstand and dresser all reading 4:47am.

She had woken before being woken, and felt more awake than ever.

Trent wasn't.

She watched him sleep beside her, this amazing man, and a kind helper.

He had taken her to this moment, she thought, seeing everything much clearer, now that trusting again wasn't an issue, and new pains were emerging. His companionship had flown her from heartache all the way up here to almost happiness, a much better view of things. So proud of what she had accomplished in life on her own, and with friends and family, and she felt appreciative that this guy had also helped her to this new revelatory point. Safe and warm beneath his covers, she remembered their journey from book bantering strangers, to neighbors, to cuddlers, to friends, to bedtime storytellers, to lovebirds without the lovemaking. They'd come so far so fast, and now they were here, with him ready to love, and her almost ready. But a cloud still blocked their sunlight, a dreadful cloud she feared yet yearned to confront, right now.

Gently she peeled off his covers, feeling the morning air chill her naked chest and arms and legs. She slipped into her clothes and gathered her bag and keys as quietly as she could. She kindly tried not to wake him, stepping her feet where his carpet didn't squeak. She made it to his doorway.

"Bren?"

Damn. She turned around.

Bare-chested, he rolled toward her and leaned on his elbow, rubbing his eyes awake, then looking at her the way she had always wanted a lover to look at her, as he gave her a grin. "Have an awesome day."

So much goodness warmed her. So much love she wanted to give him. But couldn't. Not yet. "You too," her heart shared to him, her desires longing, but her brain governing, and her soul needing. Tearing herself away, she turned, with a new plan, and began today's most unusual to do list.

* * * *

She and Kris wished each other happy Weed Your Garden Day via text.

Bren grinned, then focused on today's run, a super intense run. Jogging through the brisk morning air beside the wide Marina Green park, giving herself time to think everything through, as she listened to the mechanical steady pace of her happy yellow sneakers, as fast as her nervously thumping heart, while her mind mulled. There was still time to turn back.

She so wished she could enjoy the gorgeousness of the morning. The rising sunlight behind her bursted the Golden Gate Bridge bright red in front of her, the city's big grass field beside her left shimmered green, and the bay water to her right waved tranquil blue, but the splendor was lost on her.

With each rapid stride west she hurled herself closer to her destination, hearing Trent's words in her head: "Have an awesome day." If she jogged back to her apartment, got dressed, and went to Kris's guest reception brunch, and then the rehearsal dinner it would be a productive day. But it wouldn't be awesome. It would still be living in this cloud that hadn't lifted.

No.

No more.

That cloud had to go.

This totally needed to be an awesome day, so she could have an awesome life, and an awesome love. And the only way it could all be awesome is if she kept running forward.

She came to the end of the Marina Green, her borderline, that since her breakup she would never cross, where she had been turning around for a month. But today she raced past the edge and defiantly into the danger zone.

She looked at her watch. 6:28am. She flew faster!

Running on rage, she picked up speed to a sprint, pushing harder, breathing deeper, and now *very* focused. Dodging cars, she ran across Marina Boulevard's four lanes and continued running west up the sidewalk beside the fancy houses, her long shadow stretched out in front of her. All kinds of book references to shadows came to mind: Plath and Jung and Alcott and Martin, and got her thinking and seeing possiblilities. A metaphor for her dark side. This could be a symbol of the dark pained self inside her. Or this shadow-Bren was more reasonably the absence of light blocked by her opaque body. Whatever shadow-Bren was, she was inescapeable, forever linked, like bad with good, yin and yang, hurt and love. Why did there always have to be hurt with good stuff. That's a crummy way to do things, she angrily thought, fueling her to run even faster towards her dark self, seeing her shadow, actually seeing herself doing something wild, either making a mistake or making progress. Either way, she was now committed and flying forward, and feeling like she was finally doing something to fix her life, and it felt empowering!

Skidding like a cartoon character around the corner she veered south, barreling up pretty Baker Street, passing more beautiful houses on her left, hopefully with beautiful relationships inside, and on her right the beautiful picturesque Palace of Fine Arts. Memories of picnics on the manicured grass, feeding the majestic swans gliding through the lovely lagoon, gazing at the gorgeous pillars and massive dome, and memories of her smiling enviously at the brides and grooms in pretending-to-be-virgin-white dresses and pretending-to-be-sturdy starched tuxes as they pretended staged smiles for the beautiful wedding pictures taken in the beautiful location to get everything beautiful so they start a beautiful life together beautifully.

She hoped the best for them, but wondered if there could be so much light without shadows.

She swung left and cartooned again around another corner, zooming east, and bolting up Beach street between its beautiful two-story houses, her shadow now chasing her as she faced the blinding sun, but undaunted she continued, determined to shine light on all the her hidden questions and dark mysteries messing up her mind.

Then, right on time, she saw her target: Greg.

If only he had been as faithful to her as he was to his work schedule, predictably pulling down his garage door at exactly 6:30am and striding across his driveway and mounting his motorcycle. A dark helmet covered his face. He looked like a menacing masked monster. How perfect. Closer and closer she braved toward the monster, towards her personal dragon. This part of the Marina was a residential maze and he was her Minotaur, part man part beast, out of the maze of her mind and now in the flesh, like Theseus, but without a thread; just her body, heart, and head, she was facing him, in reality. This was happening. This was real. Her heart slammed. She sweated hot. Chills and rage and fear, oh my. But she kept running, so sick of running away, now running towards him, until she found herself in front of him, full stop. Blocking his escape, forcing his attention, challenging his danger, and . . . and . . . unable to breathe!

Maybe she was defeated before she could even fight, as she leaned forward, gasping, panting, weezing, desperate for breath.

The monster's helmet came off.

The face of a shocked and worried ex-boyfriend met her eyes. He hopped off his motorcycle. He ditched his helmet and stretched out his hands.

She stretched out hers to keep him away as she panicked and heaved for air. She struggled to stay standing; she would be damned if she fell to her knees before her actual nemesis. Like her favorite heroes, always prepared, her fingers fumbled fast through her belt pack and found her inhaler. She whipped out her lifesaver and sucked in a hit! Her "stay away" hand still protected herself from his touch that might overwhelm her feverish feelings too much. She would save herself by breathing and breathing and breathing through her slowly opening airways . . . until she could finally function normally again, and stop feeling foolish in front of her ex, her nightmare, her epicenter of hurt, the guy she wanted most to not see her be weak.

"Bren," he dared to speak her name so sweetly. "Are you all right?"

She nodded about her breathing, then shook her head about her life, noticing how lightheaded she was and out of sorts. So out of sorts that she now struggled intellectually to remember why she had run there, which was of course his next question. She stood, racking her brain and catching her breath, fighting death, and staring at the killer of their relationship. Their eyes saw each other, remembering all those memories they shared, so many good memories too, so many good feelings, and one really bad feeling, and remembering why she was there.

She could now breathe a little better, and inhaled to verbally jab pain at him.

"I'm mad at you!" she yelled at Greg's confused eyes, hot, embarrassed, and thrilled to finally vent. "I pride myself on being calm and in control, and above petty nonsense. But I'm mad at you. I'm angry. I'm *furious*. And I can't move on with my life until I say it to your face."

His face stared stunned at her.

"You cheated on me. You lied and screwed around behind my back. You disregarded our relationship. You disrespected me. You ruined us."

His eyes whipped around the neighborhood. His hands told her to quiet down.

"I gave you my heart, my trust. I bought you a book and a balloon."

"I told you I was sorry."

"It doesn't matter." She had her breathing back, and used it. "When we ended, a revelation started. I see the world differently now. I have felt sad and miserable and broken for a month. But I haven't been able to dispel the anger. All this horribleness has lived in me for a month because I haven't been able to tell Kris and talk it out and vent. I can't love again until I get this anger out of me, and at you, so you finally understand how much you hurt me!"

He stood there, looking at her, listening, and maybe finally understanding.

It felt *soooo damn good* to release this anger, empty it out of her so she had space to let new happiness in. Yes, finally! She felt hope, hope that she could now move on.

Suddenly a sliding noise whooshed above her and a voice interrupted her euphoria. "What's going on?"

Bren looked up, and saw a woman's face and draping hair leaning out the open window of Greg's second-story bedroom and looking down on them like Rapunzel. Bren's mouth opened too as she recognized Abby, his ex, the woman she'd caught him kissing a month ago, and felt herself refill with venom. The visual of the last time she saw Abby popped into her mind, the man-stealing minx. Now she had caught them again, living together?! Greg once again had a dumb look of "uh-oh" on his face. Deja vu. He hadn't changed at all. Only a week ago he pleaded "I still love you" but he was still with Abby? He was *still* lying to Bren. Abby wore Greg's bathrobe and had clearly spent the night, one short week after Greg had ambushed her at Holly's party to almost convincingly proclaim the depth of his continuing love.

Not so deep it appeared.

He was an astonishing asshole. What if she had believed him last week and went back to him? Would he still secretly be boffing Abby on the side? *Oh.* This was too much. Nothing he told her was true; there was no use yelling at him anymore. He had to be shown, to get him to understand the pain he caused her.

She breathed big.

And used her brain instead of her fists.

"I want my *Happiness* back," she ordered.

Greg looked lost. "I don't know how to give that to you," he said stupidly.

"Go upstairs and get it."

"Huh?"

"My Danielle Steel book *Happiness*. I want it back."

"Oh," he said, realizing. "That's why you came here?"

"It is *now*," she said, proud of herself for thinking this up on the spot.

He relented, probably fearing she would make an even bigger scene in front of all his neighbors, and let himself go off schedule and he rushed back toward his apartment that he now shared with *Abby*, while checking his watch to see how late he would be for work.

She watched him.

Greg went inside.

Bren scowled up at Abby's scowl, then tilted her head in defiance. Then Bren hopped on Greg's motorcycle. He was foolish to leave his keys in the ignition, foolish to teach her how to ride it, and foolish to go get her book (which was already back at her apartment).

"Noooo!" she heard Abby holler. Then she heard Greg's engine rumble to life like a big "SCREW YOU" to Greg and Abby!

Her neurons fired fast too, trying to remember what he taught her. *Clutch? Yes, pull clutch. Then, um, kick it out of neutral. Then release clutch? Yep. Slowly. Rolling forward. Give it throttle.*

Vrrrroooooooom!

She was off, slipping from the feel of Greg's fingers on her shoulder. *Wow.* She gave it gas to get away. His bike roared. Her adrenaline soared! And she burst down the street like a rocket! His furious face in the rearview mirror got smaller.

"Breeeen!" Greg's yell tried to overpower her thunder.

But the roar of his window-shaking motor overpowered him. And it felt really good to finally *roarrrr!* She throttled loud! She made a scene! She let everyone around them know the truth she had been hiding for weeks, that she was really angry at him!

She wobbled a bit, but quickly got her balance and got the hang of riding once again. The neighborhood was a maze up ahead. But she knew one way out. She clutched, braked and cranked the metal horse's handles into a U-turn, skidding her around to face Greg's rage, as he stood flabbergasted a hundred feet away. Now he looked like a monster without his helmet. A furious monster; his true self? She knew she had taken away what he loved even more than women. His big metal penis turned beautifully and the tables had turned beautifully too. His pain was her pleasure. Now she had power over *him!* She felt *electric!* He stood, staring her down, center street. Was he really sure he wanted to play chicken with her. She wanted to find out who he really was. She released the brake and throttled, thrusting forward, about to joust with the jerk messing up her life. Full speed ahead. Her mph climbed, making it clear she was not going to stop.

Would he actually try to block her? Grab her? Risk hurting her again?

His hands flung out, ordering her to stop!

No, she thought.

Vrrrroooooooooooooooooom!

Right toward him!

His face red. His mouth cussing. His hands out to grab her.

Closer. Closer! Closer!!

She *dared* him!

He spun away.

She flew passed him!

Thank goodness she didn't have to veer; she got to be the strong one.

"Ha ha!" she cackled, not looking back, knowing she now had power over him, knowing that felt fantastic, knowing she was hurting him back non-violently, knowing revenge felt so gooood, but not knowing where the heck she was going, except out, out of his reach, teaching him a lesson by taking his second most prized possession away from him. She had hoped that in the past month that Greg had learned from his mistake and matured. But with Abby there, clearly he hadn't learned his lesson. Maybe taking his toys away would finally teach him that he can't hurt people and get away with it. She got away with his bike and bee-lined west, straight toward the Palace of Fine Arts, and the golden sun had her back.

She careened the corner to the left, back onto Baker with his stolen treasure, roaring the engine, freaking out the swans, disturbing the perfection with the reality of love-gone-wrong, passing North Point Street and Bay and Francisco too. Then a curve to the right suggested what to do, and she did it. Bren broke right, braked, then burst out into traffic, taking 101 west, taking a vacation from unproductive safe normalness, seeing her stretching shadow in front her doing this *crazy* thing as she zoomed like crazy up the highway with Greg's engine thundering fast and powerful between her legs, at one with such power, riding chaos with her thighs, like horses and dirt bikes in high school, like she wanted to do with Trent. She loved this powerful feeling!

The speed, the freedom, the wind through her hair! For the first time in forever she felt so in charge! Though for once in her life she had no plan. She was making it up as she went. And this spontaneous in-the-moment living felt exhilarating!

This was crazy!

And enthralling!

She spontaneously zoomed west passed the Lucasfilm buildings, the Presidio, Crissy Field, and then north towards total *freedom!*

The blue bay sparkled out towards her right as she rode away from all the residential buildings. The morning commute was puttering along the other direction, but her lane heading out of the city was wide open and waiting. Then, tingles thrilled through her body as she saw the huge passionate red towers of the bridge in the distance in front of her, beckoning her to freedom. She accepted by forcing the engine harder. This was like nothing she had ever done. Exhilarating. So alive. So powerful. Loving this power so much that she wanted to feel even more power over anger, as much screw-you-to-everything-making-her-feel-bad power as she could feel as she twisted the throttle and roared her passion over the beautifully massive Golden Gate Bridge.

The air whooshing on her was so cold, but she was still hot with adrenaline as she rocketed over the 1.7 mile span, over the bay, the brisk rushing wind flailing her hair back like wild streamers, as she made her way through the misty morning cloud. She knew the city was to her right. She knew the hills of the Marin Headlands were to her left. She remembered staring at those hills from Holly's roof and wanting to escape to them. She finally was! A new thrill came over her as she now realized exactly where she wanted to go and exactly what she wanted to do.

Zooming from the bridge like a hotshot she banked right exiting off the highway, twisted and turned around the roads towards the west, and roared, up and up and up, non-violently taking the high road up into the hills, up into fog. She had never come up there before. She had gawked at these picturesque hills from the safe city, but now they were real. She had escaped!

Her adrenaline still flowed while flying past tourists taking pictures of the bridge and her gorgeous city that she left behind her as she tore westward toward her shadow with new purpose, swerving along the winding rural roads over the back of the dragon-like landscape, thinking of nothing and no one but her own well-being for once.

Roaring upward through the morning fog, higher and higher, the vapors thinner and thinner, until *swoosh!* She broke through the fog and into the clear. The bright road and golden hills and vast blue ocean lay before her, the whole rest of the west clear as eternity. And another clarity occurred; seeing the grand horizon, she finally saw the real target of all her angst, and on this awesome day, after escalating decades, while she had the adrenaline, it was time for a showdown!

High above everything, the air was cold, chilling her lungs enjoyably with true, uncluttered freshness. It smelled like clean honesty, reinvigorating her, and with a new sense of purpose she throttled straight for that eternity she saw ahead.

She followed the curvy coastline north as fast and loud as she could push the bike without tipping over. She was eager and nothing hindered her. She had a single focus now.

The cliffs to her left towered high over the drop. She looked and looked, then finally found an ideal spot. She steered hard off the winding road and skidded onto the dirt. Down the long slope she went toward the cliff, straight toward the edge, her heart racing, her hands gripping the handlebars, her body sweating and shaking over the rough terrain, her eyes staring straight ahead toward the edge, all her anger, all her pain, fueling her action, able to jump off Greg's motorcycle and roll it over the cliff for glorious revenge!

But . . . instead, she grabbed the brakes and careened into a violent skid, sliding. SLINDING!! *S L I I I I I I I I I D I N G ! ! ! !*

AND STOPPED!

A dust storm flew over the cliff's edge, into the air.

She and his motorcycle stayed safe, as she sat, shaking, panting, white knuckles gripping, one shoe on the dirt, wheels parallel to the cliff's colossal drop, and feeling full of *POWER!*

Her frantic heart beat as fast as the motor's pistons!

She breathed . . . and breathed . . . staring hard at the horizon.

Finally ready for this, in the bright sun, she kicked out the kickstand, dismounted and gently rested his bike upright. Still breathing hard, she dared to venture closer to edge and eyed the violent waves crashing against the unforgivable rocks far below, like the ocean licking it's chops. She appreciated the solid ground more than ever and stayed planted on the plateau, denying nature the satisfaction of his bike and a vengeful deed, deciding to be better than that, to not be completely bonkers, showing life that *she* was better than that, better than pain-causing life.

Furious, she glared at the massive thin horizon line between the ocean and sky, a horizon line that looked like a very big mouth, and the real target of all her anger.

"Hey, life, what the fuck?!"

Life didn't answer, the mouth didn't move, for obvious reasons. But she gave it hell anyway.

"I'm mad at you! Yeah, *you*. You're the one I'm really mad at. Letting crappy things happen. Letting cheaters cheat and break hearts. Letting Kris fracture her arm last year rock climbing. Letting that girl stain Holly's sofa with her spray tan. Letting Calli's vibrator embarrassingly fall out of her purse and vibrate all over the courtroom floor during jury duty. Letting Trent's dad have a heart attack from an ice cream truck. Letting horrible things happen in this world, even to nice people. What the fuck is wrong with you?! This isn't how things should be. Things should be better, nicer, more organized."

Life let her vent.

"I always knew that things weren't perfect. But when I caught Greg kissing his ex-girlfriend any hope for perfection *broke.* Now I really realize how imperfect everything is. And it really sucks. And I'm really pissed off about it!"

Life let her be pissed off.

"I'm falling in love with Trent. And, amazingly, maybe foolishly, I'm really starting to trust him. And I'm pretty darn sure I can trust Mark will be good to Kris and be a good husband to her. But I don't trust *you,* life. I don't know what horribleness you're going to let happen next. Now that I really know how indifferent you are, I'm worried that I have to be really careful, and aware, and ready. But we shouldn't have to live like that. Life, you should be like a great story: full of meaning and providence and helpful answers. Your silence is not helpful. You should be better than this. Why can't you be more loving? Why can't you make me feel as safe and cared for and not alone as Trent makes me feel?"

Life stayed silent.

"Nothing? No response? Still indifferent?"

Of course she wasn't expecting the horizon line to actually split open like a mouth and boom an answer to her, and if it had she would have totally popped a poop! But no symbolic bird flew near her as a sign that life was answering her, like in novels. No gentle gust of whispering wind. Nothing. No helpfulness at all. No love. Just silence. She stood, the morning sun warm on her back, so close to the cliff's edge that she didn't have a shadow anymore, feeling liberated of a lot of the anger she had yelled out, clearer, like the open sky. She inhaled lots more clarity and exhaled out lots more angst.

"Well, I'm not indifferent, even if you are. I'm better than your silence. I care about people, about making the world good. I help. I tell people things that I've read to help them. I straighten people's pictures on their wall when they're crooked. I tell people when they've got pasta sauce on their face so they can wipe it off. I don't stay silent. Well . . . except for this past month I've stayed silent, to help Kris be happy, to not disturb her wedding with my drama. At least I think that silence was a good thing."

Damn, she thought. Should she have not stayed silent, like indifferent life? Should she have done better? She stood, wondering, breathing, sweating, and feeling so much better for having vented out anger at Greg and at life and not having stayed silent. Now she knew how unhelpful and heartless silence was, and she really wondered if she had done the right thing by keeping quiet for a month.

She looked out at the unanswering, unhelpful horizon, and knew she wanted to be better than that, and knew she no longer wanted to be silent!

* * * *

The fog was gone and the sun was bright. The Golden Gate Bridge's suspension cables stretched out to Bren like welcoming arms as she walked back to SF triumphantly across the threshold between the land of epiphany and everyday San Francisco. Wind blew whistling pitches past her ears and she likened the sound to brass horns blowing a victory song for her.

She thought that mythologist Joseph Campbell might be proud of her. Like all those brave mythological adventurers, she had bravely ventured out of her normal world, confronted powers, gained new knowledge, and was returning home to share that vital knowledge with the world, like a hero. She *felt* like one.

After eight years of living in San Francisco, she had never walked across the Golden Gate Bridge. She was always too busy or crossing it in a car. She was glad her first time doing it could be so meaningful. She wished her first time *doing it* in the flatbed of Dwayne's uncomfortable truck on a sweat-smelling football jersey could have been as meaningful. Perhaps that inelegance really kick-started her longing for a fairytale life, an impossible life? She still didn't know.

The bridge's tall reddish towers passing over her never seemed so beautifully majestic until now. The stretching bay below her never sparkled so magically. The shimmering citadel to her far left never appeared so promising.

Colors looked brighter. Air smelled fresher. She felt enlighteneder.

She smiled caringly at all the people she marched past: joggers, bike riders, and gawking tourists. She wanted to share with all of them this feeling of euphoric insight she now carried with her, and couldn't wait to share her no-more-silence revelation with her friends!

* * * *

After a zillion-mile journey back to SF on foot she finally reached Kris's new home in this stylish Marina apartment building on busy Chestnut Street. She was so thirsty and hungry and her legs ached from the long journey, but excited, as she buzzed Kris's door buzzer.

Holly answered.

Holly sounded thrilled to hear Bren's voice.

Holly came down. *Fast!* Wearing a royal blue party dress.

Calli tagged along wearing a scarlet skirt.

Bren watched her friends shock and gawk at her been-through-a-lot-this-morning weariness and sweaty jogging attire as Bren stretched her arms open wide to be held and comforted.

"*What the flipping heck is going on?*" Holly whisper-yelled at Bren in a not-as-welcoming-as-Bren-expected tone and not hugging her.

Uh oh. Bren wondered what Holly knew. "I'm so happy to see you two," Bren exclaimed.

They didn't look quite as happy.

"Greg called me at 7am this morning and was freaking out that you stole his motorcycle. Did you? Did you steal his motorcycle? Did you?"

"Yeah, did you?" Calli echoed excitedly.

"I did."

"What the *flipping hell?*"

"Yeah, what the *flipping hell?*"

"I was angry at him."

"So you stole his motorcycle?"

"Yes."

"Are you crazy?"

"No. For the first time I feel sane."

"Then why did you do something *in*sane?"

"Yeah, why?"

"Why are you doing lunatic stuff a day before Kris's wedding?"

"I needed to."

"Not *now*. Bren, I had to talk Greg down for ten minutes and get him to not call the police on you."

"Oh," Bren didn't think he would go *that* far. "Does Kris know?"

"No. I promised him that I'd get you to return his motorcycle if he and Abby promised to not tell anyone about this so Kris won't find out."

"And they actually haven't told anyone? They must not want people to know the whole story."

"What's the whole story? Where is Greg's motorcycle?" Holly asked.

Bren did not give her friend silence. Bren courageously told Holly and Calli what she did with Greg's bike and why and finally told her friends all about catching Greg cheating and keeping her heartbreak a secret for a month! Her words fell out of her like a windstorm, *finally* unloading everything she had been hiding inside her for a miserable month. It felt *so good* for Bren to get all these pent up secrets out of herself and into her friend's ears!

Holly and Calli's mouths dropped open!

"Oh, Bren," Holly exclaimed, throwing her arms around her, so tight, actually not caring if her pretty dress touched Bren's sweaty, dirty jogging clothes.

Calli hugged Bren too.

Oooooooob. This hug felt so wonderful. Bren exhaled huge as she embraced them back, feeling such relief and love to finally share with her friends all her hidden sorrows.

"I'm so sorry," Holly said.

"I'm sorry too," Calli said.

"Thank you," Bren said to them, as they all embraced on the sunny sidewalk, feeling so relieved and loved and finally free, as people passed by their embrace with their dogs, baby strollers, and Gap shopping bags.

"Does a motorcycle vibrate your hoo-ha?" Calli asked.

Holly came out of their hug. "I knew it."

"Knew what?" Bren said.

"I just knew Greg cheated on you."

"You did? How?"

"I'm the Marina's information central. I know stuff about everyone or I figure it out, and I figured he cheated on you."

Bren tensed. "Did you tell anyone? Does anyone else know?"

"I don't think so."

"What gave it away?"

"I just had a sense about Greg, and I told you I had a sense about him, and you still dated him," Holly explained. "So when you and Greg broke up I just had a feeling the reason was that he cheated. And a month ago I asked you if that was the reason, and you insisted that it wasn't. You insisted you broke up with him because you wanted to have kids and he didn't, and I said you could talk to me about stuff in confidence and you wouldn't talk to me about it. So I felt like you weren't ready to talk about it yet. And Kris's wedding was coming up, and you seemed fine hanging out with Trent, so I figured you were doing fine and we would spill the truth after the wedding."

"Oh my gosh," Bren exclaimed, stunned.

"That's why I sent Julia to your apartment."

"*What?*" Bren exclaimed, really stunned.

"You didn't want to talk about it, but I still wanted to help you. I figured you were gonna have trust issues after being cheated on by Greg, so I tried to help you, in my own way. I knew someone who knew Julia, and they told Julia where Trent lives now, and when he would be home if she wanted to talk to him, and hopefully you could overhear their conversation, and then know for sure if you could trust Trent."

"You arranged that whole thing? And didn't tell me?" Bren said.

"And you didn't tell me?" Calli said.

"Calli," Holly said. "If I told you then everyone would know within five minutes."

"That's not . . . well . . . um . . . yeah."

"Oh my frickin' geez," Bren exclaimed really, really stunned. "I thought life was sending me a helpful coincidence. So much for that."

"Bren, I was helping you, the way I thought you could be helped."

Bren inhaled long and deep, and chuckled as she exhaled at all this insanity. "All this secret keeping is becoming ridiculous.

Enough. I'm done with secrets, done with silence, and that's why I'm going to tell Kris about Greg and everything right now."

Holly gasped! "Absolutely not."

Calli's head swung between them like watching a tennis match.

"It's not right for us to be friends and have secrets, big secrets," Bren explained.

"We gotta keep secrets," Holly insisted. "Until after Kris's wedding."

"I'm not gonna keep silent anymore."

"You have to," Holly said.

"Yeah, you have to," Calli said.

Holly and Calli didn't seem to share the enlightened joy of Bren's new revelation and proactive decision. Not one bit. Bren remembered that Joseph Campbell also wrote that the returning hero is often misunderstood and rejected. This certainly wasn't the appreciative welcome home she had expected.

"Kris is our friend and she deserves the truth," Bren insisted.

"*After* her wedding," Holly insisted.

"Yeah, *after* her wedding," Calli insisted.

"No. Now."

"You're *not* thinking clearly."

"I'm *finally* thinking clearly," Bren said. "And I'm gonna finally tell Kris everything!"

Chapter 13 – night

FRINIGHT

Bren didn't tell Kris anything.

Instead she got convinced to continue staying quiet. She went home, showered, changed clothes, avoided Trent, joined Kris's pre-wedding day brunch at Kris and Mark's apartment, mingled with out-of-town guests, and pretended everything was totally fine with her, then kept pretending as she sat politely at Kris and Mark's rehearsal dinner with a big smile on her face not telling Kris anything except words of happiness, and still keeping secrets.

Holly gave her an approving look across the table.

Calli stared starry-eyed at Trent.

Trent gave starry-eyed looks at Bren, not knowing what she did that day.

Kris's parents and brother gave some weird toast in some alien language from their alien church.

Mark's parents embarrassed the heck out of Mark with a 4th grade Halloween story when he learned that dressing up as a mummy with toilet paper isn't smart when it's raining.

And Kris and Mark looked super happy this night before their wedding.

Crrrrrrrud. Maybe Holly was right about keeping quiet, Bren thought, now feeling really confused about everything. She also felt incredibly relieved and exhausted from venting her anger out. But now felt nervous about how it would come back at her. Would Greg press charges against her? Would life punish her for yelling? Would Trent think she was a psycho for what she did and leave her? Why couldn't everything just have a happy ending like in rom-com novels?

Everyone chatted.

Everyone danced.

Everyone went home.

But Bren went home with Holly.

She was too confused to sleep with Trent again, and too tempted to sleep with him if she stayed in her own apartment. And Holly insisted she stay with her to keep an eye on her so she wouldn't do anything else "crazy." Luckily at Holly's she could have some space, and think, and come up with a new plan to fix everything, somehow, maybe, hopefully, as Bren lay on Holly's living room couch, alone, without her cuddler, wondering if he was feeling lonely too, holding the blankets, watching Holly's fish swim around randomly, and, in the quiet, made up her own bedtime story about Holly's fish and their lives before arriving in Holly's huge tank. Maybe they were swimming around in the tropics, doing daily fish tasks, when they suddenly got chased by a mean shark, and just as the shark-jerk was about to munch them they got swept up in a hurricane, and blown out of the ocean and through the air, and landed in the back of Santa's sleigh on his yearly journey. Santa happily helped out the befuddled fishies, put them in a bowl of water and flew them all the way to Holly's apartment where he knew they would be loved. For Christmas, Santa left Holly a big fish tank of beautiful fish, and the fish got a safe and happy new home with food and attention and love, and no fear of mean sharks ever again.

Bren grinned. Pleased with her improving silly bedtime story abilities, and watched Holly's fish, feeling new feelings for them, happy for them, envious of their carefreeness, hoping she could soon be that happy and carefree, as she watched them, and watched them, closed her eyes, and missed Trent's wonderful arm around her and his hard-on beside her, as she drifted off to sleep, wondering what wildness could possibly happen with her life next . . .

Chapter 14

June 14 – Saturday

Clink, clink, rattle, rattle.

Bren bolted up!

Bewildered.

Breathing fast.

Dimness.

Thoughts racing!

Looking around. *Where am I?*

Big room. Coffee table. Curtained Windows.

This was not her bedroom.

She clutched a blanket.

This was . . . mural painted walls . . . chandelier . . . fish tank . . . Holly's living room.

On a sofa.

Alone.

Except for the fish.

And someone standing beside her!

"Breakfast?" Trent's voice greeted softly.

Oooooooh, She exhaled, and breathed calmer.

Her hands fell to her lap, both relieved and nervous to see him.

"Sorry to startle you," he said quietly, while grandly lowering down a big tray onto the coffee table beside her. "This is your 6am wake up call."

She breathed the chilly air easier. She was safe. She slowly calmed, finding her sweaty body dressed in Calli's red pajamas. She looked around at Hol's curtained living room windows with muted early sunlight barely illuminating the large room.

Trent stood with a smile, jeans, and a yellow t-shirt that read: *Don't know where this story will go.*

Bren didn't either, but she knew that once again his morning noise had rescued her from Greg; she'd had a new nightmare. Her mind replayed the fresh dream of Greg kissing Abby and yelling at Bren and searching his body for his missing penis and asking her what the heck she had done with it!

Trent had also returned to her, in real life, a good to heal from a bad dream.

"One cannot think well, love well, or sleep well – "

"If one has not dined well," Bren finished Trent's Virginia Woolf quote. She looked up at his grin as her nose filled with the amazing smell of cooked food and her eyes beheld a beautiful breakfast.

Wow.

A spectacular tray splayed before her waking eyes with a big stack of pancakes made into a happy face with a bacon smile, sliced kiwi eyes, a strawberry nose and veggie-scrambled egg hair, accompanied by a tall glass of orange juice, pitcher of syrup, dish of butter, napkin, silverware, and a cheery yellow tulip in a thin vase garnishing the generous presentation. He seemed so happy to finally be able to give her breakfast.

"Wow, Trent," she thanked him. "This is so nice of you."

He smiled as big as her bizarre bacon-pancake person, clearly pleased that she was pleased.

She looked up at him, astonished that her cuddler had also become her private chef. She looked around toward Holly's kitchen but didn't see anyone else. "Did *you* make all this?"

"I did," he said proudly.

She was impressed, and bewildered. "I thought you couldn't cook."

He smiled big again. "I wanted to surprise you with breakfast in bed."

"But I'm not in bed. I'm on a couch."

"Breakfast on couch?"

"That's works."

"Lucy's a wizard in the kitchen," he said. "And, yesterday, I asked her to come over teach me how to cook a good breakfast. FYI, I have twenty burnt pancakes at my apartment. I also made five burnt pancakes here this morning, but these are the good ones."

Bren smiled, then cautiously tested his eggs. *Wow*. Lucy taught him well. She *was* surprised, at his kitchen skills and that he was there.

"I'm sorry to show up here unannounced," his said, as he sat down in the big chair beside her. "Holly asked me here and let me in. She wanted me to make sure you started your day happily."

She swallowed his delicious pancakes.

"And to make sure you didn't do anything odd again this morning."

Oh cripes, she thought. "What did Holly and Calli tell you?"

He raised his eyebrows. "They said you got all zen and the art of motorcycle stealing."

Rush of embarrassment. "Oh geez. You must think I'm a lunatic."

He grinned. "Not completely."

She exhaled.

"After meeting your not-nice ex-boyfriend here last week, after realizing your unresolved stuff all this week, I don't find it too lunatic-ish that you vented. Although, I figured it might be yelling, not trying to run your ex over."

"I didn't try to run him over. Is that what he said?"

"I'm hearing this though the gossip grapevine, so I don't know. I'm just glad you're better now, I hope."

"I'm – oh geez." She tried to organize this mess. "It just kind of happened, in the moment, without planning. I guess I did what I did because I needed to do it, and when I did it I then realized what else I needed to do. But when I returned I found that I couldn't do what I wanted to do because it would undo everything. So I didn't, once again I did what they wanted me to do, what I'm supposed to do, even though I don't think it's what I should do. And now I don't know what to do."

He grinned again. "Okay, that sounded a little lunatic-ish."

She smirked and sighed. "Maybe I am."

"I don't think so," he said, relaxing in the chair, with her on the couch, as if she was in some weird therapy session with the man who insanely built book shelves for her and wanted to install a slide to her bedroom. "I think you've been under a bunch of stress."

Kinda, maybe her whole life, she thought.

"And I probably made things worse for you this week," he said.

She sat up taller. "You comforted me this week. Without you I might have done something nuttier. Though I can't imagine what that would be."

He smirked, then sighed. "I'm sorry if I caused you trouble."

"Oh cripes. This isn't about *you*."

"Yeah it is. I shouldn't have flirted with you in bed. I stressed you out. I freaked you out."

"Lovingly."

"Selfishly. You said it yourself. I was supposed to make your week easier and I made it complicated."

"You helped me rethink."

"I pressured you."

"You pleasured me."

"I imposed my book on you."

"You invited me to read it."

"I went to bed with you."

"I invited you into my bed."

"I told you I was falling for you."

"I'm glad you told me. Trent, you didn't do anything wrong," she assured him. "Believe me, if you had done the slightest thing wrong I would have been done with you faster than reading a one-word novel."

He exhaled and smiled.

"My baggage probably burdened you this week," Bren said.

He smiled. "Actually you really helped me. Besides, you know, letting me cuddle and completely fall head over heels for you and brightening my life brighter than ever before, you also organized me, and my writing schedule, telling me to go to Back Scratch Bar every day. I did. And yesterday while at the bar I had a total breakthrough and figuring out my whole next novel and wrote a bunch of it."

"Really?" she said, excited. "Tell me."

He smiled. "I was sitting along the wall and I saw a couple sitting by the window talking, and another couple at the bar, and a couple playing pool and another couple walking in, and I thought: *that's the story*. It's about 4 different couples. Each couple gets a long chapter about their relationship or meet-cute and tells a story with them, and in the fifth chapter at the end of the book they all end up at a bar and they all meet for the first time, and we see why we've been learning about them separately, so we can appreciate them all meeting and forming a friendship together at the end. I'm really excited about it. I wrote so many ideas and lots of dialogue already. The story is just falling out of me. And I applied all the story structure stuff you gave me and I outlined the plot and organized the whole story into a really awesome structure because you helped me. It's gonna be awesome. So thank you so much for having me go to that bar, and the daily writing routine, and the story structure planning. Now there's hope that I won't be just a one-hit-wonder. You saved me. Thank you."

She smiled big. "That's amazing. I'm so happy for you."

"You totally saved me, Bren, in lots of ways. Now I'm even more enamored with you, if you don't mind."

She felt enamored with him too. Really enamored. She ached to touch his hand, but restrained herself. "Another reason I bailed on you so early yesterday morning is because I don't trust myself with you anymore," she told him. "I want you, so *badly*. I want to take off our last layer of clothing and let go with you. But I haven't figured everything out yet and I just can't right now. So we can't just cuddle again. And I don't know when, or if, we can anytime soon."

He nodded understanding.

She hoped she wasn't losing him. "I'm glad you told me you're falling for me. I told you to tell me everything. I'm falling for you. So I feel that I should tell you everything." She took a deep breath. "Julia showing up at our apartment building was not a coincidence. One of my friends knew somebody who knew somebody who talked Julia into coming to our building to see you at a time when I was home, so I could overhear you either invite Julia up to your apartment or reject Julia, to help me know if you I could fully trust you or not with your ex."

He raised his eyebrows. "So it was a test."

She exhaled. "I guess. I don't know. I'm sorry."

He grinned. "Did I pass?"

She smiled. "You did."

He nodded. "Good."

"And I'm really glad you passed, because I might have lost all hope for relationships if you had wanted Julia back, or if . . . you cheated on me."

"*You cheated on her?!*" a voice shouted from Holly's open apartment door.

Bren's head flew up.

"You cheated on my bestie! I'll pummel you!" Kris shouted at Trent, zooming towards him like a green sweat pants and shirted blur across Holly's living room and tackling Trent!

"OOOF!"

Wham!

"Noooo!" Bren exclaimed.

Kris pinned Trent to the floor!

Bren grabbed Kris's arm!

Calli rushed out of her bedroom and grabbed Kris's other arm!

Kris's lock on Trent was solid.

They all struggled!

Madness!

They were a four-bodied brawling crazy creature!

"No one hurts my bestie!" Kris shouted.

"Don't hurt Trent!" Calli shouted.

"Kris, you misunderstood!" Bren shouted.

Kris held tight.

Bren held tight.

Calli held tight.

SPLASH!

Cold water crashed over them like an ocean wave, drenching them all!

"Aaaah!" They all shrieked, and separated, and looked up.

Holly stood over them, holding the umbrella stand Calli had once peed in. Holly had put out their fire, as the water in her big fish tank sloshed around behind her, along with her frantic fish, maybe not sloshing around this much since the time they were in the back of Santa's sleigh.

Five panting people.

Four of them wet.

Three freaked out fish.

Too much confusion.

One helluva mess.

"Enough," Holly polite-yelled down to them. "This is supposed to be Kris's special day."

Bren was surprised to see Holly be sorta aggressive. All this chaos seemed to be stirring to the surface a new side of everyone.

They all sat panting and dripping on the wet carpet with wet clothes, wet hair and shock on their wet faces.

"I'm sorry," Trent said to Holly.

"Sorry for cheating on my friend?" Kris snapped at him.

"He didn't cheat on me, Kris," Bren explained. "You misunderstood. I said '*if*' he had cheated on me. He didn't cheat."

Kris sat, wet, breathing heavy, staring, then exhaling. "Oh," she said. "Well . . . good."

Bren rolled her eyes. Holly was right. Now Bren was really glad she didn't tell Kris that Greg cheated.

"Wow," Calli said. "It's a good thing you didn't tell Kris that Greg cheated."

Oh crud.

Bren and Holly both palmed their foreheads.

"*What??*" Kris shouted. "Greg cheated on you?? I'll pummel him!" Kris jumped up and started for the door.

Oh super crud!

Bren tackled Kris's right side.

Holly tacked Kris's left side.

SPLASH!

Calli threw another umbrella stand full of water on them!

"Aaaah!" They all shrieked, and separated, and looked up.

"I'm so sorry," Calli said. "I forgot I wasn't supposed to tell Kris about Greg. I'm forgetful-Calli in the morning."

Bren sighed.

Trent sat on the floor looking at all of them with raised eyebrows.

Calli dropped the umbrella stand and ran over to comfort Trent.

"Why didn't you tell me?" Kris asked.

"*Why?*" Bren said. "Because of what you just did. Overreact. Become violent. If you beat up Greg he might call the police and you'd go to jail, *again*, right before your wedding. I couldn't tell you."

"Is that why you and Greg broke up?"

"Yes."

"So you kept this a secret from me for a month?"

"Yes."

Kris looked at Holly. "Did you know?"

"I did."

Kris breathed heavy, staring at the wet floor, then at the ceiling, then she bolted up to her feet and ran the other direction, into Holly's kitchen, up Holly's stairs, and up to Holly's roof.

Bren and Holly and Calli looked at each other.

Oh super, super crud. Not a great start to a wedding day.

Holly grabbed Calli's hand and pulled her off of Trent, as they and Bren all ran after Kris!

Chapter 15

Up up up, Bren raced to the roof, hearing Holly and Calli's bare feet slapping the wood steps behind her. Kris's special day was blowing up. *Gotta un-blow it.* Out the door. On the roof. Bright morning light blasted her eyes. Wild wind iced her wet skin under wet pajamas as her bare feet raced across the roof, chasing after Kris towards the east side of the roof. Now she was driving her friend to an edge too. Guilt and panic chilled Bren, desperate to get Kris smiling again and stuff all this mess back into Pandora's Box.

Kris kept running until she stopped at the railing. Bren's feet stopped beside her.

A week ago up here they were so happy, chatting blithely like a Noel Coward comedy. This day felt like a play again, but this time, a bizarre farcical drama.

Kris spun around and looked at her friends.

Kris: First of all, happy National Strawberry Shortcake Day.

Bren: Thank you. You Too.

Kris: Second of all, *what the fuck?!*

Bren: Kris, I'm sorry about all this.

Kris: Bren, you've been recovering from Greg cheating on you all this time and you didn't tell me?!

Bren: Yes.

Kris: I can't believe you've been faking okayness for a month.

Bren: Kris, I'm sorry I didn't tell you. But I had to not tell. I didn't wanna distract your focus on your wedding with my drama.

Kris: I can think of my wedding *and* your drama. You should have told me.

Bren looked at Holly.

Holly looked at Bren

They both looked back at Kris.

Kris: Greg cheating must have crushed you. I could have been helping you.

Bren: Your focus needed to be on your wedding.

Kris: The wedding is fine. I wanna help my friends.

Bren: I know you do, and instead of enjoying your special month before your wedding you would have spent all your time trying to take care of me.

Kris: So?

Bren: So I didn't want to ruin this special time in your life with my negative stuff. Everything I didn't tell you was to protect you and your wedding from my personal problems.

Kris: You have no "personal problems." Your problems are *our* problems. We're friends. We tell each other everything. We fix shit *together*.

Bren: You overreact.

Kris: *I don't overreact!*

Bren held up her wet pajama arms as proof.

Kris sighed.

Kris: I get a bit emotional.

Bren: And when you get emotional you do things before you think, and if I told you Greg cheated on me you would have kicked his butt into his neck.

Kris: I'm gonna *kill him!*

Bren: Noooo! I can't let you get arrested for assault again. Greg might press charges.

Kris: Dammit, don't screw up my argument with logic.

Bren: Your temper needs logic.

Kris: Then you should have logically tied me to a chair and then told me about Greg.

Bren: After I did that last year you still tracked down that rude waiter and threated to tie his dick in a knot. Now I can't eat there ever again.

Kris rolled her eyes.

Bren: Look. I've just been really confused about everything lately.

Kris: Then you need to tell me about your confusion. We don't keep secrets. I thought we all agreed last year to not keep secrets.

Bren: But your wedding.

Kris: Holy dick cheese. Have you *all* been keeping secrets from me?

Bren shared a look with Holly and Calli.

Kris: Well, fuck that. What else have you all been hiding?

Bren: Well . . . um . . I . . . yesterday I kinda stole Greg's motorcycle.

Kris: You what?? You stole Greg's motorcycle?!

Bren: I was emotional.

Kris: And you think *I* overreact?!

Kris took a breath, then typed on her phone.

Bren: I did overreact. I'm sorry. Now I don't know if Greg is gonna press charges against me. So, I might be arrested before the wedding. Who knows? I don't know anything anymore.

Bren paused.

Bren: Who are you texting?

Kris: Mark. We tell each other everything. When I'm upset he calms me down.

Kris's phone dinged with a return text. Kris nodded, exhaaaaled, and looked back at her friends.

Kris: Okay. I'm calm now. So, you fucking stole Greg's motorcycle????

Calli: And Bren also stole Trent from me.

Bren: What?

Calli: You saw me and Trent last week. We were together, and you took him.

Bren: I thought you were fine with Trent and me.

Calli: I'm not fine. Why do you think I'm fine?

Kris: Because I told her you were fine.

Holly: So did I.

Calli: Why'd you tell her I was fine?

Kris: Because your lusts don't last. You like someone for two days and then you're hot for someone new.

Calli: New hot people keep showing up.

Holly: You still want Trent because you can't have him, like the time you begged me over and over because I refused to put a skylight in your bedroom so you could count stars as you fall asleep.

Calli: And so angels could watch me have sex. It's a hot voyeur thing

Holly: Oh my gosh.

Calli: Trent's different. I hung Trent's picture on our fridge and the next day he shows up in our apartment. It's destiny.

Bren: It's coincidence.

Calli: Trent said coincidence means you're on the right path in life. Trent's on my path.

Holly: Maybe the coincidence means he was supposed to be here, but not necessarily with you.

Calli: Well that's not as fun.

Bren: I didn't mean to upset you, Calli.

Kris: Trent belongs with Bren.

Calli: Why?

Kris: Because he was sent to Bren by Madeline.

Bren & Calli & Holly: *What?*

Kris: Bren, Madeline gave you Trent, to thank us for matchmaking her with Ed last year.

Bren: She did?

Kris: Ed was in Trent's book club. Ed told Madeline about Trent. Madeline moved in with Ed so Ed could tell Trent of Madeline's available apartment. Madeline put you and Trent together like two birds in a cage and hoped for the best.

Bren: Are you flipping kidding me??

Kris: It's true.

Bren: So much for fate. Kris, you've been keeping secrets too.

Kris: Kinda.

Bren: Why didn't you tell me?

Kris: I only found out last week. Madeline bragged it all to me when she stopped by Holly's party and saw you and Trent happily talking on the bench for hours. I didn't want to risk messing up anything between you and Trent, so I kept quiet.

Holly: I can't believe I didn't know about this either. It's like I've lost my knowing-everything-about-everyone superpowers.

Bren: Oh my gosh. That's incredibly sweet of Madeline, but it's also bizarre.

Kris: Ed was friends with Trent and he thought Trent was cool.

Bren: Geeeez. Did Trent know?

Kris: Not according to Madeline.

Bren: *Everyone's* been keeping secrets.

Calli: But that doesn't mean Trent wants Bren.

Holly: I think Trent does want Bren.

Calli: That's because Bren got to have sex with him for a week. I think he should have sex for me for a week also, and then he can decide to be with me or Bren. I can be logical too.

Bren smirked.

Bren: Trent and I didn't have sex. We cuddled. That's all.

Kris & Holly & Calli: Cuddled??

Bren: Yes, cuddled. So I could sleep. Because Kris said cuddling induces oxytocin.

Kris: Oh shit. Really? You got together because of what I said?

Calli: Then I should get to cuddle with Trent for a week.

Holly: Calli, don't be absurd.

Calli: But Bren gets everything she wants. She gets Trent. She gets flawless skin. She gets to be maid of honor instead of Holly.

Holly: Calli. Don't cause more trouble.

Calli: It's true.

Kris: Hol, did you really want to be my maid of honor?

Holly: It's fine. I understand why you picked Bren. She's your roommate and you guys are close.

Calli: But you knew Holly a whole year before you met Bren.

Kris: That's not how I decided.

Bren: Holly. I always felt weird about it too. I didn't mean to make you feel bad.

Kris: Neither did I, Hol. Bren, you felt weird about it?

Bren: A little.

Calli: But you did it anyway.

Bren: Kris asked me. I felt honored.

Holly: It's fine. Let's not fight about it. Let's just be happy for Kris and help her have a happy day.

Calli: See, Kris. See what a great maid of honor Holly would have been? Holly cares about you having a happy day.

Bren: I don't know what's right anymore. Kris, I feel like crap that you overheard and now this is happening.

Kris: I'm glad I overheard. I didn't know there was so many secrets going on behind my back this whole time. If I knew my wedding was gonna rip everyone apart I would have eloped in Vegas without any of you.

Holly: Everything's fine.

Kris: Everything's fucked. My friends and bridesmaids are all mad at each other.

Bren & Holly: We're not mad.

Calli: I'm mad at Bren.

Holly: Calli.

Kris: Holly. I don't love Bren more than you. I was so happy to be getting married, but so distraught that I suddenly had to rank my friends and decide who to be my maid of honor. It sucked ass and I didn't mean to hurt you.

Holly: I understand.

Kris: I picked Bren to be my maid of honor 'cause she's incredibly organized and I knew she'd work well with Ann.

Bren: Anna.

Kris: Whoever.

Calli: Oh, Bren took charge all right. She tried to do Anna's job for her and manage the whole wedding herself. Anna would call Holly and complain about Bren trying to manage everything.

Bren: She did?

Holly: Just a bit. At first. But not lately.

Bren: Oh gosh. I'm sorry. I . . . I must have backed off after I broke up with Greg. I backed off everything.

Calli: Back off Trent.

Holly: Calli, chill. You drive me crazy sometimes.

Calli: What do I do?

Holly: You do *things*. Every day. You bring home strange people that try to sniff my aura. You make weird toilet paper roll art configurations in the living room. And you drip ketchup on my couch.

Calli: Drips aren't my fault. It's gravity's fault. All I'm doing is eating.

Holly: On my couch. Some days you stress me out so much I have to take a bath to relax. But lately I can't take a bath because of the drought's water restrictions. So lately I've been extra stressed out.

Calli: Well you stress me too, with all the things you *don't* do. You don't let me be naked around the apartment. You don't wanna celebrate New Week's Eve with me every Sunday night. And you have an awesome singing talent but you don't sing anymore 'cause you're afraid people will hate you for "showing off."

Holly: They will.

Calli: And I'm tired of your quiet time after 9pm.

Holly: I'm tired of your friends eating all my food in the refrigerator.

Calli: They don't eat it all.

Holly: They ate my cheesecake on Thursday.

Calli: That was Chet. He ate your cheesecake after eating *you* on Thursday.

Holly blushed.

Bren & Kris: What??

Bren: Thursday?

Kris: Two days ago?

Bren: You're back with Chet?

Kris: You're back together with that jackass?

Bren: Don't pummel Chet.

Calli: I'm so sorry. I forgot I wasn't supposed to tell that. Me and my mouthy mouth.

Holly: It's all right, Calli. Let's get everything out. Chet and I are not back together. We've just been . . . you know . . . hooking up.

Bren & Kris: *What?*

Holly: It's not permanent. It's just a fling, while he's up here for the wedding.

Bren: I thought you'd moved on.

Kris: I thought you wanted Ron?

Calli: I thought there was a shrieking dolphin in our apartment, but it was just Holly and Chet humping.

Holly: Chet's the best sex I've *ever* had. He's ruined me for other men. I've dated some good guys in the last few months, but they don't have Chet's magic in bed, or on the kitchen floor, or amazingly in a hotel elevator. I wanted to experience that *magic* again. I've been trying to get there without him, with guys and gadgets and elevator solos. But he's the only one who can drain my fish tank, if you know what I mean.

Kris: I'm not sure how to picture that.

Bren: I'm trying not to.

Calli: I'm picturing it.

Holly: There is no magic between Chet and I beyond sex. We can't do a relationship. We tried that. We have nothing in common. But *ooooh,* I really needed to experience his magic again.

Calli: I'm glad you and Chet are having sex again. I've missed hearing your loud, animal sounds. It's like being back on my family's farm.

Holly: Oh gosh. Kris, I didn't want to distract from your wedding, so I didn't tell you.

Kris: You kept all this super sex secret?

Holly: You don't like Chet. I knew you'd be upset with me being with him again. And it's just a temporary fling. He'll be back down south after the wedding.

Calli: Yeah he will.

Holly: Not my south. San Jose.

Kris: Oh my God. I had no idea my wedding would fuck up everyone's lives. Does getting married mean all my friends have to lie and keep secrets from me to be *nice?* You've all been politely walking on eggshells around me?

Bren: We just wanted to keep your focus on your wedding. To not spoil your special day with our personal crap.

Kris: What's crap is that we all have secrets. We're all supposed to be best friends who tell each other everything, wedding or no wedding. I wanna get back to that openness. I don't wanna stand up at the alter with all of my dear friends knowing that Holly is having a sex crisis, Calli wants to clobber Bren, and Bren is so messed up right now she's stealing motorcycles. And I'm . . . I've been keeping secrets too.

Bren, Holly, and Calli looked at Kris, curious.

Kris: Bren, I felt so bad about moving out and leaving you, so guilty. And I'm glad Trent moved in. That helped me feel less guilty about leaving you alone. But, still, I've been sad since I moved out. We lived together for eight years and all of a sudden you weren't there anymore. And I've had such mixed feelings, because it's awesome living with Mark. But I've missed you, and I've wanted to talk with you more this week, and miss you less, but I didn't want to interfere with your new relationship with Trent and mess that up, because he's really great for you.

Bren: I'm so sorry, Kris. I miss you too. You can talk to me any time.

Kris: Good. Because I wanna talk more from now on.

Bren: Good.

Kris: And Holly, me and Mark didn't use the opera tickets you gave us. We gave them away and lied that we went.

Holly: I figured that when you told me your favorite part was when the nutcracker cracked his nuts.

Kris: And Calli, Mark and me don't invite you camping with us anymore because you get scared at night and constantly ask us if every noise is a bear or Bigfoot and crawl into our tent with us, and then you suggest a threesome.

Calli: Grunting threesome sounds would keep Bigfoot away.

Kris: I'm just coming clean about everything. Any *more* secrets you're all hiding since I got engaged? I want us all to go to my wedding clean, without secrets, and everything worked out between us. Let's all get it out. Everything. Right now.

They all thought . . . looked at each other . . . and hesitated.

Calli: Bren hates your "leftovers" stew.

Bren: Hey.

Holly: I hate my job.

Kris: You do?

Holly: I wanna quit working for my parents. But I'm scared they'll hate me.

Kris: They won't hate you.

Holly: They'll be "disappointed."

Kris: We'll definitely do a brunch to deep dive into that, Holly. What else?

Bren: I'm scared my twenties are coming to an end.

Holly: I'm scared Calli won't ever keep a job.

Calli: Jobs can't keep *me*.

Bren: I'm sad that you moved out.

Kris: I'm so sorry, Bren. But I'm getting married.

Bren: I know.

Calli: I love that you moved out, Kris. Now you'll spend equal time with me and Holly.

Holly: It's not a contest.

Kris: I'm sorry you think I favor Bren.

Bren: I'm sorry you think Kris favors me.

Calli: Holly, I'm sorry I talk to you through the door when you're pooping.

Holly: Calli, I dirty extra dishes when I'm mad at you when it's your turn to wash.

Calli: I *knew* it!

Bren: I used to secret-eat Kris's food.

Kris: I never knew that.

Calli: I secret-borrow dresses from the store and bring them back unwashed.

Holly: I secret-stalk you all online.

Kris: I secret-fart in public and blame it on Mark.

Bren: Sometimes I public-fake I'm a British tourist.

Holly: Sometimes I plan how I'd shoplift just for fun.

Calli: Sometimes I buy a pie to throw in my face.

Kris: Sometimes I don't listen to what you all say.

Bren: That's not a secret.

Kris: I vjazzled for my wedding night.

Bren: That's not a secret either.

Holly: I helped pick out your engagement ring for Mark.

Kris: I know. He told me.

Holly: Oh good.

Calli: I had a sex fantasy about Kris's brother.

Bren: So did I.

Holly: So did I.

Kris: So did *I*.

Bren & Holly & Calli: *What?*

Kris: Just kidding.

Holly: I painted the murals in my apartment myself.

Bren & Kris & Calli: *What?*

Calli: I don't bang the people I bring home. We just listen to my record collection, naked!

Bren & Kris & Holly: *What?*

Bren: I like Indiana Jones' Crystal Skull movie.

Holly & Kris & Calli: *What?*

A collective pause.

Bren: And I don't know if I can be with Trent right now. I'm too messed up. I don't wanna waste his time while I figure things out.

Calli: Park Trent with me. I'm ready for him.

Bren: Kris . . . I worry that married people can't be monogamous forever and you'll get heartbroken like I did. And I'm the worst bridesmaid ever to tell you that on your wedding day, and because I feel that way you should have Holly be your maid of honor instead of me. I'm so sorry.

Kris . . . siiiiiiighed . . . and straightened tall.

Kris: It pains me to see us all fighting. Fighting over stupid stuff. We can't do that. We have to stay close. We have to cherish this amazing time together 'cause –

Kris teared up.

Kris: You know, we've all seen Jane and Sara, and our other friends, and co-workers, and acquaintances leave San Francisco cause it's getting so stupidly expensive. Lots of people are having to move out of this beautiful city. And someday us four might scatter off to different cities too, and that change is gonna suuuuuuuuck. But, while we're all here, together, as friends, as kind of an amazing, dysfunctional family, let's be as close as we can by being as honest as we can. I wanna remember these fleeting years as one of the most special times in my life. And the only way it's gonna be special is if we are totally open with each other so we can work things out and stay friends and not have things secretly fester and fuck us up. So from now on we totally don't keep secrets from each other, no matter who's getting married. Agreed.

They all nodded.

Kris wiped her eyes dry.

Kris: All right. So. Everyone listen up.

They all listened up.

Kris: Holly, you didn't have to keep Chet a secret. Even though I think he's a jackass and you can do a hell of a lot better, I wanna hear all the kinky sex stuff. And once again you kept a secret talent of yours a secret. You have to stop hiding your talents. And I wanna hear about your life and hear you sharing. That's what friends do. And Calli living with you is the best thing ever. She helps you. You've brightened up so much since Calli moved in with you last year and you totally came out of your shell. You seem freer and you helped Calli get her life together. She lightens you and you give her boundaries. You two absolutely need each other. So get along with each other.

Holly looked at Calli.

Calli looked at Holly.

Holly: You're right, I'm sorry.

Kris: Calli, I think it's wonderful that you finally feel "love" for someone, and I hope you keep opening yourself up to love. But, sweetie, I think if you talk to Trent you'll find that he's head over heels for Bren. I've never seen two people more perfect for each other. You'll find someone too. Just like Bren and I did. But you gotta back off.

Calli: Hmmmph.

Kris: And Bren. You and me are friends. We share everything. You will never keep secrets from me again, even if you think I'll pummel people.

Bren: You're right. I'm sorry.

Kris: And of course you're still my maid of honor. You're the one who brought me and Mark together, you better stand up there with us. And I don't care if you have doubts. Fuckin'-A, we don't know if our marriage is gonna work out. It sure feels like it will. Mark and me are going to be faithful with each other forever. It *is* possible. And even if it's not, I'll handle it. Me and Mark are going for it and hoping for the best. We'll figure it out. We're excited to open that box with Sherman's cock.

Bren: Schrodinger's cat.

Kris: Whatever.

Bren breathed a huge exhaaaaaaaale.

Kris: And, as you can all see, I'm taking all of your secret-keeping really well. I'm not overreacting at all, even though I'm pretty pissed off at all of you. So here's how it's gonna be. I'm gonna go get ready for the happiest day of my life, and you three are gonna stay on this roof until you've all worked things out between you, so you come to my wedding the best of friends and no crap between you. And I'm the bride, so everybody has to do what I say today.

They looked at each other and hesitantly nodded.

Kris yanked them all in close for a group hug.

Oooooooh. It felt wonderful. Such relief. Such amazing friends. Such weird smells from them still wet with fish tank water.

Bren remembered her rant on this roof last Saturday that she didn't know what was true and solid. But now she remembered that her friends were solid, and she knew if she needed their help or they needed hers that they would all totally help each other. In this wild world, their friendship was the one thing she was absolutely sure of, and that security felt so damn good. She smiled with relief.

Kris released them, and smiled at her three favoritest friends.

Kris: Now, the three of you work out whatever you need to work out and come to my wedding happy.

They all exhaled and nodded.

Kris: Oh, I have one last secret. I wasn't texting Mark five minutes ago. I was texting Greg. I told him to get his ass over here, not press charges against you, apologize to you, and make everything right or I'll kick his dick to the Moon. But I'm gonna leave before he gets here so I don't kick his dick and get arrested. See you all at the wedding.

Bren stood shocked.

Kris gave them a big smile, then marched across the roof and down the stairs.

Bren, Holly, and Calli looked at each other.

Wind blew.

Silence.

Calli: I masticated Trent's burnt pancakes this morning.

Chapter 16

Bren, Holly, and Calli looked at each other, for a while, silently.

"So," Bren said. "Are we good?"

"Yes," Holly said.

"Yeah," Calli said.

Holly's phone buzzed.

Holly looked at the door camera app on her phone, and gasped. "Greg's at the front door."

Chapter 17

Bren chilled cold again.

She stared aghast at Greg's face on Holly's phone, a big problem filling the little screen.

More trouble.

His serious face stared anxious at the downstairs door, *wanting in.*

Cripes. Bren fretted. What a messed up morning. She missed the peace of her week of great sleep. Now everything was wide awake as if she'd kicked the hornet's nest.

Greg *buzzed* the button again, stinging Bren's nerves.

Was he furious at her for stealing his motorcycle?

Time to find out. No more hiding. No more keeping silent, for sure this time. Time to resolve all this messiness and close the book on it, if possible, so Kris wouldn't clobber him, if Trent could wait for her, if Greg didn't press charges against her, and if all her fear and hurt and anger didn't blow up everything even worse.

She rushed down the stairs with Holly and Calli's patting footsteps behind her.

Kris was gone, hopefully enjoying the start of her wedding day with all of them rebonded. Trent was gone too, probably walking back to his apartment, confused about everything happening. Bren hoped all this nonsense didn't scare him away forever.

Hopefully Bren, Holly, and Calli were now a united front. Bren felt like she needed her squad with her for this confrontation as they all stared at Greg's frowning face in the kitchen's camera monitor of the building's door.

Bren inhaled . . . and exhaled.

Her trembling finger *buzzzzzzzzed* him in.

He barged through the downstairs door.

She gasped.

He was inside.

She thought of all the great women she looked up to, what would they do? Would they kick Greg in the balls? If Greg said one wrong thing he might spend the night in the hospital and she might spend the night in jail.

Calli gave her a look of "wow-this-is-gonna-be-*crazy.*"

Holly gave her a look of "we're here for you, you can do this."

Bren felt the situation leaning a lot more toward crazy, but necessary, and climactic, like the exciting third act of every great story.

Bren asked Calli to open the apartment's front door.

Calli raced to the door and opened it.

Holly stayed next to Bren.

Bren's thoughts frenzied, emotions swirled, and adrenaline raged. She tried to be as brave as Joan of Arc approaching the battlefield as she daringly walked her wobbly rubber band legs from Holly's kitchen and into the living room, feeling her heart pounding with nervousness and her pajama sleeve smearing her forehead flop-sweat. Bren opened up Holly's living room curtains. She planted her bare feet in the center of the battlefield, in a power position with the window's daylight behind her silhouette and readied to face the fast approaching stomp-stomp-stomper stomping up to her high ground. She inhaled as much breakfast-scented energizing oxygen her lungs could fill with courage as she stared at the open door, clenching her fists . . . waiting . . . fearing . . . fuming . . . and . . .

Greg entered.

Winded and wearing his pajamas.

Bren's eyebrows raised.

He stopped. He stared at her. He stood where he stood last week, this time sober, but dressed in tan silk pj's with his un-matching snazzy dress shoes.

Her head tilted.

"Thank you for letting me in," he said politely.

Not the fire-breathing she was expecting from him.

"This is an unusual look for you," she said.

"It's been an usual morning."

She scoffed. "You have no idea."

"I have *some* idea," he said. "Kris just texted me to get over here, *or else*. I've been stressing all month that she would find out the reason we broke up."

"So you and Abby really didn't tell anyone that you cheated?"

"Are you kidding? I know the damage Kris did to your ex who was stealth-sexting. Every day after you left me I expected Kris to pound on my door and pound on me. But she never did."

"I never told her. Until this morning."

"Yeah. She just ordered me to come here and restore your happiness."

Bren really scoffed. "Good luck with that."

He exhaled a big breath. "Can I try?"

Aghast at his game, she squinted at him. "You can try all day, but I won't tell you where you bike is."

"I know where my bike is."

Bren was surprised. "Abby told you?"

He nodded. "Thanks for not trashing it."

"Did you really think I would?"

"Well, I'd never seen you so angry."

"I'd never felt so angry. But revenge isn't my style."

"You just wanted to scare me?"

"I wanted to *escape* you," she spoke hard and honest, not silent anymore, "escape all the heartache and anguish you poisoned me with. And I *did* escape. To the edge of the world. Then I did not roll your bike off the cliff. Then your bike ran out of gas; you keep letting me down. I had to walk your bike back to town."

"Oh," he said, actually seeming embarrassed, maybe even ashamed.

She finally felt some power over him. "I left your bike with Abby."

Greg nodded, oddly. "Then Abby left me."

Bren's eyebrows lifted.

Greg took another breath. "I told her," he said, looking at Bren like he expected fanfare. "I admitted to Abby that I came here last week and tried to get you back."

Bren was surprised that he hadn't kept that part a secret from Abby. "So she left?"

Greg smirked. "With my motorcycle keys."

Bren smirked. "Then go buzz Abby's door?"

"No," he said. "I wanna buzz *your* door."

"This is Holly's door."

"And *my* door," Calli said.

"And Calli's door."

"Whatever door gets me to you, and gets you back with me."

Bren folded her arms.

"Bren. I want you. I need you," he said, looking honest.

"You said that last week. Then I saw Abby in your frickin' window yesterday."

"I was in love with both of you. But everything's changed. I've made my choice. I want you."

Bren stood staring at him.

"Yesterday, I had never seen you so angry. Now I know just how deeply I hurt you. In that moment I had a revelation of clarity. I'll never hurt you like that again. And I'm here to tell you that I'm truly, truly sorry. You changed me. You made me better than I was. Our time together was the greatest time of my life. And if you give me another chance the rest of our time together will be even better. Let me show that to you. Please. We had something amazing."

She remembered the amazing love they had, those amazing times.

"I want it back," he said. "I'll be the man you loved. I'm still here. I slipped. I learned. And I'm still here. I made a dumb mistake. But I'm different now. We were so good together. Do you remember?"

She remembered.

"Bren. Do you remember all our fun? Trying all the cool restaurants on your To Do List."

She remembered.

"Do you remember our nights together? Meeting me at delicious restaurants. Walking to my apartment holding hands under the streetlights. Reading beside each other in bed."

She remembered. She remembered the feel of his embrace, the warmth in her chest. She remembered how much she used to love him and their bond together. He was pulling all the strings he knew would move her emotions. She felt Greg's gravity pulling her. His sincere expression, his lovely words bringing back to life all their wonderful memories of their lost relationship.

He continued. "Remember you would pick a sexy chapter from a book and you'd have us act it out from *On Dublin Street*, *Lady Chatterley's Lover*, and *Fifty Shades*?"

She remembered those fun times.

"Bren. I won't cause you pain ever again. Because I'll *never* hurt you again. I'm better. You can trust me now." He spoke softer as his loafers stepped closer. She breathed in nervously. His familiar oaky cologne reminded her of every loving time he had held her close and made her feel loved and safe and serene. He smelled clean, as if he had washed away the cheating monster that he had been and now smelled really good.

He smiled at her. "I wanna celebrate our relationship the way it should have happened," he whispered, sounding so sincere.

"I wanna celebrate your birthday with you this week. I want our new and improved relationship to be my birthday gift to you."

She stared at him.

"You know that I rarely lose a case, so for me to stand here and admit that I was wrong is a big deal for me. And this is my closing argument. We'll be better than before. Closer. Stronger. We'll have that fairytale love that you always talked about. I promise." He took a big breath and looked into her eyes. "I love you."

She smiled.

His face lit up.

She inhaled with bliss!

His arms opened wide!

"*I don't care.*"

Pause.

His head tilted.

She O-faced.

"Huh?" Greg grunted.

Bren gaped in wide wonder at her realization, stunned at how she felt, *thrilled* at how she *didn't* feel. She turned to Holly and Calli. "I don't give a darn about this conversation with Greg at all," she exclaimed, astonished. "Isn't that amazing?"

"Thank goodness," Holly said.

Calli nodded. "I was worried for second you might go with Greg again."

"I had faith you'd make the right choice," Holly said.

"The more he just kept describing everything we had done the more I realized that I just have no feeling for those experiences with him anymore. They were good times, but they're in the past and totally tainted from his cheating."

"For sure," Holly said.

"Those times did sound fun," Calli said. "Maybe I could date Greg for a while and go to those fancy restaurants and dress up as book characters for weird sex."

"You're not going to date to Greg," Holly said.

"Why not?"

"He's a cheater."

"He's single and hot."

"I'm still standing here," Greg pointed out, looking confused.

Bren still looked at her friends. "This confrontation with Greg isn't like my argument with you two and Kris, where I *truly cared* about resolving everything between us so we could stay together. This conversation with Greg feels so meaningless, because I don't care. I don't love him anymore, at all." She turned to Greg. "Sorry. It's true. And I don't feel bad about telling you that because you totally cheated on me."

Greg exhaled.

Bren turned back to Holly and Calli. "Somehow, somewhere during this week Trent slowly eclipsed Greg without me being aware of the change happening. But it happened. I feel nothing for Greg anymore, not even anger. Isn't that incredible? I broke free of my miserable catch-22."

"That's wonderful," Holly said, throwing her arms around Bren with a big hug.

"What's a catch 22? Is that an STI or something?" Calli asked.

Bren came out of their hug. "No. It's one of the books I put on your reading list, if you would just read the wonderful books I suggest for you we could talk about so many wonderful stories."

"You never listen to the music I suggest for you," Calli said.

"Your bands are so harsh," Bren said.

"Your books aren't smutty enough," Calli said.

"I think you two should keep trying to find stuff that you both will like," Holly suggested.

"We both like Trent's book," Bren said.

"We do," Calli said.

"I'm still standing here," Greg groaned.

Bren turned back to him, with a huge weight floating off her and flying away, the weight of Greg. "Look, Greg. I don't mean to be cold. That was a really good speech. And if you've actually changed then that's great. But, I don't care about you anymore. And you don't care about me, because if you did then you wouldn't have cheated on me. We're over," she said to him trying to not sound rudely indifferent, even though that's how she felt. "And now I know that if anyone cheats on me again I'll be fine. I'm not gonna worry anymore. I can bounce back. If life lets bad stuff happen, I'll just keep on going. If a lover cheats on me then they're not my soulmate and I'll keep moving on until I find my soulmate. I'll be fine. Wow. I don't feel powerless anymore. I've got this. This feels *awesome!*"

Greg's mouth stayed open.

"I don't hate you. I don't love you. I don't feel anything for you anymore. I'm totally over you. Isn't that *amazing?*"

He stood stunned.

"It's great, for me *and* for you. It's *over*. We can move on, for good. *Woooow*. You don't have power over me anymore. I'm *FREE OF YOU!*"

"Now you can love Trent," Holly exclaimed.

Bren smiled huge, then looked at Calli.

Calli sighed, then . . . nodded. "You can have Trent."

Bren exhaled. "Really?"

"Yeah," she humorously sighed. "I didn't want to admit it, but watching Trent work so hard to make you an amazing breakfast this morning, and then watching him talk and smile with you by the couch, it's super clear that he's totally into you. So, I figure, if he doesn't love me then he must not be my soulmate."

Wow. Calli was really growing. Bren nodded, and grinned. "Thank you, Calli."

"Now Madeline has to find me a cuddler too."

Bren and Holly smiled.

Bren looked down and saw the pancakes Trent learned to make for her, the pancakes with the goofy bacon smile. She smiled back at it. She looked above it at Holly's mural painting on her wall of the San Francisco bay, and the bridge, and the Marina hills where Bren had stood on the cliff yesterday. Wow, what a coincidence to have that exact cliff painted on the wall. She remembered Trent saying that coincidences mean you're on the right path. She felt that she was on the right path, to him. And she remembered what she yelled on that cliff at life: "Why can't you make me feel as safe and cared for and not alone as Trent makes me feel?" She realized she wanted to feel that safe and cared for and not alone with Trent every night. She wanted him, as her new boyfriend, right now!

Bren turned to Greg. "Thank you."

"For what?"

"For showing me a bad boyfriend so I can appreciate a *great one.*"

"Uh . . . you're welcome?"

Then Bren turned away from him, forever, no longer wasting her breath on a guy she didn't care about anymore. And she couldn't stop smiling, bigger and BIGGER!

"I gotta go get Trent!" Bren announced, jumping up and down with joy.

Holly and Calli joined her jumping as they all danced around joyously in front of Greg's puzzled frown.

"Hurry," Calli said. "We need to be at Kris's wedding."

"Yes. And thank you, Calli. And thank you, Holly." She scurried around Holly's living room. "I can't find my shoes."

Holly kicked off her slippers shaped like two blue cute fishies.

Good enough. Bren jammed her feet into them. "I love you both so much!"

Holly & Calli smiled at her.

Then Bren raced past whats-his-name to go get her soulmate!

Chapter 18

Bren ran.

Out the door.

Across the street.

Between the cars.

Down the sidewalk.

In jammies and slippers.

Horns honked.

People cussed.

But Bren kept running.

Towards the sun, on Chestnut Street.

Feeling so damn happy!

Excited!

Ready!

To love!

Ready to love Trent!

Ducking trees and weaving wild between way-too-slow people.

Passing places her and Greg used to hang.

Leaving her anger, her ex, and all those memories in her figurative dust.

Just focusing on her future, with her new love, if she could find him, finally tell him that she wanted him, and hopefully have him still want her too, even after all the bonkersness.

Screw heartbreak and hiding and feeling weak. Screw all her doubts about monogamy. She was going to keep falling in love even if each love fell apart. She would keep healing her heart if ever it broke again. And she wasn't gonna let it make her angry, because even if life and love let her down she could always believe in herself and her choice to be happy no matter what.

Every part of her yearned. Given the green light from her sex, heart and mind, from Kris to risk and just have a blast, from Holly to folly as long as love lasts, and a rally from Calli so simple yet vast: "*If he doesn't love me, then he's not my soulmate.*"

Yes!

That was it! The last nudge she needed.

She didn't need to research him endlessly like she had done while walking on this sidewalk last week. She didn't need to fear that hot Marina girls would tempt Trent away. Or that Julia would beckon him back. And no need to be angry at life for letting cheating happen

She just needed to know that she could deal with it if disrespected again. Because if Trent ever cheated on her, then he was not her soulmate.

And, instead of hiding, she would just keep on looking for her true soulmate.

This logic made her feel liberated, and fearless!

And so she ran!

Finally *FREE!*

Passing cafés and crowds she zoomed toward home. Through plumes of perfume and sweet cologne, but none as delightful as the scent of Trent's bare neck in the morning. No fancy eggs the cafes served looked as delish as Trent's kinda burnt scramble. She longed for more Trent-pancakes, for his neck, for his kindness, his arms wrapped around her, his deep magic hands, his voice, and their bedtime stories together. Now she knew what she wanted: more time with Trent, in all of these places, and fill them with amazing memories with him. She couldn't wait to book banter, cuddle, and more!

She veered right, leaving Chestnut and all her past insecure thoughts behind as she zipped around the corner onto Fillmore.

Yikes!

People.

She swerved.

Crashed into metal newspaper dispensers.

Probably looking nuts.

Not minding looking nuts.

Then she continued looking nuts, running like crazy, south, up the wide sidewalk, passing more people who gawked at her as if they'd never seen a flailing, red pajama-ed, fish-slippered, messy-haired maniac woman bolting by them before. They could stare, Bren didn't care. Not anymore. Not about anything except whatever she wanted. She flashed past them boldly, past four-story buildings, in shadow, then one-story shops, sun lighting her left, with Fillmore Street stretching out before her, just lots of distance between her and Trent that she ached to close.

She ran *faster!*

Racing across Fillmore to the east side of the street. The hard concrete, hard on her feet, but she kept slamming her guppies down again and again, getting closer and closer to having the fairytale love she always wanted in reality. She didn't have a detailed plan anymore, just to love Trent; they could figure it out as they went.

She ran in place, waiting for the red light.

GREEN!

GO!

She zoomed out of the Marina like a rocket!

Sprinting across Lombard's six-lane threshold.

Back in Cow Hollow, dodging dogs and cars, racing by Bermuda bars, crossing Greenwich, crossing Pixley, and remembering the pixie who asked Trent for a selfie as Bren's mind went ka-blooey when she first found out he was a writer. Recalling it *exciting* her. But not knowing then what a great a writer he was. What a great bedtime storyteller. What a great cuddler. What a great friend. And soon she too was a fan, not just a fan of his novel, but of his nature, his kindness, his cheer, his humor, his mind, his heart, his cuddling. *Ooooh wow.* His wonderful *cuddling.* More fun than any lover she'd ever had. Hotter than any love scene she'd ever read. She and he didn't need to act out sexy chapters from someone else's book to enliven her relationship, like she did with Greg. Her and Trent's romantic, erotic, *real* moments were far more enlivening than any fiction. Their cuddlicious chemistry made books unnecessary. *Wow.* She never thought she'd think *that.*

And the unnerving thought of living without their chemistry, without him, without her real life Romeo, stirred her and hurled her even *faster* forward! She wanted back in his non-fiction arms. Now!

Being without Trent was like being away from the city yesterday; what was dear became clear when she missed what was gone.

All she had was air.

She listened to that air now without ear-buds in, whooshing by, like singing.

She breathed that air, feeling it fill her, and feed her, steadily.

Breathing and running, simultaneously, feeling the balance.

Still, but still moving, calm in chaos, resting in motion.

And while the world was a confusing mess, she felt focused.

She could trust herself.

She felt calm.

And sure.

Like the gliding seagulls above her trusting their own wings to glide with the wind.

She finally did too as her arms soared her left around the corner and up Union Street.

Yikes!

Joggers.

She swerved.

Blundered into more newspaper dispensers.

Feeling ridiculous.

Laughing at her ridiculousness.

Then continued her ridiculous ridiculousness, running ridiculously east on the randomly peopled sidewalk, passing places she could make new memories, with Trent, restaurants they could eat at, bars they could drink at, stores to furnish his apartment, maybe *their* apartment. She passed a baby stroller. Maybe babies were in their future. Maybe a library wedding. Maybe a love that lasted a long, long time. Maybe they would start that love right now.

She could do it. She finally felt ready. And she felt a week's worth of swirling urges urging her forward, urgently, towards the bright, bright sun, towards a bright, bright future!

Hoping for the best.

Hoping she could find Trent.

Hoping he still wanted her too.

This felt so right. Into the bright. Her shadow and dark times behind her. And dawdling people in front of her. She shouted "look out!" and blurred past them, as they jumped out of the way of the wild screaming person.

Suddenly.

Up ahead.

She saw Trent's distant yellow t-shirt, as bright as the sun.

Her heart leapt up to her throat.

HOPE!

He was watching his feet as he walked, then he stopped at the curb to wait for traffic. She saw him look left, then turn away, oddly shaking his head, then quickly start to step off the edge of the curb and into the street.

"*TREEEEEEEENT!*" Bren mating-called to him.

He spun around. He saw her.

Their eyes locked on each other.

His head tilted at the pajama-slippered freak flailing towards him.

Her heart and feet pounding.

Hoping he wouldn't frown or turn around or do anything other than smile.

She breathed and ran and ran and breathed.

He smiled big!

YES! Her insides elated!

She smiled big!

The thought of them coming together again thrilled her!

This was happening!

And as this magic moment was happening, she felt the west wind on her back, as if pushing her forward towards Trent, towards love. Huh, she thought, life might be silent, but also might be silently helping her. Maybe life gifted Trent to her just when she needed him. Maybe life wasn't completely indifferent after all. Well, that's awesome, she thought, and let the gust guide her and help her towards happiness.

Suddenly a flock of girls appeared, giggling and racing up to Trent. They enshrouded him, Bren-blocking him.

Oh, heck no, Bren protested. Not now. The look on Trent's face had just told her that he was thinking "not now" too. So that's why he had turned away and shaken his head and tried to get across the street, clearly not wanting them, not even tempted. Bless his heart; he did not have a Hankering for them. Bren smiled even bigger. She knew who he wanted: her, not his fan-girls messing up the climax of their real life love story!

She would not let them mess up her and Trent's big, rom-com, over-dramatic, resolving, epic, climactic fairytale moment. A flash of possessive *primalness* surged through her hot body. She and he were going to have the most amazing, fun, and faithful love on the planet! And she couldn't wait to get started!

Full speed ahead!

Heaven help any foolish fan girl stepping between him and Bren's passion, rocketing her even faster, inhaling huge.

She shrieked and streaked through the air.

All the girls' heads turned around and saw Bren. Their mouths dropped at the sight of the red pajama-ed lightning bolt bolting towards them. They parted like human curtains and presented: Trent. Her cuddler, her love, her future. She had an answer to his t-shirt's question. She now knew how their story would end, and she couldn't wait to show him!

Then her slamming slippers pushed off of the ground!

Letting go of everything that held her down
Of past, of Greg, of woe, of hurt
Of anger, of fear, of thought, of earth
Leaping!
Off the edge!
Into the a i r . . .

Trusting Trent would catch her with care

WHAM!!!!

Onto his chest!

Into his arms!

Bodies smashing!

Hearts colliding!

Her limbs flying passed him, then wrapping around him, his muscley arms around her too, her trust rewarded with a loving catch! Slamming together their perfect match!

SAFE!

He'd caught her! *Full force!* So hard that his body swooned backward. But his strong legs braced and his solidness absorbed her momentous *crash*, with a huge smile on his face!

She made quite an impact! All her years and years of reading about love and desiring the love-of-her-life had slammed into him, along with a week's worth of swirling *desires.*

But he clearly loved her slam.

The elation was mutual.

They held each other where the sidewalk ends, where her heartache ended too, and where a whole new love began.

Together again.

On Union Street.

As one.

Her hot sweaty limbs wrapped around his body as tight as she could *squeeze.* His strong, muscular arms did the same around her back. *Squeezing* and *squeezing!*

Mouths close to each other.

Lips aching to kiss!

But . . . lungs aching to breathe.

Oh no.

She couldn't breathe.

Oh no.

Oh no.

Oh no!

She had run too fast, too hard, too long.

Her wham into him had knocked the wind out of her.

She had loved him too much.

Oh wow. Was this the price of love?

She clutched his shirt.

Panicking!

Realizing she didn't have her purse with her inhaler!

Her airways cutting off!

She gasped and gasped!

Air, air everywhere and not a breath to breathe.

Ooooh no!

She felt herself fainting, his embrace holding her vertical.

She was gonna fall asleep in his arms for the last time!

Oh no!

Love took her breath away, for real.

This was how her story would end?

With irony? Like Hamlet finally ready to be king as he lay dying. She finally found the love of her life and now she was gonna die in his arms before she could finally kiss him! *Ah cripes!*

NO!

Feeling herself weakening, freaking, and fading, dying in his arm.

But then she saw Trent see her situation and *quickly* pull from his pocket . . . an *INHALER!*

YES!

Oh yes! Yes! Yes!

He didn't let her down!

His worried eyes filled with love, as he held tight her limp body, and her real life Prince Charming kindly kissed her lips with a little plastic miracle! Oh yes! It tasted like hope.

She knew for sure right then, she saw in his ever-caring eyes, that he would always be there for her, helping not hurting, loving not leaving, cherishing not cheating, and keeping her heart flying, soaring, and near the warm golden sun in the fluffy fun clouds, up in the air!

Speaking of air.

Oh yeah, she remembered she was dying.

She sucked on his miracle!

Woooooooooooooooooooooh!

Airways opening!

Air!

Wonderful life-giving air!

OH YES!

Oh yes!

Oooooooooh, yes.

She let the inhaler fall from her trembling lips.

She breathed . . . and breathed . . . and calmed . . . and *LIVED!*

He held her.

Comfortably.

Like he would never let go.

His hug was like laying calm on a cloud, cared for, completely safe.

Love.

This felt like true love.

The love she had longed for since she could read.

And now, finally, this love was gloriously real.

She breathed . . . and believed . . . in him . . . in them.

His eyes never left her.

Hers never left him, and she never wanted to leave him again.

And his loving embrace said the same commitment to her, his arms around her body, his hand caressing her hair the magic way she loved him to.

She held onto him too. Like she would never let go. Finally breathing easy.

Wow. It felt so strange to cuddle him vertically. So new and fantastic.

Her mouth flew into a great big smile.

So did his.

They started laughing. She could breathe now enough to laugh.

"You left your inhaler at my place yesterday morning," he whispered, his sweet breath tingling over her face.

"So you carry it with you?"

He grinned. "You taught me to plan ahead."

Wow! She rejoiced. *Oh, Trent. Sweet Trent.* And he had just given her new life, in more ways than one. She held him tighter. He held her closer. They were one.

Camera *clicks*, all around them.

And there they were, cuddling in the street, with the whole world watching. Their private intimacy now public.

But Bren just laughed.

This soul wakening love she felt between them was all that mattered to her now.

She looked at him.

She loved him.

He looked at her, with lots and lots of love.

And she rewarded him with a *kiss!*

Yes!

Finally!

Fully!

She kissed him!

Wind whooshing wild.

Life was flowing. They were kissing. Everything felt *ALIVE!*

Lightning on her lips.

Thundering applause.

A perfect storm.

And a perfect ending to their romantic story.

Her head in heaven.

Her heart healed.

Her sex horny as heck.

His lips felt *amazing!* As *amazing* as she had dreamed they would feel. And his lips kissed her back, so gloriously, with soooooooo much *love!* Oh, it was the fairytale kiss she had always dreamed of, the electrifying kiss she had ached for all week long, and now it was amazingly real, and smooshing all over her smile!

Just silent body language.

Kissing like *crazy.*

Clicks like *crazy.*

The whole scene was *crazy.* But maybe it would re-inspire other broken hearts in this confusing world. To give them hope too. To tell them to keep holding out for their soulmate. At last, she was holding hers. And she cuddled the crap out of him in the heart of this fairytale land.

So tight, so passionate, gripping her inhaler, gripping his shirt, giving him her love until she needed to breathe.

She lifted her lips away and breathed again.

His electric eyes were brighter and bluer than ever, deep in hers, only hers, and nowhere else, as she inhaled a new life.

Aaaaaaaaawe.

Air, and Trent, and happiness.

Oh wait, she remembered.

There was one other thing she needed to enjoy: being a bridesmaid.

She looked at her watch. She looked at Trent. She smiled at him.

"You wanna go to a wedding?"

He smiled back and nodded.

Chapter 19

Bren burst open the door to the bride's dressing room!

Kris spun around, seated by the mirror.

Hair stylist stopped styling.

Kris's mom stopped hovering.

All eyes on Bren.

Kris's face filled with surprise in the sunlit room, then confusion at seeing Bren's strange pajama-slippers attire.

Bren's kissed lips couldn't stop smiling, as big as Kris's smile about love last week.

Kris tilted her head with curiosity as Bren pointed to the HUGE hickey Trent had sucked on her neck.

Kris's eyes popped wide! Her face lit up happy!

Bren smiled!

Kris rushed over and hugged her and hugged her, laughing!

Bren laughed too as she brightly explained everything.

Kris's mom celebrated with some weird alien language "loo loo" whistling.

And maybe it helped because all the universe finally seemed wonderful.

* * * *

Standing in the wedding ceremony, breathing much easier, Bren exhaled with relief that she hadn't messed everything up, and inhaled with astonishment that everything was working out so well.

Everyone stood around the park's baseball field on a sunny June Saturday, the wedding party all dressed in baseball uniforms. Bren was so glad she over-prepared with extra uniforms as Trent stood handsome in one, joining the groomsmen at Mark's request, Bren smiled at her bestie getting married in the Marina park's baseball field, but also eye-flirted with her new boyfriend throughout the ceremony's talk of love and funny camping stories, no longer worried about Kris and Mark's future, confident they would figure it out just fine. Mark's friend Andy officiated awesomely dressed as an umpire and the purple-haired DJ played baseball organ riffs on a keyboard between the vows and rings, and "Take Me Out To The Ball Game" during Kris and Mark's amazingly passionate kiss, and then wild applause as the bride and groom celebrated their homerun at love by jogging around the bases together. A TV news crew filmed their baseball-themed wedding, but probably edited out Kris grabbing Mark's butt while leading the forty-seven guests across the street and up to the four-story apartment building rooftop where Kris and Mark had officially fell in love a year ago.

Bren actually relaxed and let Anna impressively run the reception with military precision. The DJ played chill beats. Ashley photographed everything beautifully. Waiters dressed in baseball uniforms served chicken and pasta and pancakes to the eight round tables shaded with big green umbrellas, and also served hot dogs, Cracker Jack, and ice cream for the baseball theme. Wedding party people sat scattered at different tables with the guests, and the table arrangement respectfully left plenty of room for the seagull and its nest, and it was even appointed as the baseball wedding's official Team Kris & Mark mascot.

Holly subtly eyed Chet from a separate table as he sat beside his new giggly girlfriend, knowing what wild sex his new girl was getting, but actually feeling glad he was no longer an option; now Holly could finally move on, the end of a erotic-tastic era, and maybe the start of a new one as she sat beside one of Mark's handsome lawyer co-workers who had a talented tongue at speaking French and big, capable hands for his woodworking hobby. Holly smiled, sensing lots of erotic potential.

Calli sat next to Trent's sister Lucy. Lucy told Calli about her idea to make the story of the invention of the umbrella into a rock musical. Calli told Lucy her fashion idea to have fans in shirt collars that blow your hair around to look fascinating. And they bantered about how orgasms would be more fun if they made you float in the air for a minute, but they'd be harder to fake. And they talked and talked and smiled and laughed and Calli didn't look at Trent at all, or think about her ghost ex-boyfriend, her eyes ogled only at Lucy.

Bren and Trent sat cozy and canoodling beside Mark's watching family, Bren's mom and her new boyfriend also gawked, and Trent's sister Lucy eye-rollingly told B and T "get a room."

Kris and Mark sat canoodling too with huge smiles, loving all of their friends and family being at this super special spot, and constantly checking the score together of the Giants' game against the Colorado Rockies.

Kris's family all hollered a "woo loo loo loo" prayer to some space alien before they ate, but luckily no UFO showed up to the wedding reception.

Up on the roof, everything looked so beautiful: the blue sky above, the green park and baseball field below, the red-as-love Golden Gate Bridge way out there, sailboats on the sparkling blue bay, the bright sun in the sky like a happy eye, the big green umbrellas over the tables shading everyone, the flowers, the food, the newly married couple with his and hers hickeys, constantly touching each other, and smiling huge, and this amazing new man in Bren's life sitting beside her that she couldn't stop touching and smiling with too.

Her desires, feelings, and thoughts all swirled together, trying to comprehend all the amazingness that had happened, what was happening, and could happen next.

"We wanna hear the speeches!" Kris shouted.

Oh wow. This was happening next.

Butterflies.

Trent gave her a loving smile and an encouraging wink that conveyed all the lessons and love of every conversation and cuddle they had experienced that amazing week. She was on her own to give the speech, but she was not alone; her awesome connection with Trent and her friends was emboldenly with her.

Hopefully ready for this third-act climactic challenge, Bren exhaled, internally eye-rolled as she asked the universe for strength, giving life another chance to show her some caring, and inhaled the fresh summer air, as she rose, walked up beside the clapping bride and groom, and stood in front of everyone.

Grand silence.

A lovely, easing breeze blew.

She looked down at her well-prepared, well-worded speech with lots of literary quotes and clever baseball puns, but . . . she didn't feel connected to it anymore. Once so happy about it, surprisingly, she now felt beyond it and as an uninterested in it as she felt about her ex-boyfriend earlier that morning. Everything had changed. All the fun improv of making up bedtime stories was in her now, inspiring her to trust her new skills and actually have fun with this monumental speech. She remembered Trent's impassioned improv speech to his sister; maybe not go that hyperbolic, just find her own vibe that felt right for this wonderful moment for her sweet friends. Free as a bird from the past, now having new feelings and new focus, she looked out at all the eyes on her, and at Kris and Mark. Though this new, unplanned feeling was taking her into a totally uncertain situation, she weirdly felt all this beauty and new experiences speaking through her, and she grinned as she thought F the paperwork, and folded her speech into her pocket, and instead spoke from her heart, and she just kinda winged it.

"Love is caring. You know, it might be that simple. In varying percentages, if you care you love, and if you love you care. One year ago, in a Marina bar not far from here, Kris and Mark met. And as soon as they saw each other it was so obvious from their smiling faces that they instantly cared for each other. It was wild. Like lightning. I've read lots of romance books with instant soulmate connections, hoping for one in real life, waiting, doubting, and then to actually see it happen between these two lucky people was jaw-dropping, and inspiring. Instant connection, instant caring, and the more they talked together that night the more their smiles and caring grew."

She looked at Trent, and smiled, and cared, a lot.

"I wish us all to be that lucky."

Trent smiled back at her, a lot.

She looked at Kris and Mark.

"A few hours later, right here on this roof, Kris and Mark's caring grew so much that their elation at finding each other melted away all of their fears and they completely fell in love. They were all in, for each other, for their love, for their future, for this celebratory day, and many many innings to come. I wanted to say at least one baseball pun."

Laughter.

"Over this past year we have seen their relationship bloom; we have seen the magic that happens after most romance books end: ever-intensifying closeness. So eye-rollingly ooy-gooey with hands all over each other even in public, and lips all over each other's necks, these two are inseparable. Like quantum entanglement, even when they are apart they are linked in spirit, a magical connection. They are truly one, especially after today."

Kris and Mark smiled at Bren, their hands ooy-gooey all over each other.

Bren smiled. She felt everything about this peak moment going right, and these words somehow easily flowing into her mind and heartfully flowing out of her. "Kris and Mark care about camping, rock climbing, and really living life. They care about baseball, San Francisco, and some kind of Star Wars role play involving spaceships going in and out of docking bays that I don't want to fully understand. They care dearly about other people, their families, and their friends. Although, they don't seem to care how much noise they make in the bedroom when a roommate is trying to get some sleep. But that's because they 1000% care about each other, so much that they are deeply in love, completely committed, and deliriously happy. And we all care very much to see what adventures their amazing and kinky union takes them on." Bren raised a glass of champagne. "To Kris and Mark, thank you for being evidence to us all that fairytale love is absolutely real, and our grateful hearts wish you ever-intensifying happiness so loud that it keeps us all awake forever."

Cheers, applause, and people drank their champagnes in agreement.

Kris jumped up and threw her arms around Bren, hugging her so tight.

Joy!

Whew. That went way better than she thought it would.

Maybe life did silently help her, she thought, breathing much easier.

Kris came out of their hug with a grand smile and she got a thanking hug from Mark too, as well as Holly and Calli, and when she returned to her table she got a hug from her mom, and got not just a hug but a glorious kiss from Trent. They sat down together, hands all over each other, eyes sparkling at each other, and their elation also melted away their fears on this magical roof, freeing them to completely fall for each other, quantum entangle, and begin their adventures too.

Chet gave a nice speech, a little more R-rated, but everyone smiled and raised glasses again in celebration.

Guests gushed to Bren about her speech and her wonderful words all night. She suddenly had fans. Now *she* was the one everybody wanted a selfie with, rushing right past Trent to hug *her*, with her new boyfriend smiling proud. *Wow.* This was new and fun, she thought.

It was a helluva party! Even better than planned. The baseball diamond-shaped wedding cake was cut and devoured. The bouquet was tossed and caught by Holly. The garter was flung and caught by Kris's brother. And everyone got a commemorative baseball signed by the bride and groom.

Bren got to spend time talking and rebonding with her mom and learning that her mom and her new boyfriend Griffon were now into trampoline dancing, whatever the heck that was, but her mom seemed super happy and that was awesome and Bren wished her the same happiness that she had finally found. Bren's mom totally loved Trent and hugged him a bit longer than Bren thought was appropriate, not entirely surprised, but politely scurried Trent away from her, promising brunch tomorrow.

It was great to see Vanessa and Skip again, back from their Europe vacation, and to have Jane and Sara with them also felt like such a magical reunion. What a year, and what amazing friends. The purple-haired DJ rocked the roof as the sun set like a big red heart behind the Golden Gate Bridge, the city's million little windows and streetlights shined in the twilight like a universe of stars around them, and the baseball field below lit up its tall lights, making this awesome night even more bright.

Kris and Mark and all their friends that were with them the night they first met and fell in love all raised champagne glasses together in celebration. Then Kris and Mark, Bren, Calli, Holly, Chet, Skip, Jane, Sara, Vanessa, along with Andy, Trent, and Lucy all pulled down their pants and group-mooned the rising moon!

Balloons! Fireworks! Dancing!

The wedding and reception was a homerun!

The laughing newlyweds danced wild once again on this rooftop with even more elation and love for each other than they did one year ago, this time happily sharing this top-of-the-world dance floor with all their favorite people, as everyone shuffled, twirled, and laughed for hours. Trent impressed Bren with his moves and his couples-dancing skills as he twirled her, dipped her, and kissed her passionately under the stars. *Magical!* Foreshadowing of their next time in bed?

They totally thanked Madeline and Ed for matching them together.

Everyone celebrated with a smiling partner.

The moon joined the party, as if smiling down upon them.

Kris and Mark smiled too as they thanked everyone, then limo-ed away into forever.

Like a romance novel's happy ever after.

Couple by couple, party people slowly scattered.

Bren apologized to Anna for being too over-managey with the wedding.

Anna said "no worries" and winked that the clean up was totally under control.

Bren was free to fly away with Trent.

Yes!

Bren and Trent kissed like crazy in the elevator.

They hurried up the street to their home.

This night they'd do way more than cuddling!

Chapter 20

Door slam!

Hot damn!

Bren *whammed* Trent to their wall!

Enthralled!

In their building's stairway.

Their rhythmic grinding like rhyming, reminding her of erotic poetry, the hottest poem ever because this erotica was real.

Touching all over his baseball uniform as her hands slid and explored from his bottom to his hair at the bottom of their stairs where he stood when they first met. She tongued his lips, his cheeks, his neck. Tasting Trent, smearing sweat. His big hands sliding around her uniform too, with a grin. So ready to round the bases with him!

So fun!

After a week's-worth of wanting, they were now finally enjoying!

They kissed like a hurricane at the bottom of their stairs, where Trent had stood as a stranger in the sunlight last Saturday surrounded by romance novels as if promising to be the man of her dreams, like a foreshadowing of this glorious moment, this love, this real life rom-com come true, now happening wildly with her almost sucking his earlobes off as he picked her up, into his arms and her wrapping her legs around him *tight* as he carried her up into the night, everything feeling oh so right, so full-circle since this top-of-the-stairs area was where they first flirted, with hot words, and now with bodies, now so beyond words, because lips were now for kissing and stuff, ooooh such *gooood* stuff, she moaned!

The heck with more stairs. *Her* place was closer.

She steered him towards her door, so ready for much more. Key ready in her hand, he helped her stick it in, all the way, until it stopped, together they turned it until it unlocked. She kicked her door open to their new adventure of pleasure together as she remembered that this was the landing where he had given up Julia for her, where he had always left his door open for her, and where she had pulled him into her home to hold her. Here once again, this time him carrying her in. This time would be a sleepless, much more wonderful night.

She kicked her door closed and kicked off her shoes. He carried her into her bedroom. He knew it well and found his way through, in the dark, their hearts banging together the way she ached for their bodies to do, very soon. He clearly ached for that too.

He gently pressed her back to her bookshelves, as she let out a sigh, he gently pressed his hardness ’tween her spreading, trembling thighs. Holding her, grinding slow, feeling his hard Hank against her. She loved it, so much that her flailing hands knocked books to her floor, falling everywhere she didn’t care about messes anymore. She just wanted more grinding and thrusting and kissing and – and – and – an occasional breath.

Ooooh. So much wonderful, she thought. They could have been doing this all week. *Oh well.* They were here now, having a blast, no plan, just going with *delight*, making it up as they went along. Streetlight through her window let her see his gorgeous smile as she panted on it, and she saw his hand pull out another inhaler. Oh, bless his heart, she thought. She smiled and stuffed it back in his coat pocket. Her airways and everything about her was open, totally trusting, growing more lusting, laughing and loving like a wild windstorm gusting, around her room, all over the place, frolicking over every bookcase. Arms flinging wild, whacking novels to her floor, liberating her library in *fiery amour!* Knocking Austen and London and Shelley from her shelves, pages like wings, only thinking of *themselves* with a *passion* so *passionate* her whole athenaeum *shook* from their sex scene that felt even *better* than books!

They were in their own romance now!

He rolled away her chair and placed her on her desk!

She *r i p p e d* open his shirt and palmed his granite chest!

Passionately pressing, caressing perfect pecks!

Hot lips kissed her face, wild hands slipping off her outfit with zest!

Yes!

He freed her shoulders from clothing, bared her bra and then her tummy, as she freed him from his uniform and licked his muscles, yummy!

She gripped and pressed his hard rock wall, he laughed loud, loving it, loving her hands all the way

d

o

w

n

to his cheese-grating abs. Beautiful, beautiful. Hard as a rock.

Then her hand slid

d

o

w

n

to his –

"Ooh," she gasped, as his hands arched her back. Her mouth in the air, and once it was there he kissed her hard and heavenly, passionately, playfully, wonderfully. His tongue tasting like wedding champagne. Tonguing his tongue and feeling insane. Her body totally *tingling*, *tingling* with *delight*, his minty breath and lips like bliss, arms holding her so right, with her arms swinging wild galore, smacking her lamp down her floor, lusting for more, more *awe's* and *ooh's*! Wanting them out of the rest of their clothes!

She lapped his lips, his face, then breeeeathed.

Wow!

Fucking *electrified!*

She shoved his big shoulders back 'til he stood. Her bare foot on his bare chest launched him back onto her bed with a mighty *whooooooosh!*

They were way beyond cuddlers.

Now they were *lovers!*

She hopped off her desk. She dropped her clothes. He dropped his jaw.

She stood over him smiling, no fears whatsoever.

His *thrilled* eyes told her she was *beautiful!* Hers said "so are *you*," while panting, ready to bump their beautifuls together!

She yanked off his shoes and cotton socks, then landed her knee between his parted legs. He gasped, then smiled, as she slid her hot hands over his warm, big bare feet, then up over his pants, over his shins, his knees, up his muscular thighs. He breathed harder as her hands got closer to his zipper. His stomach quivered as she unzipped. She was so in control right now, and he was clearly *loving* it. She *loved* it too, *loving* how this felt, pulling down his pants while hearing his pants, his grunts, his groans, ready to indulge, revealing a big, beautiful BULGE!

But not revealed enough.

She rushed to her feet and *swooooshed* his pants off like a magician's tablecloth trick, leaving his dick still standing, and still covered by black boxer briefs.

But only briefly.

Like a lioness raging, she jumped in the air, heart racing, her lion caught her with care and brought her in close, his paws everywhere, on her back, on her butt, on her neck, in her hair, as he kissed her and whisked her into a wild frenzy of fun, naked and ready, tangling tongues, then he kissed and licked and savored her breasts, finally feeling this splendorousness!

She clenched her teeth and gripped his shoulders, spoiled with pleasure, he rolled her over, and spoiled her breasts even more, long sucks and licks, pleasure galore, moaning and squealing, loving his mouth, then his hands massaged as he licked his way south, hot breath, wet tongue on her goose-bumped skin, the feel of slight whiskers on his chin sliding over her ribs and naval, he tongued her tummy, erotic and playful, playing her body like a virtuoso, down, down, oh so perfect, and then *yes! Right there!* She bucked! He licked and lapped and kissed and sucked! Reeling, feeling thunderstruck, she gripped her bed and spread. "Oh fuck!" She buckled, he chuckled and gave her a grin, teasing and pleasing, her mind in a spin as he paused to tell her he loved her to her eyes, then his smile dived wild between her thighs!

Their rapturous rapport was even more glorious than any the romance or erotic poetry she had ever read, as her hands knocked books from her bed to make way for their real life awesomeness!

Finally exposed to him, free and *excited!*
His wild tongue told her he too was *delighted!*
Pleasure! Pleasure! Pleasure! Pleasure!
Gloriously lost in forever!
His tongue and her vag were like one together!
Feeling the best feeling *ever!*
ONE! TWO! THREE! FOUR!
Magic fingers, gave her *MORE!!!!*
Lost count, *shaking* to her *core!*
Wow! Never orgasming this *amazing* before!

Transcendence! Rapture! Jubilation!

True love pushing it to ELATION!

She grabbed his shoulders and pulled him up, kissed him silly, sweet and *rough*, *soooo* glad they'd found each other, loving her new friend and lover, perfect partner in the sack, she flipped him over on his back and licked his cheeks and jaw and neck and shoulders, arms and nipples, chest, *so* loving his sweet salty skin, his moans, his groans, his hands deep in her hair, completely bare to him, now fearless and alive and new, ready to taste him too!

Tonguing down his mighty abs, as rigid and delicious as she dreamed he'd taste, her happy face lapped lower to his happy place, over his undies, down below, still dizzy from so many *O's*, but so *sexcited* to indulge in his hard, massive, covered BULGE, grabbing fabric, pulling swift, unwrapping her pre-birthday gift!

Ooooooooh wow! Best birthday *ever!*

Her and Hank met at last.

And became best friends super fast.

Pleasing, pleasing, pleasing, pleasing.

Teasing, squeezing, his wild breathing.

His body shaking to and fro.

Stopping, before he could blow.

So impassioned, pulsing, pumped up, primal.

Surrendering to joy, kissing carnal.

Thoughts out of their heated heads.

Two raging souls breaking her bed.

Rolling, reeling, dropping

d

o

w

n

To her carpeted floor!
Tangling and twisting, lost in splendor!
kissing, hugging, breathing, entwining
tingling, touching, clutching, climbing
grabbing, gripping, groaning, grinding
slipping, sliiiiiiiiding, rubbing, riding
playing, pleasing, stroking, Hanking
flexing, yanking, sweating, spanking
moaning, groaning, squealing, shouting
brilliant, fingers, in and outing
wet
ready
and
s p r e a d i n g wider
stuffing HIM deep inside her
done with licking kissing sucking
finally, finally, finally FUCKING!!!!
their sex was as thrilling as mixing their minds
when making up stories together at bedtime
finally together, his Jules Verne and her Jane Austen
their Vausten was amazingly awesome!
they did every position that Bren had renamed
they did lick-the-beaters and tennis game

they did open book and heart-to-heart
bumpy-road and push-the-cart
spinning compass, surfboard swim
trading favors, please-come-in
hot-talk, spacewalk, touch-the-sky
caterpillar-to-butterfly
infinity and flapping wings

they rocked looking-for-earring so awesome that she actually found her lost earring!

and "OOOOOOOH YESSSSSSSS!!!!!!!" She GASMED one more time!

and felt his GASM BLAST IN HER, SUBLIME!!!!!!!!!

both collapsed

as they finished together

wet

hot

naked

quivering

clutched as one on her floor

together

and they kissed

their lips blending beautifully

breeeeathing . . .

. . . touching . . .

. . . loving . . .

. . . tingling . . .

. . . nuzzling . . .

. . . holding . . .
. . . cuddling . . .
. . . smiling . . .
. . . feeling . . .
. . . wonderful stuff . . .
finally
at peace
laying
in love . . .

Epilogue

Soooo, this was not how Bren planned her week to go.

But she loved how it was ending.

Happily, sweatily, lovingly.

Laying happy with Trent among books like a real life love story popped from the pages, heart pounding, panting, tingling warm all over, feeling fantastic!

Darkness, thoughts racing in afterglow.

Desk, Jane Austen poster, empty shelves, in her bedroom, clutching her new boyfriend.

Thoughts flinging, replaying all the *wow* they had just wonderfulled.

Breaths calming, sharing air, she and he laying there.

He lay collapsed upon her, with her body and smile spread wide, exhausted.

Their hot bodies cooling from the breeze of her ceiling fan that had somehow gotten bumped on amidst their reckless passion.

Slowly relaxing, breathing, smiling.

On a paper cloud of glorious books.

Beside her broken-legged, leaning bed.

And everything felt as wonderful as it could possibly be.

Their love had grown too hot to be a restrictive-clothed Austen story anymore.

She remembered how hot she got with their verbal banter on their stairs.

Their physical banter was even better.

The best sex in a library she'd ever had!

Yep, they definitely had a spark.

And he was as good a guy as the protagonist in his novel who thrilled her.

He had definitely not let her down.

And neither had life, nor Madeline for somehow sending her soulmate to her.

The best cuddler, boyfriend, lover ever!

When they let loose together and just had fun their connection was magic.

Like she had never known.

Beyond words.

Two booklovers beyond words.

She enjoyed this wonderful wordless moment.

Their bodies and beings a perfect fit, in more ways than one.

Enjoying feeling this happy feeling.

Enjoying their hearts bamming against each other as if talking in some wild love language.

Enjoying hearing his slowly slowing breathing.

Enjoying her body still wrapped tight around his.

Enjoying his body collapsed upon her like an angel fallen from the sky.

Enjoying his Hank still awesomely inside her.

"This might sound odd," his sexy voice whispered to her ear. "Would you like to go on a date?"

She laughed. Oh how *Benjamin Button* backwards their relationship had been. A normal date sounded very, very nice. She wondered what she would wear and where they would go and felt herself blushing with giddy excitement, and smiled. "Yes, I would like a date very much."

He squeezed her happily and kissed the side of her neck.

Smiles.

Feet playing footsie.

Fingers caressing "I love you."

Kisses on cheeks and hickey-covered necks until their lips found each other again.

Divine.

Except for the unusual feeling of her butt on a mess of books, a mess she surprisingly didn't mind.

"Baby," she breathed to him.

He smiled big. "Yeah, baby."

"What book is poking my left butt cheek?"

He gallantly dislodged the pesky hardcover.

He laughed. "*The Pokey Little Puppy.*"

She laughed out loud, so hard that her muscle-squeezes kegeled Hank out of heaven.

Ooooooooh.

Oh.

And a weeks-worth of Trent-tastic splooge deluge out of her.

Wow.

Now she had much more than his "potent prose" inside her.

But she calmly trusted her birth control as much as she trusted that letting go of all her fears and letting him in her in every way was absolutely the right decision.

He certainly agreed as he smiled and rolled off her and assumed his faithful position beside her hot, sweaty body, and cuddled her once again, but naked this time, and he slowly caressed his huge happy smile lovingly over her neck and cheeks and lips. "Happy anniversary," he said to her.

She grinned. "Hey, it is our anniversary."

"One week today," he said, sounding proud. "And many more to come." He continued gently caressing her and sweetly kissing. He still seemed as fond of her as before their room-wrecking fun.

"Do you still love me now that your no-longer blue-balls are empty?" she asked humorously, yet kinda serious.

His lips smiled gleefully wide, like stretching pink bubble-gum and answered. "Bren, I love you more every minute. Years from now my love for you will be so big that we're gonna need another planet."

She smiled gleefully wide too. His words "years from now" excited her. Years of this would be awesome, feeling this fantastic, years of sleeping naked with him and wonderful conversation and companionship and sniffing his first edition of P&P, visiting author's homes together, and all kinds of fun stuff together, into the exciting unknown. Their future was blank pages that they could fill with all kinds of vertical and horizontal adventures. She imagined lots of non-magazine pictures of Trent and her on her refrigerator, maybe their refrigerator.

Wow. They had come such a long way, she thought, since the first time they cuddled in this room last Saturday night. They had gone through so much to literally come to this amazing moment that had restored her belief in happy endings. In one crazy week she'd gone from a broken heart to a broken bed. Sometimes it was a two steps forward and one step back process (ready to be with Trent then not ready, deciding to not stay silent then staying silent, Holly's on/off relationship with singing and Chet, Calli constantly getting and losing jobs, Kris's indecision about whether to vajazzle or not), but little by little always striving for joy, she, and Trent, and her friends were progressing forward through life and slowly arriving at a really good place.

The more she thought about her and Trent's time together the more she saw a pattern, a silent story structure, a non-indifferent chiastic symmetry to the events of their week: first kissing Trent at the same corner where he first learned her name, him looking through her bookshelves then her looking through his, the hickeys. This whole adventure seemed . . . cosmically designed.

She stared up at the horizon line where her wall met her ceiling and wondered. Maybe life wasn't totally indifferent and had silently helped her. Lots of coincidences: Madeline wanting to move out at the same time Trent was looking for a new apartment, seeing Holly's mural painting of the cliff she had stood on, Calli's fridge-picture of Trent, and then Calli's longing for Trent instantly transferring to Trent's sister when they met at the wedding with obvious sparks flying between them.

What magical coincidences might happen next?

Blee-dee.

Her phone bleeped that she had a new text message.

She ignored it, wanting only to bask in her and Trent's afterglow. Until it bleeped again. And again. And again. And she finally she looked and saw the craziest text from Calli. With a link to a video, a video of Bren giving her speech at the wedding that a guest had filmed and posted was now going viral. Around the world! Blowing up social media with 21,492 views and 4,000 likes in just 4 hours, and the feedback comments were heart-soaringly positive, and now she really had fans, and . . . *wow!* She showed Trent.

He smiled. "You did something great."

She smiled.

"But I thought you were great already," he said with a kiss.

She looked up at her photos of her heroes with a smile, then she texted a thank you back to Calli and hoped she was having a super fun night too.

Everything felt good.

She thought of her friends now happy too out there tonight: Kris cuddling with Mark, Holly cuddling with Glenn, and Calli cuddling with Lucy, as she enjoyed cuddling with Trent. She had friends, and family, and a new boyfriend, and a good job in a magic city, and everything felt like a story's happy ending with a bright future.

She felt like she'd grown so much in just one wild week. She'd learned a lot of stuff, and learned a lot about herself. Not only did she trust Trent, she kinda now trusted herself even more, enough to improv a bridesmaid speech, and some new named and unnamed sex positions, and to be trust herself to be able to handle whatever happened in life.

She thought about her mom's slogan: "just be happy, it's more fun." Bren pulled her yellow blanket around her and Trent, together wrapped in happiness, and decided to have fun, and to trust him, and never be with anyone that she wasn't having fun with. Yep, she agreed with her thoughts while running towards Trent on Union Street, she had discovered the secret to how to trust: you just decide to, until they show you they can't be trusted. She believed in herself to be able to handle anything that happened, not be broken by it, and keep going, because now she knew her strength, she knew life was silently on her side, and she knew she could improvise a new plan.

Trusting herself, that was the secret.

Self-trust was the secret to survival and happiness, she decided, and everything else in life was just pizza toppings on her crust of self-trust. Or something like that. Whatever happened, she would be fine, and just enjoy goodness for as long as it lasted,

With this new feeling of confidence and her solid, comforting new view of life, she totally relaxed with him, and cuddled, and smiled, feeling the wonderful flow of oxytocin. No more molten anger in her, now only the feeling of serenity.

Their connection really felt true and real and good, and they would tell each other everything. It was the kind of love she'd always read about and hoped to find, and now, finally, here it was, in real life, in her arms. *Yay!* And it was a love story with a heartbreaking ex, a hot book-talk stairway meet-cute, a wild week of sensual cuddling, motorcycle stealing, friend rebonding, self-power discovering, with a joyous wedding and wild sex finale, and a happy ending with the beginning of the most amazing relationship ever! It was as fun and wild as any of the rom-com books now scattered around her bedroom, maybe a love story worth writing herself one day. Maybe she could explore writing, not just reading. She had fun verbally-writing their bedtime stories. Who knows? She'd go wherever she felt the right wind blowing. But whatever the future would be she sure didn't feel nervous about it like before.

She snuggled close with Trent, not out of need, but out of choice and happiness to embrace with the most perfect person for her to be in a love relationship with, her soulmate, and she his soulmate, finally together, holding each other, simply, contently, in the dark, surrounded by a busy city, a confusing world, and a vast, cold, silent universe. But they had each other, warm, and not alone.

She looked up at her calendar with June 18 circled. Just four days away. What a wonderful birthday present she was getting this year: a new boyfriend and the awesomest love she'd ever had. She looked over at her to do lists. Trent and she could have a couple's to do list, but there only needed to be one thing on it: their happily-ever-after plan, a plan they would make up as they went along.

They were going to have so much fun.

He kissed her again, then she watched him smile and watched his hand find his pants, and out of a pocket he pulled a floppy red balloon. "May I?" he asked.

She smiled super, super big. "Yeah. I'm ready."

She watched his smiling lips inflate it with his breaths, tie it perfect with firm gentleness, as she felt super tingles, and she watched her one-balloon-guy offer one beautiful love-red balloon to her.

"Happy birthweek," he said with a super sweet smile.

Her emotions swirled. She was totally over her fear of balloons now. It was gonna be a really happy birthweek, and a really happy future. Her happy heart floated up to the sky, even if this non-helium balloon couldn't. This balloon wouldn't slip away; it was here to stay, maybe even forever, one amazing day at a time.

Tomorrow was National Smile Power Day; what an awesome day to start their first full day as girlfriend and boyfriend, they had a lot to smile about. She looked forward to breakfast and Trent making his glorious pancakes. Pancakes every day and passion every night, with her soulmate, life was going to be flooplezoopley amazing. She was so excited to see what adventures they would have together, and what new bedtime stories they would create together. She held her happy birthweek balloon and cuddled into their delightful union, breathed in a glorious inhale of book-scented air, and looking at his big smile and into his true blue eyes she exhaled her smiling whisper over his lips: "Once upon a time . . . "

songs to cuddle to

Collide by Howie Day
Fall Asleep by Us the Duo
Hold Me by Janine
Kiss Me by Ed Sheeran
Chasing Cars by Snow Patrol
Let's Be Still by The Head and The Heart
You Are In Love by Taylor Swift
Stay by Bob Seger
All Things All At Once by Tired Pony
Always In My Head by Coldplay
The Scar by Carly Simon (from Working Girl soundtrack)
Come Back To Bed by John Mayer
Magic by Coldplay
Say (All I Need) by OneRepublic
Lost Tonight by Liz Phair
Never Gonna Leave This Bed (Acoustic) by Maroon 5
At Last by Etta James
I Can't Help Falling In Love With You by Ingrid Michaelson
Dream Beach by Michael Hedges
Beach Sequence by Passengers (U2 & Brian Eno)
Edge Hill by Groove Armada
Lullaby by Spill Canvas

This playlist is based solely on the author's opinion, and this book has no affiliation with these listed performers or songwriters.

Calli's rom-com novel coming soon!

The fun prequel to this novel is *Passion or Pancakes*

paperback & ebook on Amazon

audiobook on Audible

Check for updates on my social media stuff:

www.nathanbaylet.com

Instagram: instagram.com/nathanbaylet

YouTube: youtube.com/@nathanbaylet

X (Twitter): twitter.com/NathanBaylet

Patreon soon

Merch soon

Thanks for reading!

www.ingramcontent.com/pod-product-compliance
Lightning Source LLC
LaVergne TN
LVHW010626110826
845149LV00014B/2791
9781959920038